Praise for Angela Hunt

"Angela Hunt has penned another winner! From the opening scene, she had me wanting to find out what would happen next to the people of Peculiar, peculiar and otherwise."

—Robin Lee Hatcher, bestselling author of *Heart of Gold* and *Belonging*

"Angela Hunt is a virtuoso of emotion. She is able to not only explore and explain feelings but draw you into them with a deftness that's nearly magical. All too soon, you're reading these chapters and unable to put the book down. You need to know what happens next. Delightful, engaging, and rich with emotion, Angela Hunt's story of three sisters will make you want to reach out to your own sisters. If you're looking for a good weekend read or perhaps a book that will help bring you closer to your own family, this one is it. Angela Hunt hits it out of the park."

—Fictionaddict.com

"Only Angela Hunt could write a relationship novel [*The Fine Art of Insincerity*] that's a page-turner! As one of three sisters, I can promise you this: Ginger, Penny, and Rose Lawrence ring very true indeed. Their flaws and strengths make them different, yet their shared experiences and tender feelings make them family. From one crisis to the next, the Lawrence sisters are pulled apart, then knit back together, taking me right along with them. I worried about Ginger one moment, then Penny, and always Rose—a sure sign of a good novel, engaging both mind and heart. Come spend the weekend in coastal Georgia with three women who clean house in more ways than one!"

—Liz Curtis Higgs, bestselling author of *Here Burns My Candle*

"*The Fine Art of Insincerity* is the story of three middle-aged sisters that converge on St. Simons Island to clear away the cobwebs from their deceased grandmother's island home. But the cobwebs hiding the secret pain that each sister harbors threaten to entangle and complicate each woman's deep sense of order and decorum, especially since one of the sisters is hell-bent on a collision course with fate. Angela Hunt's womanly tale of sisterly affection and protective martyrdom is a well-woven story of self-discovery and personal growth that will melt your heart!"

—Patricia Hickman, author of *The Pirate Queen* and *Painted Dresses*

"Hunt delves into some serious issues in this family drama centered around three sisters clearing out their grandmother's house, yet still manages to add humor when it's needed most. This emotionally compelling novel is a gem."

—*Romantic Times*

ANGELA HUNT

FIVE MILES SOUTH OF
Peculiar

A NOVEL

HOWARD BOOKS
A DIVISION OF SIMON & SCHUSTER, INC.
New York   Nashville   London   Toronto   Sydney   New Delhi

Howard Books
A Division of Simon & Schuster, Inc.
1230 Avenue of the Americas
New York, NY 10020

First Howard Books trade paperback edition June 2012

HOWARD and colophon are trademarks of Simon & Schuster, Inc.

For information about special discounts for bulk purchases,
please contact Simon & Schuster Special Sales at 1-866-506-1949
or business@simonandschuster.com.

The Simon & Schuster Speakers Bureau can bring authors to your live event.
For more information or to book an event contact
the Simon & Schuster Speakers Bureau at 1-866-248-3049
or visit our website at www.simonspeakers.com.

Designed by Davina Mock-Maniscalco

Manufactured in the United States of America

10 9 8 7 6 5 4 3 2 1

Library of Congress Cataloging-in-Publication Data

Hunt, Angela Elwell
Five miles south of Peculiar : a novel / Angela Hunt.—1st Howard Books
trade paperback ed.
p.   cm.
1. Sisters—Fiction.   2. Family reunions—Fiction.   I. Title.
PS3558.U46747F58 2012
813'.54—dc23   2011047804

ISBN 978-1-4391-8204-8
ISBN 978-1-4391-8207-9 (ebook)

For Carol T.,
who learned to like Moon Pies and grits on my watch.

To turn on a dime,
Do a one-eighty,
Reverse course,
Recalculate—
When my well-paved road veered in another direction,
I had to wonder who programmed my GPS.

—Darien Haynes, "Road Warrior"

FIVE MILES SOUTH OF
Peculiar

esidents of Jackson County, Florida, held their breath the morning of July 3, 1968, when old man Caldwell took to his bed complaining of a monstrous headache. As the clock struck two, he sat up, sneezed, wheezed, and lay back down, expiring before his head hit the pillow. The doc pronounced him at 2:03, then placed a call to the county seat. Someone in the county clerk's office reportedly clicked a stopwatch and set it in the safe. County officials and city planners nodded to one another with greedy smiles, knowing that Charles Caldwell's precious estate, known to all as Sycamores, would officially become county property at 2:03 p.m. on July 3, 2018. As to what purpose the property would serve, no one dared offer an opinion. But they could spend the next fifty years dreaming . . .

Darlene Caldwell Young, who was only six when her grandpa died, would later take quiet pride in the fact that her family home was not built on the sweat of slaves or the commerce of cotton, but on the courage, cunning, and risk necessary to garner a fortune during Prohibition. Though a current visitor to Sycamores would find alcohol only in bottles of vanilla, rum, and peppermint extract, Darlene considered her grandfather a genius. He not only managed to shelter Sycamores from taxes, but also devised the charitable gift annuity that provided a monthly income for any immediate Caldwell descendant residing on the property.

That income allowed life at Sycamores to continue as it always had, with a sedate and stately elegance. "Chase" Caldwell's progeny were more than willing to let the rest of the world rush and worry and gobble meals behind a steering wheel. At Sycamores, and in Peculiar, the nearest town, life was meant to be savored.

Ready to take a load off her feet one Friday morning, Darlene sank into a rocker on her front porch. She pulled a tattered Japanese fan from her apron pocket and snapped it open, then frantically thrashed at the hot air. The porch lay in deep shade, but beyond it simmered a sun-spangled garden where roses nodded their heavy heads and sunflowers followed the blazing torch in the sky. Next to the sunflowers, Nolie was staking the top-heavy gladiolas while her dogs, Lucy and Ricky, romped across the grass edging the mile-long driveway.

Darlene frowned. The grass looked to be ankle deep, but ever since Daddy's accident Nolie didn't like to ride the tractor mower. Darlene would cut the lawn herself, but in this heat, she'd have to do it either before sunup or after sundown, and she didn't want to risk running over a possum or armadillo in the vague half-light.

"Lawn needs mowin'," she called, trusting that Nolie could hear her above the barking dogs. "Do you think we could get Henry to find somebody to come out and take care of it?"

Nolie looked up, her eyes shadowed by the wide brim of her straw hat. "Didn't we just cut it?"

"Been nearly two weeks." Darlene fanned herself again. "Those dogs are gonna be itchin' if the grass gets too long. We won't be able to keep the fleas off 'em, and I'm not gonna put up with another infestation in the house."

Nolie turned, the hot breeze ruffling her long pullover apron as she watched her pets play. "You'd better call Henry, then." She picked up her gardening basket. "Ask if he can find someone regular."

"Only till the heat passes. Might as well save some money and do it myself once the weather cools off."

Nolie waved in silent agreement as she followed the dogs and walked toward the driveway.

Inhaling the sweet scent of the honeysuckle vines, Darlene propped her hand on her chin and watched her baby sister. Oh, to be young and carefree again. Though Nolie had recently celebrated her fortieth birthday, her face was still unlined and her figure trim. Come to think of it, Nolie was still a child in many ways. Not surprising, considering she'd never been married, never raised children, and never been widowed. Darlene had borne the stress of all three, and wore the resulting laugh lines and worry ridges on her face.

Darlene straightened as an unfamiliar vehicle slowed on the highway and turned onto the property. A red pickup rattled over the gravel drive, its bed covered with a bright blue tarp and bulging like a Gypsy's wagon. Nolie slowed as the truck drew closer, then the driver stopped and leaned over to lower his passenger window.

A chill climbed the chinks of Darlene's spine as she stood and walked to the edge of the porch. This was how every TV crime show began—a suspicious vehicle pulled up beside an innocent woman while the driver asked about a missing puppy or for directions to the police station. But this road led to Sycamores and nowhere else, so the stranger had either made a wrong turn or was fixin' to kidnap one of the Caldwell women.

Darlene clenched her teeth. "Don't be a dumbbell, Nolie. Don't you get in that truck."

As if she'd heard and *wanted* to rebel, Nolie stepped over the shallow drainage ditch at the side of the drive and walked toward the vehicle. Without even a moment's hesitation she reached for the door handle and hopped into the cab.

Honestly! That girl had no awareness of danger, no understanding of propriety, and absolutely no common sense. Darlene had spent many a sleepless night worrying about what would happen if Nolie met a dangerous killer who summoned her into his car—well, now she knew. Nolie would not only get in, she'd invite the maniac home for supper.

Even Darlene's children had never been that trusting.

Darlene stood in hypnotized horror. If that truck started kickin' up dust in a sudden U-turn, she was calling the sheriff and raising holy heck—

But the pickup continued rumbling toward the house, its giant tires making soft popping sounds as it rolled over the gravel. Darlene pressed her lips together, then stepped inside the foyer, where Daddy's shotgun leaned against the marble windowsill.

The stranger in the truck might not have evil intentions, but when two single women lived only a short distance from the state hospital for the criminally insane, Darlene would rather be safe than sorry.

Nolie pushed at the brim of her hat to better see the man who'd identified himself as Erik Payne. He was certainly spruced up for a hot day in May—the middle-aged man wore a white shirt, a red tie, and dark blue trousers with a crease so sharp it might have been top-stitched. He looked like a politician on parade, but what kind of man deliberately chose to hang a tie around his neck in this heat? Then again, he said he was from Chattahoochee, and everyone knew that place was home to the Florida State Mental Hospital.

She pursed her lips, dreading what Darlene would say about her getting into this man's pickup. Darly would take one look at him and figure he was a recovering mental patient, an escaped criminal, or, given his red, white, and blue attire, a desperate politician.

Nolie tilted her head. "You say you're from Chattahoochee?"

He kept his gaze on the driveway as the truck rolled forward. "Yes, ma'am. Before I lost my job I was pastor of the First Community Church there. You ever hear of it?"

She shook her head. "I don't get over that way much." She shifted her gaze from his clean-shaven face to his hands. Smooth and pale, with clean and evenly trimmed nails, they looked like a preacher's hands.

"So." The reverend cleared his throat as he applied the brakes and stopped a few feet from the front sidewalk. "Should I be nervous about talking to your sister?"

"Why would you be?"

"Didn't you notice? The woman's carrying a shotgun."

Nolie laughed. "She won't hurt you. But she sees herself as bein' in charge of the house, so she tends to be a little overprotective. She's the one to talk to if you're lookin' for work." She gripped the door handle and grinned. "And you're in luck—I happen to know she's looking for someone to mow the lawn and all like that. Since she started having hot flashes, Darlene can't take the heat."

A wave of crimson brightened the preacher's face as he shut off the engine and pocketed his keys. "Alrighty, then. I guess I'm as ready to meet her as I'll ever be."

"Her name's Darlene Young. Come on with me and I'll introduce you."

Nolie slid out of the truck and stopped to pat Lucy's and Ricky's heads—the anxious dogs had followed the pickup after Nolie hopped in. After seeing that she was okay, they positioned themselves like armed guards between the approaching preacher and their mistress.

Erik lifted both hands. "Do those lions bite?"

"They're Leonbergers, and they've never bitten anyone—yet." Nolie stepped toward Erik, then looked at the dogs and touched the stranger's arm. "It's okay, baby dogs. This man is a friend."

The dogs' stiff tails relaxed to swing back and forth in happy arcs. "They're beautiful," Erik said, following Nolie as she led the way up the sidewalk. "I've never heard of that breed."

"Not many people have," Nolie answered, pleased by his interest. "They're a lot more common in Europe than over here. I had these two flown over from Germany when they were pups."

Giving the preacher another reassuring smile, Nolie turned toward the porch—and stifled a groan. Darlene stood between the center columns at the top of the stairs, holding the shotgun as if she meant business. "Darly"—Nolie gave her a warning look—"you can put the gun away."

Her sister eyed the stranger with a steely gaze. "I don't know this fellow."

"That's only because you've never met him. Darlene, I'd like you to meet Reverend Erik Payne. Reverend Payne, this is my sister Darlene Young."

The minister took a hesitant step forward, his hand extended. "Mrs. Young. I'm pleased to meet you."

Darlene lowered the gun and shook his hand without smiling. "What brings you all the way out here, Reverend Payne? We don't need any more Bibles—we already have one for every room and a twenty-pounder on the coffee table."

"Please, call me Erik. And I'm not selling anything." He pulled a folded handkerchief from his pocket and wiped perspiration from his forehead. "Since you asked, ma'am, I was pastoring a church in Chattahoochee until those folks decided the time had come for me to move on. With the employment situation being what it is, one of the deacons gave me your name—he said you and your sister might be willing to take in a stray. I'm not looking for a handout, mind you, but a job and a place to live for a short while. I had to leave the parsonage, so I've been staying in a cheap hotel off the highway while I look for work."

Nolie tugged on Darlene's apron. "You were just sayin' we need a man to mow the lawn. And wouldn't it be nice to have someone replace that old siding on the guesthouse? He could do that and a lot of other chores around here. I know you have a long list of things that need fixin'."

Darlene glanced back at the old house behind her. Nolie knew her sister was thinking about the shutters that needed painting, the mud-dauber nests needing to be knocked down, and the guesthouse that could use a face-lift . . .

"That's just part of owning an old house. No matter where I sit, I find myself lookin' at somethin' that needs doin'." Darlene shifted her gaze back to the minister. "Before we can commence, Reverend Payne, I have to ask somethin' and I'd appreciate an honest answer. Why did that congregation ask you to leave?"

The minister blinked. "I beg your pardon?"

"Did they catch you stealing from the offering plate? Or were you spending too much time counseling somebody's wife?"

Nolie lowered her gaze, afraid the minister would see the blush she could feel burning her face. Darly had never been one to mince words, but why did she have to be so blunt with a man of the cloth?

The reverend's mouth twisted as he loosened the knot of his tie. "Nothing like that, ma'am. I—well, I was five years married when I took the church. My wife supported me all the time I was going to school and seminary, but once we went to Chattahoochee and actually got into the work of the ministry, she decided she didn't like being a pastor's wife. She didn't like living in a parsonage, she didn't like going to parishioners' baby showers, and she didn't like sharing me with a hundred other people. So a year ago she picked up and left, and after six months she divorced me. The church was good enough to allow us some time in case God wanted to restore our marriage, but when that didn't happen, the church decided that a divorced man couldn't be a good example to the flock. They asked me to leave, so here I am. And that's probably a whole lot more than you wanted to hear."

Nolie studied her sister, but she'd never been good at guessing Darlene's thoughts. Anything could be going on behind that implacable expression.

The preacher dabbed at his forehead again, then shoved his handkerchief back into his pocket. "That's God's truth, ma'am; you can call and ask anyone in Chattahoochee."

Darlene leaned the shotgun against a porch column, then folded her arms. "What could you actually do for us, Reverend Payne?"

He glanced at Nolie as a half smile crossed his face. "Honestly, ladies, I haven't done much manual labor lately. But as a kid I did some painting, lawn mowing, and gardening. You tell me what needs to be done, and if I don't know how to do it, I'll go to the hardware store and find somebody who can teach me."

Darlene looked away a moment, then nodded. "In return for your help we'll give you use of the guesthouse and supper every day. But how long do you think you'd be stayin'?"

He took a deep breath and scratched his chin. "I don't rightly know about that. I *do* know I've been called to the ministry, so as soon as I'm settled, I'm going to start sending out resumes. God called me to preach and teach, so that's what I intend to do . . . just as soon as the Lord opens a door."

Nolie smiled. "So we'd be waitin' on God with you."

"That's the gist of it, yes ma'am. Would that be acceptable?"

"Hold on a minute." Darlene narrowed her gaze. "The man who sent you to Sycamores—he got a name?"

"Yes—Beverage Simmons."

A smile finally broke through Darlene's inflexible mask. "All right, then. I know Beverage, and I know he wouldn't have sent you to us if you couldn't be trusted." She nodded at Nolie. "I s'pose we can work something out. You agree, Magnolia?"

Nolie stared in pleased surprise, then grinned. "I don't see why not."

The minister practically melted in relief. "Thank you, ma'am. Thank you, *ladies.*"

Nolie smiled, glorying in the moment. She'd been holding her breath, hoping Darlene would see that the good and Christian thing to do would be to help this man regain his footing. He had a look in his brown eyes, the same look she saw when one of her dogs got hurt, and she couldn't bear to see any living creature in pain.

Like Momma always said, far too many people were quick to dish out advice when what a hurting person really needed was a helping hand.

"I say, 'Welcome to Sycamores.'" Nolie grinned as the dogs picked up on her excitement and began to bark. "Come on. I'll walk you over to the guesthouse. It's not fancy and it needs some work, but it'll keep you cool at night and dry in the rain."

"No matter what it looks like," the reverend said, following her, "it'll serve as an answer to prayer until it's time for me to move on."

In her doctor's Manhattan office, Carlene Caldwell looked out at the downtown skyline and couldn't resist a sense of foreboding. Where was her young doctor, and why did he have to keep her waiting? She eyed the thick folder on the man's desk. Why did one simple procedure require so much paperwork?

She folded her hands in her lap and wished she hadn't given up smoking. If ever a situation called for a cigarette, this one did.

"Are you okay?" Martin asked.

"I'm fine." She tried not to look at her agent, who sat next to her and jiggled his crossed leg more energetically than usual. "By the way, I want you to know how grateful I am that you were willing to come down here with me. I've been dreading this appointment for weeks, so it's nice to have someone along. You know, for moral support and all like that."

"You must be anxious—your Southern speech patterns are showing." Martin laughed, but his laughter had an edge that did little to comfort her. "I'm always happy to help you, Carlene. It's the least I could do after all our time together." His brow furrowed. "How many years has it been?"

She turned, grateful for the change of subject. "Let's see—I got my first part in '84, and signed with you right after. So that's—what?"

"Twenty-eight years. You never have been any good at math."

"That's why I trust you to keep my accounts straight." She smiled at him. "We've lasted longer than a lot of marriages."

"Including yours . . . and all three of mine."

Carlene glanced at her watch, then sighed and crossed her legs, struggling to get comfortable in the utilitarian chair. "Good thing *we* never married."

"Good thing I never asked. I knew you had better taste."

She looked over her shoulder at the closed door. "What could be keeping that doctor?"

Martin's eyes softened. "Are you worried about what he might say?"

"No—well, yes. I keep hoping for good news, but common sense tells me something's not right. My *throat* tells me something's not right. I don't even talk like I used to; this rasp in my voice is driving me crazy—"

"Some people might find it sexy."

"Those people know nothing about how the human voice makes music."

Martin fell silent, then reached across the space between them and squeezed Carlene's arm. "I'm sorry you're in this spot."

She choked on a desperate laugh. "If I'd known losing my voice for six months was even a possibility, I would never have had the surgery."

"Didn't they warn you about all the things that could go wrong?"

"Of course, and I signed the stupid consent form. But nobody ever expects that any of those things will actually happen."

Martin shifted in his chair, then cleared his throat. "By the way, how's your understudy doing? Are the producers happy with her?"

Carlene shrugged. "I think so. But almost anyone could play Golde. It's not what I'd call a demanding role."

"Any thought about what you might like to do next?"

"That will depend on what I learn today, won't it?"

The door behind them finally blew open, revealing a young doctor who wore a wrinkled brow and a concerned expression. He walked around the two guest chairs, then paused to shake Carlene's hand. "Thank you for coming in, Ms. Caldwell."

Carlene introduced Martin, who stood to shake the doctor's hand. She leaned forward. "I hope we can skip any other formalities, Dr. Weston. I have to know—is my throat going to get better, or will I spend the rest of my life sounding like I have laryngitis?"

The doctor twisted his mouth and perched on the edge of his desk. "You sound fine to me."

"I don't think I sound fine. I want the voice I had before the surgery."

"You haven't noticed any improvement since I last saw you?"

"None."

"Your upper register is still affected?"

"My upper register is *gone*. I used to have a five-octave range; now I can barely manage two."

"I'm sorry to hear that." The doctor rubbed his palm along the seam of his trousers, then released a rapid volley of words: "I asked you to wait for the result of the latest scan because I was hoping the scar tissue would recede. But, apparently, the thyroid cartilage has elongated and reinforced the loosening of your vocal cords. I was hoping you'd be better after several months of recuperation, but sometimes, due to factors beyond our control, our purposes are thwarted and our goal is not achieved. You are able to speak, and that may be the best result we can hope for."

Carlene blinked, her mind reeling in the verbal onslaught. Finally she grasped one word: "You thought I'd be *better*? Doctor, I can't simply be *better*. I have to be *exceptional*. I have to be able to sing like I used to. I was hoping to sing *better* than before."

The doctor's expression remained locked in neutral. "I'm sorry the results of your surgery were not what we expected."

Carlene struggled to swallow as her scarred throat tightened. *Not what he expected?* Why didn't he call this what it was—a *disaster, catastrophe, calamity,* and *tragedy*?

"Martin, I can't—" She closed her eyes as the office walls swirled and swayed. Martin barked a command, then a strong arm supported her shoulders and held her upright.

A moment later, she opened her eyes to find that the room's walls and ceiling had resumed their proper places. She fixed her gaze on the doctor's white lab coat, now only a few inches away.

Martin took her hand. "Are you all right, Carlene? Would you like to go home? I could call a cab—"

"So that's it?" She lifted her chin and looked at the doctor, who was moving back to the chair behind his desk. "My voice is ruined." The sounds rasped as she forced the words over her wounded vocal cords.

The doctor's mouth changed just enough to bristle the fashionable stubble on his cheeks. "I'm so sorry the results were not . . . optimal."

"You've already said that." She blinked, then focused on Martin. "I think I'm ready for that cab now."

Martin helped her up as the doctor stammered. "If—if there's anything I can do—"

"You can explain everything to my lawyer," she said, walking toward the door, "when you tell him how you destroyed my life."

Carlene let her head fall to the back of the seat as Martin slid in beside her and gave the cabdriver her address.

"No." She shook her head. "I'm not going home. I ought to be at the theater."

"Whatever for? Your understudy has the part covered."

"I've been helping out backstage. I don't want everyone thinking I'm some kind of invalid, and as long as I'm getting paid . . ."

Martin stared at her, then waved in surrender. "The Forty-sixth Street Theater, then," he told the driver. "And Sixth Avenue after that."

She crossed her arms. "Thanks for humoring me."

"I don't understand why you're doing this to yourself. You ought to go home; you need time to consider your options."

"What options? I'd say the doctor was pretty definite about my prognosis."

"I think you should get a second opinion. What does this young guy know? After all, he botched the surgery—"

"And I'll let my lawyer take care of that. I'm not going to confront a hotshot medical expert about his substandard surgical skills."

"So you're going to sue?"

"If I have a case, I'd be foolish not to. Isn't that why surgeons carry malpractice insurance?"

"Fine. But while your lawyer's pursuing justice, you and I need to talk about your future. Just because your voice isn't what it used to be doesn't mean you're ready to be put out to pasture. You're a fine dramatic actress, and I'm not giving up on you."

"I'm almost fifty, Martin—too old to be a leading lady."

"No one has to know how old you are. You look great, and that's all anyone cares about."

She snorted. "I look like a spit-and-polished used car. People can tell my odometer's been set back, they just can't tell how far."

Martin ignored her quip. "We could find a play with a great supporting role. Look at all the actresses who have played Broadway well into their eighties—"

"That's a pretty short list. And actresses, even great ones, are a dime a dozen in New York. I wouldn't make the cut. Any success I might have achieved has come because I could sing."

"That's not true."

"It *is* true, though you're sweet to try to convince me otherwise. But you're right about needing time to think. Maybe I should go home."

Martin tapped the Plexiglas window between the back seat and the driver. "We've changed our minds. Can you take us to Inwood instead?"

Carlene braced herself as the cab made an abrupt turn onto a congested side street.

"We could look for TV work," Martin said, settling back. "Maybe you could audition for a soap. Some of them are moving to the Internet."

"And play some up-and-coming starlet's grandmother? No thanks."

"You could interview for a network morning program, audition for a few cable shows, maybe go on *Celebrity Apprentice*—"

She glowered at him. "I don't need to grovel. I don't want to be in the spotlight unless I deserve to be there."

"But you have talent, and with that comes a responsibility—"

"I *had* a talent." Despite her intentions to remain strong, her chin quivered. "For six months I've dreaded this possibility, so I'm not going to harbor any delusions. I was an exceptional singer and a decent actress, but I'd be lucky if my reputation extends as far as the outer boroughs. No one in Hollywood is clamoring for my head shot. No one in network television even knows my name."

"They could learn it."

She snorted softly. "The market is already crowded with aging singers. I'm not going to force my company on anyone."

"You're too young to retire."

"Do I have a choice?"

"What else would you like to do?"

She pressed her fingertips to her temples. "I've never considered being anything but a singer. I never . . . I mean I don't think I ever had a choice to be anything else."

She closed her eyes as the cab jounced through a pothole. The doctor's announcement had floored her with its finality, but the news hadn't come as a complete surprise. For the last four months she had been warming up her lower register with scales and vocal exercises. But every time she approached the D an octave above middle C, her throat closed. No matter how hard she tried, she couldn't coax out any sound.

She groaned. "I should never have gone to that ENT. My coach said I needed only a few weeks' vocal rest, but that seemed too simple. So I had to go to the fancy throat doctor and he had to try a new technique . . ."

She blinked back a sudden rush of tears. Why had she thought surgery would help? Because she was hoping for a *better* voice, as if medicine could improve a God-given gift.

She wrapped her fingers around her agent's hand. "I'm sorry. I know you're trying your best to be supportive, and I appreciate it. But right now I'm not feeling optimistic."

He shifted to face her. "There's no reason this has to end your career. You take some time to think, and after you've come up with an idea of what you'd like to do next, give me a call. I'll help you get whatever gig you want."

She squeezed his fingers. "I appreciate the thought, but I'm not willing to sully the reputation I spent years building. I'm going to go back to my apartment, take stock of my situation, and maybe go for a walk in the park. That should clear my head so I can come up with a plan about what to do next."

"I'll always be here for you."

"I know you will." She squeezed his hand again. "You're not only a good agent, you're also a good friend."

Chapter Two

Standing knee-deep in a field of black-eyed Susans, Nolie stopped deadheading flowers and looked toward the main road. Through some magic of geography and air current, the breeze carried human voices to her, male and female. A moment later she saw a couple fly by on racing bikes, their bodies lean and sweaty. She stood staring long after they had disappeared, then shook her head and lowered her gaze.

She was no racer; that bold life did not belong to her, would never be hers. She belonged to genteel Sycamores, where courage and risk taking had long been bred out of those who lived beneath its roof.

She looked toward the tall trees that bordered the property and studied the tapestried swags of shadows hanging from their lower branches. Above the trees, tattered clouds crept toward the road as if they, too, had something better to do than maintain the status quo.

Sighing, she snipped the heads off another bunch of faded flowers, then stopped as she spied the new handyman walking from the guesthouse to the front porch. Overcome by a sudden awareness of her grass-stained apron and sweat-soaked bangs, she ducked behind a tall stand of sunflowers, but Reverend Payne didn't even glance in her direction. He kept his gaze lowered, his head bent, and his shoulders hunched. The man walked as if he carried the weight of the world on his shoulders, though he held only a few white envelopes.

Her heart twisted. All she knew of him was the abbreviated history he'd shared when he arrived, but his brief words undoubtedly disguised dark sorrows and painful secrets. She knew sadness and lived with secrets of her own, heartaches she had never shared with anyone but her dogs. If this unhappy man wanted to unburden himself, she could suggest that Ricky and Lucy made great confidantes . . .

But how could she do that? She couldn't simply walk up and ask him to reveal his deepest thoughts to her pets. Grief lived in a tightly coiled shell, and only time and the gentlest of entreaties could persuade grief's keeper to even admit its existence . . .

Emily Dickinson had understood. "I like a look of agony," she wrote, "because I know it's true . . ."

Nolie lopped off a few more dead blossoms, then lowered her hand and quietly snapped her fingers. Ricky and Lucy, who had been wallowing in the grass, rolled to attention. "Come, my beauties," she whispered, creeping toward the front porch. If they stayed in the shadow of the tall magnolia, the minister might not notice them at all.

Reverend Payne walked to the front door, knocked, and waited. Nolie drew a deep breath, knowing that Darlene would be trudging to the foyer and grumbling the entire way. She rarely made it out of pajamas before noon on Saturdays, and she didn't like anyone outside the family to see her in her robe and slippers. But some situations couldn't be avoided.

Nolie ducked behind the magnolia as the front door opened. Like a grumpy turtle reluctantly peering out from its armored exterior, Darlene stuck her head out.

"I'm sorry to bother you, ma'am," the pastor said, "but I'd like permission to use your mailbox to mail some letters. Is it okay with you if I have return mail sent to this address?"

Nolie bent forward and peered through the leafy screen separating her from the porch. She couldn't see Darlene's expression from this angle, but because the pastor appeared appropriately apologetic, she didn't think Darly would hold this inconvenience against him for too long.

"Fine, fine, feel free." Darlene's head drew back into the house, then reappeared. "Just remember to raise the flag or the mail lady won't stop. Anything else you need?"

"Nothing at all," the minister said, turning away. "Thank you."

Nolie stifled a giggle as the door closed. Darlene had to be burning with curiosity about their new employee, but after the inquisition she gave him yesterday, she'd think twice before asking him about his family, his background, and what side his great-grandfather fought for in the War Against Northern Aggression. Nolie was curious, too, but not so much about the preacher's history. She wanted to know more about the man himself.

She would have remained hidden until Reverend Payne was halfway down the driveway, but Ricky, bored with this confusing version of hide-and-seek, broke his stay and bolted toward the minister, his tail waving like a flag.

"Well, hey there, fella." The preacher stopped to pat the dog's big black head. "Where'd you come from?"

Ricky's impulsiveness left Nolie with no choice. She strolled out from behind the magnolia, clippers in hand, Lucy trailing like a good girl. "Silly boy"—she scolded the dog—"you know better than to bother people who aren't used to big goofs like you."

"He's not bothering me." The air of melancholy around the pastor lifted as he smiled. "I like dogs. I wanted one myself, but my wife— well, we didn't get one. But there's something unique about the bond God designed between man and his best friend, don't you think?"

Nolie nodded. "I know what you mean. I had a pug as a kid, long before they became so popular. Then I had a boxer, a Great Dane, and a Rottie. A couple of years ago I learned about Leonbergers, and well, you see the result."

The preacher straightened and tucked his envelopes beneath his arm. "They're beautiful animals."

"Thank you, Reverend."

"Please, call me Erik. I'm afraid I don't feel like much of a reverend these days."

Nolie glanced away, then gestured to the envelopes. "You walkin' to the mailbox?"

He nodded. "I figured I should get these into the mail early."

"Let me walk you down there. I can tell you everthing you want to know about Sycamores on the way."

The beginning of a smile tipped the corners of his mouth. "An unexpected treat."

They began to walk, the dogs pacing between them, and after an awkward interval Nolie feared she'd been too forward. What if this man didn't *want* to know anything about Sycamores? What if he thought her as blunt as Darlene?

Thankfully, he broke the stiff silence. "Have you lived here all your life?"

"Oh, yes." She smiled in simple relief. "I was born in the first-floor bedroom. My sisters were born in the hospital, but Momma said I couldn't wait for the drive over to Quincy. I always thought it odd she should say that, seein' as how I came ten years after the twins were born."

He hauled his gaze from the driveway to the house. "Darlene has a twin?"

"Yes—Carlene, though they don't look anything alike. Never did, apparently. They have a birthday comin' up next week—a big one, since they're turning fifty." She lowered her voice. "Don't say anything to Darlene, but the mayor and I are working on a surprise party for her. He's trying to find a room large enough to hold everbody in town."

The rhythm of the minister's steps skipped a beat. "Your mayor is throwing a citywide party?"

Nolie laughed. "Peculiar's not that big. And since Darlene has had something to do with nearly every civic organization in town, everbody knows her. Plus, the honorable Henry and Darlene have been seein' a lot of each other in the past few months. I think he's sweet on her."

"Nice. Is Miss Darlene's twin coming home for the celebration?"

Nolie stopped to pick up a stick on the side of the drive, then threw it into the grass. Ricky sprinted off to fetch it.

"Carlene hardly ever comes home. She's so busy." She glanced back at the preacher. "Carly left the area right after high school, and I don't think she's ever looked back. We don't mind, though, 'cause she's singin' on Broadway. Bright lights, big city, and all like that. Momma used to say she was born for somethin' a lot bigger than Peculiar. She's the only Caldwell that was."

Ricky came bounding back, the stick between his teeth, but he carried it to the minister. Nolie smiled as the man bent to accept the drool-covered twig. "Sorry. I should of warned you about the slime."

"That's okay. I'm washable." Erik threw the stick, too, flinging it farther and faster than Nolie ever had. Both dogs took off after it this time, and Lucy found it first.

Nolie began to walk again, knowing the dogs would follow. "You'll probably hear about Carlene when you go into town. She's sort of a local legend."

"I'm not surprised."

Lucy brought the stick to Nolie, who stopped to accept it. Rubbing the dog's ears, she glanced again at the stack of letters under the minister's arm. "Did you write all those letters last night?"

He glanced at his envelopes. "Not exactly. I had copies of my resume printed up before I left the church. I figured I'd better take advantage of the printer and copy machine while I still had access to them. Then I'd need to start fishing if I want to stay in the ministry."

"Readin' and writin' never came easy to me, so I was about to be really impressed with you." Nolie softened her smile. "I'm so sorry about your . . . situation. But since you have to be someplace, I'm glad you're here. Sycamores can be downright peaceful, as long as you don't let yourself get caught up in one of Darlene's projects. My sister stays as busy as a long-tailed cat in a roomful of rockin' chairs."

He chuckled, then looked directly at her for the first time since they'd begun their walk. "I don't want you to think I'm only camping out here while I look for another job. In fact, this afternoon I was planning to ask your sister to tell me what she wants done."

"You won't have to worry about not havin' anything to do—she'll give you a list." Nolie nodded toward the mailbox, still thirty feet away. "I'm going to stop here to keep the dogs off the road, but you go on ahead and put your letters in the box. The mail lady usually comes around lunchtime, so if you need to send any more, you should be fine as long as you run them down here by eleven thirty or so."

She put the dogs in a sit and waited as the preacher strode forward alone. As he placed his mail in the box, she considered the marks of grief on his narrow face and wondered how she could possibly help a man like Erik Payne. People often brought injured animals to Sycamores, knowing that Darlene and Nolie would either tend them or take them to the vet, and now the good Lord himself had sent them one of his wounded servants . . .

"The heart asks pleasure first," she murmured, quoting Miss Emily, "and then, excuse from pain—and then, those little anodynes that deaden suffering . . ."

Lucy looked up, her tail thumping in an inquisitive rhythm.

"It means *painkiller*, sweetie. I looked it up." Nolie rested her hand on the dog's head, then gave her ear an affectionate tweak. Erik Payne's situation was a lot more complicated than a broken wing or a sprained leg, so how, exactly, were she and Darlene supposed to help this poor soul?

Carlene stood at a narrow window in her studio apartment and watched pedestrians on the sidewalk—people hurrying to and from work, dog walkers, women in spandex and sneakers, Chanel-clad housewives laden with shopping bags, and the occasional map-toting tourist in search of a famous landmark or the diner from *Seinfeld*.

Each of them had unique reasons for coming to New York, but all of them thought they'd find something special in the Big Apple, something worth the aggravation of dealing with crowds, breathing smog, and paying exorbitant prices for everything from a haircut to real estate.

What would her neighbors do if their dreams evaporated? They wouldn't give up and go home—New Yorkers were made of sterner stuff. Pop psychology dictated that they'd probably go through the various stages of grieving. Martin had jumped headlong into denial, but Carlene lived with her ruined vocal cords, so denial was useless. Anger came next, supposedly, and she *had* felt angry enough to call her lawyer and give him the details he needed to take her case. While he pursued her victory on the legal front, she could move on to bargaining, depression, and, finally, acceptance.

But how could she ever accept that her lifelong quest had ended with a raspy whimper?

Her life had revolved around musical theater since the seventh grade, and ever since her mother pointed her toward New York, her dream had been Broadway stardom. That life might be over and her dream defunct, but she would not let a pair of ruined vocal cords destroy *her*. She had always maintained a high level of satisfaction in a job well done, so she would not settle for speak-singing her lyrics, nor would she audition for a daytime drama simply because she needed to pay bills. Her reputation for excellence would remain intact, and no one, not even her trusted agent, would convince her to offer an audience less than her best.

Retirement would be the logical answer, of course. Martin managed her retirement fund, but kept reminding her that those accounts needed to accumulate undisturbed at least until her sixtieth birthday. Yet how was she supposed to pay her bills for the next ten years? Living in New York required a sizable salary and steady employment. Her disability payments would end in a few weeks, and then she would need a job. She could advertise for voice students, but how was she supposed to afford Manhattan on a voice teacher's sporadic earnings?

Even if she found a teaching position at one of the local schools, how could she live without the theater? All her friends came from theater backgrounds; even her biorhythms revolved around the largely nocturnal world of the Great White Way. Could she ever learn to get up before noon? Could she sit in the audience and enjoy a show while every atom of her being yearned to be onstage? If she were no longer part of a cast, who could she invite out for dinner, and what would they talk about?

If she had accomplished all she set out to do, she could probably retire gracefully. Broadway stardom would have supplied her retirement nest egg and fulfilled her career goals. If she'd achieved stardom, she could stay in New York and enjoy late lunches with theater critics and directors. She would compliment them on their insights, their productions, and the outstanding new crop of singers, dancers, and actors. She could offer constructive criticism, give advice, and tell entertaining stories about onstage flubs and embarrassing miscues. She might even be able to make retirement seem enviable.

But to be forced from the stage because a surgeon could not keep his promises—

Like a bolt of lightning through her chest, a surge of rage took her by surprise. She caught her breath, her lungs burning, and managed to exhale through clenched teeth.

How was she supposed to rid herself of this fury? Not to mention the jealousy evoked by the thought of seeing her acquaintances still in the theater. She'd never be able to converse with them about their latest productions without feeling the sting of envy. If she couldn't control her emotions, if she let her feelings show, her old friends would see—maybe they would later *say*—that she'd become a bitter and jealous woman.

On the other hand, if she attended the theater as an act of support and encouragement, if she could sit in the darkness and let the glorious magic and music wash over her . . . the pain would be excruciating.

Her heart twisted with that agony even now.

Every day she struggled with not being able to sing in the shower, sing along with her exercise music, or sing in the solitude of her apartment. Sometimes she forgot and opened her mouth, but the sounds that came from her throat served only to mock the voice that had deserted her.

Feeling suffocated, she struggled with the old window and finally managed to raise it. Fresh air blew in, billowing the curtains as she leaned into a reservoir of sounds: the distant whine of an ambulance, the clip-clop of a horse and buggy on tour, the light laughter of school-girls on their way home. She loved New York . . . would love it until the day she died, but it held no place for her now. New York demanded everything a person could give, and she'd already given all she had.

She had sacrificed everything—old friends, family, and the love of her life—for the theater. But though she had given her all, she still remained a long way from conquering Broadway.

And now she had to leave.

She stepped away from the window, sank into a chair, and wondered how she could explain all this to her agent. Martin ought to understand, but he had never stood in the wings and sweated bullets while waiting to go onstage. He had never applauded and laughed during the magical Gypsy-robe ceremony held backstage before a new show opened. He had never sung from his soul and felt that mystical connection between a performer and the audience. He had never tasted the delicious realization that on a given night, in a given hour, he and his fellow cast members had grasped the hearts of every man and woman in the audience, squeezed tears from their weary souls, and left them forever changed.

Even though he was a theater insider, Martin would never understand the tumult of emotions in her heart.

How could she remain in New York? The city was too closely bound to the theater scene; she couldn't speak of one without tasting, hearing, and smelling the other.

But if she couldn't stay in New York . . . where would she go?

In all the winding years of her life, she had visited nearly every state and several foreign countries, but she had lived in only two places: Manhattan and a sprawling old house five miles south of a rural burg called Peculiar. She'd arrived in one of the world's largest and most famous cities after leaving one of the smallest and most insignificant.

She had to face a hard truth: New York had ruined her for any other town. Returning to Peculiar meant returning to inertia, and inertia felt far too much like death.

*   *   *

A five-mile stretch of Highway 90 lay between the late Chase Caldwell's estate and Peculiar, Florida, current population 493. Established as a way station between Marianna and Chattahoochee by Caldwell and a few of his cronies, the small town served as a distribution point for home-manufactured medicinal products until the long arm of the law closed down most of the operations. By that time, however, Caldwell's fortune was secure and his hands as clean as a new dime.

Pedaling over the length of highway that maintained a respectable distance between Caldwell's home and his business, Nolie tipped her head back so the breeze could catch the brim of her hat and flip it onto her shoulders. With her hat dangling over her back, she smiled and coasted through the shady Great Hall of Oaks. Nobody else called the mile-long stretch by that name, but as a child she'd taken one look at the magnificent live oaks sheltering the road to town and knew that such a beautiful place needed a memorable name.

Safe from the sun's broiling rays, she closed her eyes and coasted down the center of the road, trusting her ears to tell her if a vehicle approached. Darlene said Nolie was crazy for riding her bike instead of waiting for a ride to town, but Darlene didn't understand that a bike ride through the Great Hall—with a cool breeze on her face and the wind whistling in her ears—felt an awful lot like flying. And who wouldn't want to do that?

All too soon, Nolie's bike shot out of the shaded tunnel and the sun smacked her in the face. She sighed, then gripped the handlebar with one hand while she fumbled for her hat with the other.

The highway flattened, leading Nolie into the town center, a square bordered by four roads: Central Avenue, Main Street, Martin Luther King Boulevard, and Church Street. The roads edged the centrally located Peculiar City Park while local businesses crowded cheek by jowl on the opposite side of the streets. Darlene always said that if you couldn't find what you needed in the city square, you couldn't find it in Peculiar.

A car filled every available parking space, typical for a Saturday afternoon. Nolie rolled past the Coif It Up salon, the only salon in three counties specializing in white *and* black hair styling, the First National Bank, the Feed Store, and the narrow storefront that housed the municipal library. Finally she reached her destination: the Piggly Wiggly grocery store, known to locals as "the Wiggly."

She parked her bike outside the grocery, then pulled off her sun hat and checked her reflection in the front window. Several long strands had escaped the elastic band holding her hair back, so she smoothed the flyaway pieces and moved toward the door. She didn't have to look beautiful for Henry Hooper, but she didn't want to frighten any of his customers, either.

"Morning, Nolie." One of the cashiers waved as Nolie walked by. "How are things at Sycamores?"

"Same as always, thanks." Nolie smiled and tried to remember the girl's name. She had the rosy cheeks common to the Hooper clan, so she had to be one of Henry's relatives. Maybe a niece?

When she didn't see Henry in any of the aisles, she waited until the cashier finished ringing up Mrs. Marshall, then she cleared her throat. "Excuse me, hon, but I'm looking for the mayor. Is he around this mornin'?"

The girl jerked her thumb toward the corner of the building. "He's in his office. You can go on in."

Nolie thanked her and moved toward the paneled booth at the front of the Piggly Wiggly. Henry Hooper's office consisted of an elevated eight-by-ten platform with paneled four-foot walls and a strip of glass along the top. Apparently the space was private enough to let him concentrate and open enough for him to spot trouble brewing from fifty yards away.

As she approached, Nolie glimpsed the top of Henry's head through the glass panel. He must have seen her coming, because before she could knock he opened the short door and greeted her with a smile. "Miss Nolie! Come on in. Everything okay out at Sycamores?"

"We're doin' fine, thank you. How 'bout you?"

He sank back into his chair. "Gretel's home from college, but all she does is sleep late and complain that there's nothing to eat in the fridge."

Nolie smiled. "If you're not busy with grocerin' or mayor business, I thought I'd come by to talk to you about"—she lowered her voice to a near whisper—"the party for you know who."

"Of course." Henry's round face lit with a conspiratorial glow. He motioned toward another chair and waited for Nolie to sit, then he rolled closer. "It's all planned. I've reserved the fellowship hall at the First and Only Baptist Church, and the folks from St. Mary's are donating a cake. They want you to choose one from our bakery, and they'll foot the bill."

Nolie's cheeks warmed. "That's really nice. So everything's set for June eighth?"

The grocer crossed his arms and beamed. "It's been easier than I thought. I put a bug in Glennette Wessel's ear, so she's got the Ladies' Beautification League working on decorations. I also mailed invitations to Katie and Griffith Junior."

Glad that Henry had reached out to her niece and nephew, Nolie smiled and crossed her legs. "Any word from the kids?"

The light in his eyes dimmed slightly. "Unfortunately, neither of them can make it. They said they'd send flowers, so I told them to send any gifts to me and I'll make sure to deliver everthing to the party." He clasped his hands. "They were both awful upset about missing their mom's big day."

"They're good kids and Darlene's close to them. She'll understand." Nolie pressed her lips together. "And that reminds me—I found somethin' the other day and thought you might like to see it." She pulled a faded color photograph from the pocket of her long skirt and passed it to Henry.

He put on his reading glasses and frowned at the photo of two infants lying side by side on a blanket. One of the babies had turned and pressed its hand to the other baby's face.

Henry snorted. "Cute kids. Looks like one of them has it in for the other one."

Nolie smiled. "Not quite. I found that picture in our attic—that's Darlene and Carlene when they were about six months old. Carlene's not hitting Darlene, she's comforting her. On the back of the photo,

Momma wrote that whenever Darly lost her pacifier, Carly would stick her fingers in Darly's mouth so she'd settle down and be quiet."

"Huh." Henry winked as he handed the picture back to Nolie. "Wonder if a pacifier would keep the woman quiet now."

Nolie brushed aside his little joke. "The thing is, Henry, the twins used to be really close. I'd love to see them be that close again, so I've been thinkin' that maybe we should invite Carly to the party. After all, June eighth is her birthday, too."

Henry's mouth opened. "Why—I never even thought about it. It's been so long since anyone around here has seen Carlene—"

"I know she doesn't get home often, and she might not be able to come. But don't you think it'd be nice if we sent her an invitation? If she can't come, at least she'll know we were thinkin' of her." She propped her chin on her hand. "You may remember that Carly used to be active in civic affairs, too—she was Miss Buttercup Squash back in the day. So it'd be a real shame to leave the other Caldwell twin out of a citywide celebration."

Henry snapped his mouth shut, then pumped his fist in the air. "Bless Patsy, you're right, and shame on me for not considerin' it myself. I'll send Carly an invitation and tell her it's a surprise." His smile faded. "But I don't know how to reach the woman."

"Here." Nolie pulled a note card from another skirt pocket. "That's Carlene's address and phone number. Like I said, she probably won't be able to get away, but at least we tried."

The man's bushy brow rose a fraction. "Does she still go by Carlene Caldwell? I seem to remember Darlene mentioning that Carly got married a few years back."

"She did, but that's been over for a while. And she kept her maiden name all along—Darlene said lots of professional women stick with just one name. I suppose Carlene Caldwell does have a certain ring to it."

Henry dipped his head in an emphatic nod, then rolled back to his desk and set the note card by his alarm clock. "Bless you for thinking of this, Nolie. I'll get that invitation out today. And who knows? Carly may surprise us and make an appearance."

"I wouldn't hold my breath, but you never know." Nolie stood and patted his shoulder. "If you need anything from me, Henry, just holler. I'll be here faster than you can say 'Jack Rabbit.'"

Darlene squirted a splash of furniture oil onto her dust rag, then slowly lowered herself to her knees. Reaching for the legs of a spindly antique table, she massaged oil into the dry wood, wishing she had someone to work liniment into her stiff muscles.

Griffith had been good about things like that. He would often volunteer to rub her shoulders at the end of a long day, but she always figured he offered only because he wanted her to return the favor. The strategy was typical Griff—never one to freely share what he was thinking and feeling, he never asked directly for what he wanted, but hinted in a hundred small ways. How many of his hints did she miss?

She picked up the bottle of lemon oil and gave her rag another squirt, then scooted to the other side of the table, her knees cracking as she rocked forward. Lately her body seemed determined to remind her that she had entered the grandma stage. Even her calendar had joined the conspiracy—it kept flipping pages, moving inexorably toward the big birthday, the one destined to elicit all those tacky over-the-hill jokes. She would be fifty in two weeks, but no one had mentioned the occasion lately and she didn't want to be too obvious about reminding them. With any luck, her friends would remember her birthday in time to take her to lunch or drop by with a cake. After all, it wasn't every day that a woman passed the half-century mark.

Unlike poor Griff, who'd only made it to forty-five.

She straightened her aching back. If only the kids could come home! At thirty-two, Katie was struggling to balance her career and her family, so a quick trip to Florida with her husband and son would be impossible. Griffith Junior lived a more relaxed lifestyle, but he and his wife had settled in California so the flight home would be expensive, especially if he wanted to bring his family. Darlene had held Griffy's daughter only once, but she talked to little Marlee every

Saturday morning and Griffy tried to Skype her once a month. Even though talking over the Internet was nice, nothing could beat pressing her lips against her granddaughter's chubby cheeks and breathing in the scent of baby preciousness . . .

Darlene sighed. She shouldn't let herself think about situations that would only depress her. A visit from either of her children would be too much to hope for, so she ought to be grateful for Skype and e-mail and those Internet photo-sharing services her kids were always using. She would have to accept that she and Henry and Nolie would quietly celebrate her birthday at Sycamores, or maybe Henry would take her to Chattahoochee for a nice sit-down restaurant dinner. Seeing as how this was a milestone birthday, maybe he'd put on a sport coat and drive her all the way to Tallahassee. If he decided to go to that much trouble, maybe, just *maybe*, he'd think about popping the question.

She groaned when a ruckus arose on the lawn, then leaned on the table and peered out the second-story window. Nolie's dogs were barking, a sure sign of approaching company, but when she looked out she only saw Nolie riding her bike up the driveway. Her heart lifted when she noticed a plastic Piggly Wiggly bag fluttering in the bicycle basket. Nolie might have seen Henry today. And maybe he dropped a hint about his plans for Darlene's birthday . . .

After giving the antique table one final swipe, she took the stone stairs as quickly as she dared in her sock-covered feet, then hurried through the living room and onto the back porch. Nolie was walking her bike not toward the garage, where it belonged, but toward the guesthouse.

"Nolie!" Leaning out the screen door, Darlene cringed to hear a note of alarm in her voice. She didn't mind Nolie hearing it, but she didn't want that melancholy minister to think she was afraid of him. As long as she had Daddy's shotgun, she wasn't afraid of anybody.

Nolie turned her head. "What?"

"Where've you been?"

"I rode into town and picked up some stuff for Erik."

"The man has a truck. Can't he fetch his own stuff?"

Her sister's shoulders rose and fell in exaggerated exasperation. "I offered to help, Darly. I was headin' into town anyway."

"Whatever for?"

"Land's sake, can't a body have any privacy around here? Maybe I wanted the exercise. Maybe I just wanted to get out of the house for a while."

Darlene frowned at her sister, but she hadn't stepped outside to ask about the preacher. "Did you see Henry? Did he say anything . . . interesting?"

Annoyance struggled with humor on Nolie's face as she glanced over her shoulder. "Of course I saw Henry. And what do you consider 'interesting'?"

Darlene shrugged. "Did he say anything about comin' over tonight?"

"No, he didn't. And I don't think he will, because his daughter's home for the weekend."

Darlene went back inside, slamming the screen door as she left Nolie to her business. Gretel Hooper, Henry's twenty-year-old daughter, tended to be possessive of her father, and more than once the girl had flashed Darlene a drop-dead look that left no doubt about her feelings for her father's girlfriend.

Shaking her head, Darlene moved into the kitchen and stared out the window as Nolie knocked at the guesthouse door and handed the grocery bag to Erik What's-His-Name. They talked a minute—Darlene couldn't make out a word, but she did notice that Nolie kept twirlin' her hair—then Nolie went back to her bike and walked it toward the garage.

About time.

Darlene sighed and tossed her oily dust rag into the trash bin, then looked around to see what needed cleaning next. Cary Grant, her tuxedo cat, twined around her legs, purring like a new outboard motor. The clock began to chime the hour and her stomach gurgled right on cue—lunchtime. Might as well finish up the last of that tuna fish in the fridge; it'd be good with warmed-up hash-brown casserole on the side.

"Ready to eat?" she asked the cat. "How about a bite of tuna?"

She hummed tunelessly as she made two tuna sandwiches, cut them diagonally, and set them on two plates. She put the leftover casserole in the microwave and poured two glasses of sweet tea while the oven whirred. As promised, she spooned up a bit of tuna for Cary Grant on a fine china saucer.

Nolie strolled into the kitchen as the timer dinged. "Hmm, something smells good."

"Hash-brown casserole. Better eat before it gets cold."

Darlene sat in her usual seat, but Nolie dawdled on the way to her place. She pulled out her chair and looked at Darlene. "Do we have any more tuna?"

"Good grief, how hungry are you?"

"I was thinkin' Erik might like some lunch. He asked me to bring him some potato chips and Vienna sausages from the grocery, but I don't think chips and sausages are going to hold him very long."

"I promised to feed him dinner, and didn't I do that last night? He can get his own lunch."

"But we have extra, and heaven knows we don't need to be stingy. I want to take him a plate."

"If you start takin' him a lunch plate he'll expect one every day. Next thing you know, you'll be getting up at sunrise and servin' him breakfast in bed."

Nolie laughed. "I don't think that's gonna happen. He doesn't seem the omelet type."

Darlene tilted her head to study her sister. Why was Nolie so interested in the preacher's welfare? And how did she know he wasn't the type to like omelets? No good could come out of Nolie's interest in a divorced man, let alone a divorced minister.

She thrust the pointed end of her half sandwich toward her baby sister. "And that's another thing—why hasn't he mowed the lawn? That was the first thing on the list I gave him, but he hasn't even cut himself a path to the guesthouse. At this rate, the grass will be thigh high by the time he gets around to earning his keep."

Nolie smiled, her customary good humor missing from the curve of her mouth. "He mentioned the lawn—said the tractor needed oil and lubrication, and while he had it apart he was going to clean the engine."

"Sounds like he's stalling."

"Sounds to me like he's trying to help us maintain an old machine. Replacing the tractor would be awfully expensive."

"Having a live-in handyman who doesn't do anything handy could be expensive, too." Darlene took a big bite of her sandwich and stared at her sister, defying her to argue.

Nolie picked up her plate. "Since you don't feel inclined toward generosity, I'll take him my lunch."

Darlene mumbled around the food in her mouth: "You can't do that. You're skin and bones; you need to eat."

"I'll eat something later."

She took three steps toward the door before Darlene swallowed and signaled surrender. "Set that plate back down on this table. I'll not have my good dishes going out to the guesthouse. We're liable to never see them again."

"So you'll make him something?"

"As soon as I finish my lunch. So sit, Missy, and eat that tuna salad before you dry up and blow away. I might not need to clean *my* plate, but it sure wouldn't do you any harm."

Nolie grinned, but she obeyed and lifted her iced tea in a saucy salute. "You're not fat, Darly."

"Didn't say I was. But I am way too short for my weight."

Darlene forked up the last shreds of her casserole and let her gaze drift toward the pantry, where she'd set a store of paper plates for occasions like this. Like it or not, she had a feeling that from now on she'd be fixin' three lunches *and* three dinners every day.

She needed to find some other chores for that so-called handyman. If he had time to chat with Nolie, the man didn't have enough to do. And few things were more detrimental to a person's character than having nothing to do and plenty of time in which to do it.

Chapter Three

As a teenager, Nolie once watched a news segment about a Los Angeles gang. When asked what a neighborhood was, one boy looked directly into the camera and said, "A neighborhood is a place, once you step out of it, you get beat up."

She never forgot those words.

On Monday morning, Nolie fed her dogs in their kennels because she and Darlene had big plans for the holiday. Memorial Day wouldn't hold much significance for Ricky and Lucy, but the stores in Peculiar would be closed, the mail wouldn't run, and the town's annual parade would begin promptly at noon. Anyone who wanted to participate would head downtown around eleven forty-five and the parade would end an hour later, followed by a brief prayer service near the veterans' graves in the Congregational Church cemetery.

She squirted a few drops of liquid vitamins onto her dogs' dry kibble, then gave the waiting animals the free command. After they leaped toward their bowls, she patted each head, then latched the kennel gates and headed toward the house. She and Darlene usually grilled hot dogs and hamburgers after the prayer service, but she hadn't heard anything definite about Darly's cookout plans for this year. Last year, since her book club's selection of the month had been *Girl Meets Grill: Smokin' Recipes for Hot Women*, Darly had invited those ladies to Sycamores. This year would seem comparatively low-key unless someone besides Henry joined them. Maybe Nolie could convince the soft-spoken Reverend Payne to venture out and enjoy a burger or two.

She had to admit the man intrigued her. He'd been living at Sycamores for only three days, but the place felt different with a man around. When she walked outside, she wondered if he watched her through the window; when she swept the back terrace she found herself hoping he'd come out to keep her company. She enjoyed the few occasions they'd talked, and for the first time in a long time she'd met a man who left her wanting to know more about him, not less.

She didn't know where Erik Payne had come from, other than Chattahoochee, but his melancholy aspect seemed to reinforce the words she heard that teenage boy utter so long ago. Erik Payne had definitely stepped out of his neighborhood, and life had beaten him up.

She wanted to know why and how, but she hadn't seen much of their handyman since his arrival. He remained polite and soft-spoken whenever she happened to encounter him, and he looked almost painfully grateful when Darlene delivered his dinner tray each evening. Darly kept a sharp eye on him, keenly searching for evidence that their handyman was actually handy, so Nolie kept assuring her that the man was working hard to refurbish the tractor.

Whenever Nolie took Lucy and Ricky for a walk beside the lake, she walked along the side of the guesthouse, her ears tuned for sounds of activity. The little building wasn't currently air conditioned because the old window unit was on the fritz, so if the poor preacher stayed in his room, he had to open his windows or swelter. Last night, as she and the dogs hurried past the guesthouse windows, she heard the slow click-clack of a hesitant typist.

That was when she realized that Reverend Payne had lost not only his wife, his home, his job, and his copy machine, but also his secretary. If he was hunting-and-pecking his way through each re-sume cover letter, he might be living at Sycamores for a good long time.

By late morning, she and Darlene were ready for the parade. Though Nolie would have enjoyed taking the old tandem bike into town, Darlene refused to ride anything that didn't have a steering wheel, power brakes, and seat belts.

They parked her aging Buick sedan in the lot behind the Pig-gly Wiggly. Darlene's smile broadened when she spotted Henry in the milling crowd. He had reserved three empty lawn chairs on the bunting-draped viewing stand in front of his store, so Darlene led Nolie up the steps like a queen escorting her retinue toward a set of red, white, and blue thrones.

"There you are!" Henry greeted Darlene with a quick kiss on the cheek, then winked at Nolie. "So glad you two gals could join me."

"Gretel coming to the parade?" Darlene asked, her voice impassive.

"Gretel went back to school. You've got me all to yourself, Darly."

Darlene smiled. "All's ready at the house, your honorableness." She winked as she sank into the chair at his side. "The hamburgers are waiting in the fridge, and I fixed 'em with my special marinade."

"Then they'll be the best burgers in town." Henry patted her hand, then adjusted the glittering sash running from his left shoulder to his right hip. Nolie was about to tell him how official he looked, but just then the fire chief ran up.

"All clear to begin the parade, Mr. Mayor?" he asked.

"We're all here." Henry threw Darlene a quick smile, then ex-ecuted a crisp salute. "Lead the way, chief!"

As usual, parade participants had assembled at the city park in what appeared to be random order. The fire chief motioned to the driver in the big red fire engine, and sirens began to wail. Nolie clapped her hands over her ears and grimaced as volunteer firemen threw candy to the excited children who waited beside the red truck.

She lowered her hands as the fire engine pulled onto Main Street, followed by a horse-drawn flatbed loaded with the members of the Peculiar Community Orchestra. As long as a resident could mount a ladder; sit upright on a moving trailer; and blow, strum, or beat an instrument, they were expected to make a joyful noise at civic events.

As the orchestra began to play "The Stars and Stripes Forever," Nolie found herself whispering the alternative lyrics her grandfather had taught her: *Oh, be kind to your fine-feathered friends . . . for a duck may be somebody's mother . . .*

She watched ninety-year-old Deveny Whitlow strike the chimes on a glockenspiel mounted between two two-by-fours. Though the glockenspiel chimed about a beat behind the rest of the instruments, the bright-eyed great-grandma wielded her mallet with gusto, and Brittany Scrip, a teenage wunderkind on the trumpet, soared on the high notes.

"I love that band," Henry said, slapping his knee. "Finest community band in these parts."

Nolie might have remarked that it was the *only* community band in these parts, but she bit her tongue as the orchestra followed the fire truck and the Shining Lights Twirlers Team advanced to the viewing stand. Their batons spun, flew, and occasionally bounced on the asphalt as their theme song pounded from the stereo system in their sponsor's Miata convertible.

"Erica Brand should know better than to stuff herself into one of those sausage suits," Darlene whispered, her lawn chair creaking as she leaned toward Nolie. "Once she had an hourglass figure, but my, how the sands of time have shifted."

Nolie studied Erica, who, at twenty-six and five months pregnant, should have known better than to put on an outfit she wore in high school, but she was probably the best majorette Peculiar had ever produced. She was one of the few girls qualified to twirl with fire, and at the mayoral viewing stand she paused to set her batons alight. Despite Darlene's snide comment, Nolie couldn't help being impressed.

"Hey." Darlene elbowed Nolie in the ribs. "Isn't that our preacher man over yonder?"

Nolie straightened and followed Darlene's pointing finger. Erik Payne stood on the park side of the street, nearly obscured by a big-haired clown hawking cotton candy. The preacher's sharply angled face was turned toward the twirlers, but he watched with a detached look, his hands in his pockets, his shirtsleeves flapping in the stiff breeze.

Henry leaned toward Nolie. "Who's the scarecrow? I don't think I've seen him around before."

"He's not from Peculiar," Darlene explained. "Showed up at Syca-mores the other day claiming to be a pastor in need of a job. Nolie talked me into hiring him as a handyman, but so far all he's done is eat and ruin our tractor."

Nolie sighed. "He took our tractor apart so he could clean it. And I didn't talk Darlene into anything; she would have given him a job no matter what." She frowned at her sister. Why did Darly always try to hide her heart beneath a layer of crust?

Henry winked at Nolie and patted Darlene's hand as the Piggly Wiggly float—a crepe-paper-draped pickup towing a giant helium-inflated sow—followed the twirlers. In the face of the rising wind, several uniformed cashiers clung to ropes and struggled to hold the pig down.

As grocery employees tossed coupons to the crowd, Henry leaned toward the Caldwell women. "The pig had a hole in her this year, but we patched her up with duct tape and Gorilla Glue. Worked like a charm."

A tractor from Doc's Hardware trailed in the wake of the flutter-ing coupons, and a red convertible decorated with Styrofoam wig stands puttered behind the tractor.

Henry blew out a breath. "What in tarnation is that supposed to be?"

"It's the entry from LuAnn's Coif It Up Salon," Darlene hurried to explain. "That's her husband driving the car."

As soon as the convertible rolled by, Nolie stood and waved her hat to catch Erik's attention. His brow crinkled for an instant, then he smiled. Taking advantage of the gap between parade entries, he jogged across the street. "Good morning, ladies," he said, approaching the viewing stand. "I was hoping to get to the hardware store, but I forgot about Memorial Day."

"Small towns are at their best on days like this," Henry said. He stood, leaned over Darlene, and thrust his hand over the banner-draped railing at Nolie's side. "Henry Hooper, town mayor."

"Erik Payne." The preacher shook Henry's hand, then pointed toward the street as another parade entry rolled up for the mayor's approval: a flatbed trailer bearing the handbell choir from Peculiar's First and Only Baptist Church.

Nolie read the poster on the side of the flatbed, then glanced at Erik, who wore a confused expression. "Something wrong?"

"That church." He nodded toward the float. "Is First and Only the official name?"

She tucked a wandering curl behind her ear. "I know it sounds odd, but we're used to it."

Erik chuckled. "Small town flavor at its best, I suppose."

She was about to remark that the town he'd come from wasn't exactly a metropolis, but her thoughts scattered when a group of trim, tanned women in shorts, sleeveless shirts, and sweatbands followed the bell choir. Two women at the rear carried a banner stretched across a long pole announcing The Calorie Counters Club.

Darlene snorted. "It's those awful Methodist women!"

"Now, sweetie." Henry patted her hand. "You're not the type to bear a grudge."

How well did Henry know his girlfriend? Nolie covered her smile, but Erik had caught her midgrin. "Okay"—he moved closer to the railing and lowered his voice—"you want to explain why your sister is mad at the Methodists?"

Nolie drew a deep breath and lowered her voice. "See that empty storefront a couple of doors down? Well, a year ago Darlene decided to open a cupcake shop. Since cupcakes have become sort of a national fad, she decided that a really great cupcake shop would put Peculiar on the map. Her shop, the Cup Cakery, might have done just that. She did a bang-up business in the first six months, with a steady stream of local customers. Other folks came from as far as Tallahassee and Mobile to buy her cupcakes."

Erik's forehead knit. "People drove all the way from Alabama for a cupcake?"

"These weren't ordinary cupcakes—they were Darlene's. Her beautiful little concoctions came in flavors like Key lime, hummingbird, and pear pecan. Red velvet was her best seller; she sold dozens of them."

"I had no idea she was such an entrepreneur." Erik folded his arms, the grim line of his mouth relaxing. "I'm impressed."

"I was, too, but after about six months of eating cupcakes every day, the Methodist women decided that the Cup Cakery was a devilish temptation that must be resisted, so they torpedoed the shop by founding the Calorie Counters Club. Within a week, more than a hundred women joined the Methodists and swore to resist the devil and anything that came close to lookin' like a palm-sized pastry."

"I didn't know there were a hundred overweight women in Peculiar."

"They weren't all from around here. Last I heard, the membership included women from three counties, including Baptists, Catholics, Presbyterians, and a few Unitarians—and they don't even *believe* in the devil." She shrugged and watched the Girl Scouts' float pass by. "Two months later, Darlene had to close her shop. The Cup Cakery moved into the annals of Peculiar's history, but the Calorie Counters kept goin' strong, especially after Darlene gave away a few dozen five-pound bags of buttercream frostin'. More than a few of those calorie counters were goin' to meetings on Monday and gobbling Darlene's buttercream on Tuesday. Darly never quite got over it—she still calls 'em calorie-countin' hypocrites."

Turning her head, she was startled to find the minister so close to her. At this distance, separated only by bunting and a cheap pine railing, she could see the long silken fringes that edged his brown eyes. Those eyes touched her now, gripped her. Had his beautiful eyes been the feature that first attracted his wife?

She turned back toward the street and felt her face flush. Wherever had that thought come from? Darlene was lucky because she could blame these annoying blushes on hot flashes and hormones . . .

Erik laughed, but she heard a trace of sympathy in his voice. "Poor Darlene. I'm beginning to understand why she feels the way she does."

From the corner of her eye, Nolie saw Darlene's bosom heave as the Calorie Counters power walked past the mayor's elevated seat. Nolie would probably feel resentful, too, if her attempt to participate in free enterprise had failed so spectacularly.

Nolie let her gaze rove over the crowd. "The thing is"—she pitched her voice to a level designed to reach Erik alone—"I have my own business ambition. Fortunately, it has nothing to do with food."

"You planning to cycle around the world?"

She gave him a quick, sidelong glance to make sure he was kidding. "No. Nothing to do with bikes. My goal involves my dogs."

"Fred and Ginger?"

"Ricky and Lucy."

"Oh, yeah, the Ricardos." He grinned, and Nolie's heart warmed to see the hint of a twinkle in his eye. This man must've needed a holiday in the worst way.

"Anyway, I borrowed a lot of money from Darlene to build the outdoor runs and to bring my dogs over from Germany. I did my homework and I know they come from healthy champion stock. They're both over two years old now, finally mature and ready for breeding . . . so that's what I plan to do."

Erik's thick brows rose nearly to his hairline. "You want to raise puppies?"

Nolie held up a finger. "Only one litter at a time—I'm not talkin' about runnin' a puppy mill. But Leos are truly special dogs, and perfect family pets . . . as long as people don't mind a little drool and a little shedding."

Erik sucked at the inside of his cheek, then tilted his head. "Have

you noticed the national popularity of little bitty dogs? The kind ladies carry around in their pocketbooks?"

Nolie waved the notion away. "Those dogs are nothing but dress-
up toys for froufrou women. I want to raise dogs for people who love
animals. People who like having a bit of land under their feet and
enjoy long walks after supper. People who don't mind a dog who
thinks his duty is to protect his home and family."

Erik gave her a benign smile as if accepting her dream as a bit of
harmless Cinderella talk. He focused his gaze on the Peculiar barber-
shop quartet, now rolling by in a restored Model T.

Nolie propped her chin on her fist, assuming the conversation
was over, but Erik soon spoke again. "So do you want to raise puppies for the joy of it? Or for the money?"

His questions caught her off guard. "For the joy of it, of course. I
mean, who doesn't love puppies? But I also need to repay Darlene for
the loan. And while I suppose it would be nice to have a little money
set aside, I hear that breeding can be expensive, especially if your girl
needs a C-section."

Erik had the good manners not to ask why she didn't have a job,
and Nolie wasn't about to volunteer complicated details about the family history. He probably thought she and Darlene were wealthy because
they lived in a big house, but the fortune that built Sycamores had expired along with her grandfather. Darlene still had a bit of money from
Griff's life insurance, but the only income Nolie received came from the
charitable gift annuity Grandpa established before his death.

She stared at the pair of clowns attempting to juggle for the
mayor. She tried not to worry about what would happen in six years
when the annuity payments stopped and Sycamores became county
property, but sometimes she couldn't help feeling that she was getting
a late start in life. Darlene had become a wife, mother, and widow;
Carlene had established a career. Nolie did nothing but tend the gardens, train her dogs, and sew in her workroom . . .

Wasn't life supposed to be made of more than such simple things?

Henry leaned over to address both sisters. "So, girls, what should
I bring to the cookout today? We have some day-old doughnuts that

might be good for dessert. You put scoops of vanilla ice cream in the holes, then drizzle 'em with hot fudge sauce and top each doughnut with whipped cream and a cherry . . ."

Darlene harrumphed. "Keep your stale old doughnuts. I made a red, white, and blueberry shortcake and it's ready for the eating. Just show up, Henry, and let me take care of the rest."

Nolie turned to Erik. "You're coming to the cookout, right?"

His gaze shifted from the street. "There's a cookout?"

"When we get back to the house. It's tradition. Just come on out to the terrace; Darly will have everthing set up there."

"I don't want to intrude—"

"You won't be intruding. It's just us home folk, and now that includes you."

His face transformed, the stoic veneer peeling back to reveal surprise and pleasure underneath. Something else, too . . . gratitude? Then, as suddenly as the veneer had vanished, it reappeared.

Whatever Erik Payne's reasons for coming to Peculiar, Nolie was glad he'd taken time to enjoy the beautiful May afternoon. With all the rejection he'd suffered over the past year, the man had to be in need of company and comfort . . . and Darlene's red, white, and blueberry shortcake could provide him with both.

And a leisurely afternoon on the terrace could furnish Nolie with a perfect opportunity to get to know their guest.

Exasperated with waiting, Darlene slid off her stool and uncrossed her arms when the minister finally stepped out of the guesthouse and trudged across the lawn between his apartment and the back porch. One of the dogs trotted down the deck stairs to meet him, but the preacher paused at the bottom of the steps. "If you want," he called, catching Darlene's eye, "I can fix a plate and take it back to my room. I don't want to interrupt your party."

Nolie practically bounded over an empty chair in her eagerness to greet the man. "Don't mind Ricky, just come on up. We're always happy to welcome another friendly face."

Darlene sat and bit back the comment that leapfrogged onto her lips. The preacher's face was anything but friendly; most of the time he looked like a basset hound with an earache. Nolie said he couldn't help looking sad after all he'd been through, but Darlene was of the opinion that ministers should make a determined effort to look pleasant—after all, they were walking advertisements for the joys of Christian living.

Henry nodded at the newcomer. "Good to see you again," he said, tugging his napkin from the top of his tee shirt. "Glad you could join us."

"Thanks for the invitation." Reverend Payne slipped his hands into his pockets and surveyed the spread on the table. "My, my. Everything looks delicious."

"Really." Darlene heard the dry note in her voice and tried to smile it away. Honestly, if this was how the man reacted when he was pleased, she'd hate to see him when he was miserable.

She pointed to the empty garden chair across from Nolie. "Preacher, why don't you sit there? We have burgers; hot dogs; macaroni and cheese; green-bean casserole; and red, white, and blueberry shortcake. Condiments are on the table. If you don't see anything you like, holler and I'll fix you a peanut butter and jelly sandwich."

"Or I'll get you something from the Wiggly." Henry grinned at the handyman. "Maybe you've heard—I own the grocery store downtown."

"A man of many hats," Darlene added, reaching for the green beans. She passed the dish to Henry along with a wait-till-you-taste-this smile. "After all that hoopla at the parade today, shouldn't we be curtseying before you or some such thing?"

"I wouldn't hear of it." Henry helped himself to a double serving of beans and passed the dish to Nolie.

Remembering her manners, Darlene cleared her throat and waited until everyone looked her way. "I suppose we should ask our resident minister to say grace." She transferred her gaze to the newcomer. "Will you do the honors, Reverend?"

Color flooded the man's cheeks, but he bowed his head. "Thank you, Lord, for this food and for the generous hands that prepared it. Bless us to do your will . . . and please make it clear what that will is. In Jesus' name, Amen."

"Amen," Nolie echoed.

Darlene folded her hands as the others resumed passing platters and bowls. "So—are you all settled in the guesthouse, Reverend?"

"Please call me Erik," he said, spearing a hot dog as the platter passed by. "My first name seems to fit better than ever these days."

"I'm sure you're hot in that little apartment, but that window air conditioner doesn't need much work," Darlene continued, watching Henry ladle macaroni and cheese onto his plate. Good grief, if the man kept eating like this he'd need a new suit for their wedding—provided they ever *had* a wedding. She redirected her attention to the preacher. "If the heat becomes unbearable, I'd move that AC unit to the top of your priority list. But don't touch it until after you've repaired the sprinklers—we're getting dry patches in the lawn and we're going to lose some grass if it doesn't get water soon. Plus, if the sprinklers in the garden fail, Nolie will have to water all those perennials by hand."

"That wouldn't be so bad." Nolie shot a sharp glance at Darlene. "And the summer rains should be arriving anytime now."

"Got it—sprinklers first, AC second." Erik looked around the table. "I know Nolie was born at Sycamores—have you always lived here, Miss Darlene?"

"Since she was just a twinkle in her daddy's eye," Henry said, winking at her. "All three of the Caldwell girls were born 'n bred right here in Chase Caldwell's house."

The preacher cocked an eyebrow. "Chase Caldwell?"

"Our grandfather," Darlene explained. "He left the house to us as part of a charitable gift annuity."

"Lawyers in the county say it was the most creative will ever filed down at county records." Henry grinned. "I don't understand all the legalese, but ol' Chase nurtured a lifelong distrust of the government, especially since they shut down his business back in the twenties."

"He made hard liquor," Nolie added, shaking her head. "Sometimes I just can't believe it."

"Anyway," Henry went on, obviously warming to the subject, "ol' Chase made a fortune during Prohibition and founded the town of Peculiar—some say he did it just because he needed an out-of-the-way spot to sell his homemade hooch. On a run to Chattahoochee, though, he met a local girl and fell in love. And that was the end of Chase's illegal enterprise."

"Quite the scandal." Nolie squirted mustard onto her hamburger bun. "He was forty-three and Grandma was only seventeen."

"Scandal or not, he cleaned up his act." Darlene stared at Henry, determined that he tell the full story. "Grandma wouldn't have let him court her otherwise."

Henry chuckled. "Yeah, Lela Ruby Lee was a sweet Christian girl and a teetotaler. But that didn't stop Chase from enjoying his money—or from doing his best to see that the revenuers never got their hands on a penny of it. He wrote his will so that his estate would pass into the hands of whatever descendants were living on the place the moment before his death, then fixed it so the house would provide a monthly income to whichever Caldwells lived here for the next fifty years. After that, the house becomes county property."

The preacher's mouth took on an unpleasant twist. "Did he intend to leave his descendants high and dry?"

Henry shrugged. "I guess he figured most of his kin would have moved on by then—either that, or he thought the house wouldn't be worth livin' in. Who knows what he was thinkin'?"

"Grandpa was brilliant." Darlene lifted her chin and met the preacher's gaze. "I don't know what his reasons were, but I've always known he had our best interests at heart."

"But only fifty years? If the man lived an average life span, that term is—"

"Grandpa died in sixty-eight," Darlene interrupted. "So we have six more years to enjoy our home."

"And after that?"

Here he was, directly asking the question that kept Darlene awake for many a night. She couldn't give him an answer, but she wasn't about to let him know that Grandpa might have been a little shortsighted.

She dropped a spoonful of relish onto her hamburger bun. "The good Lord takes care of his children. I'm not worried about the future."

"I don't think anybody around here is going to kick us out," Nolie said, running a fork through her green beans. "And I can't imagine living anywhere else."

The minister lifted a brow and glanced at Henry. "Really, Mr. Mayor?"

"The town council really hasn't discussed the future of Sycamores," Henry said, his cheeks flushing. "It's too soon."

Darlene dipped her chin in an emphatic nod. "You bet it is."

"I remember when the three Caldwell girls were always together," Henry went on, clearly feeling chatty now that he had another man to talk to. "Darlene and Carlene were like two peas in a pod, and little Nolie used to trail along behind them. I went to school with Carly and Darly, kindergarten through twelfth grade. But smack in the middle of our senior year Carlene hightailed it to New York, and Darlene married the captain of the football team soon after. I might have asked her to marry me, but she didn't give me time to pop the question."

Darlene's cheeks warmed as she smeared mustard on her hamburger bun. Charming, loose-lipped Henry was venturing perilously close to subjects she didn't like to discuss, especially not before a stranger.

"I'm going to pop *you* if you don't eat your supper." She nodded toward Henry's plate. "Try that green-bean casserole and stop boring our guest."

"I'm not bored—and you don't have to consider me a guest." The preacher looked at her with an open expression, as if he wanted her to peek inside his soul and see his sincerity. "I like learning about people . . . that's probably one of the things that led me into the ministry. That and the fact that God called me, of course."

Darlene tilted her head, bemused by his offhanded comment about his calling. For heaven's sake, the man made it sound as if God had picked up the phone and dialed his number.

Nolie nodded, clearly accepting every word without question. "Of course," she said, nodding. "That only makes sense. If the Lord tells you to do something, you really have no choice."

Silence sifted down like a snowfall, broken only by the steady slap and suck of water around the old pilings, all that remained of the lakeside dock. Darlene stared at Nolie, amazed by her sister's ability to stop a conversation in its tracks.

But not for long.

"So"—the preacher picked up his hot dog—"is the other Caldwell sister still in the Big Apple?"

Henry shot Nolie a quick glance, then Nolie shook her head almost imperceptibly and turned to Darlene. Darlene frowned, mystified by the unspoken exchange. What was goin' on with those two?

"She's a Broadway star." Nolie looked at the preacher now, her eyes shining with pride. "She's been in all the big musicals: *Wicked, Les Misérables, the Phantom of the Opera,* and *Fiddler on the Roof,* just to name a few. She's amazing."

"She sings." Like a bullfrog interrupting a chorus of birdsong, Darlene's matter-of-fact tone silenced Nolie's trilling. "She sings, so off she went to conquer the Great White Way. We don't hear from her very often."

The minister's brows flickered. "You don't sing, Miss Darlene?"

"We're twins, but we're far from identical." She shrugged and lifted her tea glass. "I guess we're about as different as twins can be."

"But surely you've gone up to see her shows," Erik said, displaying the first real spark of interest Darlene had seen on his face. "That must have been thrilling."

She shook her head. "Never had time to go to New York. After Carlene left, we got busy livin' our lives. I got married, raised two kids, buried Momma, got my kids married, and then buried Grandma. Not all at once, understand, but over the years. About five years ago I buried Griff, my late husband. So you'll have to excuse me, preacher, but I haven't felt much like going to New York to celebrate my sister's success."

The man blinked hard, his cheeks flaming as if she'd slapped him.

"We've had our share of rough times," Nolie said in a gentler tone, "but we've had good times, too. And except for Carly, we Caldwell girls don't really like to travel. Last year Darlene's kids got together and gave her two tickets to Paris for her birthday, but she has yet to use them."

Henry leaned toward Darlene and waggled his bushy brows. "We could use them sometime, sweetie. We could go to gay Par-ee for the summer and have our picture taken on the Eiffel Tower."

"Or we could stay here and tend to our business," Darlene finished, hoping to conclude the discussion. "You know I can't leave all my responsibilities, and neither can you. Next week the Ladies' Auxiliary is coming to Sycamores for our weekly meeting, and the Begonia Book Club is convening on the first and I still haven't read my book. Then there's the garden club, which goes into full swing in the summer, and the planning meeting for the Preserve our Downtown League's Annual Spaghetti Dinner and Bake-off. I haven't even mentioned the Fall Festival, but the steering committee for that meets soon, too. I'm too busy to go anywhere, Henry, so there's no sense in even thinking about going to France."

Henry offered her a peacemaker's smile and reached for another helping of macaroni. "I suppose you're right. After all, tending the Wiggly and running Peculiar is more important than taking time to enjoy myself. I have the rest of my life to travel and see the sights, don't I?"

Darlene narrowed her gaze. Was that an attempt at sarcasm? She often struggled to read Henry Hooper. Though they'd been keeping company for more than six months, she wasn't exactly sure where she stood with the man. He was quick to call her *sweetie* and eager to tease her about running away together, but he didn't drop by every day and sometimes he didn't call on weekends. But he never failed to show up when she invited him for a meal . . . unless Gretel happened to be in town.

As Nolie began to talk about her dogs, Darlene sighed and picked up her hamburger. Nolie could keep tellin' folks that Caldwell girls didn't like to travel, but Darlene harbored a secret desire to see the world. Some days she stood wrist deep in dishwater and stared out the window, feelin' that the sycamores bordering the property were more like malicious guards than benevolent shade trees. She and Carly had played beneath those trees, sheltered beneath them in sudden showers, climbed in those sprawling branches. And then Carly had gone off, leaving Darly in the trees' blue shadows. Those watchful sentinels kept her tied to the house, chained to her responsibilities, and dependent on her routines. First Griff had needed her, then her children, then Momma, then Grandma, and now Nolie. One by one the others slipped away, leaving Darlene to tend to the family heritage. In a few years, though, the county would ask her to leave, and then where would she go?

If Henry didn't soon step up to the plate, she had no idea. She tried not to worry, but the future hovered over the horizon like a steadily approaching thundercloud.

She wished she could be more like Nolie, chipper and chirpy and blissfully unconcerned about threatening problems. Nolie was like Carlene in that respect, certainly not like Darlene, who'd never been good at making idle conversation, especially with men. Carly had a knack for it—in high school, boys fell in line to ask her to dances and parties, forcing Darlene to either tend the punch bowl or settle for Carlene's castoffs. Even Griff dated Carlene before he ever looked at Darlene, and as much as Darlene loved her late husband, she never really understood him.

Once, just once, she'd love to find a man who considered her the most beautiful, talented, and wonderful Caldwell sister.

She took a bite of her hamburger and closed her eyes, sighing in satisfaction. She may not have had much luck with men, but she had certainly learned her way around a kitchen. This mouthful only confirmed that her burgers, at least, really were the best in three counties.

Chapter Four

O n a cloudy Tuesday afternoon, Carlene walked up the old stone stairs and thumbed through the mail she'd pulled from her box. All the usual end-of-the-month bills had arrived: electric bill, gas bill, cable bill. Accompanied by a second notice that her Actors Equity Association dues were past due.

She sighed. She didn't see any need to renew her membership in the actors' union, but maybe she ought to. If by some miracle Martin managed to find her a part that didn't require singing, she'd need that union card.

She frowned as she flipped to a letter with a familiar postmark. Neither the handwriting nor the return address rang a bell, so who could be writing her from Peculiar?

She reached her apartment and let herself in. Dropping the other mail on a table by the door, she ripped the envelope open:

Greetings, Carlene!
 Your big day's almost here!
 Your sister Nolie and I have pulled out all the stops

to arrange a citywide fiftieth birthday party for you and Darlene. We're holding the event on your milestone day, that night to be exact, in the fellowship hall of the First and Only Baptist Church. Nolie tells me you might not be able to make it because of performance obligations, but if you can get away, we'd all love to see you.

If you can't come, would you consider sending a card for Darlene in care of my address? We'll present it to her as a special surprise.

Please let me hear from you as soon as possible, and remember—mum's the word! We want this event to be a big shocker for Darlene... and we Peculiar folk would love to honor you, too.

Cordially,
Henry Hooper, Mayor
(850) 555-3847

Carlene dropped onto the sofa as a wave of unexpected pleasure swept over her. The town was throwing a community-wide birthday party for the Caldwell twins. Unbelievable. Including her must have been an afterthought since she hadn't been home in years, but how nice of them to plan a party for Darlene. In her Christmas cards Darlene always joked about being the spine that held Peculiar together, and this Henry fellow had just proved her right.

A birthday party in Peculiar—what would that look like? She fanned herself with the letter, repelling an annoying hot flash. She couldn't help smiling at the thought of a crepe-paper-festooned reception hall. The room would be filled to overflowing with kind expressions, warm smiles, delicious food, and soft Southern accents. She might even spot familiar faces among the crowd . . . though none of them would be the face she longed most to see.

That face now smiled only in her memories.

She'd planned to celebrate her fiftieth birthday quietly in New York. She hadn't made any calls yet, but she hoped to find a handful of friends who might want to go out to dinner with her. Though she'd tell them it was her birthday, she wouldn't tell them her age. When they lifted a glass to toast the occasion, she'd give them a sly smile and say she was thirty-five—again—and fighting hard to stay there. They'd drink to her health, while she'd smile through the sparkling champagne and wonder if the Big Apple held any future for her at all.

She folded the letter, slipped it back into the envelope, and considered her choice. The party planners in Peculiar weren't expecting her to show up, so what would happen if she called Henry Hooper and told him she'd be pleased to accept his invitation? The man would probably be tickled to death. Nolie would certainly be happy.

Her smile softened at the thought of her younger sister. She barely knew Nolie anymore, but Nolie wrote occasionally and had been the only one willing to share details about Momma's illness, Grandma's funeral, and Griff's sudden death. Darlene had apparently been content to let Nolie act as the official family correspondent, because other than brief notes on Christmas cards, Darly never wrote. She'd called exactly three times in the past thirty-something years, each time to convey sad news.

The thought of Darlene cast a shadow on Carlene's nostalgic musings. Darlene had once been closer than a best friend, but over the years, life and distance came between them. Carlene missed her twin terribly when she first moved to New York, and sometimes she missed her still, but Darlene hadn't exhibited any signs of wanting to reconnect. So Carlene shoved her hurt and loneliness aside, then locked them away.

How would Sondheim describe it? Her relationship with Darlene was a dress that no longer fit, a song she no longer sang. Or maybe a hair shirt she no longer wore.

She tapped the invitation against the palm of her left hand. Though her relationship with Darlene wasn't close, they weren't at war, were they? Everything should be fine if she went home for a brief visit.

Carlene set the letter on her sofa and pulled her calendar from her desk. Ordinarily the pages would be filled with *x*'s marking performances or rehearsals, but the future weeks and months were an expanse of blank space.

Her gaze skimmed the penciled-in appointment on yesterday's page. A real estate agent had come by at eleven and her advice had been simple: declutter, removing as much personal property as possible. "And while you're at it," she said, her dark eyes honing in on Carlene's naked ring finger, "remove yourself as well. We find that apartments sell more quickly when the owner has vacated the premises, so if you want a quick sale . . ."

Carlene did want a quick sale, the quicker, the better. But how was she supposed to declutter and where was she supposed to go?

Those questions bothered her all last night, but perhaps a partial answer had arrived in the form of this invitation . . .

Maybe she ought to go home.

She needed to sell the apartment, no question. With no income, the monthly expense was draining her bank account at an alarming rate. She wouldn't have to fret about missing a casting call if she left town since no one would be calling. And the apartment should sell in a flash if Carlene stored her personal belongings and moved out. Newcomers to the city were always looking for decent apartments in good neighborhoods.

A visit to Sycamores would solve her immediate problems. She could go home to visit Nolie and try to rekindle the close relationship she once shared with Darlene. Later, after her apartment sold and she had deposited the proceeds, she could move to some pleasant city with a lower cost of living.

The thought of going back to Peculiar filled Carlene with a surprising sense of satisfaction. Perhaps the feeling sprang from her upcoming birthday and the sense that fifty was a good time to take stock of one's life. She could go home to rest, reconnect with both sisters, and figure out what she wanted to do with the remainder of her years. She wouldn't tell anyone about her vocal problems, the lawsuit, or her butchered career. She'd let her doctor, lawyer, and agent handle those problems.

Why not go home to sit by the lake and let the unspoiled beauty of her childhood home wash over her? She wanted to close her eyes and drift back to a simpler time when she had loved and been loved. She wanted to walk the hallways her momma walked; she wanted to touch the Mason jars her grandma had filled with kumquat jelly and cherry preserves. And as painful as it might be, she wanted to walk through the field where Daddy died, to visit the cemetery where so many of her loved ones slumbered beneath a lush cloak of pasture grass.

She wanted to leave flowers by Griff's headstone.

She wanted—needed—to be refreshed. And if she exercised a bit of tact and diplomacy, she might not need to get into any heavy discussions with Darlene. Couldn't they simply accept each other and be friends?

She flipped through the pages of her calendar. Early June wasn't exactly the best time for visiting Florida—even before summer officially began the oppressive heat and humidity made the air feel as thick as molasses—but New York would be sweltering soon enough. Besides, she'd have the lake only a few yards away. If she found the heat unbearable, she could simply pull on her bathing suit and take a swim.

When she wasn't swimming or sleeping, she could spend time with her sisters, doing whatever they liked to do. Peculiar had never offered much in the way of shopping, but she might be able to talk her sisters into going to Tallahassee, where the three of them could shop and eat dinner in a nice restaurant . . .

Why not go home? She smiled at the idea and consulted the letter again. Henry Hooper's name sounded vaguely familiar, so he must have attended school with her. Because Peculiar was too small to support its own school system, the Peculiar kids had been bused to schools in neighboring towns. Henry Hooper must have ridden her bus or been in her class.

She pulled her cell phone from her purse and punched in Hooper's number. The phone rang three times, then a bored female voice answered. "Piggly Wiggly."

Carlene blinked. "I beg your pardon?"

"This is the Piggly Wiggly. Did you want something delivered?"

"I—I'd like to speak to Henry Hooper."

"Hang on."

Carlene held the phone at a distance after a loud clunk rattled her ear, but even from a foot away she could hear the squawk of an intercom: "Henry, you have a phone call. Henry?"

After a long moment, a breathless male voice rasped over the line. "Hello?"

"Henry Hooper?"

"Speaking."

"Henry, this is Carlene Caldwell. I received your invitation and I wanted you to know that I'd be delighted to accept. I haven't been home in a long while, so I think I'm overdue for a visit."

She waited through an interval of stunned silence, then Henry's voice boomed over the line. "Is this some kind of a joke? Edna, is this you?"

"It's Carlene. Carlene Caldwell, Darlene's sister."

"Well, knock me over with a feather. Nolie told me not to hold my breath, but I figured, why not write the lady? I'm so happy to hear from you."

Carlene laughed. "Thank you. I'm happy to accept. Should I plan to fly down on Friday the eighth?"

"I think that'd be fine, unless you want to come in sooner. We need to keep you hidden from Darlene, though, so you can be a surprise."

"I have some business to take care of before I can leave Manhattan, so I'll plan to arrive on the eighth. Your party sounds wonderful."

"This is so great. Darlene will be thrilled and so will all the folks in town. I know a bunch of people would be honored just to get your autograph."

Carlene lifted her gaze to the ceiling. "I don't know that my career is anything to crow about."

"Don't you be modest, now. Why, hundreds of people go up to the Big Apple to make a name for themselves and never come close, but you did it! I remember you telling us that you wanted to be a professional singer. Though the other kids laughed, I never doubted you. I knew you could do it."

Carlene bit her lip, struggling to place the name and voice. "Henry—forgive me, but did we ride the school bus together?"

"We sure did. And the three of us would have graduated together if you hadn't skipped town early. Darlene was right ahead of me in the line to get our diplomas. Carlene Caldwell, Darlene Caldwell, Henry Hooper."

Carlene smiled as the memory of a stocky, freckle-faced boy crystallized in her brain. "You're *Hank* Hooper. You had a little sister— Nancy or Fancy or—"

"Darcie," Henry corrected. "She married Lowell Ranger right after high school and moved to Georgia. We don't see much of each other except at Christmas and Thanksgiving."

"That's too bad." Carlene glanced at the letter, wondering what he expected her to say next. She'd love to trip down memory lane and find out about other people from her past, but if she was going through with this plan, she needed to begin packing up her apartment, have her mail forwarded, and tell her agent she was leaving town for a while . . .

"Hank, it's been delightful to chat with you, but I need to get going. I suspect you do, too. Being the mayor must keep you terribly busy."

"Busier than you'd think," he said, a smile in his voice. "Thanks for calling, Carly. We look forward to seeing you."

"Same here," she echoed. "See you in a couple of weeks."

Southern families associate their homes with their loved ones, and no room is more family friendly than the kitchen. Clutter is allowed here, scuff marks on the wall are perfectly presentable, and no one minds if a few dirty dishes wait in the sink. Children are encouraged to cook with their parents (and allowed to lick the mixing spoon); parents pretend not to notice when kids drop bits of their dinner for the family pet; and the pot for making sweet tea resides permanently on the stove.

After serving three generations of Caldwells, the kitchen at Sycamores had an especially well-loved look. The bricks around the built-in oven had darkened over the years, the plaster had been buried under at least three different wallpapers, and a fine layer of dust cloaked the iron pot rack above the kitchen island. But the new granite countertops provided a gleaming contrast to the scuffed brick flooring and morning sunshine poured through the wide window adjacent to the scarred pine table, spangling the old chairs and shining on the antique dishes displayed above the cabinets. Not a single uptown decorator would describe the Sycamores kitchen as *fashionable*, but nearly every woman in the Southern United States would call it *comfortable*.

On June first, at precisely eleven a.m., Darlene took one last look around the circle of ladies gathered in her spacious kitchen. Satisfied that each woman had tea or coffee and a slice of brown-sugar pecan cake, she took her place at the head of the gathering and rapped on the tabletop with her knuckles. "This meeting of the Fall Festival and Miss Buttercup Squash Pageant Organizational Committee will now come to order."

"Hear, hear." Monisha Brand, committee vice chairman, rapped on the table as well, after casting a stern glance at Edna Higgins, who insisted on finishing a conversation with Glennette Wessel.

Ignoring Edna's rough whisper, Darlene flashed a polite smile and slid a sheet of paper from a manila folder. "The first order of business is good news. I have here our official letter from the Miss America organization renewing our charter of the Miss Buttercup Squash Pageant. We're the only pageant within a hundred miles to officially feed into the Miss Florida Pageant, which, as you know, feeds into the Big One. Once again, we've been honored to continue this outstanding tradition to encourage scholarship, character development, and poise among our young women."

The five other ladies greeted this news with a polite smattering of applause.

"I know the pageant and festival are still several months away," Darlene continued, "but as president of the committee I wanted to set a few considerations before you. First, the pageant venue. Are we still set on having this event at the park pavilion? We've been fortunate not to be rained out in the past, but you know our weather . . . our luck might not hold."

"We could always move it across the street to St. Mary's," Orlain Jones suggested. "They have the largest auditorium in town, don't they?"

Mary Thomas shook her head. "I'm not sure our church is set up for a pageant—or even if the priest would allow it. The Baptist church would probably be a better fit."

Darlene shook her head. "Bathing suits in a Baptist sanctuary? I don't think that's gonna work."

"And don't forget the baptistry." Orlain made a face. "Who wants to look at that big tank in the wall?"

Glennette lifted her hand. "We could fill the baptistry with potted palms or flowers so it wouldn't be so obvious."

"Or we could simply postpone the pageant until the next night if it does rain," Monisha added. "I can't remember the last time we had rain two nights in a row in October."

Darlene nodded. "Postponing might be the best idea. Easier by far to postpone than to drag all the microphones and such to one of the churches. We'll need sound equipment all day long at the festival."

"Darly"—Edna squinted through her thick glasses and waved her bejeweled hand at the window—"who is that walking outside with your sister?"

As one, the women turned toward the window overlooking the screen porch and the backyard. Darlene turned in time to see Nolie and the preacher walk past, the dogs at their sides. Nolie carried a basket of flowers while the minister toted a pair of long-handled clippers.

From his spot on the windowsill, Cary Grant watched the pair with keen interest.

"That's the Reverend Payne." Darlene's voice tightened despite her attempt to remain casual. "He's doing some work around the place for a few weeks."

Like hungry trout in a crowded pool, the women leaned in for a morsel of information.

"Who is he?"

"Where'd he come from?"

"Is he married?"

"If he's a reverend, why isn't he preaching somewhere?"

Darlene lifted her hand. "Ladies, please!" When they quieted, she launched into a succinct explanation: "From what I gather, he's a minister who lost his church because his wife divorced him. He came from Chattahoochee, and I don't know where he was before that. Nolie talks to him more than I do." She gave the group a pointed smile. "Now, as to decorations for the pageant—"

"He and Nolie seem to be getting on mighty well," Edna said, a note of insinuation sliding into her crackly voice. "Pretty sly of you, hiring him to work in Nolie's gardens."

"I'm not being sly and he's not interested in anybody, especially not my sister. He's here to work, that's all. And he does a lot more than fiddle with the landscaping."

"I think it'd be fittin' if Nolie found a new man and settled down." After dropping sideways into her chair, Monisha crossed her legs and smiled out the window. "After going through that terrible humilia- tion . . ."

Edna caught her breath in an audible gasp, and Glennette's, Or- lain's, and Mary's faces dissolved into mournful expressions. Darlene closed her eyes, chagrined that the subject had arisen. No one in town seemed inclined to forget about the age-old tragedy that clung to Nolie like a shadow.

"Nolie is anything but tragic, and the quickest way to stop gossip is for everbody to just hush up." Darlene tapped the table to refocus the group's attention. "Now, we need to discuss the pageant decora- tions. Are we going to go with the theme for the festival, or should we do something special for the pageant?"

"The theme is autumn harvest," Orlain said. "Always has been."

"Hard to get away from pumpkins and scarecrows in October," Glennette added. "I suppose we could do roses or something fancy around the stage, but wouldn't red roses clash with the pumpkins and orange and black crepe-paper streamers we hang around the pavilion?"

Monisha pointed toward the window again. "Look, they're talkin'."

When Glennette and Orlain rose from their seats for a better view, Darlene's patience evaporated.

"Listen, ladies—" But she turned, too, and fell silent when she saw Erik Payne standing in front of Nolie, his head bending toward hers as she pointed to the dogs and smiled. Nolie was putting a lot of effort into the conversation, so Darlene hoped Reverend Payne wasn't the sort of man who would break an innocent woman's heart.

"Gossip is the devil's radio," she whispered, less iron in her voice as she turned and gave the others a pleading look. "Please, please, can we *try* to focus on the festival? We have work to do."

Glennette and Orlain sat, but Monisha crossed her arms and remained standing by the window. "Nolie brought me another beautiful apron last week. She left it for me at the Wiggly's bakery counter."

"She gave me one, too," Glennette said, wrapping a curl from her new weave around her finger. "It was a really pretty pink pinafore and must have taken hours to sew. Lots of ruffles and lace trim."

"I'm sure it didn't take that long." Darlene sighed. "Nolie's a whiz with a sewing machine."

"It's not right," Monisha insisted, stepping closer to Darlene. "Not right at all. Nolie's been sewing those aprons ever since—"

"I know how long she's been sewing aprons," Darlene muttered through clenched teeth. "I know how many the girl's made. Don't you think I see 'em? Don't you think I hear that machine runnin' every afternoon?"

"She's not a girl, she's as old as me, and I've had five kids and two husbands." Monisha leaned into Darlene's field of vision. "So don't you think it's crazy that all she does is weed her garden and sew aprons and ride around town on a bicycle?"

"What about wearing white all the time?" Edna straightened her spine. "Why does she do that?"

"Some say it's because white is the Chinese color for mourning." Orlain pressed both hands to the table and looked goggle-eyed at the group. "She's been in mournin' all these years."

"I thought it was because she still thinks of herself as a bride," Mary said, lowering her voice. "Like she's still standing at that altar—"

"I find it incredible that y'all can't seem to mind your own business," Darlene snapped. "And that you, Monisha, sometimes use canned frosting when everthing behind the bakery counter is supposed to be made from scratch."

Monisha stiffened. "Why, I never—"

"Oh, yes you do. I can taste the difference between store-bought and homemade with half my tongue tied behind my back." Darlene glared at Monisha a moment more, then strafed the rest of the table with a stern gaze. "My momma always said the reason some folks can't mind their own business is because they have awfully little minds and no business at all. Now—anyone else have a comment about my baby sister?"

Edna, Glennette, Orlain, and Mary either looked at their hands or buried their gazes in their glasses of iced tea.

"I didn't think so. Okay, then. If it rains, we'll postpone for a night. As to the decorations, we'll see how far we can stretch a harvest theme with pumpkins and Indian corn. Maybe we can find some orange roses, so keep a sharp lookout. Any other business we should tackle now?"

She glared around the circle, but no one else dared offer a peep.

"Good. This committee is adjourned until next month." She stood, her chair scraping across the ancient brick flooring. "Thank you, ladies, for coming. Be sure to pick up a sampler cupcake box before you leave."

* * *

Nolie skipped down the stairs on Sunday morning and grabbed a biscuit as she passed through the kitchen. Darlene was sitting at the table in her Sunday best, her gaze fastened to the newspaper. "See ya," Nolie called, wrapping the warm biscuit in a napkin. "I'll be home for lunch."

"Where are you goin' this morning?" Darlene didn't lift her eyes from the printed page. "Visitin' Mount Zion again?"

"Thought I'd try the Morningside Church of Christ." Nolie settled her pocketbook on her shoulder. "I heard birds singing outside my window this morning, and that put me in mind of the way the Morningside people sing. No piano there, you know, though sometimes we can hear the Mount Zion folks carryin' on from across the street."

Darlene shook her head. "Whatever floats your boat. But seriously—I don't know what you can possibly get out of any church if you only visit it every once in a while."

"Maybe I don't go to get something out of it." She grinned. "Maybe I go to put something *into* it. See ya later."

She hurried across the screened porch and took the steps down to the terrace below. The air smelled of summer, blooming jasmine, and sweet honeysuckle. She inhaled a delicious breath on her way to the garage, then stopped when she saw Erik sitting in a lawn chair, an open Bible on his knee.

"Mornin'," she whispered, reluctant to disturb him but not wanting to ignore him, either.

He looked up and blinked, as if she'd awakened him from a doze.

Nolie lowered her gaze. "I, um, was wonderin' if you wanted to go to church. I've been to about all of them around here, and I could point you in the right direction if you're lookin' for some particular flavor."

She looked up in time to see his face twist in a small grimace; then he shook his head. "Thank you, but I think I'll stay here this morning. I can have a nice time of worship under these trees."

She lifted her gaze to the mature sycamores that towered over the guesthouse. "I guess you can, at that."

"Sometimes"—he went on as if he hadn't heard her—"I think someone ought to establish a church for people who've been kicked out. The ones who, for whatever reason, aren't welcome at church anymore."

He looked eastward, staring toward Chattahoochee, his features stamped by grief and his eyes shadowed with loss. In that moment, Nolie was overcome by the conviction, unanchored but strong, that she had been purposely placed before a man at a crossroad. She had to say something.

"Don't." She clung to the strap of her pocketbook with a fierce grip. "Don't let yourself get vinegary. If you can't forgive those people for what they did, you'll build up walls."

He squinted at her. "Walls?"

She nodded. "Walls between you and everthing. And soon you won't be able to see out."

He stared at her a moment longer, then closed his eyes and nodded. "I think I understand."

"I'll leave you alone, then," she said, her voice soft in the morning stillness. "See you later."

She pulled her bike from the garage and dropped her pocketbook into the basket. Ricky and Lucy barked as she pedaled down the driveway, and she needed every bit of her willpower to resist looking over her shoulder to see if Erik Payne had gone back to reading his Bible . . . or if he was watching her leave.

After taping the end of the last crepe-paper streamer to the ceiling, Nolie climbed down from the stepladder and surveyed her handiwork. The Reverend Tommy Lee Joseph, pastor of the First and Only Baptist Church, had promised she could decorate for the big birthday party anytime after Wednesday-night prayer meeting, so she enlisted Henry and Erik Payne to help her make the room appear a little less Spartan.

Why did Baptists always worship in such utilitarian buildings? The Methodists' tiny fellowship hall had been finished off with Sheetrock and pretty wallpaper, but it was too small to handle this birthday gala. The Baptist hall was bigger, but the blue concrete-block walls weren't exactly elegant.

After unloading her bag of supplies, the men helped Nolie blow up balloons, drape pink and white paper streamers along the walls, and pull a large table into the center of the room. All that remained on Nolie's to-do list was decorating the table and bringing the cake from the grocery store.

"I thought"—she said, digging through her bag for the pink paper tablecloth she'd picked up at the Wiggly—"that we'd cover all the other tables in plain white paper and save pink for the table with the big cake and the flowers from Griffy and Katie. What do you think?" She looked from Erik to Henry, but both men stared at her with blank faces.

"Um, sure," Henry finally said, shrugging. "I could get any color tablecloth you need, though."

"Pink should be good," Erik said. "Very feminine."

"That's what I thought." Nolie found a stray package of balloons at the bottom of her bag and tossed it to Henry. "Found one more. Can you blow those up for me, please?"

Henry groaned. "I'm going to be hyperventilated by the time we're done here."

Erik extended a hand. "I can help. I wouldn't want poor Henry to be left breathless."

"Henry can manage them." Her heart pounding at her own audacity, Nolie somehow found the nerve to grab Erik's sleeve and pull him away. "I need you to tie a piece of pink or white ribbon onto each balloon, then tape groups of five or six balloons to each corner of the center table." She tsked in dissatisfaction as she looked at the other balloon clusters hanging from each of the four corners of the room. "I was hoping I could get hold of a helium tank, but I couldn't find one in town."

She turned and looked at both men, half-hoping one of them would volunteer to drive over to the florist in Chattahoochee, but neither of them said a word. Henry was probably too busy to go, and Erik—well, considering the reason he left that town, she could understand why Chattahoochee might be the last place on earth he wanted to visit.

"I suppose those balloons will do." She unfolded the pink table-cloth and spread it over the table. "As soon as I get this situated, y'all can tape the balloon bouquets on the corners. Then all we'll have to do tomorrow is put the cake and flowers in the center."

Red-faced and breathless, Henry stopped puffing to tie a knot in the end of an inflated balloon. "Is Monisha making the cake at the store?"

"Yes, and she promised to use buttercream frosting. I don't know why Darlene has suddenly decided that she hates fondant, but she made a point of telling me that she likes buttercream more than any-thing else. I guess she knew I'd be getting her a cake. After all, I can't expect her to bake this one."

Henry handed his balloon to Erik, who proceeded to tie a long strip of ribbon to the knotted end.

"I can't wait to see Carlene," the grocer said, a dimple appearing in his round cheek. "I called her the other day to make sure everthing had worked out, and she asked if I could pick her up at the Tallahas-see airport. So I'll be bringing her to the party."

Nolie grinned. "That's great. I was wondering how she was going to get here because she doesn't drive, either. She says you don't need a car in Manhattan."

"Makes sense." Erik dropped a finished balloon onto the table, then slid his hands into his pockets and looked at Nolie. "Is this your church?"

"Isn't it the Lord's?" Nolie laughed when Erik gave her a puzzled look. "Yes, I come here a lot, but I don't attend *only* here. Sometimes I worship with the Mount Zion folks, then I go to St. Mary's, then I visit the Methodists, then I come here or go to the Church of Christ. I like to rotate."

Erik blinked. "Does your sister rotate, too?"

"Darlene likes this church best. She used to like the Methodists until—well, you know. Until the Calorie Counters put her out of business."

Just then one of the double doors opened and Glennette Wessel stuck her head into the room. "Hey, Nolie—is it okay if I bring my autograph book tomorrow night? I'd love to get your sister's signature, but I wanted to ask you first."

Nolie looked at Henry. "Glennette knows?"

"Shoot, the whole town knows about Carly coming." Henry pulled another balloon from the package. "That cat slipped out of the bag the minute one of the cashiers heard me talking on the phone."

"But what if Darlene—"

"Everbody knows not to speak a word to Darlene about it," Henry finished. "So don't worry your head about it."

"The dangers of the small-town grapevine." Erik chuckled as Nolie waved to Glennette. "This place makes Chattahoochee feel like a metropolis."

Henry graciously ignored Erik's comment. "We haven't talked about how we're gonna pull off the surprise tomorrow night, Nolie. If you have Darlene here by seven, Carlene and I should be coming through the door at about seven fifteen. But what if her plane is delayed? Or what if I get stuck in traffic?"

"Traffic shouldn't be that heavy at seven," Erik pointed out. "And you could always call and warn somebody if you're delayed. Nolie could carry on as if everyone's only come together to celebrate Darlene's birthday."

Henry considered this. "Sounds reasonable."

"Yeah, but—" Nolie frowned at the grocer. "Darlene will notice if *you're* not here on time. And the longer you stay away, the more aggravated she'll get. By seven fifteen she'll be ready to have a conniption fit."

"Then maybe I'll call her," Henry said, laughing. "I'll tell her I'm out picking up a surprise. She won't be mad if she thinks I'm getting her a present."

Nolie grinned—the man had come to understand her big sister awfully well. "She'll be tickled pink. And when Carlene comes through the door, Darly just might fall over. Maybe I should stand next to her in case she faints."

Chapter Five

*B*ecause Carlene had come to associate going home with funerals, she felt a pang of loss when she checked in for the Tallahassee-bound flight. She smiled at the attendant and tried to shrug off the feeling, but still it persisted. And why wouldn't it? She hadn't flown south since she went home for Griff's service five years before. She had been anxious during that flight, too, knowing she'd have to call on inner reserves she wasn't sure she possessed. How was she supposed to be strong for Darlene when she couldn't say Griff's name without a break in her voice? How could she sit in the family pew with Griff's children and pretend he was nothing more than a brother-in-law?

Those two days, the last she had spent in Peculiar, were among the most difficult she ever endured. Though she had wanted to stay with Aunt Verna, who usually opened her guest room whenever Carlene came to town, something told her Darlene would want her sister at Sycamores. So she went to the big house—she crossed the front porch Griff had crossed, walked the hallways Griff had walked, and sat in the kitchen where Griff had drunk his coffee and eaten his meals. Whenever anyone squeezed her shoulder and said it was good of her to come home, she responded with a paper-thin smile and inwardly wailed like a motherless child.

Darlene barely spoke to her during that visit. Nolie said it was because Griff died so suddenly Darlene was still in shock, but Carlene knew her twin had deeper reasons. Once claimed, Griff belonged only to Darly. She was still jealously clinging to him, unwilling even to share her grief.

Carlene went to Peculiar to be with her sisters, to honor Griff's memory, and to say a final good-bye, but the day after the funeral she had taken the first available flight back to New York, where no one knew her secrets.

Now she peered out the tiny window to her right. They were flying over acres of pines, oaks, and palms, a completely different landscape from the one she'd observed when she took off from JFK. Ninety minutes ago, she watched gray asphalt and soaring buildings recede into the distance; now miles of green woods, blue lakes, and brown farmland filled her window. Angular roads intersected the flat landscape, and in the distance she could see the rolling expanse of the Gulf of Mexico.

She smiled at the flight attendant who walked the aisle checking seat belts, then folded her hands and tried to relax. Amazing that she could be so nervous about something as simple as a trip home. She hadn't felt this jittery before her auditions, or even before opening nights. For those occasions she had rehearsed; she knew every word she would sing and say. In a few minutes, however, she would once again be with people who knew her when she and Darly used to run around Sycamores in bare feet and matching shorts sets.

She hadn't been that girl in a long time.

She closed her eyes as the jet swayed from left to right, then felt the abrupt jolt of wheels on the runway. As a flight attendant reminded passengers to remain seated, she reached for her purse under her feet.

She was going home to celebrate, she reminded herself. The occasion wasn't a funeral, but a party. Griff had been gone five years, so she ought to be able to walk through her old home without imagining him coming around every corner and sitting in every chair.

She stepped off the plane and felt hot, humid air cover her like a damp blanket. She strode into the terminal, then with a brisk step hurried toward the luggage carousels, hoping Henry Hooper would find her before she had to pick him out of the crowd.

She hadn't progressed ten yards when she heard her name. "Carlene! Carly Caldwell!"

She turned in time to see a stocky, red-faced man with glasses, a soft paunch, and a receding hairline. She recognized him—he'd been at Griff's funeral—then smiled. "Oh, my goodness, it's Hank Hooper, all grown up."

"Bigger and better than ever." He held out his arms and she stepped into them, then gasped when his enthusiastic embrace squeezed the air from her lungs. "Oh, I'm sorry," he said, releasing her. "You're still such a tiny thing. I guess I've been picturing you more filled out like Darlene."

"Darlene got Daddy's build. I inherited Momma's, and she never could put on weight." Amazing how easily those words sprang to her lips after so many years.

She stepped back and smoothed the wrinkles from her suit, but Henry kept talking. "I probably shouldn't yell your name in a public place. Wouldn't want you to be swarmed by fans wanting your autograph."

She resisted the urge to laugh. "Don't worry, Hank, nobody's going to swarm on my account. And thank you for picking me up. I appreciate your driving all this way to get me."

He grinned. "Only makes sense. Besides, I'm kinda tickled to be able to bring you in as a treat for Darlene. We've been seein' each other for a while now, so I'm glad I could do something to surprise her."

"You're dating my sister?" Carlene lifted a brow. "She always had all the luck. First she married Griff and now she's seeing you."

"Well." The man's flush deepened. "She's a sweetheart. And I should probably tell you that no one calls me Hank anymore. After I took over my dad's grocery store, everbody started calling me Henry. That's the name on the store-manager sign."

"Then I beg your pardon, Henry." She pointed to the luggage carousel, where suitcases were tumbling down the ramp. "I suppose we'd better look for my bags."

After retrieving her luggage, she waited outside an older-model sedan while Henry perspired and fumbled with the keys. "I'm glad your flight arrived on time," he said, opening the trunk. "Nolie and I worked out a contingency plan in case you were delayed."

Carlene glanced at her watch. "What time does the birthday party start?"

"Right at seven. We'll be only a few minutes late."

"Won't Darlene wonder where you are?"

"She thinks she's going to a women's missionary meeting, so she won't expect to see me at first. If she *does* notice I'm not around, Nolie's going to tell her I had to run out and pick up a special surprise. I don't think she'll suspect a thing."

He hoisted the suitcases into the trunk, then hustled around to the passenger's side, where he unlocked and opened the door. Carlene smiled at his unexpected demonstration of chivalry.

If Darlene had her eye on Henry Hooper, she'd picked a nice man. The fellow was definitely a shirtsleeves kind of guy, but he seemed to have a good heart. Honest, hardworking men like Daddy and Griff were hard to find. If only she'd run into a guy like them . . .

They pulled away from the airport and headed west on the two-lane highway that fed into I–10. "Say"—Henry kept his eyes on the road as he drove—"what do you tell people when they ask where you're from? I've always wondered what people say when you tell 'em you're from Peculiar."

"Actually," she hedged, "since no one knows where the town is, I usually say I'm from Tallahassee or, if they know Florida, I might mention the panhandle. If the person asking is from Manhattan, I say I'm from a small town near the Georgia border. Most Manhattanites don't have a clue about Southern geography."

Laughing, Henry veered onto the interstate's entrance ramp. "Is that a polite way of saying they're egotistical?"

"I wouldn't say that. But New York is the center of the world, haven't you heard?"

While Henry snickered, Carlene steered the conversation away from her other life. "Tell me what you've been doing since high school. You played on the football team, didn't you? Seems like I remember you hanging out with Griff and all the other guys."

"Oh, yeah, we always had a great time during football season." While Henry launched into memories of their senior year and his early days at the Piggly Wiggly, Carlene settled back and studied the passing landscape. Not much had changed since she left the area—a few narrow roads and gas stations had appeared on what used to be untouched acreage, but most of the flat land along the highway was still studded with spindly pines and stubby palmettos.

Before she knew it, they were slanting toward the exit ramp and Highway 90, which led to Chattahoochee and Peculiar. Her stomach tightened. Over the years, her visits to Peculiar had been quick, brief, and quiet. Unable to bear the thought of staying at Sycamores, where she'd be smacked with the reality of Darlene and Griff's marriage, she'd chosen to stay with Aunt Verna, a great-aunt who never seemed to remember much about Carlene other than the fact that she was kin and always welcome. She'd spent several Christmas mornings in Aunt Verna's kitchen, and she'd held Aunt Verna's arm through Momma's and Grandma's funerals. She would have done the same at Griff's, but Darlene insisted that Carlene stand by her side . . . a place Carlene assumed with equal parts eagerness and reluctance.

She blinked when she realized Henry had fallen silent. "I'm sorry, did you ask me something?"

Henry cut a glance toward her. "I asked how you were able to get away from your show. Darlene says you're too busy to take much time off."

Carlene's hand rose automatically to her throat. "I . . . I'm taking a bit of a break from performing. I guess you could call it a sabbatical."

"Wow. Folks goin' up to visit Broadway now have no idea what they'll be missin'."

She laughed. "They'll see a good show. New York overflows with talented performers."

"But none like you."

Unable to face the admiration in his eyes, she looked out the window. "I suppose we are all different."

"Anyway," Henry went on, "Nolie asked if we should have you sing. Glennette Wessel—I don't think you know her; she's Dr. Morgan's secretary—she was all set to play piano for you, but I told Nolie it wouldn't be right to invite you as our guest and expect you to sing for your supper. So don't worry about that—as far as Mayor Hooper is concerned, you've got the night off."

A strangled sound rose from Carlene's tight throat—a cry that was half sob, half laughter. "Thank you," she managed to say, avoiding Henry's curious glance. "I appreciate that more than you know."

Henry continued to chatter as the car rushed through the darkness, and Carlene tried to smile and nod at all the appropriate places. But her thoughts had flown ahead to her meeting with Darlene. Had her sister been able to bury the past, or would their conflicts rise up to haunt them?

Darlene glared at Nolie, who seemed in an uncharacteristic hurry to get to the missionary meeting. "Good grief, where's the fire?" she grumbled, searching for her pocketbook as Nolie tapped her foot by the front door. "You know the first fifteen minutes is nothin' but announcements."

"Maybe I *like* hearing the announcements," Nolie said, a small flame of defiance in her eyes. "Come on, Darly, I don't want to be late."

"But you never go to these meetings. What's so special about this one?"

An odd look flitted across Nolie's face; then she lifted her chin. "I hear they brought in a special speaker and I want to hear her."

"Who?"

"I don't know; some lady who works in New York. Now shake a leg. I don't want to be late."

Darlene bit back her irritation and tried to rein in her grouchy mood. The day was nearly over and no one but Nolie had even *mentioned* what today was—and all Nolie did was wish her a simple "happy birthday" at breakfast, then hand her a dry store-bought cupcake with a candle stuck in the middle. Not even Henry had remembered the day's significance.

A woman passed the half-century mark only once—so why hadn't anyone else remembered this milestone?

Trying not to feel hurt, Darlene grabbed her pocketbook from the foyer table, then followed Nolie out the door. As she drove to the First and Only, Darlene couldn't help noticing that Nolie's knees kept knocking back and forth like a hyperactive boy's.

"Did you drink too much coffee?" She glanced at her sister. "You're as jumpy as a cat with a tin can tied to his tail."

"I'm fine." Nolie ran her hands over her bony knees, then crossed her arms. "I hate bein' late, that's all."

"No one's even gonna notice, you mark my words."

"If that's your way of sayin' I'm invisible, I already knew that. You don't have to rub it in."

Good grief, what had gotten into the girl? Nolie wasn't usually so touchy.

Darlene pulled into the church parking lot, then stopped and stared. "My heavens, look at all these cars. Did someone invite the Methodists?"

"Just hurry up and park, will you?" Nolie pointed to an empty space on the thin strip of grass behind the church property. "How 'bout over there?"

"You know the pastor doesn't like us to park on the—"

"Just do it, will ya? We're already five minutes late."

Darlene heaved a sigh, but did as Nolie suggested. As they cut through the parking lot, she tugged at the waistband of her panty hose, which kept slipping southward. The situation wouldn't be so dire once she found a seat, but all this fast walking was likely to shimmy her control tops down to her thighs.

"Hang on, Missy." After glancing around to make sure no one was watching, Darlene pulled out the elastic on her skirt and tugged on the panty hose waistband, stretching the elastic power panel to its maximum length. Maybe if she took teeny-tiny steps into the building and tried not to exhale, nothing would shift for the next half hour.

Fretting on the sidewalk, Nolie groaned. "Good grief, would you come on? We're gonna miss the whole thing."

"You won't miss anything important. Baptists never start on time."

Nolie rolled her eyes at Darlene's baby steps, but they finally reached the entrance to the kitchen and fellowship hall. Darlene's confidence faltered when Pastor Tommy Lee met them at the door. He greeted Nolie with a brighter-than-usual smile, then pointed toward the double doors at his right. "The meeting's already started, ladies. Better hurry on in there."

"Thanks, Pastor." Darlene caught her breath and pushed through the wide doors.

"SURPRISE!"

Darlene gaped, words failing her. She'd swear that every last soul in Peculiar stood in the crowded fellowship hall, with all eyes focused on her. Several people wore pointed paper birthday hats, the adults smiling and clapping while gamboling kids ran through the room like frisky puppies. Pink and white crepe-paper streamers hung from the walls, balloon bouquets graced every table, and a huge banner covered the back wall.

The crowd parted while Darlene stared, revealing three floral arrangements and a gigantic birthday cake studded with candles. Someone—probably not Monisha Brand since from where Darlene stood the piping looked perfectly uniform—had baked a seven-tier cake, covered it with pearls and buttercream, and decorated it with amazingly realistic sugar roses, daisies, and wisteria blossoms. As a finishing touch, the talented baker had positioned a three-dimensional 50 on the uppermost tier.

Darlene brought her hands to her mouth and fought back tears. She hadn't been forgotten, not by a long shot. Someone had taken a lot of time and trouble to arrange all this.

She turned to Nolie, who stood by her side. "Who?" she asked, her voice strangled. "Who planned this?"

Nolie grinned. "People who care about you."

"But who?"

"Henry, mainly. I helped, but the party was Henry's idea."

"That wonderful, sweet man." Darlene turned to look for Henry, but she couldn't find him among the well-wishers. As people swept forward to congratulate her, she caught Nolie's eye again. "Where is Henry?"

"Out," Nolie said, struggling to stand in the surging mob. "He had to pick up some—" The rest of her words were drowned out by friends coming forward to congratulate the guest of honor.

Her heart brimming with joy, Darlene accepted her friends' congratulations. She'd always known that Henry was a thoughtful man and she'd seen how well he treated his late wife, but to know he cared enough to do all this for *her*—

Were all her dreams about to come true?

"Thank you, thank you." She shook every hand that reached for hers and greeted her guests with a teary smile. "It's so kind of you to come. So thoughtful."

"Were you surprised?" someone called.

"Very!" she yelled back. "As surprised as a kid stumblin' smack into Santa Claus!"

Pastor Tommy Lee stepped forward and took her hand. "Miss Darlene, do you have any words of wisdom for us now that you're half a century young?"

She grinned at his choice of words. "Well, birthdays are nice to celebrate, and I certainly appreciate this one. But too many of them will about do a gal in, won't they?"

When everyone laughed, Darlene hugged herself, realizing that this had to be one of the happiest days of her life.

As she continued to receive her neighbors' compliments and good wishes, she noticed a buzzing from the women around the center table. They were waiting, probably for her to cut the cake or blow out candles, but she still had to greet at least a dozen people who hindered her forward progress. The children, though, had to be restless and eager to eat. "You can go ahead and cut the cake," she called to Nolie, who was moving toward the center table. "Let the little ones have some—"

"Not yet," Nolie called over her shoulder. "We have to wait for Henry."

Why on earth would they have to wait for him? Unless he was bringing matches or ice cream, Darlene couldn't imagine why the women wanted to postpone the inevitable.

She froze as the group behind her emitted a collective gasp. Anticipating another surprise, she turned and saw Henry standing just inside the doorway, a pleased expression on his face. Adrenaline sparked her blood. He waggled his brows and gave the crowd a wait-till-you-see-what-I-brought grin, then stepped back to allow someone else to enter.

Darlene's mind reeled.

Carlene.

The realization hit with the force of a blow, and for an instant Darlene couldn't do anything but stand rooted to the floor, her mouth open. Then she ran forward, arms open, and wrapped her twin in a bear hug.

"Carly! What are you *doing* here?"

"Happy birthday, Darly." Carlene folded bird-like limbs around Darlene's shoulders, then stepped back and smiled. "Surprise."

Still numb with astonishment, Darlene looked at Henry. "When? How—?"

"I invited her." Obviously pleased with himself, Henry rocked back on his heels and tucked his thumbs into his belt. "I knew you wouldn't believe she was comin', so we decided you might as well be surprised. She's here, and she might even stay awhile."

Carly had come home for something as silly as a birthday party? Darlene gaped, then hugged her twin again. "I can't believe you're here. It's so good to see you!"

"It's good to be here, Darly." Carlene's eyes, still as blue as the sea, shone with affection, and her voice rasped, probably with pent-up emotion. "Happy birthday, sweetie."

The flood of people who had shaken Darlene's hand rushed forward to greet Carlene. Darlene stepped back, happy to share the attention, but she couldn't help noticing that folks approached Carlene differently. No one hugged Carly, no one yelled at her or smacked her on the shoulder. Instead, they took her hand with an almost palpable deference, they *crooned* their greetings, and several offered autograph books for her signature. They treated Darlene like a neighbor, but they treated Carlene . . . like royalty.

Darlene shouldered her way out of the mob feasting on her sister and walked toward Nolie, who had finally decided to light the candles. In that moment she understood why Nolie waited to cut the cake. The top of the bottom tier said, "Happy Birthday, Darly and Carly." The same sentiment was repeated on the gigantic banner dangling from the back wall.

Darlene stood beside the cake table and stared at the sputtering candles, her bubble of happiness deflating. Had this party been for her, or for Carlene? Or had she, the ordinary sister, been an afterthought?

Once again she'd been asked to share, and once again she ended up with the apple core while Carlene got all the deliciousness. It wasn't enough that she'd been asked to sacrifice for Carly's voice lessons, pageant clothes, and dress rehearsals. Never mind that Momma never paid Darlene as much attention or that Carly rarely had time for her sister once she caught the Broadway bug. As a teenager, Darlene gave and gave, and got—what? Leftovers. The cheaper clothes. The perfunctory displays of affection and the minimum amounts of attention.

She never got anything until she learned to step out and take what she wanted, but even then, Carlene's shadow loomed large at Sycamores.

"The flowers are from the kids," Nolie said, gesturing to the arrangements on the table. "But the center one's from me and Henry."

"They're pretty." Darlene forced a smile. "Really nice." She wanted to add that the lilies in the center arrangement reminded her of funerals, but she managed to bite her tongue.

Henry stood on a chair and lifted both hands. "Order, order please," he called, waiting for the noise to subside. "I know we're all excited to have Carlene back home, but let's not forget that this is a day to honor two sisters . . . because they're both fifty, fun, and foxy!"

The crowd laughed. Darlene stretched her smile when she felt Nolie's gaze fall on her.

"We've hung photos of several memorable moments from the twins' lives on posters around the room," Henry continued, "so after you get your cake, be sure to take a look around so you can appreciate everthing that's happened in the last fifty years. But most of all, Darly and Carly"—he glanced down at Carlene, who still stood by his side—"know that we love and appreciate you. Now . . . I think it's time for you two gals to blow out some candles!"

As Henry hopped off his chair and led Carlene to the cake table, Darlene straightened her spine. She barely glanced at Carly, but leaned over the table and waited for her sister to do the same.

Before puckering up for the big breath, however, Carlene turned toward Darlene. "Darly? You okay?"

"Everbody's waitin', so let's blow these things out before someone calls the fire department." Darlene looked up, caught Nolie's eye, and winked. "Whatever you do, Carly, don't spit all over this beautiful cake."

As the crowd around the table laughed, Darlene drew her deepest breath and blew like a typhoon, keenly aware of Carlene's delicate puffing. Even in something as trivial as this, Carlene insisted on maintaining her dignity and position. Fine, then. Let her stay up on her pedestal. Life could get pretty doggone lonely at the top.

"Who wants cake?" As the children squealed and moved closer, Darlene cut a few slices and dropped them on paper plates, which Nolie passed to outstretched hands. From the corner of her eye, Darlene saw Henry approach Carlene and place his hand on her elbow, guiding her toward the Reverend Tommy Lee. He was undoubtedly introducing those two, and after that he'd squire Carlene around the room, making sure she met everyone from the preacher to the custodian.

Darlene backed away from the cake table, knowing that for the next hour or so she'd have to nod and smile and pretend she was having the time of her life. A quick glance at some of the pictures on the wall—Carlene singing with the high school choir, Carlene in her Miss Buttercup Squash crown and sash, Carlene riding on the back of a parade convertible while Darlene drove the car—convinced her of one thing: Henry hadn't arranged this party to honor his girlfriend. He arranged all this to honor the girl who won the Miss Buttercup Squash crown at the Fall Festival, then left Peculiar and went off to become a Broadway star.

Darlene realized how right she'd been when she offered her words of wisdom earlier—too many birthdays like this might absolutely kill a woman.

"This," Carlene whispered to Henry as yet another woman approached to shake her hand, "feels like a high school reunion, except some of these people are so young I don't think I've ever met them."

Henry chuckled. "They know who you are, and I reckon that's all that matters."

"Momma says you used to change my diapers," the younger woman said, gripping Carlene's hand. "Of course, I don't remember that, but she's always told me I should feel special because a Broadway star used to babysit me."

"Oh." Carlene squeezed the woman's fingers and smiled. "Thank you."

A little girl stepped forward next. "Can I have a picture?" When she held out a camera, Carlene stared at it, unsure of what she was supposed to do. Should she take her own picture or stand with the girl?

Henry walked over to rescue her. "I'll do the honors," he said, taking the camera. "You two pretty ladies get together, and I'll take your picture."

Bewildered, Carlene drew the little girl to her side, draping an arm around the child's shoulder as Henry snapped the flash photo. As Carlene waited for her dazzled eyes to refocus, the little girl's clear treble rose above the crowd: "I want to be a famous singer like you. Momma says I can be, if I work hard and go to New York."

Not wanting to discourage her, Carlene nodded. "That's nice."

She felt her spirits lift when a woman in a patterned tunic and white pants carefully led Aunt Verna toward her. The old woman must be getting feeble if she needed a nurse's supervision at a party.

Aunt Verna, who seemed shorter than Carly remembered, peered up at Carlene. "And who are you?"

"Carlene. I'm Chase Caldwell's granddaughter." Carlene kissed the woman's wrinkled cheek. "It's so good to see you."

"So we're kin?" Verna looked to the nurse for confirmation. "Is she kin to me?"

"Yes, ma'am."

Verna repeated Carlene's name, then her eyes brightened. "I know you. You're Griffith's sweetheart."

Somehow Carlene managed to smile. "I'm afraid not, Aunt Verna. You must be thinking of Darlene."

The nurse caught Carlene's eye. "She's pretty lucid most days, but sometimes she gets confused."

Verna smiled again. "Are we kin?"

Carlene raised her voice. "I'm your great-uncle's granddaughter. I've stayed at your house."

"You have?" Again, she glanced at the nurse, then she patted Carlene's hand. "I hope you enjoyed yourself, young lady."

"I did." Carlene smiled and arched her brow. "How old are you now?"

Verna blinked rapidly. "Who are you?"

"She's seventy-five." The nurse smiled at her patient with quiet affection. "That's not so old, but she's got the dementia. I've been with her four years and I tell you, there's never a dull moment at Miss Verna's house."

"I can imagine. It's good of you to make sure she's still getting out and about. She's always been active."

Aunt Verna's bony hand fell on Carlene's arm. "So nice to see you. Are we kin?"

Carlene smiled. "We are. And I'm so glad you came to the party."

As they talked, Carlene became aware of quiet murmurs lapping all around her, like waves against the sand: "Saw her at Griff's funeral, but didn't get a chance to speak." "Will she stay longer than a couple of days this time?" "The Broadway star." "Sings like an angel." "Do you think she'll sing for us tonight?"

Grief welled in her, a cold current that threatened to drag her under. They were talking about someone who no longer existed, and about a gift that had been cruelly stolen. What would they say when—if—they learned that the angelic voice had vanished?

Another woman grabbed Carlene's hand, her grip like a vise. "Do you know Bernadette Peters? I saw her in *Annie Get Your Gun*, and I wondered if you knew her. Is she really as sweet as she seems?"

"What about the kid who played Harry Potter?" a teenage boy wanted to know. "I heard he's been on Broadway."

Carlene answered their questions as best she could. Yes, she'd met Bernadette Peters and yes, the lady was very nice. No, she'd never met Daniel Radcliffe, but she was sure he was nice, too. Reba McEntire's twang was genuine, Kristin Chenoweth really was a tiny woman, and yes, it was fascinating to watch the Beast turn into a handsome prince before Beauty's dazzled eyes. How did they do it? She didn't exactly know, not having been in that show.

She shook a dozen hands, endured several fierce embraces, and had her picture snapped so many times she began to wonder if her eyes would ever distinguish colors again. Finally, Henry stepped into the impromptu receiving line and held up his hand. "Y'all, this little lady hasn't even had a chance to enjoy a slice of her birthday cake. Let's give her a break, shall we?"

Carlene gave Henry a grateful smile as he escorted her back to the cake table. Once there, he glanced around, then spotted Darlene in a chair against the wall. "Come on over, sweetie," he shouted. "Time for you birthday girls to cut this cake for the camera."

Carlene studied her sister as Darly pulled herself out of the chair and lumbered—none too eagerly, Carlene thought—to the center of the room.

"Here's the knife"—Henry held the blade between them—"and y'all should both place your hands on it and cut together. Wait— that's right—now hold that pose so I can get a good shot. We want to put it in the display case at city hall."

Carlene arched her brow. "You have a city hall now?"

"Not yet," Henry answered, moving to the other side of the table. "But one day we will."

Carlene smiled at the camera. From the corner of her eye she could see Darlene smiling, too, but her sister's smile was fixed, tight, and displayed only a tidy row of upper teeth. "A classic insincere smile," Carlene could hear her drama coach saying, "never reveals any teeth on the lower jaw."

After the first flash, Carlene leaned toward her sister and lowered her voice. "I'm sorry for showing up without any warning. I know this was a lot to spring on you."

"You don't have to worry about me." Another insincere smile shone above their joined hands. "But I've never heard of anybody's birthday picture being placed in a public display case. It's not like either of us saved someone's life or anything."

"This isn't about me," Carlene answered, responding to the subtle accusation in her sister's words. "Maybe he wants to put the picture on display because you're his girlfriend."

"He's never put any pictures of me up before." Darlene pressed her hand over Carlene's, squeezed hard, and lowered the blade with such force that the handle cracked against the table. Then she re- leased the knife and stalked away, leaving Carlene to flex her crushed fingers.

She sighed. Though Darlene appeared genuinely happy to see her in that first moment, apparently the situation had changed now that she'd had some time to stew.

Carlene—whose formfitting performance outfits had for years forced her to refuse offers of cake, candy, or pie—helped Nolie serve the guests, then picked up her own plate. Maybe she would indulge in one or two bites of the red-velvet layer cake. After all, she spent part of the day speed walking through an airport, and surely that effort equaled at least half an hour on the treadmill. Besides, no performance outfits waited for her, not tonight nor in her future.

Ignoring the sour feeling in the pit of her stomach, she took a bite of the red velvet and closed her eyes as the flavor tickled her tongue. She'd forgotten how good Southern cooking could be. No one stinted on butter down here; no one substituted chemical additives for pure cane sugar. No wonder everything tasted so delicious.

As she stood in a quiet corner and nibbled at her dessert, her eyes sought and found her twin. Darlene had aged in the five years since Griff's funeral—apparently she stopped coloring her hair. Her waistline appeared a few inches wider than it had been, and her face seemed to be marked with more lines than before. But she still looked good—Darly had always projected strength rather than femininity, and her strength remained in full measure. If Martin were here, Carly knew how he'd evaluate her sister's appearance: *And in this corner we have the Southern sister, who stands five foot ten and fights as a light heavyweight . . .*

Though Carlene had intended to eat only a few bites, before she knew it, the entire slice of cake had disappeared. But she wasn't the only one who couldn't resist—some of the others had returned to the cake table for a second piece of the scrumptious dessert.

Carlene threw her paper plate away and walked over to Darlene. "I know this probably feels awkward," she said, sitting next to her sister, "but a lot has happened since we last saw each other. Maybe it's time we reconnected."

Darlene opened her mouth to answer, but at that moment Nolie approached with two brightly wrapped boxes. "I'm glad I found you two together," she said, handing a pastel-colored package to Carlene. "For you." She offered the box with the brighter paper to Darlene. "And for you, Darly."

For an instant Carlene could only stare at the box—she certainly hadn't expected to receive a gift. For years she and Nolie had only exchanged birthday cards, so this had to be something special.

With one eye on Darlene, who was also staring at her present, Carlene tugged at the thin ribbon around the box. "You don't have to be polite," one woman called from a table. "Just rip the paper off and have at it."

Carlene glanced at Darlene, who grinned at the woman and ripped the wrapping away. It fluttered to the floor, while a little girl dashed forward to scoop up the scattered pieces.

Carlene stopped unwrapping to let Darlene take the spotlight as she lifted the top off a thin white cardboard box, then brushed aside a piece of folded tissue paper. Something lay inside, some kind of folded fabric. Darlene lifted it out and held it to her chest, allowing the folds to fall over her long shirt and skirt.

An appreciative wave of oohs and aahs rose from the guests. Carlene squinted, trying to decide what Darlene was holding; then someone supplied the answer: "One of Nolie's handcrafted aprons!"

Nolie made *that*? Carlene had little experience with aprons, handmade or otherwise, but couldn't help being impressed by the detail in Nolie's work. The bright red and blue apron skirt had been appliquéd with images of a pie, a chocolate cake, frosted cupcakes, and a pot of tea. At the bottom, right above the hem, colorful calico fabrics spelled out Darlene's name.

Impressed, Carlene shifted her gaze to her younger sister. Nolie had become quite the accomplished seamstress, if that was the proper term for someone who made appliquéd aprons.

Nolie turned toward Carlene, her face glowing. "Now open yours, Carly."

Carlene pasted on a smile and ripped the paper from the box, then lifted the lid. Another apron lay beneath a layer of tissue paper, but this one looked nothing like Darlene's. Instead of bright, bold colors, for this apron Nolie had chosen fabrics in soft periwinkle blue and blush pink. She embellished the hem with Carlene's name, not with appliqué, but with a lovely embroidered script. While Darlene's apron was a full-coverage design that tied around the neck and at the waist, Carlene's tied only at the waist and dropped in pleated folds over her skirt. Pink fabric rosettes at each side added the perfect accent to a large strip of pastel blue rickrack over the waistband.

"It's beautiful." She smiled at Nolie. "It reminds me of those lovely aprons Beaver Cleaver's mother wore."

A blush tinted her younger sister's cheek. "Vintage aprons are all the rage right now. I hope you like it."

"Gorgeous, dear. Simply gorgeous." The stout woman sitting next to Nolie patted her arm. "You always do beautiful work. And it's so generous of you to give those aprons away."

"Hey, birthday girls," the pastor called, waving to get their attention. "I've always wanted to know—which of you is the eldest?"

Carlene stiffened her spine. She didn't need to be reminded that she was aging with every breath, but some things couldn't be helped. Darlene threw her a quick glance, then grinned at the minister. "Can't you tell? Carlene's older than me by a whole ten minutes!"

Carlene smiled at the pastor, tolerating the joke, while inwardly she grimaced. But judging from the ripples of surprise moving throughout the room, she didn't look even a second older than Darlene.

Carlene turned to Nolie and ran her hand over the embroidered apron. "Why take the time to make such personalized aprons? You could simplify the details and make something that's really commercial."

Her youngest sister shrugged. "I like the personal touch. I can be creative with the designs, and no two aprons are ever exactly alike."

"But why give them away when you could sell them?"

A dimple appeared in Nolie's cheek. "I get paid by making people happy."

Carlene sighed as a woman tapped Nolie's shoulder and Darlene drifted away to talk to someone else.

So much for Southern hospitality.

Hoping the party would soon break up, Carlene looked around for Henry. She could ride home with her sisters, but she would need to get her suitcases out of Henry's car—

Darlene intercepted her questioning glance. "Are you spending the night with us, then? Or were you planning to stay with Aunt Verna again?"

Carlene drew a deep breath. "Actually, I hoped to spend a few days with you and Nolie. I brought enough clothes for a week."

Darlene's mouth curved in a smile that seemed forced. "Well, of course you're staying with us—we have a lot of catching up to do."

Nolie dropped her hand to Carlene's arm. "You and Darlene should go on home. I'll stay here with the other ladies and make sure everything's put away." She glanced at Darlene. "I'm assuming you want me to bring the leftover cake to the house?"

Carlene was about to protest, but Darlene silenced her with a sharp look. "Sure, bring it over. We'll have it after supper tomorrow night."

"And the night after that," Nolie joked. "There are pounds and pounds of cake left."

"Maybe we should give some of it away," Carlene suggested. "Don't you know a family with a lot of kids? That big middle layer hasn't even been touched, and we certainly don't need to eat it."

Darlene's lips thinned, but Nolie snapped her fingers. "Orlain Jones has six kids and they're always hungry." She turned to search the crowd. "Hey, Orlain!"

A tall, thin woman with tightly curled hair extracted herself from a conversational knot and sashayed over.

"Carlene wants your family to take that center cake tier," Nolie explained. "So help yourself whenever y'all are ready to go."

"Oh! So nice of you!" Orlain covered Carlene's hand with both of her own and gushed like a drama critic in love with a leading lady. "I was just tellin' my kids, the bigger they are, the nicer they are. Thank you so much."

Carlene patted the woman's hand and pulled herself free, then picked up her birthday apron. She was about to ask Henry for a key to his trunk when she caught a glimpse of her twin sister's face.

Darly's hard, disapproving expression stopped her cold. Staying at Sycamores might be a mistake.

Chapter Six

*A*n army of confusing emotions waged war in Darlene's chest as she drove home alone. She had been so delighted with the surprise party, practically over the moon with joy; then Carlene walked through the door and stole the show. Just as she had in high school; just as she did every time they were together.

Darlene's heart had turned over when she first saw her twin sister—her other half, showing up unexpectedly! But a moment later the old hurt awakened, the sting that used to constantly remind her that she was the less talented sister, the less favored twin. The one who'd been asked to sacrifice again and again so Carly could have whatever she needed to accomplish her dreams . . .

Why had Carlene come back today? Year after year she popped in at Christmas, spent two days with an increasingly dotty Aunt Verna, and assured the family that she'd made New York her home. She lived in Manhattan, worked on Broadway, and socialized with friends from the Upper West Side. She'd been too busy to come home for a single Thanksgiving; she'd been too caught up in her show schedule to come back for the birth of Darlene's children. She'd missed both

Katie's and Griffy's high school graduations, yet tonight she waltzed into the room on Henry's arm as if she were the guest of honor.

Why had she come home at the exact moment Darlene had nearly convinced herself that a good man truly loved her?

She blinked back tears and tried to focus on the taillights of Henry's car. Carlene rode in that car because Henry insisted it'd be no trouble for him to deliver Carly and her suitcases to Sycamores. He would have driven Darlene, too, but her Buick sat behind the church and someone had to drive it home. Since Nolie didn't drive, that meant Darlene, one of the celebrated birthday girls, had to drive herself. So here she was, the ugly stepsister, following Cinderella and the prince.

She glanced at her speedometer. Henry seemed to be creeping down the highway; he never drove this slowly. Was he trying to stretch out his time with Carlene?

Darlene urged her car closer until she could see Carlene's shining blond head only two feet from Henry's broad shoulders. Leave it to Carlene to make a beeline for Darlene's man as soon as she stepped off the plane. By the time she went back to New York—please, Lord, let it be soon!—Henry would be smitten with the delicate rose and Darlene would seem like a fleshy, flowerless aloe.

She tightened her grip on the steering wheel as pain squeezed her heart. Life could be so unfair. She'd met identical twins who could pass for mirror images of each other, but she and Carlene were almost opposites. She weighed a whopping ten pounds at birth; Carlene barely tipped the scale at six. She grew up strong and robust; Carlene managed to feel faint after running the fifty-yard dash.

Even Nolie's handmade gifts illustrated their differences. She gave Darlene an apron made of bright and utilitarian materials; she gave Carlene the sort of thing you'd give a woman who didn't have the sense to use a pot holder when pulling a hot pan out of the oven.

Carlene had inherited their mother's petite frame and fair skin; Darlene received her father's big bones and dark hair. The girls paid little attention to their differences until they reached middle school. Then Darlene shot up like a rocket, eclipsing all the boys, while Carlene only grew more feminine and curvaceous. The boys flocked to Carlene like bees to a flowering tree; they asked Darlene to play defensive tackle on their flag-football team.

And then, sometime around the seventh grade, Carlene volunteered to sing a solo in church—and the planet shifted on its axis. Momma stopped baking after-school treats and started concentrating on Carlene's music lessons, etiquette instruction, and designer dresses, whatever it might take to launch the musically gifted daughter to stardom.

Darlene swallowed over the growing lump in her throat. Surviving adolescence was difficult; doing it in the shadow of a nearly perfect sister was next to impossible.

The cold December day Carlene left for Juilliard, Darlene went with the rest of the family to the airport, wept a few crocodile tears as Carlene boarded the plane, then came home and told herself that she wouldn't miss Carly at all. She'd been wrong—Carly's absence felt like a physical amputation. Yet part of Darly felt as though she'd been set free, too. No more comparisons. No more pitying looks from Grandma. No more competing with Carlene for everything.

But though some things were easier with Carlene out of the picture, the house seemed strangely silent without Carly's constant chirping. After dinner, Darlene missed arguing with Carly over whose turn it was to do the dishes. In the morning, she missed hearing the rumble of the pipes that meant Carly had jumped into the shower and would take all the hot water. And in the early weeks of 1981, when Darlene faced the biggest problem of her life, she missed having her best friend around. She thought about calling . . . but knew Carly wouldn't understand her reasons for risking that kind of trouble.

One night in early March she walked down to Carly's bedroom, sat on the edge of the mattress, and stared at the empty pillow. How many times had she stopped here, eager to share a bit of gossip or ask Carly for advice? Sometimes she didn't need to say anything at all— she had only to lock gazes with her twin, who knew exactly what Darlene was thinking without either of them saying a word.

Learning to live without Carly, especially during those first turbulent weeks apart, had been like learning to breathe underwater. Some days she forgot her twin was gone and would run to Carly's room, where she gaped at the tidy bureau and choked on reality. Even now she would sometimes flip through a catalog, see an outfit, and know Carly would look wonderful in that color.

Just as she had looked wonderful tonight.

Darlene clamped her lips together to imprison a sob. Her heart had swelled with love, joy, and pride when she first glimpsed her sister, but other emotions followed on the heels of those feelings. How was she supposed to handle all of them?

Darlene brought a hand to her mouth as Henry's car pulled through Sycamores' open iron gates and rumbled over the long driveway. "It's only a week," she told herself as she struggled to maintain her control. Only a week and then Carly would be off again, going back to New York and her jet-set lifestyle. If she could bear losin' Momma and Griff, she could certainly bear having Carly around for a few days.

Lifting her chin, she turned onto the driveway and sped around Henry's vehicle, small stones bouncing off her car's underbelly as she headed toward the garage.

Chase Caldwell's brick house was every bit as sprawling as and quite a bit grander than Tara in the film version of *Gone with the Wind*. Finished in 1935, the neoclassical home featured four towering white pillars atop a marble porch at the zenith of stone steps. A second-floor balcony overlooked the front porch, while over a dozen mullioned, shuttered windows gazed across the lawn and reflected the rising sun. Stately wings to the left and right echoed the classical design while a rooftop widow's walk added to the impression of grandeur.

Sycamores was no less impressive when viewed from the lake. The back of the old house opened up to embrace the lakeside lot, with screen porches on both the second and third floors to catch the early evening breeze. Staircases at each end led to a brick terrace featuring a barbecue pit and a picnic area. While shade trees dominated the front and sides of the property, the afternoon sunshine gilded everything in the back, weathering the wooden decks, warming the bricks, and feeding a lush lawn that evoked envy from homeowners in three counties.

As a child, Carlene believed Sycamores to be the most beautiful house in the world.

She stepped out of Henry's car and pulled her purse to her shoulder. She had thought a lot about this moment, wondering what she would feel when she entered her childhood home now that Griff had come and gone. Did his presence still linger in the hallways? Would she feel his essence if she ventured into the master bedroom? She never lived under this roof while Griff and Darlene were married; until his funeral she had even managed to avoid staying in the guest room. But Sycamores had been her home long before she ever met Griffith Young.

Standing beside Henry's car, she squinted to see the house through the darkness. A carriage lamp at the side of the walkway stood empty and lightless, its bulb missing or broken. The front walkway, which she remembered as being edged with fragrant rose bushes, now lay stark and plain while grass creepers encroached on the stone steps. The only available light came from a front-door lamp glowing weakly from the top of the hill.

An unexpected lump rose to her throat. What had happened here? Carlene knew very little about her siblings' finances, but surely Darlene and Nolie could see that the house had fallen into a state of disrepair. Like Carlene herself, it was no longer exceptional, no longer filled with promise or hope . . .

Had her sisters given up because they knew the year 2018 was rapidly approaching? Or had something destroyed their pride in the family estate?

"Let me grab those suitcases for you," Henry said, popping the trunk. He set both cases on the driveway, then extended the handles and dragged them over the broken stone walkway.

Carlene led the way up to the porch. As she moved through the gloom, leaves rustled and she realized that some things hadn't changed. Trees still surrounded the property, live oaks and magnolias, tall pines and sycamores. She breathed in the sweet scent of jasmine and knew that white star flowers somewhere in the darkness would soon carpet the lawn with falling blossoms. Some aspects of home hadn't changed at all.

The twin trees her grandfather had planted at the right and left sides of the porch were tall when she left Peculiar; now they were wide as well, their sprawling limbs guarding the front windows upstairs and down. As a girl she had climbed those trees; often she would sit in one and Darly in the other as they competed to see who could be the first to spot Daddy's car or a sailboat on the lake. The smooth bark appeared black in the dark, but she remembered it as gray and mottled, like camouflage. These benevolent sentinels, the grand trees that had given Sycamores its name, guarded those who lived inside.

She shifted her focus to the house. The windows appeared dingy in the moonlight, and as they moved closer she could see that peeling paint—red?—covered the shutters. Looking up, she saw that the classical wooden railing around the balcony had been replaced with black iron, and the dentil molding at the roofline was nearly obscured by mud-dauber nests.

She blinked away tears and focused on the front door, not wanting Henry to glimpse her disappointment. This house had been her grandparents' crowning achievement, and her mother had always taken pride in it. The place probably began to decline after Griff's sudden death, but Carlene had hoped that Darlene and Nolie would do their best to keep the place shining.

"Go on in." Henry nodded toward the door. "If it's locked, the key's bound to be under the mat. Darlene'll be goin' in through the kitchen door in the garage."

Carlene caught her breath and turned the knob. The grand marble foyer, dominated by a curved staircase, used to gleam beneath the light of the crystal chandelier, but now the marble at her feet appeared dull and lifeless. The staircase stood as solid as ever, but nothing short of a bomb would disturb those graceful stone steps.

She looked around, unsure how she should proceed.

"I think Darlene would want you in the guest room," Henry said. Carlene turned. "And which room would that be?"

"Upstairs, back of the house. Right across from Nolie's room."

Carlene had no idea which room Nolie was using now, but she could find her way upstairs blindfolded. Mindful of Henry's heavy load, she moved toward the elevator her grandfather had tucked beyond the foyer.

"Elevator's not working," Henry called. "That old thing hasn't worked in four years, give or take. Darlene says it's plumb wore out, but it'd take a small fortune to replace it."

Of course it would. Carlene sighed and retraced her steps. Leaving Henry to manage her suitcases, she climbed the stairs to the second floor, then walked down the wide hallway that led to the back porch. Bedrooms sprouted like branches from this passageway—two in the front and two in the rear. The master bedroom, thankfully, was downstairs, so she could avoid envisioning Griff propped up in any of these beds.

"At the back of the house," she repeated, her heels occasionally striking wood through the worn carpet. That meant she'd either be staying in her old bedroom or in Grandma's. The memory of her grandmother, quickened by the familiar surroundings, brought a new tightness to her throat.

She glanced at the doors to her right and left, remembering what lay behind them—the elevator, a closet, a narrow staircase to the kitchen. A bathroom.

Reaching the farthest bedrooms, she peered into the suite at her right. Her grandmother had lived here during Carlene's childhood, and she remembered it as a spacious area with a fireplace and two doors that opened onto the back porch. She stepped into a short hallway, walked past a big bathroom, and blinked at the space beyond. Her grandmother's massive antique oak bed had been replaced by a virginal twin bed with a pink spread. Paperback volumes lined a bookcase between two mullioned doors, and beyond them, a screen door opened to the backyard. A faintly doggy odor permeated the entire area.

"This is Nolie's room, I believe." Henry jerked his head toward the hallway. "You'll be over here."

"Just a moment, please," she said, wanting to linger. "I haven't been here . . . in a long time."

Carlene stepped through the doorway that used to lead to a playroom. The doll house, rocking horse, and teddy-bear collection beloved by two generations had disappeared, replaced by cardboard boxes, antique trunks, and a long pine table burdened with mountains of fabric in every conceivable color. Bits of old lace spilled out of a basket, while a stack of neatly pressed vintage handkerchiefs sat on the lid. A smaller table near the two square windows held a lamp and a sewing machine, while a long white cord spiderwebbed from eave to eave and corner to corner. Aprons dangled from this cord, beautiful bits of new and aged fabric in various shapes and textures, long sashes trailing and shifting in a breezy current from the open window.

Carlene breathed deeply. Not only did this area smell of dogs, but clumps of black and white hair clung to the worn carpet.

She gestured to the dangling aprons. "Let me guess—this is Nolie's lair?"

Apparently Henry had never been here before. "Wow." He tipped his head back and studied the assortment of fluttering fabrics. "I knew she liked to make aprons, but I had no idea she liked it this much."

The sound of heavy footsteps drew their attention. "Henry?" Darlene's voice held a sharp edge. "Are you up here?"

"At your service." He quickstepped toward the hallway. "I was just helping your sister with her luggage."

Not wanting to abandon Henry to Darlene's ire, Carlene hurried back to the hall. When she arrived, Darlene was staring at Henry with her arms crossed and her gaze focused to an ice pick's point. "Carly, I think you should stay in the guest room over on this side. You and Nolie can keep each other company up here."

Carlene followed Darlene across the hallway and into her childhood bedroom. She glanced at Darly, surprised that her sister hadn't mentioned the connection. She had grown up in this room while Darlene had the bedroom at the front of the house. When Nolie arrived, Momma turned the front bedroom across from Darlene into a nursery.

"My old room," Carlene said. The place had changed since her youth—the once pale yellow walls had been painted pink and her quilted bedspread replaced with a polyester version that could have found its match in any Motel 6.

But the sight of the massive oak bed ripped aside a hazy curtain, revealing dozens of shadowed memories. She and Darly used to sit on this bed and play with their paper dolls, pretending the carved wooden finials were turrets in their dolls' castles. She'd sit on one pillow and Darlene would take the other, their paper-doll families spread out at their feet.

"Grandma's bed." Carlene smiled at her sister in open delight. "I'd forgotten all about it until I stepped into Grandma's—I mean Nolie's—room. I realized the bed was missing, but here it is."

Darlene nodded. "Right."

"Do you remember how we used to play on it?" Carlene moved to the headboard and curled her hand around one of the ornate carvings. "Do you remember how we'd tape our paper dolls to these posts so they could live in a tower like Rapunzel?"

Darlene stared at the bedpost like a woman pondering a problem in trigonometry. "I don't remember that."

Carlene looked at Henry and smiled. "Maybe she doesn't, but I do. Grandma would sit in the rocking chair and read her Bible while we climbed up to play on her bed. Paper dolls, Barbies, or long games of Candy Land . . ."

Darlene flashed a smile of upper teeth and transferred her gaze to Henry. "You want some coffee? I was fixin' to put on the pot."

"Only if it's decaf." Henry put a hand to his back and grimaced. "I plan on sleepin' good tonight."

"Then come on down to the kitchen."

Carlene tilted her head and studied Darly, aware that her sister's voice held a note of warmth that had been missing a moment ago. She'd been in Peculiar less than five hours, so what could she possibly have done to offend Darly?

"I'll be down in a bit," she said, even though Darlene hadn't asked if *she* wanted coffee. "I want to unpack a few things so the wrinkles don't set."

Darlene led the way out of the room, but Henry paused in the doorway. "Sure is good to have you home, Carlene. And I hope you had an awfully happy birthday."

"Henry!" Darlene's voice sharpened.

"Oops," Henry whispered. "I'd better run. If you need anything, just holler, okay? We're all mighty excited about you bein' here."

"Thank you." Carlene offered him a fleeting smile, then closed the door and lifted one of her suitcases to the bed. If Darlene didn't change her attitude, Carlene might need to buy a sweater. This Florida summer was shaping up to be a lot chillier than she'd expected.

Chapter Seven

The morning after the big surprise party, Nolie slipped into a white blouse and worn white denim overalls, then whistled to her dogs and tiptoed down the back-porch stairs. She stepped outside, where the morning sun had gilded the earth with a shiny glow. After giving Ricky and Lucy their vitamins, she released them into the backyard where they rolled in the dew-drenched grass and chased a few butterflies.

She sank into a lawn chair, wrapped in a blanket of contentment. Last night's party had gone so well she expected everyone who attended to wake up in a delicious mood, happily hungover from sheer festivity. Henry had been pleased, and for the first time in five years all three Caldwell sisters spent the night in the family home. She sensed that her mother and grandmother were smiling from heaven, overjoyed to see the house brimming with life. Darly and Carly hadn't exactly turned cartwheels when they finally reunited, but they'd come around. They'd been separated far too long.

She rose and crossed the stone terrace to the spot where the dogs' food and water bowls waited. After filling each bowl with kibble, she whistled and smiled as Ricky and Lucy came running. "Don't gobble it all at once," she warned, standing back to let the dogs eat. "You don't want it to come right back up again."

As the dogs crunched their breakfast, she settled into a chair and pulled the slim leather volume of Emily Dickinson's poetry from her overalls pocket. She thumbed to a well-worn page, read the poem there, then closed her eyes to ponder a line: *I'm nobody! Who are you? Are you nobody, too?*

"You're an early riser."

She startled as a male voice intruded on her thoughts. Erik Payne stood behind the overgrown viburnum hedge, a pair of garden clippers in his hand.

She smiled and closed her book. "Looks like you're working your way down Darlene's list."

"Some of her projects are going to take a lot of time, but if there's one thing I've learned while living in Florida, it's that plants grow like mad once warm weather arrives. If you don't keep 'em trimmed back, they'll eat the house."

"If you mean to get serious about trimming that hedge, I think we have some electric clippers in the garage."

"I saw them—but it's so early I didn't want to wake anybody. I'll pull out the heavy machinery in a bit." He nodded at the small book in her hand. "Let me guess—you're reading *My Utmost for His Highest.* That's a great devotional book."

She lowered her gaze, heat creeping up her throat. "Um, I tried that book once. I read the first paragraph five times and still didn't understand it."

He gave her a sympathetic smile. "Oswald Chambers can be quite deep. I often find myself trying to understand something he said."

"That's not what I meant—I meant I couldn't *read* it." She looked up and met his gaze, wanting to be honest with him. "I have a learning disability. Sort of like dyslexia, but not quite. The words and letters often don't make sense to me."

"Oh." He studied her, a spark of some indefinable emotion in his eyes. "Then what are you reading?"

"This?" She waved her little book. "A teacher gave this to me when I was going through a hard time in the twelfth grade. It's a collection of Emily Dickinson's poems."

"And you can read those?"

"She uses simple words, mostly. And she thinks like I do."

Finished with their breakfast, the dogs slurped from their water bowls and then ran to Erik, who didn't seem to mind them dripping on his shoes. He bent to rub their heads.

"They like you." Nolie slipped her book back into her pocket. "Dogs have good intuition about people."

"Do they? I thought they loved anyone who'd pet them."

"That may be true in some cases, but my babies have genuine discernment."

He chuckled. "So what made you decide to get these Whatchamaburgers?"

She laughed. "Leonbergers." Her gaze shifted to her dogs' stately dark masks. Now that they had finished greeting Erik, they were surveying the backyard with alert ears and dignified expressions. "I guess you can tell I like big dogs."

"I gathered that you're not into toy poodles."

"Everbody needs someone to lean on, right?"

He smiled, but a thoughtful crease crept onto his forehead. "Most people lean on other people."

"Yeah . . . but in a place like Peculiar you have to be careful who you trust with your secrets. There's not much to do in a small town, but there are plenty of folks whose favorite activity is crankin' the ol' rumor mill."

She bent and snapped her fingers, then called Lucy. As the dog stood and walked over, Nolie met Erik's gaze. "Dogs never blab your secrets and they don't complain. Can you say that about anyone else you know?"

He lifted a finger in a silent touché. "You've got a point there."

"And they're really great animals." She put Lucy in a sit, then rubbed the dog's ears. "Darlene says I'm crazy, but Lucy'll go into heat again in a couple of months, and I really want puppies this time. She's ready."

Erik lowered his clippers and reached out to stroke Ricky. "I know you have room here for all kinds of pets, but some people would say there are already too many domestic animals in the world—"

"Created through irresponsible breeding," Nolie interrupted. "I'm not one of those silly people who think having puppies will be fun. I know raising puppies is hard work, but I'm okay with that." She put her hands on Lucy's silky ears, then pressed a kiss to the dog's dark head. "My sisters have made lives for themselves while I've been a homebody. I'd like to show them I can support myself if I have to."

She softened her smile. "And if you need another reason, maybe it's because I'm a sucker for . . . babies." She coughed to cover the catch in her voice, then lowered her gaze lest Erik focus on her flushing face.

Doggone it, why did her voice crack every time she talked about babies? She'd already come to terms with the realization that she'd probably never have one. Because the love of her life deserted her, he'd taken that possibility with him.

So she'd learned to avoid things that hurt—romantic comedies, sappy melodramas, and baby showers. Acceptance was healthy; torturing herself was not.

Fortunately, the man behind the hedge didn't seem to notice the crack in her composure.

He gave Ricky a final pat and picked up the clippers again. "Well, I hope the puppy thing works out for you. I don't know much about dogs, but these two are awful nice even"—he wiped his hand on his jeans—"if they do dribble a lot."

Nolie summoned up a bright laugh. "You get used to that. And don't forget, the other day you said you were washable."

"That I did." Erik grinned and clipped an overgrown branch from the hedge. "That I did."

* * *

Darlene and Carlene peered into the ditch beside the road that led to Sycamores.

"I see something shiny down there," Carly insisted, dropping her schoolbooks in the dust. She kicked off her sneakers.

"You're crazy." Darlene reached to grab the suspenders that crossed in the small of Carlene's back, but Carly toppled into the ditch before Darlene's fingers could grip the material. When Carly splashed and disappeared, Darly knew she had no choice—she had to go in after her sister.

She held her nose and jumped in feet first, remembering too late that she hadn't removed her shoes. As bubbles rushed past her ears, she opened her eyes underwater and searched for some sign of Carly, but the water was dense and murky. She dove again and again, her lungs and eyes burning, her ears filled with muffled sounds. Finally, she had to face the possibility that she had failed and Carlene had drowned.

She felt the muddy bottom beneath her shoes and launched herself upward, then broke the surface and gasped for breath. Her blurry eyes scanned the grassy bank, but she didn't see Carlene. She took another deep breath, about to dive again, but then heard someone singing "Tea for Two."

She whirled. Carly was sitting cross-legged on the opposite bank, her long braids dripping, her skin shining with water. She had peeled off her knee socks and was calmly squeezing the water out of them as she sang.

"Carly!" The name burst out of Darlene like a roar. "Why on earth did you do that? There are snakes in this ditch. You could of gotten us both killed!"

Carlene smiled the innocent smile of an angel. "I don't think we'll be dyin' in a ditch, Darly."

And as Darlene stared, rage rising in her chest, she was also unbelievably, indescribably, wonderfully *grateful* that nothing had happened to her twin because she couldn't imagine walking home alone. They were meant to be together, no matter what, no matter where.

"A gator could have grabbed us," Darlene said, starting in again, but then she looked up, aware of other voices. Someone was nearby; people were talking. People who didn't belong here.

In the sprawling first-floor master suite, Darlene groaned and gripped at the dream, reached for it as it faded away. Muffled sounds rattled the old window, male and female voices, and she knew without looking that Nolie and the minister had run into each other in the backyard.

She'd been dreaming. For some reason her mind had carried her back to elementary-school days, when she and Carly traipsed all over Peculiar on their walk back from the bus stop. She opened her eyes, the details of the dream fading like a weak radio signal. She could no longer remember why she and Carly had been standing by the ditch, but the strong emotions of her dream self still tugged at her. The irritation felt familiar, but the determination to save Carly . . . she hadn't experienced that one in years.

She shook herself awake and sat up, remembering the voices outside her window—Nolie and the preacher were talking in the backyard. She wasn't surprised. They were both early birds, and neither of them had a serious care in the world. Neither of *them* had just celebrated a milestone birthday, and neither of them stood in jeopardy of losing true love because a rival had swept onto the scene.

She let her heavy eyelids close. As images of the previous night crystallized in her mind, a fresh surge of hurt rose and crested over her heart. She'd hoped a good night's sleep would ease her mind, but the memory of Henry and Carlene alone in his car still made her wince.

How could the sight of two people she loved make her want to scream?

The pain was not unfamiliar. Years ago, long before her marriage, she had watched Carlene and Griff walking together at school, their hands intertwined, their heads bent toward each other, her blonde hair lightly strafing his broad shoulder. The sight of them had been enough to make Darlene queasy, and now her stomach roiled again—

She threw off the covers, forcing Cary Grant from his comfortable spot by her side. The cat mewed in complaint, but Darlene wasn't in the mood to spoil him. Carlene was upstairs at this very moment, probably sleeping beneath a silk beauty mask, probably dreaming of Henry just as Darlene had once dreamed of Griff.

She sat on the edge of the bed, straightened her spine, and drew a deep breath. Maybe these fears were the result of paranoia. Maybe she was worrying for no reason. After all, Henry didn't seem like Carly's type, but who knew what Carly's type was these days?

She ought to be happy. Last night Nolie assured her that the birthday party had been planned for *her*, and that inviting Carlene had been an afterthought. Nolie and Henry had put in a lot of effort, and she'd be ungrateful if she didn't give them credit for their hard work.

So maybe the time had come to let bygones be bygones. Perhaps she needed to look out for Carly again, to remember how desperate she once had been to keep Carlene close. After all, they were still sisters and nothing could change that.

Five long years had passed since Griff's funeral; surely she and Carly could put their history behind them. They ought to be able to share their experiences, tell their stories, and learn how to be close again. They were twins, after all, and had once been as close as hand and glove.

This was a new day, a good beginning for the future. She and Carlene could renew their relationship with a clean slate. Griff, God rest him, was gone, so they should bury all those hurts and renew their friendship.

What did Momma always say? "Anyone with a thimbleful of brains can hold a grudge, but to forget an injury is truly beautiful."

So she would be beautiful. She would be gracious. And she would welcome her sister with open arms.

And as for Henry . . . she would simply have to keep him away from Carlene. After all, Carlene couldn't help being a star. No more than Henry could help being a man.

If Henry's natural affections began to pull him toward Carlene, Darlene would simply have to reel him in and get him to the altar. She'd done it before, so she could do it again.

But just once she'd like to marry a man who loved her before he loved Carlene.

Carlene dreamed of a trombone, a flat, raspy instrument that erupted in a *blaatt* at all the wrong moments and disturbed the singers on-stage. They were performing the costume-ball scene from *Phantom,* and right before the chandelier was due to crash, the director called a halt and glared into the orchestra pit. "What *is* that awful noise?"

She woke with the same question in her head. The elaborately costumed players vanished as she opened her eyes and stared at the water-stained ceiling, yet the sustained droning continued.

She rolled over and glanced at the clock. Ten forty-five, still early according to her biorhythms. After a long night at the theater, she usually slept until noon, lunched at one, and headed to the gym at two. By five she would be on her way to the theater, and by seven, she'd be ready to step onstage and sing her heart out.

But no one would ask her to sing today. Or tomorrow, for that matter.

She groaned and tossed the covers over her head. The filmy cotton curtains did nothing to block the bright morning light, and the old double-hung windows made a poor sound barrier. She couldn't go back to sleep now, not with sunlight in her room and that annoying drone in her ears.

She swung her legs out of bed and took a moment to survey the room. Her old bedroom had no fireplace, but it did have its own bathroom and two doors that opened onto a porch overlooking the backyard. The current furnishings were far from plush, but they would certainly suffice for a visit.

She stumbled into the bathroom, splashed cold water onto her face, and reached for a towel. Holding the towel to her damp throat, she left the bathroom and thrust her head into the main hallway, listening for any sound that might reveal her sisters' whereabouts. A thick silence lay over the second floor, and no wonder—from the sound of the ruckus outside, everyone was out in the yard.

After taking a leisurely shower and dressing in slacks and a sleeveless sweater, she took the back stairs to the kitchen where she found Nolie and Darlene eating sandwiches, warmed-over casserole, raw carrots, and leftover birthday cake. The clock over the sink said eleven thirty.

"Good mornin'." Darlene smiled and nodded toward the spread on the kitchen island. "Help yourself to some lunch. We didn't know when you'd be up, so we didn't wait."

Was she implying that Carlene was lazy? "I didn't expect you to wait," she answered, picking up a plate. "And I have to ask—what *is* that awful noise I've been hearing all morning?"

Nolie grinned. "That's Erik—he's trimming the hedges around the terrace. He waited until nine to start up the electric trimmers, but those bushes are so overgrown it'll probably take him all day to finish the job."

Carlene opened the drawer that used to hold silverware. Now it served as a repository for rubber bands, pens, assorted coupons, a pair of tongs, a box of matches, and a spool of dental floss. *Floss?*

She picked up the container and turned toward her twin. "You clean your teeth in the kitchen?"

Darlene's face twisted in revulsion. "Are you nuts?"

"Then why do you keep floss—"

Darlene shook her head as if any three-year-old should know the answer. "To slice cheesecakes. And for replacing stray buttons."

Carlene sighed and dropped the floss back into the drawer. "Your lawn guy—did I meet him at the party last night?"

"No." Darlene finished the last of her sandwich, then tapped her lips with her napkin. "He's a preacher we hired to be our handyman. He's looking for a church, so if you know anybody—"

"Sorry." Using her fingers, Carlene plucked a hunk of turkey breast from a package and dropped it on a slice of wheat bread. "I don't know many church people these days." She paused before a rectangular dish and peered at the jumbled contents.

"Chicken-and-rice casserole," Darlene said, a note of pride in her voice. "Very popular around here."

"I'll pass." Carlene kept her voice light, but when Darlene stiffened, she added a quick explanation: "Too many calories. Professional preservation has trained me to consider my waistline."

She hopped on a stool, but one look at Darlene's face revealed that her explanation had not soothed her sister's pride. Darlene sat with her lips pressed together and her hands folded, her eyes narrowed into an I'm-ready-to-strangle-someone squint.

Best to change the subject.

Carlene blew out a breath and smiled at Nolie. "Thanks for your hard work on the party last night. Everything was delightful. The cake was amazing, and your gift—well, I've never worn an apron, but I'm going to wear that one at my next dinner party."

"I hoped you'd like it." Nolie propped her chin on her hand. "Everyone seemed to enjoy themselves, didn't they? Of course, most folks were absolutely thrilled to meet a Broadway star. After you left, I heard so many comments about how beautiful you are and how honored they were to meet someone who had hit the big time—"

"Stop." Carlene held up her hand. "Nolie, honey, I'm not a big star. Honestly. Big stars get big money and their names on the marquee. I got my name in the playbill and was lucky if they spelled it right. And most of the time I worked for scale, which doesn't go far when you live in Manhattan."

"Doesn't matter," Nolie said, her eyes wide and shining. "You're a star to us no matter what. How many girls from Peculiar have performed professionally on a New York stage? Or any big-city stage, for that matter? Zero, other than you."

"But I'm not famous."

"You're famous to us, so you'd better get used to the attention." Nolie rapped the table as if she'd settled the matter. "Everyone was tickled to meet you, so don't be surprised if a few folks happen to drop by this week. I've a feeling lots of people will want to see you again before you head back up north."

"When is that, by the way?" Her face composed into a blank mask, Darlene looked at Carlene. "When are you leaving?"

Carlene nearly choked on a stubborn hunk of bread crust. How could she answer? She'd hoped to stay until her apartment sold; then she'd take a quick trip to New York to settle her affairs before deciding where to move. The tone of Darlene's voice, however, seemed to indicate that an early departure would be best for all.

"I-I have an open-ended ticket," Carlene stammered, "but I hoped to fly out next Friday or Saturday. After a week, you'll probably be glad to see me go."

"Never!" Nolie proclaimed, but as Carlene finished the rest of her sandwich, she couldn't help noticing that Darlene didn't utter a word of protest.

Darlene's lack of enthusiasm was understandable. They had been separated for far too long; it would take time to get to know each other again. Until they did, Carlene would approach Darlene cautiously, taking care to avoid hidden land mines.

With no future prospects remaining in New York, she needed time to lick her wounds and pull her thoughts together. Now that she was no longer capable of fulfilling her goals, she needed space to dream new dreams and figure out what the future could hold.

In Peculiar, where few people dreamed and ambitions grew small, surely she could manage to do that.

After eating lunch with her sisters, Nolie crept back into the kitchen, opened the refrigerator, and pulled out the turkey, the mayonnaise, and the casserole dish. Because her sisters were somewhere in the house, she quietly made a turkey sandwich and set it on a china plate, then added a generous helping of casserole, a few raw baby carrots, and a generous slice of birthday cake. She grabbed a glass and filled it with cold lemonade and extra ice, then pulled a plastic fork and napkin from the miscellaneous drawer.

Though Darlene had promised to feed Erik lunch every day, Nolie couldn't resist a compelling urge to fix his meal herself. Darlene would slap food on a paper plate, a decent sandwich with chips and lettuce as a token green veggie, but she wouldn't be lavish with the cake, nor would she trim off the thready ends of the carrots or heat the casserole until it was piping hot.

After sneaking a glance across the living room to be sure Darlene was nowhere in sight, Nolie set the plate and glass on a tray, then slipped out to the screened porch overlooking the backyard. Wooden stairs led down to the terrace, where Erik was slowly making progress on the overgrown viburnum. She set the tray on the iron table, then moved a few steps down the staircase, remaining safely out of the way of flying greenery.

Erik Payne was nothing like the other men Darlene had occasionally hired to do yard work at the house. Most lawn men ran a gas trimmer over the hedge, snipping only the protruding branches, and then moved on, but Erik seemed to see through the overgrowth to the ideal shape within. As sweat streamed from his brow and dripped from his nose, he used the clippers to remove the overgrown branches, then ran the shears over the hedge again, taking off another two inches of growth. Steadily and patiently, he kept working, bringing the hedge down to its proper shape.

He must have been an extremely patient pastor—the type who didn't expect saints to be formed in a day. The world surely could use more pastors with a gentle touch.

Intent on his task, Erik didn't notice Nolie until she put two fingers in her mouth and produced the sharp whistle she used to call her dogs. Then he looked up and cut the noisy engine.

"You really should wear goggles when you're using that thing." She moved farther down the stairs. "We wouldn't want you to get a sliver in your eye."

He gave her what looked like a perfunctory smile, then lifted the trimmer again. "Maybe I'll go get my glasses when I'm ready to take a break."

"It's way past time for a break. I brought you some lunch."

"Thanks, but I don't need anything."

She crossed her arms. "If you're going to work all day in this heat, you need to eat and drink. And while you're at it, you should probably go get those glasses and a hat."

He shook his head as if to refuse again, but when she didn't budge he sighed and lowered the hedge trimmer.

She gestured to the wrought-iron dining set on the screened porch. "You can eat up there, or anywhere else you like. That old iron table may not be pretty, but it's perfectly functional."

"I'm not fussy," he grumbled, stomping toward her.

She led the way up the staircase and smiled when he dropped into the chair like a sack of potatoes.

"You know," he said, bending over the peeling tabletop, "this set would look pretty good with a fresh coat of paint. We might have to sandblast the rust and remove this old finish—"

"I'm glad to hear you say that." Nolie sat in the wobbly chair across from him. "I'd love to help you spruce this place up. I've wanted to do something for ages, but I haven't known where to start."

He shook his head. "I couldn't ask you to—"

"Why not? If I want to work on this house, seems like you have to let me. Grandpa set it up so all of us girls would be caretakers of his estate, so technically, you're workin' for the three of us."

A spark of curiosity lit his eyes as he swallowed a bite of the sandwich. "What are you plannin' to do—you know, when the time comes to move on?"

She shook her head. "I don't plan on goin' anywhere. I've been hopin' they'll let us girls stay on. We could take care of the house until . . . well, until there aren't any more Caldwell girls left to take care of things."

Erik turned his head, his gaze drifting over the back of the house. "It's a lot to take care of. Why would you want to stay in such a big old place?"

"Because it's home. Because I've never lived anywhere else."

He snorted softly and reached for his lemonade. "This house is quite a contrast to the parsonage where I lived—until last month, that is. I was grateful for it, don't get me wrong, but my wife hated it. Two tiny bedrooms, a skinny kitchen with no real place to eat, and a living room that opened straight onto the street—no porch or anything."

Though she had begun to feel relaxed with the minister, Nolie tensed at the mention of his ex-wife. When they talked about Sycamores or the dogs or the weather, she could almost forget he'd ever been married, so the reminder that he'd recently experienced a broken heart brought a host of unwelcome memories crowding back . . . along with feelings of loss, memories of painful adjustment, and a load of public humiliation.

"Worst of all," Erik continued, oblivious to the shift in her mood, "the house was right next to the church, so anytime anybody wanted me, they'd just walk over and bang on my door. One man came in the middle of the night. Because he knew I'd be in bed, he walked around and pounded on our bedroom window. Nearly scared Kelly to death."

Nolie stared into space, struggling to keep her imagination from picturing him in bed with a woman named Kelly. A young, pretty blonde, surely. A woman with China-doll features and crystal blue eyes . . . someone who deserved Erik, or at least thought she did.

Nolie slammed the door on those unwelcome thoughts and choked out a reply. "You're kidding."

"I kid you not. Finally, Kelly couldn't cope anymore. We'd only been at that church only about a year when she decided she couldn't handle another day. She packed up and went back to her hometown. I kept writing her, promising that I'd get another church where things would be better, but she wrote back and said it wasn't just the church; she was unhappy with everything. She didn't want to be a pastor's wife, period. When I said I couldn't stop being a minister, she filed for divorce."

He sipped from his lemonade again, then turned, leaning forward with his elbows on his knees. "Funny thing," he said, his voice heavy with irony. "I told her I couldn't deny God's calling and stop bein' a minister, and now look at me—I'm a handyman. What I couldn't quit because Kelly asked me to, I had to quit because the church asked me to. And nothin' about the situation makes any sense."

Nolie remained silent, realizing that he was probably saying more than he'd intended. His grim expression and the way he stared into space seemed to draw a curtain between them; a one-way curtain that did not invite further conversation.

Still, she couldn't resist one question. "Did you"—she hesitated— "I mean, maybe it's none of my business, but I can't help wonderin' if you and your wife had—"

"Kids?" His eyes widened, then lowered. "No, thank the Lord. No children, and I'm grateful. I wouldn't want to put them through this kind of trouble."

Nolie lowered her gaze, wondering if she'd trespassed by asking too much. But the preacher kept on talking.

"A week after my divorce became final," he said, his strained voice seeming to come from a great distance away, "a group of deacons came to the parsonage after a Wednesday-night prayer meeting. Someone had heard about my divorce decree, so they told me they'd have to let me go. They were going to look for someone else, someone who had married wisely, they said, so they needed me to vacate the parsonage right away."

He closed his eyes, and in that resigned gesture Nolie glimpsed the magnitude of his grief.

"One of the men, though—Beverage—told me about Sycamores and said y'all had been known to hire people who were down on their luck." A hint of a wry smile played around the preacher's mouth as he glanced at Nolie. "He must have been thinkin' about Darlene when he told me not to mind the woman who lived here because her bark was worse than her bite."

Nolie felt her smile twist. "Ouch."

Erik shrugged. "Your sister's a good lady . . . and so are you." He gestured to the now-empty glass and dinner plate. "Thanks for thinkin' of me. You didn't have to bring me lunch."

"I wanted to help." Nolie stood, biting back the other things she wanted to say. She wanted to do more than feed him; she wanted to comfort and encourage him. She wanted to hop on her bike and pedal over to that Chattahoochee church and tell them they'd made a mistake sending Erik away without helping him find a place to live or even giving him a referral. Worst of all, they had sent him off without offering any kind of comfort or hope . . .

But she couldn't confess those desires to a man who still agonized over losing his wife.

She picked up the plate and gestured to the empty glass. "You can leave that on the table and I'll refill it in a bit, unless you'd prefer a Co-Cola or water. The sun gets mighty warm once it crosses to the back side of the house."

"Lemonade would be great," he said, standing. "And I shouldn't bother you anymore. Darlene's gonna look out the window and wonder why I'm not earning my keep."

He jogged down the stairs, then powered up the hedge trimmer. Nolie watched him go, realizing that she'd been mistaken. That church hadn't left Erik completely bereft. One grace-filled deacon had stopped to tell him about Sycamores, a place where someone would be willing to offer an opportunity . . .

When God closed a door, he always found someone to pry open a window.

Nolie turned and hurried into the kitchen, timing her steps to match the pounding beat of her heart.

After lunch, Carlene went upstairs to brush her teeth, then decided to take a look around to see how the house had changed since her last visit. Since she'd already seen Nolie's room, she walked to the two front bedrooms.

The room on the right had once been Darlene's, so she wasn't surprised to discover that it had most recently been Katie's. Though Katie was now grown with a family of her own, Darlene kept the room as it must have been when Katie went away to school. The lavender walls complemented dark purple curtains, while violet carpet covered the hardwood floors. A photo of Katie's five-year-old son, Matt, sat on the bureau in a wooden frame.

Carlene found herself drawn to a portrait that hung between the two front windows. The oil painting must have been commissioned when Katie was nine or ten, because the girl's face still held a hint of childlike roundness. The wide hazel eyes were Darlene's, but the cleft in the chin came from Griff.

Blinking back tears, Carlene spun on the ball of her foot and left the room. Silly, really, for her to be so emotional about an unchangeable reality. After all, she knew Katie—had met her on several visits and occasionally remembered to send the girl birthday cards and Christmas gifts. But the way Katie held her head in that painting was painfully familiar—and Carlene didn't want to be reminded of Griff.

Fortunately, the blue bedroom across the hallway held no paintings of Griffy Junior. The twin bed was made up in a masculine navy coverlet, rows of basketball and football trophies lined a shelf between the windows, and the student-sized desk was as neat as a GI's footlocker. Carlene bent to look at the titles on his bookshelf: a Boy Scout manual, a couple of *Hardy Boy* adventures, one of the *Harry Potter* books. Unread, from the pristine look of the dust jacket.

She felt her mouth twist. Apparently, Griffy was very much like his father. Griff had never been much of a reader, either. Carlene read most of their American Lit assignments, summarizing stories and poems for him. She couldn't believe it when he passed the class.

She opened the closet and saw a letter jacket and varsity sweater hanging with a few worn shirts. Darlene must have kept these things for sentimental reasons, or was she thinking that Griffy might ask for them later? Did grown kids do that? Carlene didn't know.

On the nightstand, along with a lamp, stood a pair of framed photos—Griffy's senior picture and a small picture of Marlee, Griffy's daughter. Carlene picked up the larger frame and felt her throat tighten . . . Griffy looked so much like his father did at that age. She ran her fingers over the image. This was how Griff looked when she said good-bye at the airport, when he promised to love her forever. This expression—happy, confident, proud—was how he looked when she said she could never love anyone else.

She pulled the photo to her breast and bowed her head as tears spilled down her cheeks. She had lost not only Griff but also the opportunity to have children and grandchildren. She always wanted kids, always thought she'd be a good mother, but somehow babies never came along. She did get pregnant after she married Evan, but she miscarried and Evan never wanted to put her through that kind of grief again.

So here she was, back at Sycamores where she began, but now she was fifty, menopausal, and childless. Her Christmases would never be filled with the laughter of little ones around the tree, she would never have to fight the crowds at a toy store, and she would never need a shelf for picture books in her apartment.

She never meant to end up like this.

She pressed her hand to her mouth and steeled herself against an overpowering sense of loss, then gently returned the photo to its place.

After moving down the grand front staircase, she took the lower stairs that led to what her family had always called the basement, though the rear portion of the lowest floor opened into the backyard. This had been her daddy's domain, the place he went to escape the estrogen overload that resulted from living with three daughters, a wife, and a mother.

Though a three-car garage occupied nearly a third of the square footage, the stairs led to a vestibule that opened into a spacious rec room where her father kept his pool and Ping-Pong tables. The air here was thick with a damp stickiness unknown in New York, and Carlene's bare arms pebbled with gooseflesh as she fumbled for the light switch. Giving up after a moment, she crossed to the wide sliding doors and pulled back the curtains, releasing a chorus line of dust motes to dance in the slanting sunbeams.

Despite the warmth of the afternoon sun, the skin at the back of her neck tightened in an instant of déjà vu. Her daddy never talked much; like Griff, he said far more through his posture and his actions. She leaned against a supporting pillar and closed her eyes as a memory, a precious one, brushed her cheek.

She and Darlene had just turned twelve in the summer of '74. The family attended the Congregational Church because that was where Momma had grown up, and the children's choir was slated to sing a special in the worship service. That morning Maxine Harper, who directed the choir, asked Carlene to sing the second verse of "How Great Thou Art" as a solo. While Darlene gaped in astonishment, Carlene agreed.

Stepping to the microphone with quiet assurance, Carly began to sing as the choir hummed behind her. A hush fell over the sanctuary, a quiet so thick that the only sounds were the strains of the organ and Carly's voice. The other children joined her on the chorus, but Carly's clear soprano soared above the other voices, pealing like a crystal bell on the high note at the end. She'd never heard herself sing into a microphone before, but she liked what she heard.

Apparently other people did, too. After a prolonged interval of sustained silence, voices from the congregation erupted in shouted "amens." No one applauded during church in those days, but Carly knew those amens were meant for her and the Lord, who had bestowed a special gift on one of his daughters.

Her cheeks burning, she lowered her head and sat with the choir, grateful for the modesty rail that hid her from view during most of the sermon. When the service dismissed, she grabbed Darly's hand and raced to the station wagon, ready to be home.

Momma was already at the car by the time the twins arrived. She greeted Carly with a bemused smile as she opened the back door and let the twins climb in beside two-year-old Nolie.

Daddy, however, was nowhere to be found. In the passenger seat, Momma rolled down the window and waited, smiling at the occasional worshipper who walked by and said hello. Then Aunt Verna approached.

"I saw Charlie Junior," she said, bending to peer at the three girls in the back seat. She gave them a fleeting smile, then patted Momma's shoulder. "He's standing at the back of the church. Asked me if I'd seen Carly."

Momma blew out a breath. "He knows she always goes straight to the car."

"Course he does." Aunt Verna swiveled to face the church and waved at someone in the distance. "He's really standing there to collect congratulations. He'd never brag, you know, but he's awfully proud of that little girl."

Aunt Verna turned and bent again, her blue eyes seeking Carlene's. "I'm proud of you, too, sweetie. You keep singing for the Lord, you hear? If you don't use that voice for him, he just might take it away."

The threat in those words soured the happiness in Carly's chest. By the time Daddy appeared, strolling through the parking lot with his hands in his pockets, Carly felt as though she'd swallowed some large, cold object that pressed against her breastbone. Daddy got in the car, Momma sighed, and Darlene leaned forward, her chin resting on her fists. "Can we go now? I'm starving."

Daddy turned the key and pulled out of the lot without another word. But over the years, whenever Carlene questioned her father's love, she had only to remember the day he'd stood at the back of the church, collecting congratulations.

Though Daddy died later that year, Carlene could still feel him in the rec room. He used to wait patiently on the opposite side of the pool table, a cue stick in his hand as she framed her shot with her thumb and index finger. She'd shoot, she'd miss, and he'd try to give her pointers, but she didn't want advice; she wanted to win. If she couldn't win—and the odds of beating Daddy were slim, even when he went easy on her—she didn't want to play.

Occasionally Darlene came downstairs to accept Daddy's challenge to a match, but Carlene played him far more often, telling herself that one day she'd beat him at his own game. But one afternoon Daddy went out to mow the lawn and never came back inside. Momma found him pinned beneath the heavy tractor, which flipped after encountering a small sinkhole that opened after a storm.

After Daddy died, Carlene couldn't summon up the enthusiasm for pool or Ping-Pong games. She kept singing, though her venue shifted from church to school, to competitions, and, ultimately, to the stage.

She shivered in the damp humidity and moved back toward the

wide windows. She hadn't thought of Aunt Verna's warning in years, but in retrospect it seemed strangely prophetic.

In search of warmth, Carlene stepped onto the stone terrace and rubbed her arms. The sun tingled her fair skin. She'd soon have to put on sunscreen or risk a bad burn . . .

"Hello. You must be Miss Carlene, the New Yorker."

She turned toward the male voice and saw the handyman standing behind the hedge. He didn't look like any minister she'd ever seen—he was far too thin and unkempt in a sweat-stained tee shirt. His arms were filled with clipped branches, which he dumped into a wheelbarrow as she stared at him.

"Sorry—you've been so quiet I forgot you were out here." Remembering her manners, she crossed the terrace and held out her hand. "I'm Carlene Caldwell."

"Erik Payne. And I don't think you want to shake my hand right now—I'm awfully grubby."

She smiled. "Maybe you're right. And you're the minister?"

"Last time I checked."

She chuckled, appreciating his wry humor. "Well, welcome to Sycamores. We should get along fine as long as you don't try to save me. I went through all that when I was a child."

The minister lifted a brow. "Are you saying it didn't take?"

"I'm saying I've grown up."

He bent to pick up a stray branch. "Well, since I can't save anybody"—he straightened and gave her an easygoing smile—"looks like we'll get along great."

She might have stayed to make conversation, but he seemed eager to get on with his work. She turned, then from an open window heard a mechanical whirring noise. She glanced up, struggling to place the sound, and smiled when she recognized it. The sewing machine. Nolie had to be in her hobby room.

After waving good-bye to the preacher, Carlene climbed two flights of deck stairs and entered the back of the house through the second-floor porch. The door to Nolie's suite stood open, so a moment later Carlene found herself watching her youngest sister.

She breathed deep and felt a pang of memory, another shadow from her former life. After the initial shock, she'd been thrilled when Momma told them she was expecting a baby, and as an infant Nolie was adorable . . . but then Carlene turned her attention to music, boys, and friends. Like most adolescents, she began to spend more time away from home, so she gave little thought to the eight-year-old urchin who stood at the airport gate and waved good-bye through tears. On subsequent trips home, she and Nolie shared a few scattered conversations. Those, plus a few letters over the years, added up to a scant knowledge of the woman at the sewing machine.

Carlene sat on the edge of a chair in the room. The movement must have startled Nolie, because she glanced at Carlene, offered a shy smile, and went back to work on the fabric she was guiding beneath the needle.

Carlene studied her sister. Nolie had grown from a scrawny, quiet child to a slender, quiet middle-aged woman. Wearing a simple white blouse and matching jeans, she had tied her long brown hair with a ribbon in a pointedly no-style style. Despite her tanned arms and neck, no wrinkles had yet appeared on that luminous face and only the barest touch of makeup—a swipe or two of mascara—adorned her features.

She looked, Carlene realized with a wry smile, like some kind of benevolent angel. Or an aging flower child.

"I used to change your diapers, you know." Carlene slid back and made herself comfortable in the wooden chair. "Seems hard to believe now."

"I used to think you hung the moon." Nolie pulled the fabric from the machine, snipped the threads with scissors, and held it up to check her handiwork. Then she stood and grinned. "Maybe I still do."

Carlene snorted as Nolie crossed to the ironing board. "I wish Darlene was happier about my being here. I don't know what I did to upset her, but I get the feeling she's not exactly thrilled that I came home."

Nolie laid her fabric on the board and picked up the steam iron. "For years I've thought that Darlene has something stuck in her craw when it comes to you. I've chalked it up to her being jealous."

"Jealous? Of me?" Carlene blinked. "Why would she be? Momma would have given her anything she gave me—"

"Darlene didn't have your talents," Nolie said, her voice low and soothing. "Grandma always said Darlene's singing sounded like a butter knife caught in the garbage disposal."

"She had other skills," Carlene said, thinking of the delicious treats her sister used to whip up for their bake sales and parties. "She cooks like a dream. She made my dress for the Miss Buttercup Squash Pageant, and it was as nice as anything the other girls wore. No one could believe I'd won in a homemade gown."

"I'm not saying she's not talented." Nolie set the iron on the end of the board and examined the pressed fabric. "But your talent attracted a lot more attention. No one awards scholarships for sewing or baking cookies."

Carlene shrugged, silently conceding the point.

"I was hoping time would make things easier for her." Nolie slid back onto her sewing bench. "I guess I figured she'd be past all her bad feelings. But I guess nobody ever forgets where they buried the hatchet."

"When I first saw her at the party, I could have sworn she was honestly happy to see me."

Nolie laughed. "She may have been, but she's a little touchy where Henry is concerned. He was paying a lot of attention to you last night, so I'm guessing that's what ticked her off. She wasn't really mad at you; she was irritated with Henry because he seemed a little too eager to chauffeur you around."

Carlene stared at her younger sister. "You've got to be kidding."

"I wish I were." Nolie picked up another piece of fabric and pinned it to the one she'd pressed. "She and Henry have been seeing each other for a while, but their relationship hasn't been made official, if you know what I mean. I don't think Darlene is in any hurry to tie herself to another man, but seeing him with you might have persuaded her to consider Henry in a more serious light."

Carlene stared at the fluttering aprons on the makeshift clothesline, convinced she'd managed to step back in time. If Nolie was right, Carlene had returned not only to her childhood home, but also to the role she played when she and Darlene competed in affairs of the heart.

"If you're right, I can fix this." Carlene smiled and stood. "I'll go downstairs and tell Darly I could never have feelings for Henry Hooper; the man isn't my type. I came here to relax, not to compete with my twin sister."

One of Nolie's brows lifted. "Watch what you say. If you're not careful, you might make it sound like Henry's not worth having."

Carlene smiled, realizing Nolie was right. She'd have to be diplomatic when she spoke to Darlene. She'd have to make Mayor Hooper sound like the most desirable man on earth—a task easier said than done.

"Thanks, Nolie." She gave her baby sister's shoulder a squeeze. "I'll go see if I can find her."

"Try the kitchen," Nolie suggested. "If I know Darly, she's trying to bake something that will make your charms pale in comparison. Henry's favorite cake is Toffee-Mocha Cream Torte, so if you see a jar of instant coffee or a couple of Heath bars on the counter—"

"I'll know to wave the white flag of truce." Carlene winked. "Wish me luck. I'm off to make peace so I can enjoy my vacation."

Carlene paused at the bottom of the stairwell and ran her hand over the oak beam where Daddy had recorded their heights. Horizontal slashes and initials peppered the right side of the wood, but the DC slashes—Darlene's—always seemed to be at least two inches ahead of hers.

The last slash, Nolie's, brought up the rear, at least two feet beneath the others. After Daddy died, Momma must not have had the heart to continue the tradition.

Carlene looked at a slash seventy-seven inches up the beam. Daddy's height. She closed her eyes and reached for it, remembering how as a child she stood on tiptoe and tried to touch her father's bald spot. She never managed it. Even though she was probably tall enough to do it in middle school, she forgot to play the game . . . until it was too late.

A tear rolled down her cheek and she quickly wiped it away. For years, whenever she wanted to cry onstage or summon up a choked voice, all she had to do was think of her father. She ought to be crying all the time these days, because something in every room at Sycamores reminded her of Daddy. Darlene hadn't made many changes during her reign as lady of the house, so this place reminded her not only of Daddy, but also of Griff.

How could Darlene live with so many ghosts in the house? She ought to put up new wallpaper or get some new furniture. The library windows still wore curtains Momma picked out, and Grandma's rocker still stood by the fireplace in the rec room. This house held too many memories, many of them painful . . .

She turned the corner and noticed new markings on the beam closest to the kitchen. Apparently, Darlene's family had copied the old tradition, because several horizontal marks bore the initials for GJ, Griffy Junior, and KY, Katie Young. And above them all she saw another mark, seventy-six inches up the wall . . . Griff's.

Carlene bit her lip to keep from sobbing. She'd heard that girls tend to marry men who remind them of their fathers, and Griff was a younger version of Daddy. Tall like Daddy, kind like Daddy, and, like Daddy, the salt of the earth. Griff probably had a better sense of humor than Daddy, at least when he was young. Maybe marriage mellowed both of them into strong silent types.

Odds were that she and Darlene had both been attracted to Griff because he reminded them of their father. For years Carlene harbored a secret fantasy that Griff would come to his senses, leave Darlene, and marry her. But he never would have done that because he was too good a man. And just like Daddy, he died far too soon.

She leaned against the wall, pressed her hand over her lips, and struggled with the knot of emotion that seemed to have taken up permanent residence in her throat. She and Darly ought to talk about these things, but she had a strong feeling that Darlene wouldn't sit still long enough to analyze why they had both been drawn to the same man. Darlene had little respect for psychology, and didn't even like Dr. Phil . . .

Carlene drew in a deep breath. Then, when she was certain her emotions were under control, she summoned up a smile and turned the corner. After walking into the kitchen, she first noticed a jar of Nescafé on the counter—along with three cake pans, two cartons of heavy cream, and a measuring cup filled with brown sugar. Darlene stood at the end of the kitchen island, wearing a bold apron and an equally bold expression as she monitored the progress of whatever she was beating in the heavy mixer.

Carlene moved into her sister's field of vision and offered her a weak smile. "Darly, can we talk?"

"Talk away, but don't mind me if I keep working. I want to get this cake baked for dinner tomorrow night."

"Is that, by chance, a Toffee-Mocha Cream Torte?"

Darlene's brow lowered. "How'd you know?"

"Just a hunch." Carlene settled onto a bar stool at the granite-topped island. Nolie obviously knew Darlene better than Darlene knew herself.

Maybe she should open with an oblique topic and approach the matter of Henry from an unexpected direction.

"Darly"—she raised her voice to be heard above the whirring of the mixer—"I was thinking that maybe you should redecorate the living room. That space could use a fresh coat of paint in a more modern color, and that plaid sectional went out of style about twenty years ago. The piano's fine, of course, but perhaps you should consider one of those new digital models? It could play anything you like when you're entertaining." When Darlene didn't answer, she forced a laugh. "I almost hate to mention those early American end tables. They have about a zillion coffee rings in the finish. We could take a day to go shopping together in Tallahassee, or maybe we could sit at the computer and look for bargains on the Internet—"

"And who do you think is going to pay for this new furniture?" Darlene dumped a teaspoon of dark liquid into the mixing bowl, tapping the spoon on the edge with far more force than necessary. "My living room is perfectly serviceable, thank you very much. My book club likes it, and as long as they don't complain about sittin' on that sofa and usin' those end tables, I don't see why my furniture should bother you."

Carlene swallowed the rest of her argument. So much for easing into a conversation.

She held up both hands and shook her head. "Forget the furniture. I'm sorry I mentioned it. But while we're talking, I want to apologize for something you may have misinterpreted. I know you and Henry have an understanding, and I did not intend—I would *never* intend—to get in the middle of your relationship. When he wrote me, I had no idea you two were an item; I thought he was simply writing as the town mayor. If I'd known that you might feel threatened when he picked me up at the airport—"

"I didn't feel threatened." Darlene's voice went as cool as the granite countertop beneath Carlene's palms. "And I wasn't upset with you. That man should of known better than to make me drive home alone."

Carlene tilted her head, tempted to point out that Henry and Darlene had arrived in two vehicles, so what else was he supposed to do? But caution urged her to overlook the obvious. "I'm sure you've learned"—she shoehorned a trace of laughter into her voice—"that men simply don't think like women. Henry is a fine man. I'm sure he was only trying to be practical when he insisted on driving me."

"He could have driven me and let you take his car."

"He could have, if I still had a license."

Darlene's brows triangled into a sharply pointed V. "What do you use for identification at the airport?"

"My passport."

"How do you get around when you travel to all those other places?"

"Taxis, trains, subways—our shows play in major cities and urban transportation is a wonderful thing." She pressed her lips together. "Anyway, I wanted you to know that I came home to help you celebrate our birthday, to get some rest, and to reconnect with my family. A lot has happened since we were last together, and I was hoping we could catch up and maybe learn how to be sisters again."

Darlene had been about to crack an egg on the rim of her mixing bowl, but she set the egg on the counter and turned off the mixer. As silence settled over the kitchen, she propped her elbows on the island and leaned forward to look Carlene in the eye. "You know, I can't help feelin' kind of silly right now. I kept tellin' myself that Henry wasn't your type, that you weren't flirtin' with him, and that nothin' would come of it because you were staying only a week or so, but doggone it, Carly, you do it every time!"

"I do what?"

"That thing you do to show me up! You attract men like a garbage can attracts flies. They buzz around you, they rush to bring you cups of punch and slices of cake, and now they stand in line for your autograph! It was hard enough watchin' all that when we were eighteen, but I couldn't believe you were still doin' it even though we're *fifty*!"

Carlene blinked. "You're wrong about that, Darly. And I never meant to make you feel bad."

"But you did. And I was *glad* when you went away. Momma would have popped me if she'd known how happy I was the day you got on that plane and flew away, but Momma never stood beside you at a dance feelin' as ignored as the floor tiles. I did, and I was thrilled when you left because I knew I'd finally have a chance to shine."

Carlene swallowed a sudden lump that had risen in her throat and forced words out: "And shine you did." She slid off her stool and leaned across the island, meeting her sister's gaze head-on. "Look at what you've done, Darly. You got married, you raised two kids, and you kept this place going. Plus, judging from what I hear, you're the backbone of this town. Henry said you run practically every committee and club in Peculiar, and that nothing would get done without you. So you *did* shine, Darly, and you're still shining now."

Darlene straightened and picked up the egg, apparently mollified. "Well . . . sure. Henry was right about that, I guess."

Carlene smiled. "We're supposed to be adults now, so can we call a truce?" She propped her elbow on the island and extended the pinky finger of her right hand. "That man adores you, by the way. He talked about you practically the entire time I was with him."

A spark lit Darlene's eyes as she offered her own pinky. "Really?"

"Would I lie to you?"

Their two fingers met and locked, sealing their unspoken compact.

Carlene smiled as her nagging conscience waggled a warning finger. Henry hadn't talked about Darlene all that much, but a little white lie couldn't hurt, could it?

Chapter Eight

The rest of the weekend passed in relative peace, Saturday sliding seamlessly into Sunday morning. Carlene agreed to go to the Baptist Church with Darlene, and even pulled out a good dress so she wouldn't embarrass her sister with any perceived lack of respect. Darly gaped in surprise when Nolie came downstairs to join them, but she didn't comment. She simply picked up her purse, pointed toward the garage, and led the way toward the Buick.

Carlene enjoyed the service more than she thought she would. Though the worship leader insisted on singing a group of unfamiliar choruses that sounded alike, he included a few old hymns that filled her with nostalgia. A few people cast pointed looks in her direction when the music began, probably expecting her to perform in the pew, but she ignored them. Let them think she was modest; let them think she'd forgotten every hymn she ever knew.

But she found herself whispering the words without having to look at the hymnal—the old songs were buried more deeply in her psyche than she realized.

The preacher spoke on a passage from the Sermon on the Mount, then he and the worship leader gave an altar call, and several people went down front to kneel and pray. Carlene found herself staring at the bottom of a stranger's black shoes. She couldn't remember the last time she'd seen a man voluntarily put himself in such a vulnerable position.

During the benediction, she gripped the back of the pew in front of her and wondered how long it had been since she turned her attention toward God. Sometimes she thought of him as a habit she'd left behind in Peculiar, but occasionally she'd been keenly aware of him in New York. She glimpsed him in the faces of caring strangers, heard him in the Brooklyn Tabernacle Choir, and inhaled him in the crisp breath of autumn. She tasted his goodness in sparkling sunsets and felt his presence in the quiet night . . . but why did she so rarely stop to notice him?

Maybe he was punishing her by taking her voice, but that notion didn't mesh with all she'd learned of God as a child. The God she remembered allowed people to suffer the consequences of their own foolish mistakes. Then he offered comfort and second chances.

When she'd learned her lessons about pride and ambition, maybe he'd offer her a second chance, too.

Henry came for Sunday dinner, a Crock-Pot roast and Darlene's renowned Toffee-Mocha Cream Torte. Carlene watched Henry and Darlene banter, and decided they were indeed a good match. So why didn't the man propose? She was beginning to believe that people in the second half of life should seize happiness whenever they find it.

Determined to be a good sport, she spent most of Monday with Darlene, traveling from one civic meeting to another: Monday morning they visited the Peculiar Quilting Society and Peculiar's Begonia Book Club; Monday afternoon meant meetings of the Restore Our Downtown Focus Group and the Buttercup Squash Festival Planning Committee. By five, the hour Carlene usually reported to the theater, she walked through the door of her childhood home and sank wearily onto the foyer steps.

"I'm bushed." She peered at Darlene from beneath a fringe of tattered bangs. "How do you do it?"

"Want to help me fix supper?" Darlene didn't miss a beat, but kept marching toward the kitchen. "I was thinking about making candied pork chops, yams, and maybe a banana-custard pie for dessert," she called over her shoulder.

Carlene groaned. No wonder Darlene was built like a tank—she *lived* like one, bulldozing through her day and moving anyone who got in her way.

With great effort, Carlene pulled herself off the step and turned, debating which staircase would require the least amount of energy. She hadn't yet decided when Nolie appeared on the upstairs landing. "I thought I heard voices." She waved a slip of paper. "I took a phone message for you."

"For me?" Carlene blinked. "But no one knows I'm here."

Nolie trotted down the steps and pressed the note into Carlene's hand. "Here you go. I'm going to talk to Darly about inviting Erik to join us for supper. No sense in him eating all alone when we were going to make him a plate anyway, is there?"

Carlene stared at the paper as Nolie slipped away. Dr. Jonathan Carlisle from Florida State University had called and left his office number. Beneath the number, Nolie had written *Please return call ASAP.*

Carlene checked her watch. The professor had probably already left his office, but she could at least leave a message.

Rather than climb the stairs, she crossed the foyer and stepped into the library, where her parents' desk stood before the two front windows. An old rotary phone sat on the corner of the desk, and she smiled as she dialed the professor's number. Was Darlene keeping this old thing as some kind of relic, or was she simply too stubborn to change out an old gadget that still worked?

After two rings, a man surprised her by answering. Darlene identified herself, then sank into the rolling chair as Dr. Carlisle thanked her for calling.

"When I read that you were coming to town, I knew I had to contact you. Many of our voice majors are intent on going to New

York after they graduate, and I thought it'd be great if we could hold a forum and allow you to speak to them. We're always looking for people with actual experience in the field—"

"I'm so sorry," she interrupted, "but I'm probably going back to New York at the end of the week."

"I'm sorry to hear that." Disappointment echoed in his voice. "Will you be back in our area anytime soon? Perhaps near the holidays?"

Carlene glanced around the room as if she could spot an answer hidden on the bookshelves. What should she tell him? If all went well this week, she'd probably be welcome to come back to Sycamores. But if Darlene turned chilly again, a return trip might not be such a good idea.

"It's possible," she hedged. "My future plans are still unsettled."

"I understand. But if you do come back, Miss Caldwell, please call me. We don't often have singers with your track record in our area, and I know our students could benefit from your experiences. You've been in so many fantastic shows and sung with so many incredible performers . . ."

She held her breath, expecting him to say something about her presumed stardom, but he didn't. Dr. Carlisle, at least, seemed to understand the limit of her success.

"I will save your number, and I have to ask—how'd you learn I was in town? No one knew I was coming home."

He laughed. "I take it you don't subscribe to the *Jackson County Gazette*."

"That's a newspaper?"

"Sure. And the weekend edition featured a nice article about the birthday party Peculiar threw for twins Carlene Caldwell and Darlene Caldwell Young. The writer made a special point of noting your outstanding Broadway career."

She sighed. "I keep trying to tell people my career is hardly stellar."

"But you made it to the Great White Way, Miss Caldwell. That, and the fact that you're a Juilliard graduate, is more than enough to impress my students. Call me when you're coming back to town, please. I'd love to meet you and introduce you around campus. If you like what you see, perhaps you'll consider working with our students on a more long-term basis. We're always looking for talented voice teachers."

"Thank you. I will."

She wished him a good day and hung up, then leaned back in the desk chair. Florida State was only a half hour away, and Dr. Carlisle seemed to intimate that anyone with professional experience in the performing arts could get a job teaching. After all, voice majors needed individual coaches, and who would be better than someone who had already achieved a measure of success in the professional music world?

She pressed her fingertips to her lips, imagining herself capped and gowned as a professor, then shook her head. An interesting idea, but about as likely as a country mouse falling in love with a cat.

When Carlene announced that she didn't want to shadow Darlene for the rest of the week, Darlene smiled to hide the fact that those words left a welt on her heart. She had actually begun to enjoy having Carlene around, but with Carlene's announcement, images of the two of them laughing and reminiscing over a bowl of popcorn vanished like a burst balloon.

"I know you're busy," Carlene went on, looking like a wilted blossom as she dragged herself up the stairs Monday night, "so if you don't mind, I think I'll stay home for the rest of my visit. I'd like to dredge up a few old memories, so maybe I'll search for some of the family photo albums. Maybe Nolie and I can do something together, too."

"Suit yourself," Darlene said, her smile frozen as she and Cary Grant headed toward her bedroom. "See you in the morning."

But she didn't see anything of Carlene the next morning. The woman hadn't even begun to stir by the time Darlene walked out the door, and she was still wearing some kind of fancy lounging pajamas when Darlene came back at three.

"Henry's coming for supper," Darlene announced, giving her sister a pointed look. "Maybe you should think about changing into something more appropriate for mixed company."

Carlene left the kitchen without a word; when she came back an hour later, she had showered, put on half a dozen layers of makeup, and managed to zip herself into a sleeveless sweater and a pair of leather pants.

Leather pants? As if anybody in Florida needed another layer of skin to hold in the heat.

On the other hand, maybe Carlene was flaunting the fact that she could fit into leather pants. Darlene couldn't recall ever seeing leather pants for sale in her size . . . probably because one pair would require the murder of too many cows.

She managed to forget about Carlene's wardrobe while she worked on supper, but the phone rang thirty minutes before Henry was due to appear. Up to her wrists in soapy water, she paused until she realized no one else was going to answer it. She grabbed a dish towel and scooped up the receiver. "Hello?"

"Darlene? Henry."

She turned to lean on the counter. "Don't tell me you can't come. I've got your favorite brisket in the oven."

"I'm coming, don't worry. The thing is, Gretel showed up here a few minutes ago, and she's making noises about being hungry. Can I bring her, too?"

Darlene hesitated, then felt guilty for her hesitation. Henry's perpetually petulant daughter was prone to unannounced drop-ins, particularly if she needed food or wanted money.

"Sure, bring her," she said, struggling to maintain an appropriate level of enthusiasm. "The more the merrier."

Henry and Gretel arrived twenty minutes later, coming in through the back door. Henry paused to kiss Darlene's cheek, but Gretel clomped by without a word, her high-top sneakers tracking mud across the kitchen floor.

"Sorry about that," Henry said, following Darlene's gaze. "I'll get the mop."

"No, no, leave it." Darlene forced a smile. "Kids will be kids, won't they?"

Henry hesitated, probably wondering if he should follow Gretel into the living room; then he pulled out a chair and sat at the kitchen table. Darlene's heart flowed out to him. If he had gone into the living room to talk to Carlene . . . but he hadn't. He stayed in the kitchen, smiling and stroking Cary Grant as he waited for her to tell him about her day.

Bless heaven above, she loved that man.

She asked about his day at the Wiggly and listened with one ear while she kept the other tuned to the conversation in the living room. Carlene was talking to Gretel about New York and—wonder of wonders—Gretel was actually responding. Darlene made a mental note to ask Carly what she'd said to bridge the generation gap. Gretel always acted like talking to Darlene was only slightly less torturous than having her fingernails ripped off.

Once the brisket was safely out of the oven, Darlene called everyone to the old dining-room table. A lump filled her throat when she realized that every chair had an occupant. She hadn't been able to say that for years. Carlene sat at one end and Darlene at the other; Erik sat across from Nolie; and Henry sat at Darlene's right hand. Silent, Gretel took the seat across from her father.

Closing her eyes, Darlene drifted back to the days when Momma and Daddy presided over family dinners; when Nolie sat next to Momma in a high chair and she and Carly kicked each other under the table and fought over the best pieces of fried chicken and chocolate cake. She struggled against the boulder in her throat. Those days were long gone, and she shouldn't waste time wishing for them.

Now the second half of her life stretched before her, so she'd better keep her focus on the future.

She lifted her head and nodded at Henry. "Why don't you say grace for us?" She shared her smile around the table, ending with a deliberate nod at Gretel. "We're delighted to have you all here at Sycamores. Good food, good friends, and good fellowship—I think that's what meals should be about."

"Hear, hear." Henry patted her hand, then cleared his throat. "Shall we pray?"

Darlene bowed her head. She liked Henry's prayers because, like her daddy, he prayed in King James English, sprinkling his prayer with "thees" and "thous" and calling God "Our most gracious heavenly Father and Lord." When Henry prayed, she felt awed and humbled, as though she were standing on the threshold of heaven.

As Henry thanked the Lord for the food and the hands that prepared it, she sneaked a peek at Gretel. The girl hadn't bowed her head or closed her eyes, and was staring at her father with a supremely bored expression. And then—in the dimple of Gretel's nose—Darlene spotted the winking diamond chip.

Darlene tried not to stare as she struggled to make sure she was seeing a piece of jewelry and not a new freckle or a stray sequin from some sweater. Yes, Gretel was wearing a tiny diamond in her nose. Bless Patsy, what was that about?

She looked down as her appetite waned. Had Henry noticed this monstrosity? Had he said anything to the girl?

Knowing Henry, he had voiced his alarm, then shrugged and changed the subject. After all, Gretel was twenty and living away from home. What was done was done, and part of parenting meant learning to let go . . .

Darlene closed her eyes and thanked God that her children were living a good distance away. She missed seeing her grandchildren, but in nose-ring and tattoo situations, ignorance was definitely bliss.

After dinner, once Darlene, Henry, Nolie, and Gretel had settled around the TV in the living room, Carlene slipped away and went out to the guesthouse. She found Erik sitting in a lawn chair, his eyes focused on the quiet lake. He turned his head to look at her.

"I hate to bother you," she said, "but I wondered if you'd mind doing me a favor. It's something—well, it's something I don't want to ask Darlene, and Nolie doesn't drive."

The crows'-feet along the preacher's eyes deepened as he smiled. "You're not bothering me. I take it you want to go somewhere?"

"It won't take long—half an hour, tops. I think we'll be back before the others even notice I'm gone."

He nodded and stood, the lawn chair creaking. "I'll just get my keys."

While he disappeared into the guesthouse, she went into the garage and picked up the small basket she'd filled with flowers earlier in the afternoon. Erik looked at the flowers when he returned, but didn't ask questions. He only led the way to his truck.

He waited until she was seated next to him before speaking again. "Where to?"

"The cemetery," she said, glad that her voice was as smooth as calm water. "It's near the end of Church Street."

He turned the key. "I've seen it."

He drove to the town square and she stared out the window, effectively drawing a curtain between them. Her thoughts were too heavy to share, and far too personal. She needed to sort through them in private, and she needed to pay her respects to someone she'd been missing ever since stepping off the plane.

Erik's pickup stopped outside the fence around the cemetery. "You want me to go in with you?"

She shook her head and lifted her flower basket. "I won't be long. You can wait in the truck—it'll be cooler."

"And no mosquitoes." A smile underlined his voice. "I hope they don't carry you away."

Her heart twisted—Griff used to say that.

She managed a trembling smile and slid off the seat, then walked through the gate. Chase Caldwell had purchased several plots at the back of the cemetery, and these were allotted to family members as needed. Griff had been buried just behind Grandpa, with empty plots to his right and left. One of these was reserved for Darlene . . . Carlene coveted the other one.

As awkward as a girl on her first date, she stood before the headstone and clutched the handle of her basket. What was she supposed to do now? People in movies always started chattering whenever they visited the grave of someone they loved, yet she'd always thought such scenes were silly. Griff was gone, hopefully to heaven, and she wouldn't have come at all except she couldn't imagine visiting Sycamores without acknowledging him in some way.

"I brought you these." The words slipped from her tongue as she placed the flowers by his headstone. She arranged the blossoms in an empty vase she found nearby, then picked up the empty basket and stared at the engraving through a sheen of tears: Griffith L. Young, 1962–2007. Beloved husband and friend.

Darlene's husband; Carlene's friend. Though things might have worked out very differently.

She brought her fingers to her lips, pressed her fingertips to the name carved into the gray granite, and turned for the truck.

No matter how long she lived, she would never willingly come back here to visit Griff. His presence was far more real at Sycamores than in this desolate place.

Chapter Nine

Darlene had just pulled out of the garage Wednesday morning when she saw Nolie pedaling down the driveway, her bicycle basket overflowing with colorful aprons. She pressed the gas and pulled the car alongside her. "Want a ride? You're going to get hot and sweaty riding into town."

"I don't mind." Nolie smiled, her cheeks already rosy from the heat. "I want to deliver these aprons to some new folks who've moved into the area. Bernita Creveling gave me a list of names and addresses."

"I'm on my way to a meeting of the Committee to Establish a Peculiar Municipal Fire Station, but I could drive you over—"

"You have someplace to be. I'm in no hurry, so I'll take my time."

Darlene adjusted her steering to keep the car from rolling into the ditch. "Bernita still up to runnin' the Welcome Wagon?"

"She still manages to get around, but I'm happy to help her. Because so many corporate sponsors have pulled out of the program, Bernita gives their info to me so I can deliver a stack of flyers and a welcome apron."

Darlene sighed. The Welcome Wagon used to give newcomers

a quart of milk and a boatload of free samples, but nowadays they would be lucky to get a map and a few coupons. Or an apron.

She eyed the fluttering fabrics in Nolie's basket, then glanced back at the house. "Was Carlene awake when you came downstairs?"

Nolie laughed. "No—and I didn't hear a peep from her room."

"Well, she can't say she isn't getting her rest. Okay, then. You be careful on the road."

With a final wave, Darlene pulled to the end of the driveway and stopped. Why did things have to change? She grew up with a mother at home, and even though Momma worked hard as a homemaker, the culture had shifted by the time the twins graduated. Carlene bought into the new ideas, leaving Peculiar to go off and establish a career, but Darlene never wanted anything but her mother's job. To form a new family, oversee the household economy, plan and create nutritious meals, understand and provide for the special needs of children—those skills were rare these days. The old rituals like eating dinner around a table and graciously entertaining visitors were vanishing, too. Why, her grandparents used to throw open the gates at Sycamores and invite the entire community to come for a barbecue . . .

Her brain tingled with an idea as she turned onto the main road. Who said everything had to change? Traditions became traditions only because people continued to observe them. If Henry could pull off a citywide birthday party, she could host a citywide cookout. Couldn't she? The old barbecue pit hadn't been used in ages, but she could ask Erik to clean it out. He could paint that old swing set by the lake. If the chains were rusty, she'd send him to the hardware store for new chains and sturdy seats. The old dock and the sailboat were gone, but the lake remained, so kids could splash around in the shallows.

But how could she afford to feed the entire town?

Cold reality swept over her in a terrible wave. A free meal would draw people like a carcass drew buzzards, but the family budget was not what it had been when Grandpa hosted all-day barbecues.

So . . . she wouldn't have a cookout; instead she'd announce a citywide potluck and let her guests bring dishes to share. Erik could set folding tables on the terrace, and the ladies from one of her committees could supply jugs of sweet tea. She'd tell people to bring blankets, and folks could spread 'em on the lawn and relax while the men played baseball and the ladies talked. Some people might congregate around Carly like they did at the birthday party, but sooner or later they'd move off and join in the fun.

A Friday-night potluck dinner would be just the ticket. She could put up a sign in the Wiggly window—within two days, half the town would see it, and the other half would hear through the gossip mill. If the potluck began at five, the sun would be lowering in the sky so the heat wouldn't be unbearable. People could bring towels if their kids wanted to cool off with a swim, and she'd bake one of those chocolate-éclair cakes Henry loved . . .

With a citywide potluck at Sycamores, she could send Carlene back to New York in spectacular style. Carly would enjoy being the guest of honor, everyone would have a fabulous time, and Henry would be impressed by Darlene's generous effort.

And on Saturday morning, when she brushed her teeth before taking Carly to the airport, she could look her reflection in the eye and know she'd done her dead-level best to rise above her turbulent emotions and make her sister feel welcome.

When Darlene announced her plans for a farewell potluck, Carlene excused herself and headed to the lake, struggling with mixed feelings about the event. Darlene said the party was to honor Carlene's homecoming, but Carlene couldn't help feeling that Darlene really wanted to celebrate her departure.

Despite her cynicism, something in her delighted in the prospect of seeing the old house come to life again. Chase Caldwell used to throw open Sycamores's iron gates and invite everyone from Jackson County, but the area had been less densely populated in those days. She remembered hundreds of people milling about the grounds, strolling through the gardens, sailing on the lake, and fishing from the dock. Kids would snatch wieners off the grill and chase one an-other while Lulu belted out "To Sir with Love" on transistor radios and teenagers crept away to make out behind the boathouse. Mothers in breezy summer dresses would pull lawn chairs into a circle and sip sweet tea from sweating glasses while they talked about their hus-bands, their children, and their soaps, usually in that order.

She crossed her arms and swished through the grass, remembering how she'd held Darlene's hand and wandered over the same lawn with a sense of awe. Even as a child she knew that she was part of something significant, and would one day be expected to take her grandmother's place as hostess. Now, of course, the locals might see the potluck as a sneak peak at the property they'd be inheriting in a few years.

Well, if that was the only reason they came, fine. At least they'd come, and the party's success would make Darlene happy.

She stopped by the big live oak that spread the western half of its canopy over the lake. Daddy hung a tire swing from one of the branches once the girls learned to swim, and she and Darly wore that swing out. The other town kids helped, preferring the risk of the swing to the relative safety of diving from the dock.

The tire swing was gone now; not even a bit of rope remained. Carlene studied the lowest branch, searching for a scarred spot where the rope had bitten into the bark. She saw nothing, not a trace of those lazy summer afternoons.

She leaned against the solid tree trunk. Sycamores hadn't hosted a big party since Chase Caldwell died. After he passed, ivy grew over the barbecue pit and the dock began to rot. Her grandmother stayed inside more than she went out, and Daddy and Momma took over the running of the household. Guests no longer came for dinner, so Momma sold the extralong dining-room table and replaced it with a simple oak set that seated only eight.

The changes, Daddy assured his family at dinner one night, were temporary because he had big plans: Sycamores was to become a gracious Southern inn. He would somehow find the money to build a row of cottages beside the lake. The big house would serve as a dining hall and recreation center, and people would come from miles around to walk in the gardens and swim in the lake. He'd hire a cook to prepare meals for the dining room and the terrace, where waitresses in black dresses with white aprons would serve. A professional piano player would provide dinner music and Carly would sing.

"What will Carly wear, Daddy?" Darlene asked.

"Why, the most sparkly dress in the state," Daddy answered, winking at Carly. "And you'll have one just like it, Darly."

Darly clapped while Carly tilted her head, wondering what she was supposed to sing.

Daddy hired an architect and a surveyor; he met with men from the bank and officials from the county. He had been completely confident in his dream.

Carlene stared at the sparkling lake, where waves rolled gently onto the shore and gracefully retreated. Now she found it hard to imagine a row of tourist cottages along the waterfront, but as a girl the idea had been bright and believable. She and Darly spent hours playing "Innkeeper's Daughter," pretending they lived in the big house with a personal maid—Nolie—to bring them lemonade and cupcakes whenever they got hungry.

Then Carlene and Darlene came home from school and learned that Daddy had died under the tractor.

The smile that consistently lit her mother's eyes faded, reappearing only when she took Carlene's hands and spoke of the importance of dreaming big. "Sycamores may never be what it once was," Momma whispered, "and Daddy's not here to make things better. But you have a talent no one else in the family has, so set your sights high and don't settle for anything else. New York is the place for you, darlin.' You belong on the stage."

The first time Carlene heard those words, they stung—did Momma want her to go away? Even later, when she learned that an exceptional voice was truly a gift, she couldn't help feeling that once Daddy died, her mother directed all her efforts toward pushing her musical daughter out of the house.

Momma dropped out of her clubs and abandoned her social responsibilities, focusing all her energies on Carlene's future. She made dozens of calls, not settling until she found the best voice teacher available. Every week she drove Carlene all the way to Tallahassee so Carlene could study under a renowned vocal coach from Florida State. And as soon as the twins turned sixteen, she encouraged Carlene to send video and cassette tapes to television stations, newspaper offices, and the finest music schools.

In the twins' senior year, as the days grew shorter and the breeze carried the scent of wood smoke on its breath, Momma urged Carlene to prepare for the Miss Buttercup Squash Pageant. "Don't think that local crown means nothing," she said. "It's a ticket to the Miss Florida pageant, and Miss Florida leads straight to Atlantic City. And Atlantic City is only a stone's throw away from New York."

Carlene never made it to Atlantic City, but she did earn a trip to New York, undoubtedly because of her mother's prodding. She left Peculiar with her mother's encouragement ringing in her ears, and she obeyed her mother's instruction to never look back.

Except when she looked for Griff. Even now, she found herself looking for him.

She turned toward the west and blinked in the blinding dazzle of the sun's long reflection on the lake. The wind tugged at her hair as she searched the watery horizon for some sign of the small sailboat Griff used to bring over and tie up at the dock.

She saw nothing. Heard nothing but the tree frogs and crickets warming up for their evening concert.

She was beginning to understand why her mother had been so insistent about always facing forward. Looking back made one long for things that could never appear again.

Nostalgia had the power to taint even the happiest occasions with melancholy.

With a heavy basket on her arm, Nolie opened the kitchen door, then stood back and held it as Ricky and Lucy strolled into the house, their tails like regal plumes above their backs. Carlene sat at the kitchen island, and for the first time since her arrival, didn't stop what she was doing to gawk at the dogs. She simply kept writing, stacks of envelopes in front of her and one of Darlene's lists by her right hand.

Without being told, Nolie knew why Carly was writing letters. Darly was big on sending thank-you notes and, apparently, she felt Carlene owed a handwritten letter to everyone in town. Darly would have written her notes the day after the big birthday party. She would also have shamed Carly into getting hers out today because the city-wide potluck was only twenty-four hours away. The sign had been in the Piggly Wiggly window for a full day, and the phone had been ringing with people asking what Darlene needed them to bring.

From the sink, Darly released a heavy sigh. "I just mopped those floors, and here you bring in Mutt and Jeff to track it all up again."

"Ricky and Lucy aren't muddy," Nolie said, lifting her foot to catch the screen door that would otherwise slam behind her. "We were working in the garden, so we didn't go near the lake."

"Fertilizing?"

"Not today. I cut these roses and trimmed the stems. Thought maybe you'd like to arrange them for your big shindig."

She set her basket on the counter, and Darlene didn't hesitate to pounce on the peace offering. "My, my, you do grow some nice blooms." She pulled on her rubber gloves and began to count the unfurling buds. "That's one, two, three, four—how many red roses did you cut?"

"Should be at least half a dozen. And I think I counted a dozen each of the yellows and pinks." Nolie tossed a grin in Carlene's direction, then moved to the fridge. "That Mr. Lincoln rose is doing great. I think it might do better, though, if it could climb on an arbor. Do you think we could ask Erik to make one?"

When Darlene didn't answer, Nolie glanced over her shoulder. Carly and Darly were looking at each other, Carlene wearing an I-told-you-so expression and Darly looking like the cat who just swallowed the canary.

Nolie frowned as she pulled a pitcher of iced tea from the refrigerator. "What's up with you two?"

Darly didn't answer, but bent to open the cupboard where she kept her vases. Carlene went back to her letters, but a smile curved her mouth. "You know what red roses symbolize, don't you?" she asked, a teasing note in her voice.

"Sure do," Darlene called, her voice echoing in the cupboard. "I'm pretty sure they stand for *loove*." She dragged out the last word as if it were molasses candy, a decidedly un-Darlene-like behavior. When she finally pulled her head out from beneath the sink, she was grinning like a churchgoer holding four aces.

Nolie took a glass from the dish drainer. "I don't know what y'all are talkin' about, but you're being silly."

"Are we?" A dimple appeared in Carlene's cheek. "Admit it, Nolie—that Erik is a nice-looking guy."

As if she hadn't noticed. Nolie had memorized every detail of his face: the cleft in his chin, the bend in his brow, and the shadow of stubble that appeared on his jaw around eight o'clock every night. His eyes had mesmerized her ever since the day she hopped into his pickup, and more than once she had wondered how his hair would feel on her fingertips . . . like silk, probably.

Darlene reached for the edge of the counter and pulled herself up. "Don't forget *available*. That's the most important thing."

"Hello?" Nolie paused, pitcher in hand, and looked from one twin to the other. "What part of *not interested* do you not understand?"

"You should be interested." Carlene dropped her pen and folded her hands. "It's about time you considered leaving the nest, baby sister. Your biological clock is ticking away."

Nolie stared at her sister. Carly had been away from home for years, yet here she was, divorced, childless, and restless. If leaving Sycamores was such a great thing, why was Carlene here and not busy with a family of her own?

"*He's* not interested," Nolie corrected as she poured the tea. "He's still grieving the end of his marriage. He came here to find a job, not a wife."

"Seems like he could do both." Darlene set a cut-glass vase in the sink, then turned on the water. "I wasn't keen on the idea at first, but you could do a lot worse than a handyman."

"And you'd have to be blind not to notice that he's a real cutie patootie," Carlene added. "He's well educated, too. I Googled him."

Nolie nearly dropped the pitcher. She turned and gaped at Carlene. "Were you *spying* on him?"

"And why shouldn't I? The man's living here with three unarmed—"

Clearing her throat, Darlene jerked her head toward the shotgun propped near the back door.

"—okay, three *solitary* women. If he was lying about who he claimed to be, I figured we should know it. So I did a little factchecking. That's all."

Nolie blew out her cheeks, then took a long drink from her glass. Maybe Googling Erik wasn't such a bad idea—after all, he'd never know Carly had been snooping. And she was dying to know more about him.

She swallowed as questions bubbled in her mind. What had Carly learned? She had to swallow three times before Darlene finally asked the question she didn't have the nerve to ask herself.

"So what'd you find out?" Darlene shut off the water and turned to lean on the island, her eyes gleaming. "Do tell."

Carlene rose from her stool and leaned on the island, too, her eyes alight, her posture an exact imitation of Darlene's.

"Okay." Carlene took a deep breath. "Erik Dion Payne is forty-two years old—"

Darlene tipped her head back and roared with laughter. "*Dion*? Who names their kid *Dion*?"

"His parents, obviously," Nolie answered, her patience thinning. She looked out the window, half-afraid she'd see Erik on the other side of the glass, but he was nowhere in sight. Thank heaven.

Carlene smiled. "Born in Mississippi, ran track in high school, apparently played basketball for Old Miss. One website said he was captain of the basketball team. Got married right after college, and apparently worked in some kind of lawn-care business, but he quit and entered seminary sometime in 2004."

"Kinda got a late start, didn't he?" Darlene said.

"Maybe God didn't call him until 2004," Nolie said.

Darlene's chin jutted forward. "Feelin' defensive?"

"I'm just sayin'." Nolie nodded at Carlene, hungry for more details. "Are you finished?"

Carly shrugged. "Not much else to tell. He accepted the pastorate of that Chattahoochee church in 2009; they called a new preacher last week. The Internet doesn't give many details about what happened there."

"Then what's the good of it?" Darlene grumbled.

Nolie lifted her iced tea and took another sip. She didn't need to verify every detail to know Erik Payne was a good man. But it was nice to learn a few things about the person who was beginning to occupy more and more of her thoughts.

"At least he's a nice Southern boy," Darlene said, moving back to Nolie's flower basket. "I can sleep easier now."

Nolie was about to remark that a Southern boy could cause just as much trouble as a Northern one when an unexpected thought occurred to her: during the past five minutes, Darly and Carly had behaved like the close twins she knew in childhood; they had acted like sisters.

Maybe all they needed was a bit of mischief to bring them together.

With Darlene busy organizing the participants in her potluck and Nolie sewing aprons for children who would attend the big event, Carlene took a nap, then fixed herself an afternoon snack of cereal and milk. After eating and then putting away every sheet of Darlene's blasted stationery, she climbed the narrow back staircase and reentered the bedroom that felt as if it had always been hers.

She sat on the bed and placed a quick call to her Realtor, hoping to hear that someone had made an offer on her apartment. Unfortunately, no one had.

"I know I promised you a quick sale, but the market's really tough right now," the agent said. "I was planning to have another open house on Sunday."

Carlene pressed her lips together. She had planned to be back by Sunday; she'd hoped everything would be settled. But nothing shut down an open house faster than an owner on the premises, and she'd put most of her belongings into storage. She'd be making do with one bed, one sofa, one plate, one cup, and one set of flatware if she went back to New York now . . .

She thanked the agent for her time, then dropped her phone back into her purse.

Should she start packing? Though her real estate agent wanted her to stay in Florida, Darlene was busy planning a big farewell party. She had been bright and breezy when they were teasing Nolie in the kitchen, but her happy attitude undoubtedly sprang from her delight in knowing that her twin would soon be miles away . . .

Carlene fell back onto the bed and stared at the whorls and swirls in the plaster ceiling. Truthfully, she had no real reason to remain in Peculiar; she might as well call the airline and see which Saturday flight had available seats. She could go back to New York, pick up her mail, and dust the apartment. She'd make herself scarce during the open house, maybe spend the afternoon in Central Park. Or she could play tourist and take the Staten Island Ferry across the Hudson River, get a few photos of the Statue of Liberty on the way. If she moved, she didn't know when she'd have that opportunity again.

So she might as well pack.

She stood and opened the closet door, where most of her clothes dangled from wire hangers. Reaching for a blouse, she noticed a small door built into the closet wall. The sight triggered a host of old memories, which flooded back and shivered her skin in vivid recollection. The tiny door led to an attic space her family had used for storage. As a child she loved to hide in that room, pretending that her life depended on escaping the mad killer rampaging downstairs, a part usually and unwittingly played by Darlene . . .

She tried to open the door and discovered that humidity had swollen the old wood, effectively sealing the space. She pushed her clothes out of the way, spread her feet, and crouched to the level of the door. Gripping the handle with both hands, she threw her weight into the effort. After a second of strain, the door flew open, dropping her onto her behind.

Grateful no one saw her land in such an undignified position, she crawled into the attic. A wave of stifling, dry air struck her in the face.

Once her eyes adjusted to the dim light, she saw several plastic boxes, a few Styrofoam containers, and four old trunks from her grandparents' era. Dusty baskets hung from nails in the rafters, strings of ancient Christmas lights dangled from random hooks, and a silver aluminum Christmas tree stood like a pop-culture relic in a far corner.

She knelt on bare wooden planks and pulled the first cardboard box toward her. She opened the lid slowly, half-afraid a rat or roach would leap out at her, but nothing stirred inside. Vinyl records filled the box: the Cowsills, the Carpenters, the Broadway cast recordings of *Hello, Dolly!* and *Oliver!*, along with a sound track album from *The Sound of Music*. The music of her childhood. She had listened to these records over and over, inadvertently learning about stylization and diction long before she took her first voice lesson.

Smiling, she flipped through the albums she'd loved, then spotted others: the Broadway cast recordings of *Les Misérables* and *The Phantom of the Opera*. She'd never owned these albums, but she recorded them.

Who bought these? Momma? Grandma? Or Darlene?

Touched by this small sign of support, she flipped through the remaining albums but didn't find *Mamma Mia!, Hairspray, Wicked,* or *Jersey Boys.* No *Gone with the Wind.* Nothing after 1994, the year Momma died.

Carlene sat flat on the floor as understanding dawned. Momma must have saved Carlene's old albums and bought the cast recordings from her shows. After she died, Darlene packed everything up and lugged the boxes to this attic room, storing them out of sight and out of mind. She probably didn't intend to be malicious, but finding the albums here was like finding personal awards missing from the family trophy case and hidden at the back of the garage.

Carlene ran her fingertips over the photo on the *Phantom* recording. Though she was virtually unrecognizable in her makeup and wig, Momma would have spotted her. Though at least a dozen other singers of the chorus crowded around the principal players, Momma would have recognized the slant of Carlene's head and the shape of her painted mouth. In listening to the album, she would have been able to pick out Carly's voice from so many others.

Had Darlene resented the attention Momma heaped on Carlene? She always seemed to understand, but she was not immune to jealousy. Carlene tried not to flaunt her accomplishments. While she lived at home, she made sure to complain about her music lessons and piano practice so Darlene wouldn't think Carlene's life was a barrel of fun. At Juilliard, she wrote long letters about being homesick, working too hard, and being so cold she thought her fingers would freeze.

Oddly enough, every word in those miserable letters was true. That first semester she disliked Juilliard, hated New York, and despised the weather. She wrote that she would happily give up her voice if she could go home to stay.

Had Darlene believed her?

Momma never made it to New York. The woman sat through myriad school concerts and recitals; she listened to hours of rehearsals and vocal exercises. She encouraged when Carlene grew weary and prodded when Carlene wanted to quit. She spent much-needed money on voice lessons and costumes and music books. Though Carlene attended school on a full scholarship, including room and board, each week her mother dutifully sent a check for spending money.

Carly owed everything to her momma. Some town folks probably thought she owed Darly something for all the times Momma favored her, but Carlene had already taken care of that debt.

In spades.

Chapter Ten

*I*n an effort to make herself useful on Friday afternoon, Carlene went outside to check the back lawn and make sure everything was ready for the potluck. Erik had mowed the lawn and installed new swings on the old swing set. He and Nolie cleaned the barbecue pit of fallen leaves, dirt, and trash, and a shiny stainless-steel grate now lay over a pyramid of coal briquettes. Peculiar's Begonia Book Club stopped by to bring six folding tables, which they lined up on the terrace. A vase of fresh-cut summer roses stood in the center of each.

Nolie spent the afternoon taping paper tablecloths so they wouldn't blow away. The Restore Our Downtown Focus Group provided four huge coolers of sweet tea and positioned them at the drink station near the end of the buffet line. Darlene and Erik set folding lawn chairs and white plastic pool chairs on the grass in groups of twos and threes, but Carlene knew their guests would soon rearrange them into more natural groupings.

She hadn't attended a potluck in years, but she'd soon be standing amid a friendly crowd. If her New York castmates could experience even a tiny taste of effusive Southern hospitality, maybe they'd be more steadfast in their friendships.

When a rumble of thunder threatened in the west, she frowned at the ominous gray cloud on the horizon.

"Do you think that storm will hit us?" a man asked.

She turned and saw Erik standing in the shade cast by the upstairs porch, his face flushed and his hair damp with perspiration. Between the hem of his baggy shorts and the top of his tennis shoes, sweat and grass clippings streaked his muscular calves.

"I can't say." She looked at the sky again. "Depends on which way the wind's blowing, I suppose."

"If it rains, do you think Darlene will move the party indoors?"

Carlene blew out a breath. "I doubt it. If a storm comes, most people will simply stay home. And that's a good thing, since we're not really set up for an indoor party."

When a door opened, she looked up to see Darlene on the kitchen porch, her hand shading her eyes, her face pinched with worry. "Well, bless Patsy! It can't rain on us, it just can't!"

Carlene jerked her head toward Erik. "You've got a preacher here. Why don't you ask him to pray the rain away?"

She'd been kidding, but Darlene stalked over and gripped the porch railing. "Erik? You hidin' down there?"

A little reluctantly, Carlene thought, the man stepped out from beneath the shelter of the porch. "I'm here."

"Can you do that?" she said. "Pray the rain away?"

An expression almost like bitterness flitted across his face. "I don't rightly know. I've been praying about a few things for a while now, and either the Lord's not hearing me, or I'm not hearing his answer."

"Well, someone has to do something." Darlene stomped back toward the kitchen and let the screen door slam.

Erik strolled to the drink station, poured a glass of tea from the jug, then held the paper cup to his forehead. "I have a feeling it's going to be an interesting night."

Chuckling, Carlene retreated to the shade of the terrace. "You might be right."

* * *

By five o'clock, Carlene surmised that someone's prayers had been effective. The dark clouds held steady over the western horizon.

As the guests began to arrive, Erik greeted people on the driveway and directed them to parking spaces; Nolie stood by the side of the house and gave each arriving youngster a special vinyl apron designed with narrow pockets to hold hot dogs, and square pockets to hold cookies. Darlene kept vigil in front of the food tables, directing each dish to the proper station: appetizers, salads, vegetable sides, breads, entrées, or desserts. Darlene gave Carlene strict instructions: as the guest of honor, she was to mingle freely, greet the new arrivals, and assure everyone that a handwritten thank-you note was in the mail.

Several families arrived bearing two-liter bottles of soft drinks and giant bags of potato chips. When the second jumbo bag of chips passed by, Carlene was close enough to Darlene to hear her mutter, "Can you believe these women are bringing store-bought food to a potluck? I would be surprised if some of these young gals know how to turn on an oven."

Carlene bit her tongue, not having the courage to tell Darly that she never cooked, either. Why should she when she lived in a city famous for fine restaurants and twenty-four-hour diners?

At five thirty, Darlene slipped her hand through Henry's arm and climbed the steps to the first-floor porch, then walked to the railing to address the crowd. Carlene glanced over her shoulder and guessed that more than a hundred people stood on the lawn, their faces expectant and their stomachs growling.

Nolie's whistle, sharp as a knife, effectively silenced the crowd.

"Welcome to Sycamores." Darlene smiled as she extended both arms in a gesture straight out of *Evita*. "Thank you for coming, and thank you for bringing so many delicious-looking dishes. I can't wait to try a little bit of everthing."

Including the factory-produced potato chips? Carlene chewed her lip, disguising a wry smile. When the audience applauded she joined them, realizing she was participating in a drama with roles as well defined as those in any Broadway play. Darlene starred as the gracious hostess, Henry was her faithful gentleman friend, and the people on the lawn played guests who'd dropped everything to benefit from the gracious lady's noblesse oblige.

"And now," Darlene continued, "I've asked the Honorable Henry Hooper to say grace. Mr. Mayor?"

Darlene stepped back as Henry walked to the porch railing, bowed his head, and offered a simple, heartfelt prayer. When he finished, Darlene sashayed to the railing and gestured to Carlene. "I invited you all here today to say good-bye to my dear sister, who many of you have known since she was knee-high to a grasshopper. She's leaving us tomorrow, going back to Broadway, so be sure to give her a warm hug before she goes away." She gave Carlene a sincere smile that seemed to stretch across the distance between them. "We're proud of you, Carly. You'll always be our shining star."

The crowd erupted into applause again as a flush heated Carlene's cheeks. Was this a hot flash? No—this was honest embarrassment. In a moment she'd be all weepy unless someone distracted the people who were staring as if she hadn't grown up among them. What would they do if they knew she never had been and never would be a star?

"All right, y'all," Darlene called, smiling. "Let's eat!"

Carlene exhaled a sigh and hurried across the terrace as the guests converged on the tables. Ducking into the rec room, she fanned herself with the apron Nolie had tied around her waist and wondered when she'd be able to sneak into the line.

"She meant that, you know. Every word."

Carlene flinched, then turned to see Nolie standing at the sliding glass door a few feet away. "What'd you say?"

"Darlene meant what she said a minute ago—she is proud of you. She loves you a lot, in her own way. She may never be awfully open about her feelings, but tonight—well, it probably cost her a lot of pride to say those things in front of all those people."

Carlene nodded, not quite sure Nolie understood Darlene's dramatic nature. But she should probably keep quiet and smile. By this time tomorrow, she would be back in New York, readjusting to the real world and struggling to redefine her life.

All this—all of Peculiar, in fact—would seem like a vague dream.

Nolie studied her older sister's face as they stood in the shadowy rec room and waited for the buffet lines to dwindle. Darlene and Carlene may have begun their lives side by side, but even though they'd been getting along pretty well in the last couple of days, Nolie doubted they'd ever be truly close again. Something stood between them. She couldn't put her finger on what it was, but the barrier was bound to be more significant than sibling rivalry.

She walked up behind Carlene and adjusted the drooping bow of her sister's apron. "Come on, the lines are manageable now. I think you can get some dinner without being hugged to death."

"Smart thinking," Carlene said, following her through the doorway. They dodged a pair of boys who were running to the dessert table, then slipped into the line behind Doc Hensley. He flashed a welcoming smile as they each took paper plates from the stack.

"Good to see you, Nolie," Doc said. "How are those pups of yours doin'?"

"Just fine." She nodded toward Carlene. "Have you had a chance to meet our guest of honor?"

"I think I managed to wave at her at the birthday party." Doc dropped the fork with which he'd been about to scoop up a helping of green-bean casserole and shook Carlene's hand. "We're so glad you could return for a visit. Most people come back to Peculiar only if there's been some kind of tragedy, so it's a downright pleasure to see folks who just had a hankering to come home."

Carlene lifted both brows and wondered what he'd say if he knew she really belonged to the first group he mentioned. "I don't think I'd have phrased it that way, but maybe you're right."

He winked at her. "I understand. I went to school in Boston, and by the end of the first term I was so desperate for Southern cookin'

I was tempted to drive to Virginia for some fried chicken and grits. I toughed it out, but Boston baked beans and clam chowder are no substitutes for the dishes you'll find on this table."

Nolie turned to look over the spread. Their friends and neighbors had generously entered into the spirit of the event, bringing some of their most celebrated specialties. She spied a dish of Edna Higgins's sugared pecans, Orlain Jones's eggplant casserole, and Monisha Brand's candied strawberries. Mary Thomas brought her Mock Spinach Soufflé, Bernita Creveling made corn pudding, and Glennette Wessel had filled a huge platter with Cherry Salad Supreme, a jiggly concoction that featured *two* boxes of flavored gelatin and at least a pound of cherries, all of which had to be pitted before being dumped into the mix.

Nolie resisted the urge to laugh when Carly squinched her eyes shut. "Oh, the calories," she moaned. "I don't suppose anybody around here bakes with a sugar substitute."

"Only if they have diabetes," Nolie said, dishing up a helping of a chicken salad. "I hear those things lose their sweetness once they're baked, but you'd have to ask Darlene for details."

"Maybe I can take a spoonful of everything," Carlene said. "Or maybe I should take only one bite. That's all I need, really, to get a taste."

Nolie smiled, realizing that Darlene often said the very same thing. Why couldn't those two see they were meant to be close friends? "I don't know that a bite's gonna satisfy." She waved a spoon at the dessert table ahead of them. "I see a French silk chocolate pie and Darlene's chocolate-éclair cake—"

"Hush." Carlene picked up a pair of tongs and heaped lettuce onto her plate. "I'm going to fill my stomach with grass. I've already eaten so much this week that I'm not going to fit into my—"

A child's shrieking laughter cut her off, and every head turned toward a little boy who was running across the lawn, his eyes wide and his plate clutched to his chest. Behind him, energized by all the activity, loped Ricky and Lucy, their tongues hanging out as they scattered the crowd.

"Oh, brother." Nolie set her plate on the table. "I had the dogs put away in their kennels. That kid must have let them out."

Carlene went a shade paler. "Will they jump up and get after people's plates?"

Nolie snorted. "My pups have better manners than that. But they get excited when they smell food, and people are liable to start feedin' them stuff that's not good for them. Once, we had a few people over and I found a kid feeding Lucy sugar cookies, which she later threw up all over Grandma's Karastan carpet. I'd better get her."

"You need some help?" Doc Hensley called, but Nolie waved him off. She was already marching across the lawn and contemplating the best way to catch her canines. They were racing through the guests, still chasing that screaming kid, but at any moment they could catch a whiff of something succulent and stop beside someone who wasn't accustomed to giant fuzzy dogs with saliva slingers trailing from their muzzles . . .

"Ricky! Lucy!" She tried to whistle, but the sound didn't carry above the kid's high-pitched screams. "Ricky!"

A rumbling growl answered, and the crowd grew quiet as fat raindrops began to spatter plates and upturned faces. Nolie turned toward the lake and froze as a falling curtain of rain pebbled the surface of the water and began to advance toward the crowd.

"Under the porch, everyone!" she shouted.

The guests surged toward the terrace to shelter under the back porch while women hurried toward the tables to cover the exposed dishes. Raindrops beat out a rhythm on tinfoil and Pyrex lids; guests abandoned already soggy paper plates on the lawn; children dashed through spilled potato salad, fried okra, and green-bean casserole. In the center of it all, Ricky and Lucy frolicked from one abandoned smorgasbord to the next.

"Don't your dogs hate the rain?"

Having ducked under the porch in a vain attempt to escape the downpour, Nolie turned to see Erik standing next to her, raindrops streaking his face as he surveyed the wild scene with a look of mild amusement.

She blushed at his unexpected proximity, but somehow found her tongue. "Leos are water dogs. Unlike me, they love being wet."

"They're also lovin' this party."

"That means I'd better roll up the carpets." She shivered and took a side step to avoid water dripping between the wooden planks overhead. "I should have set out umbrellas and raincoats."

That was when she spotted Darlene. Darly had stopped to help Aunt Verna out of a folding chair, but the old woman was clearly having problems keeping up with Darlene. Erik ran out to help, and Nolie watched through rain so thick she could barely identify the struggling figures. Erik did reach the pair and once he took Verna's arm, Darlene broke into a run.

Nolie held her breath as Darlene sidestepped paper plates and skirted overturned lawn chairs. Darly glanced up as she neared the terrace, then lowered her head against the pouring onslaught and blindly ran forward—

Nolie flinched when a sharp crack ripped through the growling thunder, followed by a hair-raising scream. She shaded her eyes with her hand, struggling to see through the liquid curtain. Henry grabbed an umbrella and dashed toward Erik and the old woman. But Aunt Verna wasn't the woman who'd screamed; that sound came from closer by.

Where was Darly?

Nolie shouldered her way through the growing crowd under the porch and ran into the downpour. She hadn't gone more than a few steps when she halted. Darlene lay on the ground, her arms flung above her head, her clothes drenched, and her right foot twisted at an awkward angle. Forgetting everything else, Nolie hurried toward her sister, untying her apron as she went. Once she reached Darlene's side, she knelt and draped the apron over her sister's head in an attempt to keep the rain away, then peered at Darly's agonized face. "Can you walk?"

Darlene's complexion had gone the color of a paper plate. "My foot," she shouted, forcing the words through clenched teeth. "Something snapped. I-I don't think I can walk."

Nolie looked up, realizing someone had joined them. "I'm going to get Henry and some of the men," Carlene yelled, rain-soaked and wide-eyed as she met Nolie's gaze. The two stood, then Carlene lowered her voice. "I saw her foot—you need to keep it wrapped, and don't let Darly look at it. It's not pretty."

"Can Doc Hensley help?"

Carlene considered for an instant, then shook her head. "I'm afraid this calls for a human hospital. Put Darlene in the nearest vehicle and get her to the emergency room as soon as you can. I'll take care of things here—the party's over, anyway."

"How do you know she needs—?"

"I saw her fall." A tremor rippled Carlene's face. "She needs a doctor."

Nolie bent back down and gripped Darlene's forearms, unsure how to help her stand; then Erik appeared beside her. He got behind Darlene and slipped his hands beneath her arms, lifting her with his wiry strength. His gaze met Nolie's. "My pickup is right around the corner. Grab Henry and I'll meet you in the truck."

"Can all of us fit?"

"Henry will need to drive his car." He glanced around as if searching for something else, then nodded. "We're good. You can take off now."

Nolie ran toward the crowd, screaming Henry's name with every step.

"I feel so stupid!" For some reason, Darlene kept repeating the uppermost thought in her mind. "I am so clumsy! And I've ruined the party."

Erik gave her an odd look, then helped her hobble to the passenger door of his truck. She managed as best she could, lurching and hopping, leaning on him in a way that felt far too familiar.

"Here you go." He opened the door and stepped behind her. She hesitated, not knowing how she could clamber into the seat, but Erik put his hands on her waist and spoke in her ear. "On three, okay?

One, two, up you go." Before she knew it, she was on the seat and
Erik was swinging her wet legs into the cab.

"You wait here," he said. "I'm gonna run and get Nolie. I'll be as
quick as I can."

Darlene gritted her teeth and nodded as he slammed the door
and sprinted through the rain. Thank heaven she'd had the good
sense to hire him the day he came rolling down the driveway. She
closed her eyes and tried to move her leg, then stiffened as a hot wave
of pain radiated from her swelling foot. How could something as silly
as a *foot* cause such discomfort? Not only was she in physical agony,
but she had most certainly made a fool of herself when she fell only
inches away from the terrace. Every person present had been staring
out at the lawn, which meant every person at the party had seen her
tumble into the mud like a drunken fool.

She closed her eyes as rain thrummed the roof at an even deeper
pitch; then Nolie jerked the door open and jumped in, nearly landing in Darlene's lap. She scooted over as best she could, then stopped
when Erik climbed into the driver's seat. He revved the engine and
she shivered.

Nolie gripped her hand as the pickup backed over wet gravel,
then rumbled up the driveway. Darlene glanced at the long row of vehicles parked on the lawn and gave Nolie a halfhearted smile. "Looks
like we had a good crowd. Too bad everbody had to see me make a
complete fool of myself."

"You didn't make a fool of yourself." Nolie squeezed Darlene's
hand. "You were a wonderful hostess. As I ran up the walk, people
were talking about how you took the time to keep poor Aunt Verna
from being drowned in the deluge. Her daughter stayed safe and dry
under the porch, but you risked your neck and ran out in the rain."
Her smile widened. "Don't worry about a thing, Darly. By the time
this is all over people will be sayin' you're a hero."

Darlene sniffed and wiped raindrops from her cheek. Nolie was
only being Nolie. The others wouldn't be so kind and—she stiffened
as a momentary horror shivered her skin—what if someone had been
using a video camera? If anyone filmed her fall, she could be on the

Zoo Tube, or whatever they called it, by nightfall. Other people had become famous for a lot less.

She shuddered in her wet blouse. She needed someone to lean on, someone who could make her forget about her embarrassing flub. Her voice came out in a whimper. "Where's Henry?"

"I found him," Nolie assured her. "He's on his way. He had to get Ed Jones to move his car."

Darlene closed her eyes and moaned as fresh tears stung her eyelids. She couldn't do anything right these days. Her grand send-off for Carlene had imploded; her beautiful potluck would be talked about for all the wrong reasons; and Henry, who had never seen her do anything so embarrassing, would now think of her as clumsy. Next to petite, graceful Carlene, she would seem like a stumbling moose.

She opened her eyes. "You promise Henry's coming?"

"Yes."

"And Carlene?"

Nolie shot a quick look at Erik, who kept his eyes on the rain-slicked road. "Carlene was making sure everyone was okay at the house. I'm sure she'll be along later."

"Right. Carly shouldn't come to the hospital. Someone needs to stay at the house to—"

"Don't fret about your party." Nolie patted Darlene's arm. "Carlene will make sure everone gets away safely and with their own dishes."

Darlene closed her eyes, but she wasn't worried about her guests. She was concerned about Carlene riding to the hospital with Henry.

Nolie paced in the lobby by the emergency room, her arms crossed as she searched the parking lot outside the double glass doors. Henry should be here by now, shouldn't he? Darlene had waited ten minutes before they called her into an exam room, and she'd been with a doctor or nurse for at least half an hour. The doctor sent Nolie out of the curtained cubicle, telling her to relax, but it was hard not to fret when Darlene seemed more concerned about Henry than about her black-and-blue foot.

At times like this, Nolie missed having someone to tell her not to worry. Grandma had been good about that, but she wasn't around anymore. Darlene usually took charge in a crisis, but what was Nolie supposed to do when Darlene *was* the crisis?

She turned toward Erik, who was reading a magazine, a hospital towel around his shoulders. A kind nurse had handed out towels when they came in, dripping with every step. "Where do you think Henry is?" Nolie asked.

He looked up and shrugged. "Maybe stuck in traffic?"

"We didn't hit any traffic. Do you think they had a flat tire?"

A lopsided grin split his face. "Doubtful. Nobody could have that much bad luck in one night."

She tried to smile back at him, but her mouth only wobbled and her eyes filled with tears. She turned away, embarrassed, but Erik must have seen the glimmer of wetness in her eyes.

"Hey, what's this?" He stood and caught her hand. "Everything's going to be fine. Miss Darlene probably has a sprained ankle."

Nolie shook her head. "Carly said it looked bad."

"How bad could it be?"

Nolie gaped at him, amazed that he couldn't visualize a thousand possible disasters. "She could have a broken bone, she could have ruptured an artery, a blood clot could go to her heart and kill her. And now that she's in the hospital, she could pick up that awful flesh-eating bacteria bug. Someone could give her the wrong medicine. She could have an allergic reaction and stop breathing—"

"Hold on, now." With a smile in his voice, Erik pulled her head to his shoulder. As she clung to him and rattled off her worst fears, he patted her back and murmured soothing sounds.

When she finished listing every terrible thing she could think of, he stepped back and lifted her chin. "None of those things are going to happen to your sister," he said, his voice as comforting as a warm sweater. "Didn't your parents tell you never to borrow trouble?"

She hiccuped a sob. "M-momma didn't talk to me much, and I—I don't remember my daddy. He died when I was two."

"I'm sorry—really sorry to hear that. But God prepares us for the trials that come our way, and he won't allow any trial you can't bear with his help. You've got his word on that."

She hiccuped again, then covered her mouth with her hand. As she looked at him, grateful for his company, she realized he had stepped into pastoral mode as easily as he stepped into his tennis shoes every morning. She liked Preacher Payne, but couldn't help wondering about the man behind the mode.

"So God prepared you"—she lifted her gaze to meet his—"for when your wife left and you lost your church?"

He blinked rapidly, then took a half step back. He turned his head, his long lashes hiding his eyes, then smiled and studied her with a curious intensity. "You're an insightful woman, Miss Nolie. More insightful than your sisters realize."

Nolie would have asked what he meant, but from the corner of her eye she saw Henry's car turn into the lot and nose into an empty parking space. "Henry's here!"

She hurried to the door and watched as two umbrellas appeared, both of them making a beeline for the ER.

Nolie stepped outside, where a soft drizzle was all that remained of the storm. Henry and Carlene were walking across the parking lot, both of them wearing raincoats. Carlene, she noticed, carried a small overnight bag. Did she plan to camp out in the waiting room?

Henry greeted Nolie with a nod. "How's she doing?" he asked, shaking water from his umbrella. "Have they seen her yet?"

"She's been in the exam room awhile, but I think they were going to take her for X-rays or something."

Carlene's brows knit with concern. "Did the doctor say it's broken?"

"Her foot was completely numb and purple by the time we got her shoe off. The doctor didn't seem worried until he mashed on a spot and Darlene screamed like a bobcat. That was when he said he'd have to call a specialist."

"Poor thing." Henry stepped into the foyer and propped his umbrella against the wall. "Do you think we can see her?"

"I know she wants to see you. Why don't we go on in? I'll walk back to the cubicle and see if she's fit for company. If she's not there, I guess all we can do is wait."

She led the way into the lobby. Henry and Carlene sat near Erik while Nolie went to see if Darlene was still in the exam room. She and her gurney had vanished, but a moment later Nolie spied the wheeled bed coming around the corner. Darlene lay flat on her back, her mouth tight with frustration.

"The orthopedist will be in soon," the nurse said, rolling the gurney back into place. "In the meantime, you close your eyes and take it easy. Have those pain pills kicked in yet?"

"A little." Darlene pressed a hand over her face. "Is my sister still here?"

"I'm right beside you." Nolie stepped closer as Darlene parted her fingers and peered through the gaps between them. "And I'm not alone. Henry's in the waiting room with Erik and Carlene."

"Will you ask Henry to come in?" Darlene spoke slowly, her words slightly slurred. "Tell him I'm feeling better."

Nolie smiled. "I'll get him. Just a minute."

She went into the lobby and motioned to Henry, then pointed out the appropriate exam room. Henry disappeared into the cubicle as Nolie sank into the empty seat next to Carlene.

"So." Nolie took a deep breath as a burden she didn't know she'd been carrying rolled off her shoulders. "Is everything okay at the house?"

Carlene nodded. "Everything's fine. Everyone was pretty much waterlogged after the storm, so as soon as the rain slowed, they all picked up their dishes and headed home. They seemed to have enjoyed themselves, despite everything. A couple of older people mentioned that it was nice to see the Sycamores tradition revived again."

"At least folks will have something new to talk about for a while." Nolie closed her eyes as a cocoon of weariness settled around her, then opened one heavy eyelid and peered at Carly. "What took y'all so long? Darlene kept asking for Henry."

"We had to see everyone out, and a lot of people stayed to help us clean up," Carlene said. "And I started thinking about a friend of mine, a dancer, who broke his ankle and had to have surgery. If the same thing happened to Darlene, I knew she'd want some things from home, so I packed a few necessities." She gestured to the small bag on the floor. "I brought her nightgown, robe, toothbrush, comb, and some deodorant. Oh, and some fuzzy socks. I've been in the hospital only once, but I remember thinking my feet were going to freeze if I didn't get some nice warm socks."

Nolie blinked. "You really think Darlene's situation could be that serious?"

"Hard to say. But don't forget, Darlene and I aren't spring chickens anymore. Mature bones fracture more easily and take longer to heal. But it was good you brought her to the hospital right away. I've known people who limped around for days before going to a doctor and then had to have their feet rebroken. That's definitely no fun."

Nolie's stomach tightened as an unfamiliar man in a white lab coat walked down the hallway. When he turned into Darlene's cubicle, she elbowed Carlene. "The orthopedist just went in to see her. We should hear something soon, shouldn't we?"

Carlene checked her watch. "I expect so—and that's pretty good. She's seeing a specialist barely an hour after arriving at the ER. In New York, it can take hours to get to that point, especially if you come in on a Friday night."

Nolie gripped the arms of her chair and watched the exam-room curtains until the doctor left. "Can we check on Darlene now?"

Carlene stood with her and picked up the overnight bag. They walked forward, but Nolie paused outside the cubicle. She was afraid she might hear distraught moaning or weeping, but she heard only the soft mumble of a television announcer.

She led the way through the curtain and stood at the end of Darlene's gurney. Henry sat on the edge of the bed, Darlene's hand in his. Though Darlene looked as though she'd been crying, her eyes narrowed when Nolie and Carlene stepped into the space.

At least her temper was intact.

"Well?" Nolie asked, afraid to hear whatever news had made Darlene cry. "What'd the specialist say?"

Darlene's gaze flitted toward Henry, but he seemed to be study-ing the backs of his hands. Then she sighed. "You want the simple answer? I broke my foot. You want the long answer? I broke several bones in my foot."

"She won't be going dancin' for a while." Henry glanced over his shoulder at Nolie. "She won't be goin' anywhere at all. Last year I heard about a football player who had the same kind of injury. He was out for the entire season."

"I have to have surgery first thing in the morning." Darlene's voice trembled. "They'll put steel screws into my bones to hold them in the right place."

"Twenty-six bones in the foot," Henry added. "Imagine that."

"I'm so sorry." Nolie tried to give Darlene a sympathetic smile, but all she could manage was a wavering grimace. Carlene was leav-ing tomorrow and Darlene talked as if she might be in the hospital for at least a few days. That meant Nolie would be alone at the house. Of course she'd have her dogs, and Erik would be only yards away, but she had never stayed by herself, not ever.

Somehow she managed to shape her dread into a question. "How long will you be here?"

Darlene sighed. "Altogether too long, if you ask me. A couple of days, the doctor said. Then I'll have a cast for eight weeks."

"You'll be in the hospital *eight weeks*?"

"Heaven forbid." Darlene scowled. "I'll be home in a couple of days, but I have to stay off my feet for two months. After the cast comes off I'll have to use crutches and be supercareful for a while."

Struggling to stay calm, Nolie slipped her hand into her pocket and fingered her damp poetry book. Miss Emily had often worried about being alone, but she conquered her fears by remembering that her heavenly Father had everything under control.

Just like Erik said. The Lord wouldn't allow any trials his chil-dren couldn't handle with his help.

Reassured, Nolie lowered her hand to Darlene's uninjured leg. "You can manage whatever lies ahead, Darly. We'll put lots of stuff in your room so you'll have plenty to do. I'll make you a special apron with pockets for books, your cell phone, and maybe a crossword puzzle collection—"

"I'll be miserable," Darlene moaned.

"You'll be fine." Carlene dipped her head in an emphatic nod. "Because you're not going through this alone. Nolie will be there, and so will I."

Darlene's eyes sprang open and in them Nolie glimpsed real fear—an emotion Nolie hadn't seen in her big sister since Griff died. Nolie was grateful Carlene wanted to stay, but why should Darly be afraid of having Carly around?

Both Nolie's and Darlene's faces registered shock when Carlene announced her decision to stay, yet no one was more surprised to hear the news than Carlene herself. What sort of madness had possessed her when she said that?

Yet after her announcement, as Darlene stammered and Nolie blinked in confusion, her abrupt decision began to make complete sense. Why shouldn't she stay? Her apartment hadn't sold and her real estate agent wanted her to stay away. Sycamores was as much her home as it was her sisters' and in the last few minutes, when she heard the tremble in Nolie's voice, she realized that her baby sister needed her. Nolie was more than capable of caring for her dogs and her garden, but running the house? Carlene wasn't sure Nolie had ever been asked to take on that responsibility.

Henry was the first to find his tongue. "That's—that's mighty nice of you, Carlene. But don't you have to get back to a show or something?"

Carlene shifted her gaze to Darlene, whose eyes gleamed with either surprise or painkiller-induced euphoria, she couldn't tell which. "I'm in no hurry to go back. Broadway will carry on without me, I'm sure. I'll call my agent and tell him I've decided to stay in Peculiar for a few months—"

"Weeks," Darlene interrupted, her voice cracking. "I won't be laid up more than a few weeks."

"But your plane ticket." Nolie's forehead crinkled. "Won't you waste a lot of money?"

"My ticket is open-ended," Carlene answered. "I can go home anytime there's an available seat." She turned to Darlene and patted her arm. "Take all the time you need to get better. To tell you the truth, I've found myself enjoying the pace of life down here. It's a nice change from all the running around I have to do in New York."

With a parting smile, she slipped out of the exam room, hoping Nolie would follow. Henry and Darlene needed time alone together, and Carlene didn't want to intrude on that relationship.

When she entered the waiting area she saw that Erik had left his seat, but she spotted him standing before a row of vending machines in the hallway. Poor guy—either he never had time to go through the line at the potluck or he hadn't felt like an invited guest. Once things settled down she'd have to assure him he would be welcome at Sycamores as long as he wanted to stay.

Seeking a moment of solitude, she walked to the window overlooking the parking lot and smiled at the impulsive woman reflected in the glass. "Now you've done it," she murmured, barely suppressing a surge of hysterical laughter. "Martin won't believe it when you tell him."

Her agent wouldn't understand why she wanted to stay in a burg with a population of fewer than five hundred. He wouldn't grasp the entertainment value of a storm-stressed backyard potluck, or appreciate the beauty of a sister who couldn't eat breakfast until she had deadheaded every wilted flower in her garden. He would think she was crazy for considering buttery grits a genuine treat, and he'd probably have her committed if he knew she was secretly growing fond of two leonine, hairy dogs who tracked mud into the house and sprayed the living room with saliva every time they shook their heads.

Then again, Martin had never lived outside Manhattan, never washed down a Moon Pie with an RC Cola, and, like many other New Yorkers, never realized that significant activities could take place somewhere other than his overcrowded urban island.

Maybe this change of perspective was a necessary part of rebuilding the bonds that once linked her and her sisters. If she pitched in with a few household chores and helped bring new life to the estate, maybe Darlene would stop thinking of her as a vamp out to mesmerize every man in sight. Maybe her heart would soften and she'd learn how to relax around Carlene again. Maybe they'd rediscover how to understand each other intuitively, the way they had as children.

By remaining in Peculiar for a while, Carlene could get to know Nolie better. Maybe she could help her younger sister find the courage she would need when it came time to leave the nest, spread her wings, and fly off to discover a glorious, waiting world.

So many possibilities in Peculiar . . . and so few waiting in New York.

Chapter Eleven

*D*arlene fumbled for the button to elevate the head of her hospital bed, then held it down until she was sitting nearly upright. Two days had passed since her surgery. Despite the fuzzy feeling in her brain, she was ready to go home—if the hospital would let her. The orthopedic surgeon stopped by her room an hour ago and cleared her for release, but the nurse said only her attending doctor could sign her out . . . and Dr. Morgan had yet to put in an appearance.

She glanced at Henry, who was snoring softly in the only chair in the room. He'd come to see her at noon, hoping to drive her home, but the hospital frustrated his plans. He paced and jingled the change in his pockets until Darlene asked why he was so tense; then he confessed that the Wiggly was having double-coupon day and that always meant more foot traffic. "Plus, we have fryers at forty-nine cents a pound," he said, "so they'll be flying out the door. I like to be there when chickens are on sale. If I'm not watching from my office, the birds have a tendency to run away, if you know what I mean."

Darlene frowned. Maybe it was the painkillers, but she couldn't understand—

"People steal 'em," he said, interpreting the puzzled look on her face. "Over the years I've found whole chickens in purses, diaper bags, wrapped up in baby blankets, and strapped into strollers. You'd be surprised what some people will do to get a couple of free drumsticks."

"At that price you might as well give 'em away," Darlene mumbled. "That's cheap . . . cheep, cheep." She giggled at her little joke.

Henry lifted his gaze to the ceiling as if begging for heavenly help. "Those drugs are making you giddy. What if I go to the store and come back when you're ready to check out—"

"Please don't leave me," she begged. "I don't want to stay here a second longer than I have to. Dr. Morgan will be here soon; he has to be."

"What's *your* hurry?" Henry furrowed his brow. "You worried about something?"

Darlene bit her lip. She was concerned about a lot of things, and most of them began with the letters C A R L E N E. The Sister Who Would Not Leave might be taking over Sycamores, riding roughshod over Nolie, or rearranging furniture. The woman could do an amazing amount of damage in a couple of days, but Henry wasn't likely to understand.

"Cary Grant is bound to be missin' me," she finally said.

Henry dropped into the guest chair and soon fell asleep. Darlene had been waiting ever since, growing more fretful by the minute.

Young Dr. Morgan finally arrived, rushing through the door in dark trousers and a wrinkled dress shirt. "How are you feeling today?" he asked, examining her chart. "No plans for break dancing, I hope."

"Or for running through the rain," Henry answered, wiping his face as he straightened in his chair. "Caught her foot in a hole and down she went."

"Ah. Your sister told me about the thunderstorm. Too bad it had to ruin your party." The doctor lowered Darlene's chart and lifted the bedsheet to examine her bandaged foot. "By the way, I hear you have another sister, visiting from New York. Sorry I missed meeting her. Would have been a treat to meet a Broadway star."

Darlene stifled a groan. What'd Nolie do, hire a plane to trail a banner with the news?

Somehow she managed a smile. "Yes, Carlene is home. But she'll be going back to New York soon."

"Still, I'll bet you're glad to have her around for a while. I'm surprised you haven't scheduled a little concert. I know people who'd pay plenty to hear a few tunes from a Broadway actress."

Darlene gripped the edge of the bedsheet. "I wouldn't dream of asking Carly to perform like a trained dog."

"Of course, but how often do professional singers travel through this county?" He ran his hand over the stiff wrappings on her foot, then nodded. "Everything looks good here. Did the orthopedist explain what he did in surgery?"

"He did. And I know I have to stay in bed and take my pain meds, so I'm all set. Please, please, *please* will you sign me out so I can go home?"

Dr. Morgan grinned. "In a hurry to get away, are you?" He picked up her chart again. "Okay, but you have to promise to be good and keep *all* weight off this foot. Tomorrow I'll send a home nurse to check your bandages, and we'll get you back on your feet as soon as we can. But we're dealing with fifty-year-old bones, Miss Darlene, so the healing process will take time and you'll also need a few weeks of physical therapy. Be sure to take your pain medications around the clock—don't try to be a martyr and skip a dose. Once the pain overtakes you, it's hard to get out in front of it again."

Darlene gave him what she hoped was a meek smile. "Yes, sir."

"All righty, then." He flipped the cover over her chart and jerked his head toward the hallway. "Let me give this to the nurse. She'll stop by in a few minutes to go over your postoperative care."

When Darlene and Henry groaned in unison, Dr. Morgan shot her a lopsided smile. "Trust me, you're going to want those pain meds in an hour or two, so you'd better know how to take them." He gave her a jaunty wave and headed out the door.

*   *   *

After helping Henry carry Darlene up the front steps and put her in bed, Carlene made sure her sister was comfortably settled and tiptoed out, leaving Henry alone to say good-bye.

A few minutes later, the grocer joined her and Nolie in the living room. "She's going to sleep for hours," he said, winking, "and I've got fryers on sale, so I need to get back to the store. But here are her meds"—he pushed a pharmacy bag into Nolie's hand—"and she's to take one of those white pills every four hours no matter what. Keep her in the bed; the nurse said she could get up to go to the bathroom, but she has to have help, and she has to keep her weight off that foot."

Carlene nodded. "We understand. We're here to help."

"Thank you, Henry." Nolie stood to walk him to the door. "Thanks for everthing."

Grateful that Darlene was safely settled in her room, Carlene strolled into the garage, crossed her arms, and stared at Darlene's Buick. The tank-like sedan was probably a gas guzzler, but it looked solid and safe—probably why Darly kept it instead of trading it in for something more economical.

Once she convinced herself the vehicle wasn't too intimidating, Carlene went in search of Erik.

Every morning she'd been getting out of bed thinking this could be the day her Realtor called to say her apartment sold. Once it did, she'd have a tidy nest egg for beginning the second act of her life . . . somewhere. And while she had no idea where her future might lie, one thing was clear—she needed to be better equipped for life away from New York.

She hoped Erik would be willing to help her. She checked the guesthouse, then found him holding a shovel by the edge of the terrace. "You planning to bury someone?" she asked, keeping her tone light. "Or maybe you're thinking of digging for buried treasure."

He looked up and grinned, then pointed to the spot where Darlene had fallen. "It's a wonder no one else has turned an ankle in that hole. I was going to fill it in with dirt, but now I'm wondering if maybe it'd be smarter to use rocks. Dogs like to dig in soft places, but they don't usually mess with rocks."

Carlene folded her arms, impressed with his reasoning. In New York she occasionally hired men to repair something in her apartment, and they usually did exactly what she asked, never anything more. But here was a man who not only recognized a problem and how to fix it, but also wanted to prevent bigger problems from occurring in the future.

Forward thinking and handsome, too . . . The man's wife must have been crazy to leave him.

She met his gaze. "So you think we should blame the dogs for that hole?"

He shrugged. "Could be. Or an armadillo or possum. Hard to tell, but a mixture of rocks and dirt would keep whatever it was from digging in that spot again,"

"Sounds like a good plan, then." She nodded. "When you're done with that, I wondered if you could find some time to do me a small favor."

His brow crinkled. "Does Miss Darlene know you're editing my to-do list?"

"This has nothing to do with Darlene. This is a personal request."

The crinkled brow rose an inch. "What'd you have in mind?"

"Nothing unethical or immoral, I assure you. I need"—she drew a deep breath—"I need someone to teach me to drive."

He waited, probably expecting a punch line, then snorted. "You've got to be kidding. You never learned to drive?"

"When we were sixteen, Darly and I both took driver's ed in school. But two years later I went to New York and I haven't been behind the wheel since. So you'd not really be teaching me. You'd be giving me a refresher course."

He scratched at his chin. "You got a license?"

"No."

"Did you *ever* have a license?"

"Thirty years ago. But it expired and I never got it renewed."

He blew out a breath and braced his arms on the shovel. "You're gonna have to take the test again. You'll have to take the eye exam, the driving exam, and the written exam."

She made a mental note. "Anything else?"

"You'd better find the online driver's manual and start studying. Once you know the rules, I'll work with you. I figure you can drive up and down the driveway until you get the hang of it." He grinned. "But no turning the key until you've studied the manual, and no driving on public roads until you get a license. You can practice by driving around the property here."

"Sounds good. Agreed."

She turned to walk away, but he called out a question. "After thirty-odd years, why the sudden urge to drive?"

"Because Darlene can't and Nolie won't," she answered. "But somebody's got to be able to go downtown for groceries and take Darlene to the doctor for her checkups."

She wasn't sure if he found her answer satisfactory; after all, she could have asked Erik to play chauffeur for a few months. But if he didn't accept her reasons, he kept his doubts to himself.

A good thing—because at times like this she didn't understand her own impulses.

Determined not to fail at something most sixteen-year-olds could manage without any problem, Carlene turned on Darlene's ancient computer and scrolled through the pages of Florida highway regulations. How could she commit all these rules to a fifty-year-old memory? She had never heard of Florida's "Move Over" law, and a section on ABS brakes perplexed her. Brakes were part of the car's mechanics, so why did she need to learn about them in order to drive?

She jotted a question about the brakes onto her notepad. She'd ask Erik about them later, maybe when he had agreed to take her for a practice run on the driveway. After all, if she was going to spend several more weeks in Peculiar, she needed to be mobile. Taxi service was almost nonexistent in this part of the county, and she'd rather be trampled at a Loehmann's clearance sale than be seen on Nolie's pink bicycle.

She left her bedroom and headed for the kitchen, but the sound of the sewing machine stopped her. Carlene shook her head, amazed by Nolie's consistency. Even though she had undertaken the main burden of caring for Darlene, somehow she still managed to stick to her daily routine.

Carlene thrust her head into the sewing room. "Hey, Nolie, I thought you were listening for Darly."

"I am."

"But how can you hear her up here?"

Nolie's face lit with an impish smile. "I gave her a cowbell. They can probably hear that thing downtown."

Carlene laughed and leaned on the door frame, searching for a way to tactfully approach the topic on her mind. "Did you hear? Erik's going to teach me how to drive so I can get my license. Isn't that a good idea?"

Nolie barely glanced away from her sewing. "I guess so."

"Don't you think that'd be a good idea for you, too? I thought you might want to study with me."

Nolie bit her lip. "Thanks, but not now."

"Maybe later, then?"

One apron-clad shoulder lifted in a shrug. "I don't really need to drive, do I?"

"You might enjoy being able to . . . you know, if you ever wanted to move or take a job somewhere outside Peculiar."

"Why would I want to do either of those things? Besides, I don't have time for driving lessons."

Carlene blew out a breath and moved toward the back stairs. If Nolie could disrupt her sacred schedule to help Darlene to the bathroom, why wouldn't she take the time to learn how to drive? And she seemed to have forgotten that in just six years Sycamores would no longer be her home. Grandpa Caldwell had all but decreed that his descendants would move on from this place, yet Nolie seemed to want nothing more than the freedom to cocoon in the aging house.

What would it take to build a fire under that woman?

Darlene, on the other hand, had a knack for landing on her feet, so Carlene didn't worry about her twin. When they were teenagers, Darly carried on about how much she'd miss Carly once she left for school, but she didn't seem to mourn very deeply or very long. When Carlene came home for spring break only three months later, Darlene had not only recovered from missing her sister, but also gotten herself engaged to her sister's boyfriend.

Even now the memory had the power to frost Carlene's blood.

Shoving that remnant of the past aside, Carlene trotted down the stairs, then peeked into the master suite. Darlene sat on her bed, her head propped against a mountain of pillows and the television remote in her hand. Judging from her lifeless expression, she wasn't enjoying whatever was on TV.

Carlene strolled in and gripped a pillar of the four-poster bed. "You need anything, Darly? I was going to ask Erik if he'd take me to the Wiggly. I'd be happy to pick up anything you want."

The corner of Darlene's mouth dipped. "We don't need groceries. I stocked the pantry last week so we'd be ready for the party."

Trying her best to be pleasant, Carlene laughed. "I don't know what to do with a pantry full of cake flour, bread flour, and self-rising flour. I looked at those shelves last night and came away confused. So I thought I'd pop into the store and grab some frozen dinners."

Darlene closed her eyes and shook her head, clearly believing Carlene had sunk to a gastronomic low. "The food you've been eating the past two days—where'd it come from?"

"Leftovers, mostly. A lot of people left food after the picnic. But we're running low, and I need to get all those dishes returned to whoever owns them."

"Nolie will deliver them," Darlene said. "She likes to return dishes with a new apron tucked inside. It's just something she does."

"Well . . . okay." Carlene hesitated. "Do you need me to help you to the bathroom now?"

Darlene shook her head.

"Want me to give Henry a message?"

"No."

"Are you sure you don't need to pee? I might be gone for a while—"

Darlene's scowl deepened. "Just leave me alone, will ya? For heaven's sake."

"Okay." Carlene twiddled her fingers in a wave and slipped out of the room. Darlene had to be feeling woozy from all the pain medications she'd been taking, so maybe that was why she was out of sorts.

Carlene found Erik in the garage, his head and shoulders bent beneath the Buick's hood. "Is something wrong with the car?"

He straightened and acknowledged her with a nod. "I thought I should check the oil if you're serious about learning to drive. I have a feeling your sister doesn't keep up with regular oil changes."

"I suspect you're right." Carlene leaned on the side of the car and peered into the dark engine. All she could see were grease-encrusted thingamajigs and whatchamacallits, so if Erik wanted to maintain the mechanical bits, she'd be happy to let him. Once she found a place to settle, she'd get her own car and hire a mechanic to maintain it.

"I wanted to ask you about ABS brakes," she said. "They're mentioned in the driver's license manual. Why do I need to know about parts of the car?"

He wiped the back of his hand across his forehead, leaving a greasy smear. "I would imagine that's probably because you feel a thumping in ABS brakes when you apply them suddenly. Some folks are so startled they release the brakes and rear-end the vehicle ahead of them."

"Are the brakes supposed to thump?"

"Yep." He wiped the long piece of metal on a strip of old toweling and shoved it back into the slot it'd come from. "It's a safety feature."

She filed the information away for future reference as he pulled the strip back out and peered at the end of it. "So—how's our oil level?"

"The oil level is fine, but it's dirty."

"So we should clean it?"

"We don't clean oil, we replace it. And the sooner, the better."

"I guess we could take the car to the shop—"

"I can change the oil for you. You don't have to worry about it."

"Okay, I won't." Playfully, she rapped her knuckles on the window. "By the way, I'm ready for that practice run whenever you are. I asked Nolie if she wanted to learn how to drive, but she said no."

Erik slid the thin metal strip back into the engine, then wiped his hands on a clean towel. "Why is that? Why is she so—well, I guess the word is *introverted*, though she doesn't seem to have a problem talking to people."

Carlene propped an elbow on the sedan and let her gaze drift to the grassy spot where Ricky and Lucy lounged in the shade. "I don't know why she's the way she is. Honestly, Erik, I don't know her very well. I'm hoping to change that in the weeks ahead."

"Just seems a shame, the way she sticks close to home. Maybe it's not my place to say, but I can't help thinking that a woman like her ought to be out meeting more people, creating a life for herself."

"I happen to agree with you." Carlene shrugged. "But maybe she's living the life she wants."

Erik lowered the hood of the car with a slam so loud Carlene jumped. "Are you ready for that practice spin now?" he asked.

"You mean right this minute?"

He shrugged. "Why not?"

A sudden jolt of fear twisted her stomach. "Are you sure I'm ready?"

"Can you think of a better time?"

"No, but . . . do I need my purse?"

He laughed. "Why would you? We're not going anywhere."

"Okay." She took three steps back as a horde of anxieties assailed her. "You—you pull it out onto the driveway for me. I'll get in once the car's out of the garage."

Erik shook his head. "No, ma'am. You can't be asking people to get you out of tight spaces. If you're going to do this, you have to learn how to do it all."

She swallowed hard. The garage was so tightly packed, the car parked in such a narrow slot. What if the thing leaped forward and crashed into the wall? What if she hit one of the beams supporting the house? She could bring the whole place down on their heads.

"Look." Erik patted the hood and sent her a reassuring smile. "If you go slowly and listen to what I tell you, you'll do fine. We're not training for the Grand Prix; we're just going to pull out of the garage. I think you can do it. Do you?"

If she was going to invest in her own future, she needed to be brave. She needed to set an example for Nolie, and she needed to prove something to herself. She was far from old, and while her future might not be the one she'd envisioned, it could still be bright and filled with promise.

She could learn to drive a dad-burned car.

Drawn by the sound of popping gravel, Nolie left her sewing machine and strode to a window from which she could see the front lawn. Darlene's car sat idling on the long driveway. It lurched forward, rolled a few feet, and stopped so suddenly that the tires slid over the pebbles. The unusual sounds attracted the dogs, who left their shady spot beneath the trees and trotted toward the drive, their attention focused on the unsteady vehicle. The sedan rolled forward again, halted with a squeal, and then the motor revved to a roar. Agitated by the noise, Lucy dashed forward, her ears at attention, her eyes focused on a front tire.

Nolie fumbled with the stubborn latch on the window and finally managed to lift it a few inches. "Lucy!" she called, trying to fit her head through the six-inch opening at the bottom of the frame. "Stay away from that car!"

Ricky swiveled and looked around, but Lucy barked again and growled at the tire. Nolie's dogs had never developed the habit of chasing cars, and this would not be a good time to begin . . .

Nolie flew down the stairs and bolted out the front door, then ran to the edge of the porch and whistled for her pets. Ricky cocked his ears and obediently trotted toward her, but Lucy had developed a case of selective hearing. She lowered her head near the hubcap and barked again, ignoring Nolie and a flustered-looking Carlene behind the wheel.

What was wrong with Carlene? Couldn't she see that she was putting Lucy in danger? The car rolled forward, a longer distance this time, then the brakes squeaked again. Lucy's tail went erect as she raced after the car, snapping at the front tire as if she'd decided the sedan was possessed by an evil entity.

"Stop!" Nolie sprinted off the porch and flew over the walkway, her skirt billowing around her legs. As she drew closer she could see Carlene arguing with Erik, who sat in the passenger seat and kept pointing to something on the dashboard.

"Stop!" Nolie screamed again, feeling the sharp edge of pebbles through the thin soles of her slippers as she ran. "Carly!"

Her sister turned and looked out the window, her eyes going wide. Grateful that she finally had Carlene's attention, Nolie caught up to Lucy and grabbed her collar, using both hands to hold the agitated dog.

Carlene's door opened and Erik shouted, "You're not in park!" Gravel popped as the car rolled forward. A grinding noise filled the air, then the vehicle shuddered to a stop.

Ignoring Erik's sputtering and the car's movement, Carly stepped out and marched up the walkway with her lips set in a straight line and her fists clenched. Erik, now sprawled over the seat with one hand on the steering wheel and one on the brake, gave Nolie a look of pure exasperation.

Relieved that the car had died, Nolie released Lucy, who ran over and sniffed suspiciously at the front tire.

She folded her arms as Erik pulled the key from the ignition and wiped perspiration from his forehead.

"I was doing fine," Carlene called from the porch, "until that dog started barking. All that noise distracted me."

"You have to be prepared for more distraction than that," Erik yelled back. "You have to stay focused on what you're doing."

Carlene spun on her heel and went into the house, slamming the door behind her.

Erik shook his head, then looked at Nolie. "Remind me," he said, his voice calmer than it had been a moment ago, "never to teach a grown woman how to drive. I had no idea something so simple could be this difficult."

Nolie lifted her chin. "I guess driving's not as easy as Carly thought it would be."

Erik's Adam's apple bobbed as he swallowed. "That's just it; driving *is* easy," he said, his voice flat. "It's teaching that's hard. It's especially hard when your student has the attention span of a gnat."

Irritation filled his eyes, a look that swam up through the years and reminded her of another afternoon when she'd been scared out of her mind.

Buddy hadn't shown up. She waited and worried, then walked to the front of the church and told her friends and neighbors that something terrible must have happened. After making a complete fool of herself, she moved toward the church door, confused and concerned, as she overheard a snappish woman say, "Why, I never. How stupid do you have to be to plan a wedding for a no-show groom?"

How stupid? Plenty stupid. As stupid as a rotted tree stump.

On that day, everyone in Peculiar learned just how stupid Nolie was.

The sound of Erik releasing a breath snapped her back to the present. "My sister," she said, her voice like chilled steel, "is not stupid. She got flustered, that's all."

Erik drew back. "I didn't say she was stupid."

"It's what you were thinkin'. It's what everbody thinks when things don't go the way a woman planned."

Erik studied her for a long moment; then his brow wrinkled and something moved in his eyes. "I think a lot of you and your sisters, Miss Nolie. Y'all are some of the strongest, brightest women I know."

"You don't have to lie."

"As God is my witness, I'm not lyin'." He tilted his head and nodded as if he just realized why she'd come out to the driveway. "And I'm sorry I scared you. I didn't see the dogs, and your sister was too busy trying to learn the controls on the dashboard to pay much attention. Then when she heard the barkin', well, things got a little crazy. I should have helped her stay calm."

Nolie pressed her lips together, resisting a wild rush of emotion. "I don't know why Carly has to do this." Her voice came out jagged, torn by threatening tears. "Things don't always have to change, you know. Some things are meant to stay just the way they are."

Erik's forehead crinkled, but Nolie didn't care to explain further. Wrapping herself in resolve, she grabbed Lucy's collar and hauled the dog toward the house.

With her dogs safely resting in her room, Nolie sat before her sewing machine and tried to concentrate on her work. She was making a patchwork apron, the simplest thing in the world, but her mind refused to focus. Like wayward children, her thoughts kept tottering off to explore things she didn't want to think about: Darly's broken foot, that sickening grinding sound as the car shuddered in the driveway, Carly's extended stay, the friction between Erik and Carly, the friction between her and Erik . . .

Why in the world should she care what he thought? He was the hired hand, for heaven's sake. He was simply a man—okay, a nice man—who needed help, so they'd helped him. That was all.

But if she were being honest, she'd have to admit they needed him, too. Sycamores needed a man's strength, a man's know-how, and Nolie had to admit she felt better knowing that a man slept on the property. Erik might not have done anything that she and Darlene couldn't have eventually managed, but she couldn't deny that life had been better since he arrived. She also couldn't deny that her heart did strange things and her pulse beat double time whenever he approached. She remembered every word he ever said to her, even every inflection—was that normal?

Surely it wasn't. But she couldn't be falling for him, couldn't possibly have feelings for him. He was too recently divorced—well, perhaps not, since his wife had been gone over a year—but he was still grieving. He hadn't come here looking for a wife, so he certainly

couldn't be interested in her. She shouldn't be interested in him, period.

Carly, on the other hand, was a different story—she was her sister, and a woman had to be interested in what happened to her sister.
But life had been crazy since Carly came home. And what did it matter if Nolie learned how to drive? She was fine just the way she was.
Carly was fine, too.

And so was Erik.

A trembling rose from someplace deep within her, a steady quivering that threatened to unravel her composure. She hadn't felt this
way about any man in years; hadn't found her thoughts spinning in
an endless loop that seemed to begin and end with one person. She
had gone through this with Buddy Hopkins; she had met him, liked
him, loved him, and then he broke her heart. For years she struggled
with the pain and humiliation of that experience; she still struggled
with it, but perhaps the time had come to stop.

Stop struggling.

The words echoed in her head as if someone had said them aloud.
Stop struggling with Buddy? Stop thinking about him? The idea felt
unnatural. She might as well stop reading her poetry and stop breathing. She'd carried Buddy Hopkins in her heart and head for so many
years; to give him up would be like a cripple surrendering his crutch.

But she wasn't a cripple. She was whole and complete and—
what had Erik said? One of the strongest, brightest women he knew.

She set her fabric on the table, dropped her hands into her lap,
and straightened her spine. Inhaling a deep breath, she closed her
eyes and let the words wash over her: she was *strong and bright*. She
wasn't stupid. No matter what her schoolteachers said, no matter
what her scores on those standardized tests. She was strong. Bright.
And Erik believed in her.

A smile tugged at the corner of her mouth. Buddy had never
thought her strong or bright. He always told her not to worry because
he would take care of everything. Yet that fool couldn't even manage
to show up for his own wedding.

Her smile broadened. Oh, what she'd love to say to him now.

On countless nights she had fallen asleep imagining what he must look like these days. She envisioned running into him by the lake, at church, in the beer aisle at the Wiggly. She dreamed of opening the front door and finding him there, in his arms, a bouquet of roses and on his lips, a story about being kidnapped by a motorcycle gang.

Then her imagination supplied the image of bosomy Joni Leigh Grayson coming up the steps, a child on each hip. At that point the fantasy soured.

Buddy Hopkins had never been a hero. He had used her for his own enjoyment; he probably laughed about her with his friends or with Joni Leigh. He enjoyed his little flirtation, he lapped up her adoration and wide-eyed earnestness, and then he left town with the woman he really wanted . . . the one who carried his baby.

And Nolie had been foolish enough to mourn a man who wasn't much of a man at all.

But her situation had changed. A real man—imperfect, mature, troubled, spiritual, wounded, and strong—had entered her life, and her heart had done a double take. Her head was spinning with confusion, her instincts screamed *caution!* while her heart was already reeling.

Bleary-eyed and exhausted, Carlene stepped into the shower, turned the water on full force, and waited for the stream to warm. The date, June nineteen, felt like a burden on her shoulders, heavy with significance and portent. The date was an intensely personal anniversary, a monument to the frailty of flesh and the fragility of dreams.

Perhaps she shouldn't have been surprised last year when the unthinkable happened on this date—after all, the number nineteen had always marked her life's most noteworthy events. Griff kissed her for the first time on April 19, 1979; on October nineteen of the next year she won the Miss Buttercup Squash Pageant. On July 19, 1992, while starring with her in *Phantom*, Evan Parker asked her to marry him. Because she had learned how to be content with less than her heart's desire she said yes, and because she didn't want a long engagement they married on August nineteen, a quiet Wednesday morning. After five years of separations, delights, betrayals, and a sometimes frightening intimacy, their divorce became final on the nineteenth of November.

The number nineteen dabbled in more than her love life. On December 19, 1980, she learned she had won a scholarship to Juilliard. On the nineteenth of April 1987, she won a coveted part in *Les Misérables*. On January 19, 2009, a man stole her purse at a subway station. And exactly one year ago, on June nineteen, she stepped onstage to sing the part of Golde, the long-suffering wife in *Fiddler*. She had sung the role on 220 other occasions, so she breathed deeply, opened her mouth, pushed air—and discovered that nightmares could come true.

She simply couldn't sing.

The actor playing Tevye covered for her, but during intermission the director sought her out and insisted that her understudy fill in until she recovered her voice. For all she knew, the understudy was still playing her part.

One year ago, her voice gave out and her career died without any warning. Though the doctor said the damage would be permanent, something inside her yearned to see if today, another nineteenth, might bring an unexpected miracle.

Quiet reigned over the rest of the house. Darlene snored softly in her bedroom, probably enjoying a drug-deepened dream about the most effective way to can peaches or pickle zucchini. Silence emanated from Nolie's room, so Carlene assumed she had taken her dogs out to the garden.

Good. She needed solitude for her shower. For this shower, anyway.

She drew a deep breath, pulled the curtain back, and stepped into the stream, gulping lungfuls of moist, damp air. Seven months had passed since her surgery, and during those seven months she had been careful not to push her voice too hard. For the six weeks immediately following the procedure she hadn't said a word, using only notepads and hand gestures to communicate. For the next two months she spoke in a low, measured voice and never allowed herself to shout. Fragile tissues, especially when healing, deserved respect.

But seven months was a long time and the human voice was like a muscle. Like every muscle, her teachers always told her, it needed to be worked in order to remain strong. It needed to be gently stretched, worked out, and then allowed to cool down and rest . . .

She'd been resting for months. Time to see if her voice had returned.

Breathing through her mouth in order to bathe her vocal cords in warm air, she began to sing an *aah*, directing the sound toward her nose. The resulting nasality made her smile, and the ease with which the notes flowed bolstered her courage. "A-mazing grace," she began, deliberately choosing a low key, "how sweet the sound . . ." Her vibrato was a little out of control, but she could restrain that with a little tension. Her chest voice sounded okay—warm and resonant—so perhaps the doctor had made a mistake. Perhaps she could push things a little, take it up a few keys, and sing in her upper register.

She took the song up a fifth and began again: "A-mazing grace, how sweet the sound . . ."

Her voice flowed over the rushing water in a thin stream, fluid and weak, but undeniably present. This wasn't the voice of a coloratura soprano or even a mezzo, but it might suffice for a church choir or singing carols door-to-door.

Time to put herself through some vocal gymnastics. She switched to Mozart's "Alleluia," a soprano solo that contained numerous scales in the key of F. She ran through the opening segment, then began the passage that ended on an A above the staff—

Her voice quit. In the middle of the scale, without even a dying squeak. The air flowed, but her vocal cords simply refused to cooperate. In her mind's eye she could see the scarred pair stiffening in rebellion, locking their formerly lithe bodies, and rejecting the command to proceed no matter how her mind prodded them forward. She tried again, pushing air and straining her neck. And though she urged her voice upward with everything she had, the talent that had carried her through many a play and audition simply gave out.

This nineteenth would be significant only in its finality.

Hope died in that instant and with it, her dreams of ever re-claiming the life she had known. She would not be featured on the *Today* show as an incredible comeback story. No one would hold a welcome-home party for her at Lincoln Center. The *Times* would not call for an interview. Her theater friends would not hug her and tell her they'd always known nothing could stop a true artist.

As her eyes flooded with tears, she clung to the soap dish on the wall and felt sobs rack her body. Her vocal cords would not sing, but another voice, a deeper and more primal wail, gave vent to her loss and filled the steamy air with the ugly noise of grief.

Nolie couldn't help hearing the pretty sound of Carlene's singing as she came upstairs, so she stopped in the hall to eavesdrop with her ear pressed to the wall between the upstairs hallway and Carlene's bathroom. She was thrilled to listen, realizing that it'd been years since she heard Carlene sing, but then the melodic line broke and the sobbing began. Even above the sound of the shower, Nolie heard her sister's heartrending grief. After a moment of confusion, she took a wincing breath and realized she was learning one of Carlene's secrets.

Carly had been home more than two weeks, and not once during that time had she said anything about her current work or future plans. As a high school student, she sang from morning till night, practicing vocal exercises, rehearsing performance songs, and bab-bling foreign phrases in Italian, French, and German. Momma called her their songbird, and as a child Nolie found it impossible to sepa-rate Carly the singer from Carly the sister, so closely were the two intertwined.

Why hadn't she said anything about losing her voice? If she con-fessed she was suffering from laryngitis, a sore throat, or even simple fatigue, no one would have questioned her. But she hadn't said or sung a word. And Carly without music didn't seem like Carly at all.

Nolie shook her head, dismissing the disloyal thought. Her *sis-ter* wept behind this wall, and no matter what happened to Carly's music, Nolie's sister was alive and frustrated by what she was no longer able to do. And the fact that she hadn't mentioned this problem meant she intended to keep the news from them. But why? Nolie couldn't come up with any reasonable explanation.

She stepped away from the wall and tiptoed back down the stairs, the dogs trailing after her. The clear sky and warm sun had delivered a glorious summer day, but Carlene wasn't feeling much joy and Nolie didn't know how to help her. Until Carly opened her heart and shared her problem, Nolie could only wait, pray, and hope that Carlene would one day trust her sisters enough to confide in them.

After the hot work of driving practice—and the humiliating task of apologizing to Erik for running off in the middle of a lesson— Carlene tugged her blouse free of her damp chest and pushed her grocery cart toward the frozen-foods section. Darlene might pride herself on baking from scratch, but few twenty-first-century women took the time or had the inclination to cook the hard way. No matter what Darlene said, Carlene wanted to fill the freezer with frozen dinners, ready-to-eat entrées, and meals-in-a-bag by such beloved gourmets as Chef Boyardee, Marie Callender, and the Jolly Green Giant.

And she was in luck—the Piggly Wiggly had buy-one, get-one-free specials on more than a dozen heat-and-serve meals. She tossed several into her cart, enjoying the chilled air as she strolled along the freezer case. Erik, who'd driven her downtown in his pickup, walked a few feet ahead and caught her attention when he waved at someone behind the meat counter.

She tilted her head and smiled when Henry stepped out from the cutting room, a bloodstained apron stretched over his expansive belly. "Hey, y'all." His smile quickly faded to a look of concern. "How's Darlene doin'? Is she holdin' up okay?"

"She's sleeping most of the time," Carlene assured him. "Those pain pills make her drowsy."

"Be sure and tell her howdy for me." Henry wiped his hands on his apron, then held up his index finger. "And wait—I have something for you. You tell her I saved the best piece for Sycamores."

He bent and reached for something in a refrigerated chest, then straightened and handed Carlene a package wrapped in butcher paper. "It's a brisket," he said. "I know she loves 'em. There's no price sticker, so you just tell the cashier that package is on me. She'll understand."

Carlene squinted at him. "Are you sure? You don't have to feed the entire family."

"I like doing a little somethin' special for Darly ever now and then. So you tell her to hurry and get better."

Carlene set the bundle in her cart. "I'll be sure to tell her. Thank you, Henry. That's quite generous."

Erik glanced at Henry, then looked at Carlene. "You know, the mayor's known your sisters a long time. Maybe he knows the answer to the question I asked you earlier."

Carlene lifted a brow. "Which question would that be?"

"The one about Miss Nolie. About her reasons for keeping so close to home."

"Aah." Carlene looked at Henry. "Maybe he does."

Henry glanced from Carlene to Erik, then back again. "What are you talkin' about?"

Carlene smiled. "Erik's teaching me how to drive. I thought Nolie might like to learn, too, but she wants no part of it. So we were wondering why she's so . . . reclusive."

Henry drew a long deep breath, then tucked his thumbs into the bib of his apron. "You know how things are in a small town—your neighbor is known by his first name and his last scandal. So everybody around here knows about Nolie."

Carlene's thoughts scampered from one wild possibility to another. "What, exactly, do they know?"

"Nolie's tragic history." He leaned closer and spoke in a hushed, conspiratorial voice. "She's never gotten over it."

Carlene frowned. In all the letters that had come from Sycamores over the years, had she read anything about a tragedy affecting Nolie?

She knew about the family deaths, of course, and had come back for the funerals, but what happened to Nolie?

She pushed her cart closer to the freezer case. "What could have—?"

A dim ripple moved through her mind, bringing with it the memory of a simple wedding invitation. Nolie's wedding. It had arrived in the midst of frantic rehearsals for *Phantom*, and Carlene was so involved at the theater she had no time to go home for any reason. She dashed off a quick letter expressing her regret and two weeks later, Nolie answered with a brief note: *I'm glad you didn't come home. The wedding never happened.*

Carlene assumed Nolie called the wedding off, but maybe she'd been wrong.

"Does this have anything to do with Nolie's wedding?" Carlene stared at Henry as the realization took shape. "I got an invitation, but then Nolie wrote and said the wedding was canceled."

"It wasn't exactly canceled." Henry lowered his voice to a confidential whisper. "Everthing happened when Nolie was a senior in high school. Darlene was married and had two kids by then and of course, you were in New York, singing up a storm. No one knew much about Buddy Hopkins 'cause that sly one didn't spend much time in town. Then me 'n my wife got an invitation to the wedding, so we showed up at that little white church way out on Highway Ninety. Nolie was there, wearin' a white lace dress she made herself, carrying a bouquet of roses and daisies she picked from her garden."

His gaze grew wistful as he stared at packages of ground beef. "I remember it like it was yesterday. When we got out of our cars, Nolie greeted us and told us to go inside and take a seat, so we did. We waited. And waited. Finally, Nolie walked to the front of the church, cryin' her eyes out, and told us that something must have happened to her fiancé. She asked if someone would call the highway patrol and tell 'em to look for Buddy Hopkins, but then Doc Hensley, the only vet within miles back then, came runnin' in and apologized all over the place. He said he was sorry that a difficult foal birthin' had made him late, but he'd heard that Buddy Hopkins eloped the night before with Joni Leigh Grayson. Nolie dropped to the floor like a heart-shot deer."

Carlene stared as Henry shook his head. "A downright heart-breaker, it was. Once Nolie came around, Darlene tried talkin' to her, but Nolie clammed up and wouldn't say a word. She just went home, and ever since then she's been quotin' poetry, wearin' white, and keeping to her little routines. Darlene says it's her way of findin' comfort, but I don't think it's healthy for a body to be set in her ways like that. Sometimes I think you couldn't pry Nolie out of Peculiar if you blew up Sycamores and set the town afire."

Carlene listened with a rising sense of disbelief, but when Henry finished, she thanked him for sharing the story. Not knowing what else to say, she looked at Erik and thought she saw a flicker of sympathy in the depths of his eyes. As they wheeled her cart toward the checkout counter, she realized that everyone in town knew her younger sister better than she did. How could she not have known about Nolie being abandoned at the altar?

The thought disturbed her. She should have known; she should have come home. She should have been around to comfort her baby sister.

Guilt, thick and bitter, coursed through her veins, but what good would feeling guilty do now? Remorse wouldn't help Nolie, but it might help Carlene understand what she should do with the rest of her life.

She was from Peculiar, she was one of these people, yet time and distance had built a wall between them. They thought her something special, and while that notion was outwardly flattering, it also kept people at arm's length. Nolie and Darly were lucky—as third-generation Caldwells, they were loved and accepted. But Carlene was also a third-generation resident of Grandpa's town, and Peculiar was as much her home as it was her sisters'. This little town was in her blood . . . so how could she show people that it was also in her heart?

A thin magazine advertising available Jackson County real estate pointed her toward the answer. *If you want people to think of you as home folk,* she could almost hear Grandma saying, *then you need to become one of the home folks.*

Why not move back home to stay? The move made sense financially—once her apartment sold, she could invest her profit until she and her sisters had to leave Sycamores. Then she could find a little cottage in Peculiar, maybe something near the lake, or look for a house in neighboring Chattahoochee. Depending on how well she and her sisters were getting along, she might even want to live with one or both of them.

But how could she show her support in the meantime?

She discovered a good lead while standing in the checkout line. As Erik went to get his truck, she spied a flyer in the store window: the Peculiar Community Theater group would be meeting to discuss a new play. They would meet Saturday morning at the city-park pavilion, and all Peculiar residents were welcome to attend.

"That'll be fifty dollars and forty-nine cents, please."

Distracted, Carlene handed the cashier her credit card. "Here you go."

She didn't even know Peculiar *had* a community theater. The group couldn't be very big, but they could certainly draw on talent from Chattahoochee and surrounding communities if they wanted to put on a decent show. And if their upcoming production shone with exceptional quality, word would spread and people might come all the way from Tallahassee to enjoy a little night of drama . . .

Carlene smiled, overcome with the delicious feeling that she'd inadvertently stumbled onto buried treasure.

After giving Darlene her pain medication and tucking her into bed for the night, Nolie closed the master-bedroom door and breathed a sigh of relief. A twilight sense of calm settled over the house as she went from room to room checking locks. She whistled for her dogs and went upstairs, pausing at the threshold to Carlene's suite. She heard nothing but silence within, but maybe Carly was awake and in the mood for a cup of cocoa or something . . .

She rapped on the door, heard "Come in," and found Carlene sitting on the big bed, a photo album on her lap. "I brought this"— Carlene blushed—"thinking I might show it to Darly. If only I could get her to sit up and stop complaining about being stuck in bed."

Nolie tilted her head to look. "What is it?"

"Pictures. Of my productions." The color on Carlene's cheeks deepened. "Darlene will probably think these are silly."

"I won't," Nolie said, climbing onto the mattress beside her sister. "I love looking at old pictures."

"Truth is, I haven't looked at these in ages." Carly's voice brimmed with happiness as she flipped back to the beginning. "Let me walk you through some of the more interesting highlights."

Nolie propped her chin on a pillow and listened, letting Carly prattle on about this production and that. She studied pictures of Carly in costume, on the stage, and on the town in glitzy after-show finery. In those photos, a parade of ever-changing faces surrounded Carlene, many of them in obvious theatrical makeup. Not until they stumbled across Carly's wedding photo did Nolie recognize any recurring characters.

"Was this your husband?" She tapped the handsome man standing with Carlene before a spray of white flowers. "He's nice-looking."

"Evan was—I mean, he is." Carlene peered at the photo as if she'd forgotten some of the details. "He proposed the first night we went out. Handsome, talented, charming . . . I couldn't believe he was interested in me."

Nolie tilted her head. "How did you know he was the one you wanted to marry?"

Carlene's expression shifted as memory softened her eyes and a wry thought tightened the corners of her mouth. "How do you know you want to eat a piece of Darlene's pecan pie when you see it? You get a feeling in your gut, a visceral reaction. I saw him and I wanted him, as simple as that. He wasn't the love of my life, and I never thought of him as a soul mate, but I was lonely and he was a great friend. After a couple of years I learned that wanting someone isn't as important as loving them, and I'm not sure Evan and I ever really loved each other. When he got fired from our show and had to take a part in a production that wasn't as well received, he grew hard and resentful . . . and I didn't want him anymore. Of course, by that time he didn't want me, either."

"If he wasn't the love of your life—who was?"

Carlene lifted her gaze and stared straight ahead. A spark of humor filled her eyes, then the light dimmed to the quiet glow of unspoken pain. "I fell in love with a boy I met at school," she said, her voice as warm as a cozy blanket. "He made me laugh. I could tell him anything, and he understood. In a way, he was closer to me than Darly."

"Really?" Nolie straightened, desperate to hear more. "Who was he? Was he from Peculiar or Chattahoochee?"

Carly hauled her gaze to the window and seemed to study memories reflected in the glass. "He played on the football team. He was so cute"—her smile deepened—"and my, he was tall! He had to step down from the porch so I could kiss him good night."

Why didn't Carly want to reveal his name? Obviously, she had her reasons. Nolie closed her eyes and searched her memory for some clue as to the mystery man's identity. She must have been six or seven in those days, and since her bedroom was in the front of the house she might have looked out the window and caught the couple saying their farewells. But her memory was fuzzy, and Griff was the only guy she could remember hanging around Sycamores. He, of course, had fallen in love with Darly.

"We had to break up." Carlene lowered her gaze and shrugged as she turned the page. "I was going off to New York; he was a small-town boy at heart. We were so different—it would never have worked."

"But you don't *know* that. And you're not such an urbanite, Carly—Peculiar folks think you fit in just fine."

A wry but grateful glint appeared in Carlene's eyes. "Enough about me." She closed the photo album. "I'd like to hear about your young man."

Nolie felt the edge of her smile twist. Had Carlene noticed something between her and Erik, or had someone in town been gossiping? "Who says I have a young man?"

"Let me rephrase that—tell me about Buddy." She lifted a manicured brow. "People say you've been mourning him all these years, and that's why you wear white."

Nolie snorted. "Truth is, I don't care much about what I wear. But after Buddy broke my heart, I was—well, I was eighteen and overly dramatic. When I learned that Emily Dickinson always wore white, I figured she was onto something."

"Emily Dickinson?"

"*The Belle of Amherst*. Most people believe she wore white to mourn a lost love."

"Oh." Carlene's mouth quirked with a half smile. "I know what it feels like to grieve over a lost love. Seems like I spent years trying to replace mine, and I should never have married Evan. I wasn't being fair to him or to myself. You can't replace someone you've lost—I had to learn that lesson the hard way." She shot Nolie a pointed look. "You're not still mourning Buddy what's-his-name, are you?"

"Buddy Hopkins? No. I gave him far more time and attention than he deserved." Nolie's gaze fell on her hands—freckled, tanned, unadorned. Years ago, on the altar of romantic melancholy, she sacrificed all hope of ever seeing her ring finger circled with a golden band. She'd been so young, so foolish, so pitifully *grateful* that someone seemed to love her . . .

"I'm glad you feel that way." Carlene smiled as a tiny flame lit her eyes. "Because you're a beautiful woman, Nolie, and it's time you began to believe that. Any man would be lucky—no, *blessed*—to have you. I can't believe the guys around here haven't beaten a path to your door."

Nolie felt her mouth twitch. Carly was only being nice, but her sister's words did make her feel better. "Sometimes," she whispered, curling her bare fingers under her chin, "I wish I could go back and do some things over again. I wouldn't waste so much time wallowing in self-pity."

Carlene hugged her photo album as her mouth relaxed in a thoughtful smile. "I know just what you mean."

Chapter Twelve

arlene gripped the edge of the DMV's computer monitor and adjusted it to reduce the on-screen glare. The mouse felt slippery in her right hand, and some fastidious part of her brain wondered how many sweaty teenagers had gripped the same device in the last week. Hundreds, probably. But none of them could have been more nervous than she felt in that moment.

She had been studying the material for the past four days, but her heart fluttered beneath her silk blouse and her kneecaps kept jumping like jerked puppets. Had she been this nervous when she took the driver's test at sixteen? Perhaps, but all she remembered from that experience was proudly showing off her new license.

Maybe she could experience that thrill again. She completed the multiple-choice test as quickly as she could, then clicked *submit* and watched the screen go black. She glanced toward the next desk, where her score would appear before a DMV employee. He would soon call her name . . . with good news or bad.

She didn't even have time to take a seat.

"Caldwell," the bald man called, not even looking up. "Carlene Caldwell?"

She turned on shaky legs and approached the state employee.

"Congratulations," he said, his blue eyes dull with boredom behind his glasses. "You passed—barely. Take this card, go outside, stand on the painted line, and wait for the instructor to administer the driving portion of the exam."

Her heart pounding, she accepted the paperwork he gave her and moved toward the door, flashing a thumbs-up sign to Erik as she passed. After five minutes of tedious waiting, she slid behind the wheel of Darlene's tank. A grumpy-looking examiner in a sweat-stained white shirt took the passenger's seat.

"All right," he said, his breath reeking of tobacco as he pulled a clipboard onto his lap. "Put the car in gear and drive to the first stop sign."

Carlene held her breath and ran through her mental checklist: Seat belt on. Glance in rearview mirror. Put car in drive. Signal intention to pull away. Look in mirror again. Gently step on gas pedal.

The DMV was located in Marianna, the county seat, so the area was completely unfamiliar. Carlene drove at a snail's pace to the stop sign in the middle of the parking lot, braked, and looked at her instructor for directions. They hadn't gone far, but she wouldn't mind if this fellow didn't want to leave the property.

He propped his elbow in the open window and gripped the roof of the car. "Turn right, drive thirty yards, and apply the brakes in a sudden stop."

She took another deep breath to quell her trembling, put on her signal, looked both ways, and turned. She had no idea how long thirty yards was, but when she felt the man tense, she slammed on her brakes and felt the *thump thump thump* Erik had described when she asked about the brakes.

"ABC brakes." She gave the man a confident nod. "And I didn't freak out."

"ABS, you mean—and good for you." Without smiling, the man told her to pull onto the road and drive around the block. She did, her pulse racing when they entered heavy traffic, but she relaxed after making a right turn onto a quiet residential street. Sprawling live oaks canopied the shady road; she drove slowly, her gaze darting left and right, keeping an eye out for children, dogs, and homeowners backing out of their driveways. At one point she braked for a squirrel that stopped in the middle of the road, but though the examiner put a hand on the dash to brace himself, he didn't say anything. Carlene exhaled slowly and kept going.

She made the other necessary turns, finding herself on a commercial street and then on a narrow road that led back to the DMV. When they finally approached the license bureau, the examiner told her to pull into a convenient spot and park the car.

"Anywhere?" She bit her lip, dismayed to hear a quaver in her voice. She'd never been this nervous onstage.

"Close to the building, if you can find a place. It's too dang hot to walk far in this heat."

She made a face and kept rolling forward, careful not to get too close to people strolling toward the building. She finally found an empty spot and pulled into it, managing to follow the examiner's instructions without hitting a light pole or another vehicle. She turned off the engine and held her breath while he scribbled on his clipboard.

Finally he pulled off a page and handed it to her. "Take this to the woman at licenses. She'll take your picture, administer the eye exam, and print your license. Congratulations, be careful, and always remember to buckle up."

Carlene waited until the man left the car, then grabbed her purse and hurried back into the building. "Erik! I passed!" She blushed when a dozen strangers turned to stare, then sat next to him and proudly displayed her final report. "I'll be just a few more minutes. Can you believe I pulled it off?"

Erik grinned and went back to his newspaper as Carlene headed for the counter as happy, as her Grandma would have said, as a high-water clam.

* * *

Darlene lay submerged up to her chin in the bathtub and gloom-
ily considered the fact that she looked like a beached walrus with a
wounded flipper. Nolie had helped her into the bathroom and modestly retreated, leaving Darlene alone to slip off her robe, maneuver to
the edge of the tub, and lower herself while keeping her injured foot
propped on the tiled edge. Nolie had wrapped Darlene's temporary
cast in a Hefty garbage bag and sealed it with duct tape, but Darlene
wasn't worried about ruining her cast. She worried about getting out
of the tub.

She'd been soaking for so long her fingertips were as wrinkled
as raisins. "Nolie?" she called, but no one answered. She lowered her
arm and slapped the side of the tub. "Nolie! I'm ready to get out!"
Again, no response. Where was everyone? Why hadn't she brought
that stupid cowbell into the bathroom? Didn't anybody care that she
could slip and drown or break something else?

She pulled her hand out of the soapy water and pushed her
bangs from her forehead. Her hair needed washing, but she wanted
to wait until she could shower before she attempted a shampoo.
Her face felt oily, even after a good cleaning, and lately she'd been
sure she could feel invisible creatures crawling over her skin beneath the cast.

She sat up, grabbed a loofah from a nearby basket, and scrubbed
her arms. She told Nolie she wanted to soak for an hour, but the
mountains of fragrant bubbles had disappeared and the water was
going cold.

Shivering, she listened to the drone of the lawn mower and the
sound of barking dogs. Nolie must have stepped outside, which
meant she wasn't around to help Darlene . . .

Unbidden, a tear rolled down her cheek. Everyone had abandoned her. Even Cary Grant, who had remained faithfully by her
side, grew bored and hopped off the ledge of the tub, leaving to find
more interesting company. Nolie, Carlene, and Erik were so caught
up in their own projects they had forgotten about the family invalid.
Tonight they'd gather in the kitchen to eat their microwaved mish-
mash and finally someone would remember the forgotten Woman

in the Tub. Until then, she could only sit here, frozen and naked, vulnerable and alone.

She pressed her hand to her mouth and fought against the tears that stung her eyelids. This ordeal was too hard, too much, and it was taking too long. For the last five days she had drifted through a drug-induced fog. Nolie was an attentive nurse most of the time, and Carlene checked in at least twice a day, usually in the morning and late afternoon. Darlene didn't know what her twin was doing with the rest of her time, but Nolie mentioned something about Carly going to get her driver's license . . .

The thought of Carlene driving free and happy around town drove Darlene crazy. Why was Carly suddenly so interested in community theater and civic affairs? Was she going downtown to see Henry? Or did she have some other motive in mind?

Darlene let her hand fall back into the tub, then shivered as tepid water splashed her face. She closed her eyes, envisioning Nolie and the dogs walking by the lake, the dogs chasing ducks, and Nolie lost in her usual contented haze. Carly was probably in the Buick, driving slowly through downtown, waving like a celebrity at anyone who stopped to gawk at her. And Henry . . . he was probably beside Carly, beaming at her grand accomplishment.

Darlene frowned. At some point in the last few days she thought she heard Carly mention that Henry had sent a brisket, but what kind of man sent a slab of meat to the woman he loved? Furthermore, Henry hadn't come by to check on her, so what did his indifference say about the state of their relationship?

"I think he misses you a lot," Carlene reported one afternoon, smiling beneath her yellow sun hat and perching on the edge of Darlene's bed like a saucy little canary. "I put the brisket in the freezer because I didn't know what else to do with it."

"It'd be easy to cook," Darlene mumbled. "Just thaw it and put it in the Crock-Pot after breakfast. Add a little vinegar, a couple of garlic cloves, and a sprinkle of dry mustard. Oh, yeah, and chili powder. Pour a can of Coke over the top. Throw in some onions and beef bouillon cubes—"

"Too many ingredients." Carlene brushed off Darlene's instructions as if they were annoying insects. "The brisket can wait until you're up and about. Now—what do you want for dinner tonight, pasta primavera or a chicken pot pie?"

For five days Darlene had been eating prepackaged foods that tasted like cardboard and were laced with cancer-causing chemicals. Nolie hadn't complained, but she wouldn't protest if Carlene served roach casserole. Erik wouldn't say anything, either, and Carly didn't have the sense to know what good food tasted like. Eating from street-vendor carts and spicy foreign restaurants probably killed off her taste buds years ago.

Meanwhile, Darlene knew how to cook, how to run a home, and how to keep an eye on things, yet she was stuck in the tub—

Well, she didn't have to stay put.

She reached under the water and lifted the drain plug. "Nolie?" she called, not expecting a response. "Have you remembered me yet?"

No answer, but she didn't expect one after hearing the commotion with the dogs. Nolie was probably busy with them, tossing a ball or combing the loose hair out of those lion-like manes.

As the water drained away, Darlene braced herself on the deep tub's armrests and struggled to push herself up. When one hand slipped, she smacked her shoulder against the side, then set her jaw and tried again. Finally, her good foot found purchase on the bath mat and supported her weight as she pulled herself up out of the tub. She sat on the tiled rim, one leg in the bath and one leg out, and reached for the towel Nolie had set on the vanity. Thank heaven she remembered to do that.

As Darlene wrapped the towel around her chest, she caught her reflection in the mirror and shivered in a frisson of unease: her mother was staring back at her. No, not her mother, but her own stocky, sickly, pale-skinned self. Momma never looked this bad, at least not until the end.

That unsettling thought dredged up another: she was no longer necessary to the running of this household. When she'd been married, when she was raising her children, her word was law. No one at

Sycamores did anything without consulting her or Griff. But the situation had changed, and this past week served as an eloquent testament to that evolution. Now she was only one of three sisters living at Sycamores. If Carlene wanted to serve processed mush at the supper table, Darlene couldn't stop her.

She let the thought twirl in her head like one of Henry's rotisserie chickens. This must have been how her grandmother felt when Daddy married Momma and moved her in, and how Momma felt when Griff arrived and became the head of the house. Momma stepped aside gracefully, behaving as if it were an honor to move into one of the upstairs bedrooms, surrendering the master suite without so much as a whimper.

But Darlene wasn't ready to surrender yet.

She swallowed hard and wrapped her arms about herself, drowning in self-pity until she remembered the one bright light in this crisis: Carlene wouldn't stay forever. In eight weeks, ten at the most, she would go back to her perfect home and fancy New York friends. After that, life would return to normal. Even Erik would eventually find a permanent position elsewhere, and then Nolie could relax and make a million aprons without interruption.

In eight weeks, maybe ten . . . life would be good again.

Chapter Thirteen

*S*aturday morning, after dressing, applying her makeup, and giving her reflection a positive pep talk, Carlene hurried downstairs to the kitchen. Nolie and Erik, who were both sitting at the table and munching on bowls of cereal, stopped eating and gaped at her.

"You're up early." Nolie's eyes widened. "Are you feeling okay?"

Carlene forced a laugh. "I think my internal clock is adjusting to small-town life. I set my alarm this morning, but I woke up before it went off. Can you believe it?"

Erik eyed the purse dangling from Carlene's shoulder. "You going out? Need me to drive you someplace?"

"I have my license now, remember?" Carlene gave him a teasing smile, then squeezed Nolie's shoulder. "I don't want to wake Darly, so tell her I'll stop in and see her later, okay? I'm going downtown."

"Anyplace special?"

Carlene lifted her chin. "Let's just say I'm ready to do my part for the members of Peculiar's community theater."

Ignoring their curious glances, she grabbed a granola bar from a box in the pantry, tossed it into her purse, and waved good-bye.

She knew her sisters had questions about her new interest in Peculiar, but for some reason she couldn't bring herself to tell them she'd decided to stay. Maybe she was dragging her feet because she dreaded Darlene's reaction . . . or maybe she was subconsciously protecting her career, waiting to announce her decision until she knew a more exciting opportunity wouldn't come along. Perhaps her secretiveness sprang from selfishness—the last time she lived at Sycamores, she shared nearly everything with Darly, but now she wanted to keep something to herself. Whatever the root of her reluctance, the heart had its reasons, and she would trust her heart.

The prospect of backing the Buick out of the garage no longer terrorized her, and Carlene felt proud of her progress as she carefully pulled away from the house. Jackson County looked different now that she'd decided to stay in Peculiar. The hometown she once considered a dead end had proven to be a well of opportunity. She had been welcomed by friendly people, she had stretched her wings and renewed old acquaintances, and now she was ready to share her talents with the Peculiar Community Theater. She couldn't forget the flyer announcing auditions . . . and who better to help a drama group than a veteran of Broadway theaters?

She pulled into a space beside the park and smiled when she spotted five or six other vehicles. After locking the car, she tucked her purse under her arm and strode toward the pavilion. She could see several people sitting on benches beneath the open structure—a few older folks and some younger people, too. Excellent. They would need a variety of actors if they hoped to pull off a professional production.

She lowered her gaze as she neared the group. Had any Peculiar residents heard she'd decided to stay through the summer? Her appearance here might lead them to suspect that she decided to extend her visit permanently, but better to have people think she *wanted* to stay than to have them know that events had left her so hopeless she had nowhere else to go.

"Carlene Caldwell? Is that really you?"

She lifted her head as someone called out a greeting, then struggled to remember the name of the petite, gray-haired woman who stood in front of the dozen or so people seated on benches. The lady had been at the potluck and the birthday party; she had an adult daughter, and she'd asked Carlene several questions about Broadway.

Of course. Now Carlene understood her motivation. She had theatrical aspirations for her offspring. "I hope you don't mind if I join you."

"Of course not." The woman returned her smile. "Have a seat; we were just chatting. I usually wait a few minutes to give the other laggards time to appear."

Carlene blinked. The *other* laggards? How late was she?

She sat in the second row and smiled at the teenage girl beside her.

"Miss Higgins?" A man in the first row waved his hand. Carlene lifted her head as the woman's name came to her: Edna Higgins, the librarian at the Peculiar library.

Edna answered the man's question, then glanced at her watch and pressed her hands together. "Welcome, everyone, to the first meeting of our fifth theater season. Welcome, newcomers"—she smiled at Carlene—"and veterans. I am excited about the prospect of a truly stellar year."

Carlene set her purse on the concrete floor and crossed her legs, preparing for the inevitable questions.

"Of course, we veterans know each other," Edna continued, "and I usually ask the newcomers to introduce themselves, but I think everyone knows you, Ms. Caldwell."

"Please, use my first name." Carlene smiled. "After all, I'm one of the home folks."

"So you are." Edna slipped her hands into her skirt pockets. "All right, then. Before we form a committee to decide on a play for this year, the most important thing we need to do is vote on our leadership positions: stage director, director of publicity, director of fundraising, and decorating director. Does anyone have a question about what those responsibilities entail?"

Carlene glanced around. She'd never heard of organizing a production like this, but she'd never done community theater. And of course they'd need someone to help raise money to promote whatever play they chose to perform. She wasn't certain what a decorating director did, but she wasn't about to interfere with previously established traditions.

The group had begun to buzz, so Edna clapped for their attention. "All right, then, let's handle the most important position first: director of fund-raising. Do I have any nominations?"

Someone pointed to a red-haired woman, and someone else nominated the bald man in the front row. The teenage girl sitting next to Carlene leaned over and whispered, "Walt Jenkins owns the bank. He's also a good actor. He played Willy Loman last season."

"Oh." Carlene nodded with what she hoped was a properly impressed expression.

They voted, and the bank manager became director of fund-raising. Carlene got the impression that the fund-raiser's main responsibility would be contributing a hefty donation.

A middle-aged woman in the second row was the only person nominated for publicity director. After lifting her hand in the unanimous vote, the teenage girl told Carlene that the new publicity director wrote a weekly column for the *Jackson Gazette*.

Naturally. A newspaper writer would be a perfect choice for publicity.

"And now, stage director." Edna drew a tight smile over her perfectly white dentures. "And, please, don't feel pressured to nominate me just because I've held the post ever since the group's inception."

The banker nominated Edna despite her weak protest, and Carlene lowered her gaze, waiting for someone to call her name. How could they *not* nominate her? She was almost certainly the only professional entertainer in the county, and she'd spent her entire adult life acting and singing in the world's best theaters. She could bring real expertise to the troupe, as well as dramatic coaching they wouldn't be able to get anywhere else.

Silence fell over the gathering, then Edna cleared her throat. "If there are no more nominations—"

Carlene coughed, then reached for a tissue in her purse. Best to look busy when her name came up.

"All right, then, I suppose we'll have another unanimous vote. All in favor?"

Carlene straightened as every hand rose but hers. What happened? How could the Peculiar theater group nominate a librarian to direct their play when an experienced and battle-scarred Broadway actress was sitting in the second row?

She looked around, searching for some logical explanation. Did they think she'd be too tough on them? Were they intimidated? Maybe they thought she'd dropped by only for a visit; that she had no intention of remaining in Peculiar for the theater season. That had to be the reason they overlooked her. No one in his or her right mind would ignore this opportunity unless they thought it didn't really exist.

She clenched the tissue in her hand. What should she do? Should she explain that she'd come to the meeting with every intention of working with the group? Should she ask for another vote? Or should she simply go to Edna afterward and explain that she planned to stick around for the season? Edna might be so impressed and grateful that she'd *give* Carlene the job of stage director.

"Finally, we need a director of decoration," Edna said. "Do I hear any nominations?"

Her curiosity piqued, Carlene lifted her hand.

"Miss Caldwell? Would you like to nominate yourself?"

"No, no—I was curious. Since I'm not used to the way you do theater around here, I thought you might explain exactly what a director of decoration does. I assume you're talking about set decoration."

"Heavens, no." Edna released a charmless three-noted laugh. "Since we perform at the old high school auditorium in Chattahoochee, the decoration director is in charge of furnishing the lobby, making sure the outside sidewalks are swept, and decorating the ladies' lounge."

"The ladies' lounge—as in *bathroom*?"

Edna smiled without humor. "We want our theater nights to be special for our guests. We want them to feel like they're experiencing a genuine treat, and that bathroom—well, it's the typical high school restroom, a real mess. So we hang ivy on the stalls; we put baskets on the counter; and we stock the baskets with toiletries, toothbrushes, safety pins, and sanitary items. Most of all, we clean the place until it shines." Her eyes brightened. "As a matter of fact, why don't I nominate you for decoration director? Everybody, let's welcome Carlene by giving her something important to do."

Carlene's mouth went dry as every head turned in her direction, someone seconded the motion, and Edna called for a show of hands. Tragically, the vote was unanimous.

"That settles it, then," Edna declared, satisfaction ringing in her voice. "Congratulations, Carlene. You're the Peculiar Community Theater's director of decoration for the coming season. Unless"—her face went slack—"unless you aren't planning to be here that long."

Carlene gripped the edge of her bench and hoped her face wouldn't reveal the emotions churning at her core: irritation, incredulity, astonishment . . . and pain from severely wounded pride. "I'll be here," she said, her voice soft with disbelief. "Since my apartment in New York hasn't sold, I've decided to stay in Peculiar for a while."

The group applauded as Carlene looked up and smiled through clenched teeth, wondering if Edna would believe that scrubbing toilets violated the rules of the actors' union.

Probably not. The older woman might be an amateur, but she was no fool.

Instead of walking away with the others when the theater meeting dismissed, Carlene wandered through the park and stopped at the statue of Major Nathan Cutler of the Second Maine Cavalry. Though she remembered racing around the statue as a girl, she had to reread the bronze marker to recall that during the Civil War Battle of Marianna, Major Cutler rushed into the burning St. Luke's Episcopal Church to save the Bible on the altar.

Carlene pressed her hand to the statue's bronze plaque and closed her eyes. What had she expected the theater group to do, raise a statue in *her* honor? Long ago she learned that newcomers never walked into an open audition and won the starring role. They began backstage or in the chorus, and after a few seasons of demonstrating their constancy, they might win a supporting role. Only after they had proven their mettle, tenacity, and professionalism would they have been considered for a lead.

No one ever became a star without paying dues.

Someone needed to explain that truth to young thespians, tempering their hopes for a future on the stage. Someone needed to recite that maxim to older thespians, too, lest they be offended or disappointed when they were assigned to bathroom beautification.

Yes, an actor could make a living in the New York theater, but even those who regularly won supporting roles had beaten the odds. Stardom was awarded to one in a thousand, maybe a million if you included all those who yearned for Broadway from small towns and out-of-the-way bus stops. After thirty solid years in the business, Carlene had never won a leading role. Why did she expect to walk into one here?

She should have known she'd be starting over in Peculiar.

She smiled at her vain foolishness. Darlene would no doubt get a kick out of hearing what she'd been anticipating, and even Nolie might find the situation humorous . . . if Carlene ever confessed what she'd been expecting.

She gave the statue of Major Cutler an affectionate pat, then strode toward her car. Her days on the stage were finis, and the sooner she realized that truth, the better off she'd be. Now she would start at the bottom and learn how to decorate ladies' rooms . . . and Darlene would certainly have a few suggestions about that. Nolie might even be persuaded to sew liners for a couple of baskets.

But volunteer work wouldn't satisfy Carlene's need for a steady income. No matter where she lived, she was going to need money and a reason to get out of bed every morning. Fortunately, she might know where to find both.

She drove back to Sycamores, then went directly to the library. Sitting at her mother's desk, she picked up the old rotary phone,

called information, and asked for the home number of Jonathan Carlisle in Tallahassee. Carlene dialed the number, then leaned back and
counted rings. Saturday morning, so the odds were good. Please,
please, let the professor be home . . .

She caught her breath when a man answered. "Dr. Carlisle?"

"Speaking."

"This is Carlene Caldwell. I've had a change of plans and it ap-
pears I'll be moving to Peculiar. With that in mind, I'd like to run an
idea by you."

"Please, I'm all ears."

Sighing in gratitude, Carlene shared the idea that had sprouted
in her heart.

Wedged into the uncomfortable wing chair in Darlene's room, Nolie
lowered the apron she'd been hemming and smiled when she heard
the front door open and close. Thank heaven, Carlene had finally
come home. Maybe she could sit with Darlene for a while. The patient had been awake and grumping for hours, so she was obviously
feeling more like herself . . .

"I need to ask Carlene something," Nolie said, standing.

Darlene's face crumpled with frustration. "Will you come right
back? I'm going stir-crazy lying here with nothing to do. And we still
haven't solved the problem of my promise to—"

Nolie exhaled slowly as her gaze roved over the piles of maga-
zines, the crossword-puzzle books, the stack of newspapers. Darlene
had plenty to do, if only she'd take her mind off her misery. "I'll be
back soon. But I have to take care of a few things."

"Land's sake, Nolie, your sewing can wait."

"But my dogs can't—and they're hungry." Nolie tried to smile,
though her face felt as tight as the skin on a grape. "Be back in a few
minutes."

She practically sprinted out of the room. Why had she been
tapped as the full-time sitter? She'd asked Henry to invite Carlene
to the big birthday party because she wanted the twins to rediscover

each other, but instead of using this opportunity to do that, Carlene kept inventing reasons to drive here, there, and yonder.

Time for the twins to rediscover the closeness they once shared . . . even if she had to tie them together.

Breathless, Nolie met Carlene in the foyer. Carly was coming out of the library and heading for the stairs, probably to take a nap or change her clothes—things she didn't need to do, not when Nolie had reached the end of her rope.

"I need you," she said, her voice sharper than she intended. "I need you to sit with Darly. She's driving me crazy."

Carlene seemed preoccupied, as if she were thinking about something far away, then her perfect brows slanted in a frown. "Crazy, huh? Trust me, I know the feeling." She cock-a-doodled a laugh. "All right, I'll be back down soon. I need to change my clothes and—"

"You need to go sit with her *now*." Nolie underlined the word with delicate ferocity. "Darlene is all hyper about some ladies' meeting tomorrow afternoon. Apparently she promised to bring twelve dozen cupcakes, and she doesn't want me to bake them because I burn things, but she doesn't want me to find someone else who could bring them, either. I told her she could ask Henry to get cupcakes from the Wiggly, but she won't hear of it. She says she promised delicious homemade cupcakes, so store-bought, even store-bought bakery cupcakes, just won't do."

She realized she'd been yammering almost nonstop when Carlene's jaw dropped. "My goodness, Nolie, I don't think I've heard you string that many words together since I've been home."

Nolie gritted her teeth. "Maybe I haven't been this aggravated since you've been home. That stupid cowbell—big mistake!—has been ringin' all mornin'. It's getting to the point where I hear that dad-gum bell five minutes after I leave her room—"

She lifted a finger as the loud *clunky-clanky-clunky* began again. "See what I mean? Her foot's getting better, so she's been refusing her pain medications. She's definitely feeling spunkier 'cause she doesn't want me to do anything but sit and listen to her gripe."

"I'll go. Now." Turning from the staircase, Carlene gave Nolie a sympathetic smile. "You poor thing. I'm sorry you have to deal with all this, but it's nice to see you're as human as everyone else."

"I don't like being like this," Nolie answered, trudging with Carly through the foyer hallway. "So I'm sorry I'm snippy. I usually try to forgive people as soon as they get under my skin, but Darly's been getting under my skin every other minute—"

"I'd say you manage pretty well." Carlene stopped, her eyes sparking with speculation. "How do you do it? Most of the time you seem completely unruffled by things that would send anyone else into hissy fits."

Nolie lowered her gaze. "Whenever I get irritated by things or people, I remember what Buddy did to me . . . leavin' me at the church and all like that. Nobody else has ever come close to what he did, so if I can forgive him, then everthing else is just small potatoes."

Uncertainty crept into Carlene's expression. "Small potatoes, huh?"

"That must sound really silly to you."

"No . . . actually, it sounds really smart."

Nolie smiled and gestured to the kitchen. "If you'll go sit with Darlene, I have to feed my dogs. Lucy's only a couple of months away from her next heat, and I want her in tip-top condition so we can—"

"Go do whatever you have to do. I'll tell Darlene not to worry; I'll bake her cupcakes."

Nolie stopped in midstride. "I don't think you ought to *lie* to her. She'll learn the truth."

Carlene laughed. "I won't lie. I can bake a few cupcakes."

"Twelve dozen isn't exactly a few. And do you even know how to cook?"

Carlene tugged on the fashionably knotted scarf at her neckline. "How hard can cupcakes be? I saw Darlene's recipe box when I was digging in the pantry this morning, so I'll simply follow her instructions. I don't have anything crucial to do for the rest of the day, so you tend to your responsibilities and I'll take care of Darlene. We'll be fine."

Nolie took a hesitant step toward the kitchen, but Carlene

walked toward Darlene's room with a confident stride, looking for all the world like a woman who knew what she was doing.

Nolie could only hope she did.

When Carlene walked into the master bedroom and announced she'd bake the promised cupcakes, Darlene put on the same doubtful expression Carlene had seen on Nolie's face. "What is wrong with everybody around here?" She crossed her arms. "Cupcakes can't be that difficult."

"Heaven help us." Darlene buried her face in her hands. "Now I know how Scarlett felt when she saw Atlanta burnin'."

"Oh, come on." Carlene braced her hands on her hips. "I found your recipe box this morning, so I'll just follow the directions. Now—what kind of cupcakes did you promise to deliver?"

Darlene squinted at Carlene as though she were a bomb that might blow at any moment. "You'd better make the chocolate caramel—that recipe's practically foolproof. And use chocolate frosting. That's easy."

"Twelve dozen chocolate caramel cupcakes, coming right up." Grateful for a good reason to leave, Carlene smiled and moved toward the doorway. "Anything you need from the kitchen before I get started? More water? Ice cream? Would you like another sandwich?"

Darlene moaned again and shook her head.

Carlene walked toward the living room. Good grief. The way some people carried on, you'd think she had just announced plans to assassinate a world leader.

Energized by the thought of proving herself to her doubting sisters, Carlene ran up the back stairs with more zip than she'd felt in days. She had come through a dark period of uncertainty, but now she could see an answer to her problems. Dr. Carlisle had been thrilled to hear from her, promising to speak to the board of directors about approving her new teaching position as soon as possible. The community-theater group had accepted her, and though her responsibility would be small, she was willing to work hard and prove herself. She had shown Erik and the state of Florida that she was qualified to drive a motor vehicle.

Now she was going to prove to Darlene that she wasn't completely inept in the kitchen.

She stepped into her bedroom, closed the door, and leaned against it, smiling at the thought of the future. She would soon have a job, a steady income, and work that wouldn't require singing. No more wrapping her throat in wool scarves and dreading the advent of flu season. No more avoiding ice cream before a performance. No more worries about competition from younger, stronger singers.

And for at least six years, no need to pay rent. She could live at Sycamores until Grandpa Caldwell's gift clause kicked in. Once her apartment sold and she established legal residency at Sycamores, she should even be eligible for a monthly annuity payment.

Best of all, in a few weeks she would be teaching young voice majors, and as a teacher she would be granted the respect and authority she had earned after so many years of study and professional performance.

She smiled at the thought of "Florida State University Instructor" appearing on her resume. If life in Peculiar didn't pan out the way she hoped, after a few years of teaching at FSU she might consider moving back to New York, where her education and teaching experience should enable her to get a position at Juilliard or one of the other colleges.

A few weeks ago she had despaired of even having a future, but blossoms of hope now jutted through the barren surface of her hopelessness.

She changed into a pair of jeans and an oversized cotton shirt, then remembered that Nolie had created an apron for just such an occasion. She found the embroidered apron still in its gift box, so she pulled it out and tied it around her waist, marveling again at the lovely stitching. She glanced in the mirror—if she didn't look like a mini Martha Stewart, no one did.

After grabbing Darlene's recipe box from a shelf in the pantry, she shuffled through the cards until she found the recipe for chocolate caramel cupcakes. She checked the ingredients list and pulled items from the shelves: all-purpose flour, baking soda, cocoa powder, sugar, vegetable oil, vanilla extract, chocolate chips. The recipe also called for eggs, butter, and buttermilk—which Carlene couldn't find in the fridge—so she pulled out regular milk instead. The recipe also required one teaspoon of "light agave nectar," but because she had no idea what agave nectar was, she figured she'd skip it. What difference could one teaspoon make?

With all the available ingredients arranged on the kitchen island, she rummaged through cupboards until she found a set of mixing bowls. Darlene's industrial mixer stood on the counter, so she pulled off the cover and began to measure her ingredients. Since her reading glasses were upstairs by her bed, she squinted at the tiny print on the card and tossed heaping cupfuls of flour and sugar into the mixing bowl. When all the ingredients listed on the card had been measured into the bowl, she hit the switch and grimaced as the paddle blade kicked flour and cocoa onto her face.

"Looks like you're gonna need a mask." Nolie grinned as she entered from the screened porch and held the door for her dogs. Lucy and Ricky followed her into the kitchen, took a perfunctory sniff of the canisters on the island, then ambled into the living room.

Carlene glanced at her formerly white shirt, now dusted with flour and cocoa powder. "Do you know where Darly keeps her industrial-sized aprons? This one is pretty, but it only covers my lap."

"That's because I never thought you'd do any actual baking." Grinning, Nolie opened the pantry door, pulled out a full-coverage apron, and tossed it to Carlene. "This one should do the trick. Have fun."

"I will." While the mixer churned on the countertop, Carlene tied on the apron and searched the bottom cabinets for baking pans. She thought she remembered Momma keeping them near the oven—that seemed logical—but Darlene had moved them closer to the sink.

She blew out her cheeks and knelt, removing round pans, square pans, a Smurf-shaped pan, and a Bundt pan designed to look like a circle of Christmas trees. Finally she found muffin pans—five of them—and pulled them out. Darlene had promised twelve dozen cupcakes, so she'd have to fill all five pans twice, and two pans three times. Or something like that.

As the mixer continued to whir, she stuffed the other pans back into the cupboard, then grabbed a notepad to keep track of her total. She set the oven to 350 degrees, exactly what the recipe stipulated.

She turned to the mixer, which had surely done the job by now. She powered it off and lowered the big stainless-steel bowl. Then she moved to the pans waiting on the island and carefully spooned out the batter, filling each cup before moving to the next.

Bummer. The first batch filled only two pans, which meant she'd have to make several other batches. But since the oven had only three racks, she might as well start baking.

She slid the filled pans into the oven, turned on the light, and smiled at the pretty sight of chocolate-filled baking cups. Being a domestic goddess wasn't so difficult; surely anyone could manage it if they took the time.

Humming an old tune her mother used to sing in the kitchen, Carlene grabbed a measuring cup and scooped out another generous heaping of flour.

Chapter Fourteen

A metallic grind and steady whirring woke Darlene from a shallow doze. She frowned, trying to place the sounds. The coffee grinder? No, the mixer. Apparently Carlene was actually attempting to make the chocolate caramel cupcakes, but she might as well try to turn water into wine. The recipe wasn't difficult, but Darlene didn't think her pantry held all the necessary ingredients. She'd planned to send Nolie to the grocery this morning, but Nolie had been in a fretful mood and hadn't seemed inclined to grant any favors.

Darlene sat up, felt her head swim, and waited, propped on her elbows, until her brain steadied and her eyes focused. Then she threw back the covers, swung both legs off the mattress, and gingerly lowered her injured foot to the floor. From across the bed, Cary Grant's accusing stare burned a hole in her back.

"Aw, stop it," she told the cat. "If I can only hop into the bathroom, I can grab my crutches and go see what kind of disaster Carly's creating in my kitchen. Don't you think that's a smart idea?"

The cat declined to answer.

She stood on her good leg and reached out, trying to coax her body forward, but as she shifted, her weight came to rest on her injured foot. A stabbing, searing pain flamed along her shinbone as color ran out of the world. She clawed at empty space, but with nothing solid within reach, she fell hard.

A moment later, Nolie ran into the room. "What on earth!" Her eyes widened when she saw Darlene on the floor. "Land's sakes, Darly, are you trying to kill yourself?"

Darlene grimaced as wasps of agony flew along her leg and swarmed in her bandaged foot. "I thought I could . . . reach the crutches."

"Well, that was a stupid idea. I put them in the bathroom for two reasons—first, because I knew you'd need them on the toilet and second, because you're not supposed to be out of bed without help, not for a few more days. You could have broken the bones again. How could you do this to yourself? Why would you?"

Because Carlene is destroying my kitchen, Darlene wanted to shout, but she only gritted her teeth as Nolie struggled to lift her onto the bed. After much sweating and straining on both their parts, she lay on her mattress with a pillow under her head and a bolster under her leg.

Nolie glared down her nose like an irritated guardian angel. "Did you hurt yourself?"

"I might have bruised my kneecaps, but they'll heal."

"I want you to take one of your pain pills. It's time, anyway."

Darlene lay still while Nolie filled a glass with water, then handed Darlene the medicine. "Swallow," she commanded, her eyes narrowed.

Darlene grudgingly obeyed. How had her situation deteriorated to this point? She was usually the one who took care of people.

"I'm gonna get bedsores if I have to sit on this mattress much longer," she complained, handing the empty glass to Nolie. "You've gotta find a way that I can get out of bed."

Nolie bent to tuck the edge of the sheet beneath the mattress. "You can talk to Dr. Morgan about that when he comes by on Monday. In the meantime, you need to mind him and do exactly what he says."

"But Carlene's in my kitchen. She doesn't know what she's doing and it sounds like she's waging World War Three—"

"Come on, give her some credit. I was just in there and your kitchen's still standing." Nolie straightened, mopped her face with her apron, and placed both hands on her hips. "You need to relax. Turn on the TV; watch one of those reality shows you like. Paula Deen is on, isn't she?"

Any other time Darlene would have preferred watching Paula Deen to almost anything else, but not while an unpredictable dervish was destroying her domain. "You don't understand—"

"I do."

"—but you'd feel the same way if Carly wandered into your garden with a weed whacker."

Nolie straightened, her jaw tensing, then she nodded. "Tell you what—I'll pop into the kitchen one more time to see if Carly needs any help."

"Thank you." Darlene pulled the sheet to her chin and folded her hands over it. "I can relax if you make sure Carly's not wreaking havoc. If anything in my kitchen *is* destroyed, don't give me details. Just make sure none of my bakeware has to endure needless suffering."

Nolie smiled, patient amusement in her eyes. "You know"—she squeezed Darlene's hand—"some people suffer in silence a lot louder than others."

Then she left the room, whistling as she went.

When the smoke alarm began to shriek, Carlene cringed and uttered a word she usually reserved for New York traffic. Smoke streamed from the edges of the oven door and she had no idea how to stop it.

She flew to the oven and turned off the heat. Coughing on the acrid smoke, Carlene opened the door that led to the screened porch and lifted the window above the sink. After peeking through the oven window to make sure the cupcakes hadn't burst into flame, she lowered the door and ducked as a black cloud rolled into the room.

Flapping her apron to fan smoke away from the detector, she coughed and moved toward the window, hoping she wouldn't see Erik staring up at the kitchen. How embarrassing! But what on earth had she done wrong?

Once the smoke thinned, she grabbed two oven mitts and pulled the cupcake trays from the baking racks. Batter had risen and spilled out of the individual cups, coating the bottom of the oven with a thick chocolate ooze that was rapidly turning to charcoal.

Nolie burst through the kitchen door. "What's burning? Is the place on fire?"

"Not quite."

Carlene dropped the ruined cupcakes onto the center island as Nolie rushed in, her wide eyes like dark holes in pale parchment. She grabbed a straw broom, turned it upside down, and began to fan the air. "Can you help me get this smoke out of here? We're going to suffocate."

Carlene grabbed the back door and swung it on its hinges, pushing air with every movement. "Does this help?"

"Can't hurt." Nolie turned, her irritated eyes brimming with tears. "What on earth happened?"

"They bubbled up." Carlene felt the sting of tears in her own eyes. "The mix overflowed and went everywhere. I don't know why they spilled, but the oven's a mess and I still have to bake twelve dozen cupcakes. I have another batch ready to go, but I've got to get the smoke out of here first."

Nolie shook her head. "You can't bake anything with burned food in the oven—the finished product will taste like soot. Trust me, I've tried it."

Carlene swiped her hair away from her forehead. "What am I going to do? I still have to bake all those cupcakes, and now I have to clean the oven, too. I'm never going to get everything ready by tomorrow afternoon."

The smoke alarm finally stopped whooping. As the sound of silence rang in her ears, Carlene looked at Nolie, her shoulders slumping. "I hate to admit it, but I think I bit off more than I can chew."

Nolie turned an obvious burst of laughter into a cough, then patted her chest and walked toward the oven. She peered at the smoldering mess, then looked at the half-baked goop in the muffin trays. "Okay." She pulled another apron from the pantry. "I'll clean the oven while you tell me exactly what you did. I'm not the baker Darlene is, but if we put our heads together, maybe we can come up with something that looks like cupcakes."

Carlene dabbed at her streaming eyes. "I set out all the ingredients"—she pointed to the items on the island—"and poured the amounts into the bowl, then mixed them. Then I spooned the batter—"

"Hang on a minute." Nolie held up a finger and reached for Darlene's recipe card. "Did you cream the butter and sugar? Did you add the dry ingredients first and then the wet?"

"What does it matter? It all gets mixed up in the end, doesn't it?"

Nolie smiled as if she were explaining something to a very young child. "It matters. And where's the agave nectar? I don't see it here."

"I figured I could get by without it. The recipe called for only a little bit."

"Agave is the sweetener for the caramel center . . . but it doesn't look like your cupcakes even *have* caramel centers."

Carlene stared at the misshapen lumps on the center island. "I thought I could help."

"I think we need a professional," Nolie said, tying her apron around her waist, "and it's four o'clock, so Henry will be leaving the Wiggly soon. You run over there while I clean up this mess. Tell Henry you need to make twelve dozen cupcakes for tomorrow. If you tell him they're for Darlene, he'll do whatever he can to help. But you'd better hurry if you want to catch him before he leaves the store."

Carlene pulled off her sooty apron and moved toward the back door, but hesitated when Darlene's cowbell began to clang. "Nolie?"

"Yeah?"

"Don't tell Darly about this, okay?"

Nolie gave her a grim little smile. "Knowing her, she's probably on the verge of a nervous breakdown. She's gonna ask about the smoke alarm."

"Tell her anything you want, just don't tell her"—Carlene looked at the mess and sighed—"every awful detail."

Nolie moved toward the kitchen door. "I'll do what I can. But you're right; Darly is better off not knowing that you nearly burned down her kitchen."

Frazzled and distracted, Carlene pulled up to the downtown curb, dropped a quarter into the parking meter, and ran into the Piggly Wiggly, her hair uncombed, her eyes stinging, and her white shirt streaked with soot and chocolate. The cashier gave her a curious look as she scooted past, but Carlene had only one thought on her mind: salvation lay in Henry Hooper, so she had to find him. Immediately.

She found the mayor in the produce department. Through a flood of words and tears she explained her predicament. A burden of humiliation and responsibility rolled off her back when he patted her shoulder and told her not to worry, he'd be happy to provide her with twelve dozen cupcakes for the ladies' meeting.

"But Darlene doesn't want store-bought," Carlene said, still hiccuping from her crying jag. "She'll die if people thought she sent cupcakes not made from scratch."

"They'll come from the Sycamores kitchen," Henry promised, gently prodding her toward the door. "Now get along home and wash your face. I'll be over soon."

His comment about washing her face forced her to look in the rearview mirror before driving home—and what she saw horrified her. Her New York acquaintances wouldn't recognize her. Her face was streaked with black, the result of either mascara or soot, and her lipstick had completely disappeared.

She drove carefully back to Sycamores and even managed to wave to Erik after she parked the car. She had just finished repairing her makeup in her bathroom when pebbly tire noises announced a vehicle on the driveway. The cavalry had arrived.

Henry was already in the kitchen when she came downstairs. Nolie was helping him unpack shopping bags, and Carlene gasped when she saw him set six boxes of chocolate cake mix on the table. "Cake mix?" she hissed, keeping her voice low. "Darlene hates cake mixes. She says they're full of chemicals—"

"Does that woman have to know everthing that goes on in this house?" Henry winked at her. "We're going to doctor the mix a bit, and I promise these cupcakes won't taste like chemicals. Now help me unload the rest of these sacks so we can get started."

He lowered the oven door and peered inside. "Good job on the cleaning, Nolie. Looks spic and span, but"—he made a face—"I can still smell smoke."

"That'll fade once we get the cupcakes in the oven," Nolie promised. She pulled out a package of caramel candies and sniffed them before setting the bag on the table. "I love caramels."

"Then you can unwrap them." Henry grinned. "I need one hundred forty-four caramel squares, and I don't mind if you eat a few as you count. Have at it."

Nolie pulled up a chair and began to take the cellophane off the delicious treats. Henry picked up the big mixer bowl—which, Carlene noticed, no longer held anything at all—and read the directions on the cake mix.

He glanced over his shoulder. "While I mix ingredients, Carly, you can put paper liners in all those muffin tins. I brought pink ones, seein' as how these are for a ladies' meeting."

Carlene ripped open a bag of fluted cupcake liners and began to set them in muffin cups. So many little things to consider, details she had never noticed. Who knew baking could be so complicated? And when did they start making frilly cupcake liners?

Overcome with gratitude, she looked at Nolie and Henry. "I can't believe you two have dropped everything to help me," she said, her voice trembling. "Especially after I said baking cupcakes was so easy anybody could do it. I can be such a know-it-all."

Nolie shrugged. "I love you anyway."

Henry dumped the first mix into the bowl. "Don't worry about it. I learned a long time ago that the best way to forget your troubles is to help others out of theirs."

Carlene pushed past the lump in her throat. "You got troubles?"

"I've got a daughter," he said, his voice light, "who's twenty, spoiled rotten, and determined not to like my girlfriend. But don't say anything to Darlene about this. It's my problem and I'll handle it. I just haven't figured out how to do it."

Carlene gave him a sympathetic smile. Long ago she learned she could tell a lot about a man by how much he *didn't* say, and Henry was to be commended for not broadcasting his daughter dilemma to anyone who would listen.

She had her own predicament to consider. Several times over the last couple of days she thought about telling Darlene she'd decided to stay in Peculiar permanently. But every time she turned the subject toward Sycamores, real estate, or her New York apartment, Darlene interrupted with a comment about how much Carlene had to be missing Manhattan, or how nice the New York weather would seem after a sweltering summer in Peculiar.

Darly was obviously not ready to hear her sister's announcement. Carlene hadn't even been able to bring up the Fourth of July parade and the Fall Festival float she'd agreed to ride on.

And as much as Carlene wanted to share her news with Nolie, she couldn't bring herself to do it. Darlene would be hurt if Nolie learned about any of Carlene's plans first.

When Henry finished mixing the first batch of cupcake batter, he used an ice-cream scoop to put the batter into the paper liners. Because he filled each cup only half full, his first mix filled three trays. Then, while Carlene watched, he took an unwrapped caramel square, placed it on top of the batter in each cup, and pushed it until it disappeared beneath the chocolate.

"Voilà," he whispered. "This will be our little secret. Instead of piping the caramel into the center, we'll let it bake inside the cupcake. Same gourmet effect, but much easier."

"Much," Nolie agreed.

Carlene grinned. "Ha! Even I could do that."

"Then get busy. Because we still have to whip up the frosting, and Darlene will know if we don't use her recipe for *that*."

She dropped caramels into filled tins as Henry opened another box of cake mix. Soon the first three trays were ready. Henry slid them into the clean oven, and as they baked, he worked on the second batch while Carlene helped Nolie unwrap caramels.

Baking wasn't quite as simple as she'd expected, but it didn't have to be difficult. With friends like these around, she could learn to enjoy working in the kitchen.

A tear slid from the corner of Darlene's eye as she struggled to ignore the sounds of laughter from the kitchen. Why had she ever decided to have that darn potluck? The idea was stupid, and the disastrous outcome only proved that the time for potluck picnics had come and gone.

Because of that stupid party she'd broken her foot, and because she broke her foot, Carlene decided to stick around for the rest of the summer. Because Carlene decided to stick around, she was now in the kitchen with Darlene's boyfriend, laughing and batting her lashes and no doubt doing her best to charm the small-town man who had never ridden on a subway or been dazzled by Times Square. How could he not be dazzled by Carlene? Griff certainly had been.

The words to the old nursery rhyme whirled in Darlene's drug-hazed brain like a merry-go-round. *This is the cat that killed the rat that ate the malt that lay in the house that Jack built . . .*

Now that she'd had time to think about it, Darlene suspected that Nolie suggested a pain pill so Darlene would sleep through all the noisy shenanigans in the kitchen.

But there wouldn't be any shenanigans if she hadn't held that potluck. But no, she wanted to play mistress of Sycamores, to reenact the role her mother and grandmother used to fill when they served as examples of gracious Southern hospitality. She wanted to appear magnanimous and loving; she wanted to show her uptown sister that downtown folks could cook and laugh and have a great time simply by being themselves. She wanted Carlene to see that life in Peculiar could be rich, that she didn't need to feel sorry for the people who chose to remain at home . . .

But then the skies opened and Darlene found herself lying on her backside in the mud, her foot shattered and her pride destroyed.

This is the maiden, all forlorn that milked the cow with the crumpled horn, that tossed the dog that worried the cat that killed the rat that ate the malt that lay in the house that Jack built . . .

After all her scheming, maybe she deserved to suffer an accident. Maybe she deserved to lose Henry, just like Carlene lost Griff. Darlene had devised and carried out a plot back when she and Carly were constantly competing and victory over her sister tasted sweet. But the resulting encounter had changed everything, and the ripple effects of her actions still rocked Darlene's world.

That was why Carly was exacting her vengeance. Whether she realized it or not, she was working to snatch the only man who had ever liked Darlene for being who she was, and not for being Carlene's sister.

Darlene rolled over and buried her face in her pillow so the merrymakers in the kitchen couldn't hear her sobs. She had never been more miserable, not even when Griff told her he planned to go back to Carlene. She'd been *unhappier* when she learned Momma had cervical cancer and when a heart attack took Griff, but unhappiness and misery were two different things.

Misery—that time, at least—resulted from problems she'd brought on herself. And if she kept being stupid and self-destructive, she'd only make herself more miserable.

This is the man all tattered and torn, that kissed the maiden all forlorn, that milked the cow with the crumpled horn, that tossed the dog that worried the cat that killed the rat that ate the malt that lay in the house that Jack built.

She stifled her sobs when someone knocked on the door without speaking. "Nolie?" Her voice came out muffled by the pillow, so she lifted her head. "That you, Nolie?"

The door opened and a masculine hand eased through the crack, a chocolate-frosted cupcake sitting on the palm. A single candle flickered from a mountain of frosting.

Darlene sat up and swiped at her cheeks. "Henry?"

The door opened wider, revealing the mayor's sparkling blue eyes. "Hello, sunshine. Thought maybe you could use a little cheerin' up."

"Wait a minute." She reached for a tissue, blew her nose, smoothed her hair, and modestly arranged the sheet over her chest. "Come on in."

He walked into the room and offered her the cupcake. "Make a wish, then you can blow out your candle."

She gave him an uncertain look, then closed her eyes and wished that Henry would remain forever and foremost hers even though she didn't deserve him. Then with a single quick breath, she blew out the flame.

He perched on the edge of her bed and plucked the candle from the frosting. "You can be our official taster. This is one of the one hundred forty-eight cupcakes your sisters and I whipped up tonight."

She ran her finger through the icing and tasted it. "Pretty good." She narrowed her eyes. "Did this come from a can?"

He gave her a look of mock horror. "Would I do that? We used your recipe—milk and butter and cocoa and confectioners' sugar. I promise, no cans were involved."

"And vanilla." She took another taste. "You didn't leave out the vanilla."

"No, sweetie, we didn't." He dropped a napkin onto her lap. "You can eat the whole thing. That's number one hundred forty-nine. I didn't think it'd be right to deliver cupcakes in your name without first getting your approval."

"And if I don't approve?"

Again the horrified expression; then he shrugged. "Then I suppose we're going to have a long night."

A long night of Henry and Carlene working together in her kitchen? Not going to happen.

She pulled the paper liner from the base of the cupcake, then took a bite. "Pretty good," she said, swallowing. "Light and tender. But plain—where's the caramel?"

"Keep eating," Henry urged.

She took another bite and found a solid patch of caramel that tickled her taste buds.

She gave him a surprised smile. "Mission accomplished, sir. You can go home and get some rest."

"Your sisters will be glad to hear it." He stood and dropped a kiss onto her forehead. "How are you feeling? Nolie said you had a bit of trouble earlier tonight."

She lowered her gaze and hoped he hadn't noticed her puffy eyes. "I'm okay. Can't wait to get out of this bed, though. The doctor's coming Monday, and I'm hoping he'll give me something to help me get around. A walker would make me feel about a hundred years old, though—"

"I'm sure the doc will have what you need. He knows it's impossible to keep a good woman down." Henry lifted her hand, squeezed it, then pressed his lips to her fingertips. "I'd better skedaddle, or Nolie will put me to work washing dishes. Good night, sugar."

"Night, Henry." He took a step, but held her hand until he absolutely had to let go. She smiled, keeping an eye on him until the door closed. Then she lay back and steeled herself to endure a few more frustrating days of bed rest.

Nolie would tell her to count her blessings, so maybe she ought to try that. She was getting better. The promised cupcakes would be delivered. And though Henry had come running when Carlene needed help, apparently he hadn't been *completely* charmed by Carlene's enticements.

He still cared enough for the ordinary sister to bring her a cupcake.

*   *   *

After two weeks of fuzzy thinking, Darlene rejoiced when the doctor told her she should begin to ease off her pain medication. Then he wheeled in a motorized scooter, an unexpected delivery. Though the scooter was too heavy to carry upstairs, it did allow Darlene to navigate the main floor of the house without putting weight on her broken foot. She was finally able to visit her beloved kitchen, and wasn't surprised when Nolie and Carlene happily stepped aside so she could resume her role as head cook.

Dr. Morgan also removed Darlene's temporary cast and replaced it with a giant black boot—an unsightly, heavy encumbrance she hated. She couldn't remove it and shouldn't get it wet, which meant she had to keep wrapping her foot in plastic garbage bags if she wanted to take a bath or a shower.

But at least she could hobble around under her own power.

The Fourth of July fell on a Wednesday, and Darlene had never been more grateful for her motorized wheels. Nolie and Carlene left for the parade early, and though Darlene felt her face warm when Erik put her scooter in the back of his pickup and delivered her to Henry like a piece of furniture, her friends quickly surrounded her and made her feel welcome. Once again she sat in the mayor's box to watch the parade, and her heart stirred with gratitude and patriotism when the color guard and local scout troops marched by.

She gaped in surprise when Nolie appeared behind the Girl Scouts, her bicycle trailing red, white, and blue streamers as it towed a child's wagon loaded with coin-filled Mason jars. Someone had taped a large poster to the side of the red wagon. "Dogs and cats are dying," the poster read. "Will you give a dime?"

Darlene elbowed Henry. "Did you know about that?"

He followed her pointing finger. "About Nolie? Sure. She's been working with the ASPCA for a while. She wanted to surprise you."

"I'm surprised, all right. I always thought she was too shy to do that kind of thing."

"Even shy people will do a lot to support a cause they believe in."

Henry swiveled to see the next float, then nodded at the approaching tractor and trailer. "Here's another example."

Darlene tilted her head to see the next entry. Several women stood on a simple float, its sides decorated with crumpled napkins stuffed into chicken wire, its surface covered with plastic pumpkins, faded scarecrows, and bales of hay. Edna Higgins's crackly voice came through a battery-powered megaphone: "Support the Fall Festival. Sponsor a Pumpkin Squash Pageant contestant today."

Darlene was about to remark that Edna didn't have a shy bone in her body when she spotted Carlene standing on the raised platform, a rhinestone tiara on her head and a sash draped over an overblown red chiffon dress that would have looked better on a girl of twenty. On the sash someone—probably Edna—had spelled out *Miss Buttercup Squash 1980* in glittering three-inch letters.

Misreading Darlene's stunned expression, Henry grinned. "I knew you'd be pleased. The committee kept begging Carlene to do this; she kept saying she didn't want to, and finally Edna asked me to tell her we'd consider her participation a favor to the community. So she agreed, but like I said—she didn't want to at first. Your famous sister is a lot shyer than I realized."

Carlene, shy? Darlene recoiled from Henry's eager expression and tried on a smile that pinched like a bad pair of shoes.

Carlene wasn't shy . . . though she could certainly be aloof.

But Henry hadn't grown up in the same house as Carly, so he didn't know her well. He hadn't asked for movie money only to be told Momma had no extra cash because Carlene needed new music books. He hadn't begged to spend the night with a friend from school only to be told no, Carlene had a recital that evening. He hadn't been told to stay home and watch Nolie while Momma and Carlene went off to Tallahassee for another audition. He hadn't lain in the soft darkness of his room and listened to Momma and Carlene whisper about their exciting plans for the weekend.

Momma may not have intended to treat Carly like her favorite, but she did. And Carly may not have meant to act like a prima donna, but since she usually got special treatment, she came to expect it.

Once the world discovered Carly's voice, it didn't take Darlene long to realize that some people—because they were powerful or rich or talented or smart or royal—were treated differently than ordinary people. Carlene was one of the special ones and Darlene wasn't. As a teenager, life really seemed as simple as that.

The rest of the parade passed uneventfully, and Darlene sighed in relief when Erik appeared to help her load her scooter back into his truck. They rode home in silence, and though Darlene sensed that something weighed on the preacher's thoughts, he didn't mutter a word of complaint when she asked him to drop a stack of bills and a birthday card in the mail for the next day's pickup. Maybe he was discouraged by the lack of mail—as far as she knew, he hadn't received any positive answers to the resumes he'd sent to churches in need of pastors.

Back at Sycamores, she gave Erik directions as he pulled hamburger patties from the fridge and fired up the grill. Then, wheeling from pantry to counter to table, she arranged the hamburger buns and trimmings on the table. Doing something with her hands felt good. She'd keep busy until Carlene, Nolie, and Henry arrived. They'd eat together and then she'd go inside for a nap. The holiday had worn her out.

Carlene swept through the back door, still wearing that red chiffon dress and high heels. She stopped in the kitchen and pointed at Darlene. "By the way," she said, tilting her head as if she'd just remembered something. "I have a question for you."

Darlene had questions, too—why was Carlene still wearing that ridiculous getup, and why had she painted herself like a hussy for a Fourth of July parade? Somehow it seemed sacrilegious to preen and peacock on such a hallowed holiday.

But she bit her tongue as Carlene ducked into the garage, then staggered back into the kitchen, her steps impeded by two huge garbage bags, both of them bulging.

Darlene eyed the bags with suspicion. "What's in those?"

"Garbage, what else?" Carlene smiled as if surprised by the question. "This one"—she nodded at the bag in her right hand—

"is filled with soft-drink cans, and the other is stuffed with paper goods. Yesterday it occurred to me that we haven't been sorting the trash since you got hurt, so I need to know where you keep the recycle bins. I'd have asked Nolie, but she wasn't around much yesterday." She laughed. "Guess we now know why—she was busy at the ASPCA. I'm so proud of her, getting out of the house to do something different."

Darlene stared wordlessly at the bags, each neatly sealed with a twist tie, one clinking with cans and the other rustling with paper. Carlene must have spent a couple of hours picking through the trash, getting her manicured hands filthy while she sorted aluminum cans from paper and dog hair and fabric scraps and potato peelings . . .

Stifling a sudden urge to laugh, she rubbed a finger over her upper lip.

"Darly? Your recycle bins?"

Darlene looked at her twin with amused wonder. "Honey, trash is trash. We take it to the dump a couple of times a month, and it all gets burned up or buried. So I'm afraid you did all that work for nothin'."

Carlene's patient expression hardened into disapproval. "What do you mean? Surely the county recycles."

"I don't think so. In fact, I'm pretty sure they *need* trash to fill in that marshy area around the river. You big-city people may have to help your trash collectors out by sorting garbage, but we don't. So you might as well get used to the idea of tossin' stuff away. It all goes back to the earth, anyway."

Carlene lifted her chin. "Recycling isn't a big-city idea! It's simple common sense. If you cared about the environment—"

"If more people cared about the environment, they wouldn't buy so much doggone stuff in the first place," Darlene interrupted, certain that Carlene was about to launch into a lecture. "We reuse what we can around here and what we don't eat, the dogs usually do. We compost for the garden, we use natural fertilizers, and we print on both sides of our computer paper. We don't splurge on chiffon, we think red is too brash for a lady, and we don't paint our faces with so much goop that we glow in the dark. So save your breath before you deliver a big-city sermon, Miss Recycle Bin. Just set those bags out for Erik and he'll take them to the dump next week."

Carlene snatched a breath, probably preparing to say something else, but Darlene put her scooter into gear, executed a perfect three-point turn, and smiled a grim smile as her tires squealed on the kitchen floor.

She hadn't rolled five feet before her mind blew open, unveiling the reason for the spark of irritation that had been smoldering since the afternoon. In her filmy dress and sparkly sash, Carlene had unearthed memories of that other Miss Buttercup Squash Pageant, the event Carly won.

The afternoon before the big night, Carly ran around upstairs in shorts and a tee shirt while everyone else at Sycamores indulged her whims. Fluttering around Carly like a moth drawn to the light, Grandma plied Carly with dainty sandwiches and slices of fruit. Momma brought in a woman to set Carly's hair and do her nails, and enlisted Nolie to wash the car so Carlene would arrive at the festival in a gleaming chariot.

Griff, who'd been a fixture at the house in those days, wasn't allowed upstairs, so Carlene went down and took a stab at making him feel needed by modeling her pageant gown for his approval. "I need you"—she twirled slowly on a leatherette footstool with her hair in curlers—"to tell Darlene when the hem is right."

Sitting on the floor, barefoot and bedraggled, Darlene held a row of straight pins between her tight lips and looked at Griff.

"I don't know nothin' about hems," he protested, leaning on the sofa pillows.

Darlene would have offered advice, but she couldn't speak with pins in her mouth.

"You want to see just a hint of shoe," Carly said, "but you don't want the dress to drag on the floor."

Darlene shook her head and turned the raw edge under, then stuck a pin in the fabric. She pinned about ten inches around the dress, then looked pointedly at Griff.

He grinned, understanding her unspoken message. "There—that looks perfect."

"Are you sure?" Carlene peered downward, lifting the skirt slightly as she pressed the fabric against her abdomen. "It looks short to me."

"It looked fine until you touched it." Griff winked at Darlene, and she smiled her thanks.

Her heart flowed toward him as she resumed her pinning. Griff was more like her than he was like Carly, but opposites were supposed to attract . . .

A few minutes later, Carlene came back into the living room wearing shorts and a blouse. Darlene said nothing as her sister dropped a kiss on the top of Griff's head and then dropped her pageant gown into Darlene's lap. As Carly went back upstairs to be made even more beautiful, Darlene threaded her needle, smoothed out the pinned-up hem, and cast a quick smile at the young man trying to focus on a televised football game.

And as she sewed, she made a decision: she wouldn't mind if Carlene won the pageant and left Peculiar for greener pastures. But she'd do anything she could to prevent Carly from taking Griff with her.

The heartache of that day resurfaced as Darlene gripped the handle of her scooter. Some memories could not be eradicated, no matter how much time passed.

Chapter Fifteen

*T*he remaining weeks of summer blew by like falling leaves, inevitable, monotonous, and depressing. Darlene chafed at the restrictions imposed by her broken foot, but with each passing week she was able to participate in more of her usual routines.

Early August brought an unexpected surprise when Carlene announced that she'd found a job. One hot afternoon she flew into the kitchen grinning like a crazy woman. When Darlene asked what was up, Carly said that a Dr. Jonathan Carlisle from FSU had officially secured a position for her as a part-time voice instructor. And because Carlene mentioned she was staying at Sycamores in order to help her incapacitated sister, he arranged for three voice students who lived in the area to come to Sycamores for their weekly voice lessons.

While Nolie offered congratulations, Darlene stiffened at the word *incapacitated*. Dr. Carlisle probably thought Darlene bedridden and Carlene some sort of Florence Nightingale.

"Of course I'll need to have the piano tuned," Carlene said, practically giddy with the news, "but it probably needed tuning anyway. How long has it been, Darly?"

"Hmm?" Darlene looked up, distracted by the unsettling possibility that Carlene might be around even longer than expected . . . how many months was this teaching job supposed to last?

Carlene jerked her thumb toward the living room. "The piano. When did you last have it tuned?"

Darlene frowned. "Let's see—we had someone come out when Katie started taking piano lessons."

"And when was that?"

Darlene hesitated, but Nolie answered for her. "Nineteen ninety. I remember because I embroidered a little piano and the date on Katie's birthday apron that year."

Carlene settled the matter with a satisfied smile. "Okay, then. We're definitely having the piano tuned. Let's hope the instrument doesn't need a complete overhaul."

Her voice students—two young women and a young man—showed up the second week in August, their arrivals followed by hour-long sessions in which the living room echoed with opera arias and endless notes floating up and down a melodic road to nowhere. Darlene quickly discovered that she couldn't escape the noise: because the living room occupied the center of the house, the music reverberated through the building, echoing through the marble foyer and vibrating the floorboards of the second floor.

One night at dinner Nolie joked that her dogs liked to howl when the voice students sang. "But they never howl when Carly sings." She tilted her head and looked at Carlene, her eyes wide and guileless. "Why is that, I wonder?"

Carlene shrugged off the observation, but Darlene stopped eating to consider the question. When she was younger, Carlene sang all the time—she'd practice in the living room, in the shower, and in the foyer, where the stone floors amplified the sound and bounced it to the high ceiling. She sang like a canary when they were in high school, but Darlene couldn't remember Carly singing anything since she'd come back.

"What's up with you?" She stared at her twin. "You've been as silent as a ghost since you've been home."

Carlene smiled a lopsided smile and winked at Erik. "Hard to satisfy, isn't she? You'd think she got her fill of me while we were growing up."

"I did," Darlene said. "You used to sing so much it drove all of us crazy. But now—not a peep."

Carlene forked a bite of chicken and dragged it through a pool of gravy. "Maybe I'm tired of music, did you ever think of that? After thirty years on the stage, doesn't a woman deserve a bit of rest?"

Darlene shrugged. "Sure. But I thought you liked to sing."

"I did, back then." Carlene swallowed hard. "But when you do something professionally, it's not so much fun after a while. It's work."

Sensing that she'd stumbled onto a touchy topic, Darlene let the matter drop.

While Carlene taught her students, Nolie worked with her dogs. Darlene wished Nolie well, but warned her to keep her dogs, thermometers, calendars, and temperature charts out of the kitchen. "I don't want to know anything about canine reproduction," she said, pressing her hands over both ears, "and I don't want you turning my kitchen into a puppy factory. Do what you have to do, just don't give me details."

After Darlene spent seven full weeks of hobbling around with the help of crutches, the scooter, and the shoulders of various friends, Dr. Morgan came by to free her from her burdensome boot. "I still want you to take it easy for a while," he said, his expert fingers probing her oddly naked foot. "No jumping, no running, and don't let anyone step on these newly set bones. I'm going to fit you with a device that will probably make all those things impossible, but you'd be surprised how some patients manage to circumvent my instructions."

She groaned when she saw him lift another device from a box. "Not another boot!"

"Easy there," he said, smiling. "You can take this one off when you need to."

Dr. Morgan then fitted her with a "bubble boot"—a cast she

could remove when she wanted a shower or bath. In three months, the doctor assured her, after she completed her physical therapy, she could leave the bubble boot behind and do everything she'd been able to do before her fall.

After the doctor left, Darlene flipped the pages of her pocket calendar and counted weeks—she should be finished with boots, therapy, and canes by the end of October, just before the Fall Festival. What perfect timing!

When her bubble-boot days were over and the college semester ended, surely Carlene would realize how bored she was in Peculiar. How could this little town compete with the bright displays of Christmas lights in the Big Apple? Right after the holidays, if all went well, Carly would say her farewells and go back to New York. She would probably feel like she'd spent months living in exile, and surely she missed her friends and neighbors . . .

One night as they sat in the living room watching a movie on TV, a commercial for a traveling Broadway show flashed across the screen. From the corner of her eye, Darlene noticed that Carlene watched the commercial with wide eyes and a frozen expression. When it finished, Carly wiped a tear from her cheek and continued eating her popcorn as though nothing was wrong.

Quietly stroking Cary Grant, Darlene peeked at her sister. "Do you miss it?"

Carly picked up a few more popcorn kernels. "Miss what?"

"The theater. Momma always joked that you loved it so much we might never see you again unless we bought a ticket."

When Carlene turned away, Darlene braced herself for a joke or a snide remark. But a sad smile curved Carly's lips. "Sure I miss it," she said, her voice low. "But if you spend all your time missing what's missing, you'll miss all the good things you could be enjoying." She released a false, three-noted laugh. "Sounds like something Nolie would embroider on an apron, doesn't it?"

Darlene smiled, remembering another movie and another night years before. She'd gone to the drive-in with Carly and Griff, a so-called double date with Jimmy Joe Miller, Griff's cousin from

Atlanta. She sat on the back seat of Griff's Volkswagen Beetle and squirmed to see the movie screen. Carly and Griff were in the front, but Carly left her seat to sit on the small pillow Griff carried in his car so she could be next to him—practically in his lap. Her arms went around his neck, her lips pressed to his.

This wasn't a movie date; this was a make-out session.

Darlene sighed heavily and tried not to look at Jimmy Joe. He leaned against the door of the car, his head propped on his hand, apparently intent on following the adventures of Superman. Carly had picked the feature—she liked Margot Kidder and Griff had always liked Superman comic books. But neither of them was paying much attention to the movie.

"Hey." Darlene kicked Carlene's posterior with the toe of her shoe. "Some of us might like to see the screen, you know."

Carlene and Griff kissed a minute longer, then Carly giggled and pulled away. "Sorry. It's just that we really don't get to see each other much."

"You see each other all the time," Darlene groused, trying not to stare at Griff's mesmerizing profile. Every kiss he gave Carly felt like a dagger in Darlene's heart, so if they intended to make out all night—

"Maybe you're right." Griff settled his arm around Carly's shoulder, then looked at her with tender concern. "You comfortable? We could get out and sit on the blanket—"

"You don't have to do that," Darlene said, panicked by the idea of being alone with Jimmy Joe, a virtual stranger. "Just stay put so we can see the movie, okay? That's all I'm askin'."

They watched the film in silence—saw Superman grow up on the farm, then head to the big city—and when Clark Kent walked into the *Daily Planet* office, Griff looked down into Carly's eyes. "I love you, girl," he said, a teasing note in his voice, "but if you decide to stay in the big city, I don't know if we're gonna work out. I'm pretty much a small-town guy."

"You could learn to like the big city," Carly purred. "After all, a city is the same as a small town . . . 'cept there's more of it."

Griff playfully tapped the end of her perfectly powdered nose, then gestured to the on-screen images of Superman's Metropolis. "In a town like that, I'd feel as out of place as a bucket under a bull."

Carlene gave him a quick kiss, then nestled back into the curve of his arm. "Home is where the heart is, haven't you heard?"

Jimmy Joe shot the couple an irritated look, then tilted his head to see the screen again. He had been ignoring Darlene for half an hour, but she really didn't care. She had an unobstructed view of Griff and could eavesdrop with ease . . . and what she'd just overheard made all the awkwardness worthwhile.

Carlene was bound and determined to have a career on Broadway . . . and Griff had just declared that New York wasn't for him. They may have been teasing each other, but some teasing was as serious as a snakebite. She only had to look at Griff to know he wasn't joking, but Carly wouldn't see the truth. She was too set on her dreams to ever see that Griff would despise New York City.

For months Darlene prayed that God would honor her heart's desire and grant her prayers. Hadn't she spent years sacrificing for Carly's sake? She hadn't complained nearly as often as she could have, hadn't been too terribly resentful, and she honestly wanted Carly to accomplish her dreams. With all that to her credit, couldn't God find a way for Griffith Young to look at her and see *her* gifts? To realize that she loved him every bit as much as and maybe even more than Carly?

That night she'd seen the first glimmer of hope. Carly and Griff might have been head over heels with each other, but life would force them apart because Carly was set on New York and Griff was set on staying put. And once they separated, Griff would be lonely . . . and then he'd need Darlene.

Darlene shifted in her chair as guilt seeped into her memories. Maybe she did take things into her own hands, or maybe it all worked out the way God wanted it to. Who could say?

"By the way"—Carlene said, gesturing with a handful of popcorn—"I'm supposed to decorate the bathrooms of Chattahoochee High School's auditorium for an upcoming community-theater production. Can you help me make some pretty baskets filled with all the goodies you'd ever want to see in a women's restroom?"

"Sounds like fun. What's the play and when is it?"

"*The Mikado.*" Carlene released a heavy sigh. "And it's on the fourteenth and fifteenth of next month."

"Is it going to be any good?"

"It's going to be interesting. The first time I heard Walt Jenkins sing, the hair at the back of my neck snapped to attention." She shook her head. "I don't think that man knows how to hit a pitch straight on. He slides from note to note like a steel guitar."

Darlene broadened her smile in approval. Maybe this theater commitment was another obligation keeping Carlene in Peculiar. But soon, with her help, Carlene's theater involvement would become a promise kept.

Then surely Carlene would be going home.

Wearing her favorite apron—made of paw-print fabric and custom designed with pockets for a thermometer, treats, dog brush, ovulation chart, and fertility test strips—Nolie stood at the kennel gate and warily eyed her beloved girl. If the outward signs could be trusted, Lucy's ovaries were preparing to release several eggs.

Standing by Nolie's side, Ricky whined and pawed the gate. "Sorry, bud, but you can't go in," Nolie told him. "We want you to wait for the perfect moment."

From the corner of her eye Nolie saw Erik approaching, a shovel and trash bag in his hand. Bless his heart, every couple of days he armed himself with the appropriate tools and went out to scoop poop. She never asked him to do it, figuring that her dogs were just enriching the soil, but she'd never been able to walk through the lawn without watching her step, either.

"Hey." Erik adjusted his ball cap to keep the sun out of his eyes. "How's Lucy doin'?"

"Getting close, I think." Nolie pulled the fertility strips from her pocket and held up the package. "Got these from Doc Hensley, who swears by 'em. He said not to let Ricky near her until I was sure the time was right."

Erik dropped his trash and shovel, then leaned on the kennel fence. "And how do you know when that is?"

Nolie squinted at the thin strips. "Apparently the tip of this little slip of paper will turn red when you, um"—she felt herself blushing—"follow the directions. Then I can let Lucy out and hope she lets Ricky approach."

Erik grinned. "Are they like those strips you dip in a pool to test the chlorine level?"

"I've never had a pool, but probably."

"In another lifetime, I spent one summer as a pool boy. But let's keep that between you and me, okay?"

She giggled, struggling to imagine him in sunscreen and swim trunks. "Doesn't seem very pastoral."

"It wasn't. But I wasn't born a minister, you know. And at this rate, I may not die one, either."

Nolie softened her smile. She wanted to say something comforting, but he probably knew every assuring Bible verse and cliché.

"You'll find something," she finally said. "The right thing will come at the right time. I really believe that."

"You do?"

"I do. You're too special for God to leave you on a shelf, Erik." Though she could feel her cheeks burning, she forced the words out because he needed to hear them.

"Thanks for that." Erik propped his chin on his folded arms as he studied Lucy. The dog lay in the shade of her doghouse, calm, relaxed, and smiling. "She doesn't seem to miss Ricky very much. Poor boy's goin' crazy out here, and she's just bidin' her time."

"I think she enjoys being pampered." Nolie brushed sweat-soaked hair from her temples. "But that's only fair—most of the time Ricky beats her to the food, the toys, and the best dog bed. Maybe she deserves special attention every now and then."

Erik looked at Nolie as if he would say something else, then pulled himself off the fence and picked up the shovel and trash bag.

"I guess I'd better get busy. Wouldn't want Miss Darlene to look out the window and think I'm not earnin' my keep. By the way, how's she doin' with her foot today?"

"Just fine." Nolie smiled. "She's done with that scooter, though she'll probably be relyin' on crutches or a cane for a while yet. Dr. Morgan is making her go to physical therapy twice a week in Tallahassee."

"Does she need me to drive her?"

Nolie giggled. "Believe it or not, Carly wants to do it. Darlene didn't want to trust her—kept saying Carly hadn't been drivin' long enough to go out on the interstate—but Carly kept goin' on about how they needed to spend more time together, so Darly finally gave in. Then she pulled me aside and said she'd be awfully grateful when Carly went back to New York, because all this togetherness is wearin' her out."

Erik laughed. "You do a good job of keepin' them straight. If you need any help with the Ricardos, let me know. I don't know much about dogs, but those two must be quite a handful for a lady." A flush rose from his neck. "Not that you can't handle them. Looks to me like you've got the situation pretty well covered."

"I just hope I don't totally mess things up." Nolie squinted in the bright morning light. "My Leonberger breeding business isn't goin' anywhere if we don't have a litter this year. If I don't have puppies, I'll never get Darlene paid back."

He turned, then hesitated, a frown puckering the skin between his dark eyes. "Is your sister holding your feet to the fire?"

"Not at all. But no matter how hard I try not to think about it, the clock is tickin'. Soon I'll have to leave Sycamores. I want to show Darlene and Carlene that I can make my own way in the world." For some reason she didn't completely understand, she wanted to show him, too. Maybe she wanted to show everyone in Peculiar that she wasn't a tragic, lonely figure. She might not be the brightest bulb in the box, but she could take care of herself.

Erik smiled, touched two fingers to the brim of his cap in a quick salute, and struck out across the lawn.

Nolie looked at Lucy, then studied the bag of test strips. If she was going to test Lucy's hormone levels, she might as well begin.

Darlene gripped the passenger's armrest and tried not to stiffen as an eighteen-wheeler pulled to the left and overtook them, horn blaring the entire time. Not until the semi settled back in the right-hand lane did she relax enough to turn her head and glare at Carlene. "If you wouldn't poke along like a turtle, we might not have truckers risking their lives to pass on a two-lane highway."

Carlene smiled, but her knuckles had gone white on the steering wheel. "That guy doesn't have to be in such a hurry. I'm going forty miles an hour, and that's perfectly legal on a state highway."

"The speed limit is generally sixty-five."

"That's the highest allowable speed. Would you take the slice of cake with the highest allowable number of calories? No, you'd take a small one. Besides, we get better gas mileage if we go slower, and I thought you'd want to save money."

Darlene lifted her eyes to heaven in mute appeal, then propped her elbow on the door and chewed on her thumbnail. Her leg ached from the workout she'd given it in physical therapy and now, when she ought to be relaxing, she'd become as tense as a fiddle string from riding with the rookie driver. But who else was going to play chauffeur? Nolie still wasn't interested in getting her license, Henry was stocking shelves at the Wiggly, and Erik had finally gotten around to installing new siding on the guesthouse. Besides, Carlene had begged for the job, saying she needed more experience behind the wheel before she would consider herself a truly competent driver.

Maybe she ought to set herself a new goal.

"Darly," Carlene said, her hands in an exact ten-and-two position, "I've been meaning to talk to you about Magnolia."

Darlene stopped biting her thumbnail. "What about Nolie?"

"I'm worried about her. I know you've lived with her so long you probably don't even notice, but I think there's something wrong with her. Was she ever tested in school?"

Darlene gave her sister a black look. "Tested for what?"

"I don't know . . . maybe autism? Asperger's? I saw a movie last year about this girl with Asperger's. She was highly functional and brilliant in some ways, but something was *off* about her and other people noticed. Nolie's different, too, and plenty of people have noticed, but around Peculiar they simply chalk it up to Nolie being Nolie."

Darlene turned to stare directly at Carlene. "Let me get this straight. Are you saying you think our sister is mentally ill?"

"Of course not." Carlene cast her a reproving look. "Just . . . wired differently."

Darlene turned back to face the road. "Nolie's different, but so am I and so are you. Everyone is different in his or her own way; that's how the good Lord made us."

"I remember Momma saying that Nolie had learning disabilities."

"She had trouble reading, that's all."

"Reading is tied into learning. You need words to think and if you don't know words, you can't think efficiently."

"You seem to know plenty of words, but that hasn't stopped your thinking from getting all screwed up."

Carlene stared out the windshield, only a twitch of an eye revealing she knew she'd just been insulted. "I think Nolie might have OCD."

Darlene closed her eyes. "What's that?"

"Obsessive-compulsive disorder. Have you noticed her little rituals? She spends every morning out in the garden with her dogs. She spends every afternoon in her sewing room, making apron after apron. Every night she walks through the house and checks all the doors—three times. I've counted."

"Maybe she was letting one of the dogs out."

"Three times?"

"Well, she has two dogs. They go out, and then they come in. That's a lot of trips to the door." Darlene opened her eyes and wearily considered the stretch of highway that lay ahead. "And so what if Nolie has habits? You get up every day at eleven and head to the kitchen for a cup of coffee. So Nolie has a routine. You have a routine. We all have 'em."

"No one I know has a routine as exact as Nolie's. And they have drugs, you know, that can help people break habits they've become addicted to."

Darlene pressed her lips together. "No way am I letting Nolie go on drugs. She doesn't need 'em."

"Don't you realize what you're doing?" Carlene tore her gaze from the road long enough to give Darlene a sharp look. "You're acting like her mother, and why should you? Nolie's a forty-year-old woman, so she ought to be able to think for herself and make her own decisions. But she's never gone anywhere. She's never done anything but live at home, make aprons, and let you handle things for her."

"She *likes* making aprons." Darlene crossed her arms. "Other people like gettin' Nolie's aprons, and where's the harm in that? Her aprons are beautiful—she's an apron *artist*."

"Some people would say she's nutty," Carlene countered. "If I told my New York friends that I had a sister who's done nothing in the last twenty years but stay home, talk to dogs, and make aprons, they'd either sign her up for therapy or put her onstage as a performance artist. She's not normal, Darlene."

"Who wants to be normal? Nolie's fine."

"Why don't we let Nolie decide if she's fine or not?"

Darlene blinked. "What *are* you talking about? If something was bothering Nolie, she'd say so."

"Would she? Or would she be too caught up in her routine to even consider breaking out? You've made life so comfortable she's never had to make any significant decisions. She's never worked outside the home, never been married, never—"

"Hush now. That's enough."

Carlene's words raised a specter Darlene did not want to resurrect. After the Buddy Hopkins incident all those years ago, Nolie entered a black depression that didn't lift for months. She moped around the house like a grieving widow, she took to wearing white pants and white shirts, and she stopped washing her hair. Darlene worried about her and so did Momma, even though Grandma said Nolie's melancholy spell was a phase that would pass. Later Darlene couldn't help wondering if all those stressful months didn't hasten the onset of Momma's cancer, weakening her so she went much too quickly in the end . . .

"You weren't here," Darlene whispered, her voice falling to an intense note that reverberated through the car, "during that awful situation with Buddy Hopkins and the wedding. We really did worry about Nolie's sanity in those days. Momma and I were beside ourselves with frustration. Nolie would go out on the lake every afternoon; things got to the point where we'd stand on the dock with binoculars and look for her, half-afraid we'd spot an empty boat because she'd jumped in and drowned herself out of grief."

Carlene said nothing, but kept her gaze on the road.

"After nearly a year of that, Griff got Nolie hooked on making aprons—not that he meant to. She'd made a couple before Buddy, probably for her hope chest, but when Griff said he could use a leather apron, she went back to her sewing machine and made him a really nice tool belt. We praised her to high heaven, grateful she was finally doing something constructive, so she made me an apron and then made aprons for Momma and Grandma. I think she made you one, too, and mailed it off, though I don't remember Nolie sayin' that you acknowledged it."

A deep flush rose from Carly's neckline, streaking her complexion with ruddy blotches.

"So we didn't care when she started makin' aprons for practically everyone in town. We were thrilled that she was takin' regular showers again. She'd sit upstairs and sew and recite poetry, but she seemed better. She may be a little different, but she's so much happier now. So if she wants to sew aprons all day, I say we should let her."

Carlene's expression softened. "I meant to send her a thank-you note."

"Well, hooray for your good intentions. But Nolie's sewing isn't hurtin' anyone, and it may be helping her. So leave the girl alone."

"The *woman.*" Despite the softening Darlene had detected, Carlene's voice held a firm rebuke. "She's a woman, and it's time she moved past whatever happened all those years ago."

Darlene propped her elbow on the door and looked out the passenger window. "I'm not going to bother her."

"Then I may have to take care of things myself."

"Please . . . whatever you do, don't meddle," Darlene said. "If you care about Nolie at all, leave her alone."

Carlene didn't say anything else on the ride home, but Darlene couldn't relax. Beneath that composed actress's face, Carly could be plotting almost anything.

The day after her not-so-pleasant drive to Tallahassee, Carlene stepped out of the Buick, then pulled the drugstore bag from her purse and walked toward the guesthouse. Erik was working on the last wall that needed new siding, and he'd made good progress. He would certainly finish the project by sundown.

"That looks great," she called as she approached. "You've made it look like a new building."

He ran a nail gun across another piece of vinyl, then stepped back to appraise his work. "It does look a lot better. Is Miss Darlene happy?"

"Miss Darlene is hardly ever happy, but I know she thinks you've done a wonderful job." She crossed her arms. "Speaking of jobs—how's the employment search going?"

His shoulders rose in a faint, frustrated shrug. "I keep sending out letters and resumes; I keep receiving polite replies that can be summed up in two words: no thanks." The suggestion of a smile brushed his lips with ruefulness. "Sometimes I wonder why the Lord called me to ministry in the first place—I mean, surely he knew what was going to happen, right? I find myself getting angry—at the church, at organized religion, and sometimes even at God. I can't figure out what possible use he has for a divorced minister no church wants to hire."

Carlene exhaled a slow breath. "I'm not the one to ask because

I'm certainly no theologian. But Nolie said something to me the other day that made me think."

"Miss Nolie?" Lines of concentration deepened under his eyes. "What'd she say?"

Carlene folded an arm across her middle as she searched her memory. "She said that whenever she gets irritated, she remembers the worst thing that ever happened to her. And since she's forgiven that, everything else seems like small potatoes."

A change crept onto Erik's features, a shock of realization. Apparently he was taking those words to heart.

"Before I forget"—she offered him the plastic bag in her hand—"I picked up the razor and shaving cream you mentioned at breakfast. Thought I'd save you a trip into town."

He shook his head as if clearing his thoughts, then accepted the bag. "You didn't have to do that. I was going to go when I finished here."

"I had to go into town anyway, and it took only a minute to run into the drugstore."

"How much do I owe you?"

"For heaven's sake, forget it. Especially considering all you've done for us."

"Thank you." He tossed the bag onto the grass near his tool belt, then bent to pick up another strip of vinyl. "Did Miss Darlene send you off on one of her errands?"

"Actually, today I went on Nolie's behalf."

"Really?" He spoke in a tone of mild curiosity. Odd, considering how interested in Nolie he'd been a moment ago.

Carlene shifted her stance, firmly planting herself on the grass. "I went to the Wiggly to ask Henry to spread the word—for Nolie's sake, I don't think anyone should accept her aprons from this point on. Since everyone in town has to have at least three or four, it's not like they need another one. So it's time to start saying no if Nolie comes toward you with an armful of aprons."

The siding slipped from Erik's grasp as he turned to give Carlene an incredulous look. "I thought she enjoyed giving those away."

"Well, sure, she does. But she spends her life upstairs sewing aprons for people who don't need them and don't really want them. So if everyone will stop accepting the silly things, maybe she'll find something better to do with her time."

A frown settled between Erik's brows. "But . . . she's giving people a gift. To reject a gift from a woman like Nolie . . . seems downright cruel."

The words stung, but Carlene tried to grasp the motivation behind them. Maybe his comment sprang from his own pride; maybe his statement had more to do with his own situation than Nolie's. He'd been hurt by that church in Chattahoochee, so he put himself in Nolie's shoes. But their situations weren't at all the same.

"Nolie's stuck." Carlene crossed her arms. "She's had a hard time getting over a hurt she suffered years ago. That, plus her tendency to be a little obsessive-compulsive, has mired her in a rut. And if you're too comfortable in a rut, sometimes caring people have to pull you out of it."

Shaking his head, Erik picked up the fallen piece of siding. "Maybe it's none of my business, and maybe it's not my place to say this, but I think you're making a big mistake. Don't you see what those aprons represent? Nolie gives them to people she cares for, so what she's really giving is her heart. The world could use more people who are willing to do that."

"You think so?" Carlene narrowed her gaze as a current of irritation sparked her blood. How could this man dare to presume so much about her sister? He was obviously no judge of character, or he'd have seen that his wife wasn't suited for the ministry and that his church people weren't exactly loyal.

The preacher stood still, the siding in one hand, the nail gun in the other. "I do think so."

"Is this an insight you picked up in seminary, or is it something you learned from your ex-wife? Because I find it impossible to believe you have the temerity to stand there and lecture me as if I don't know my own sister."

He flinched as a wounded look filled his eyes, but he spoke in a quiet voice. "Maybe I know her better than you think."

Or better than you do.

He didn't actually verbalize the thought, but Carlene heard it nonetheless.

"Now look here, Erik—"

"Miss Carlene, when I look at Nolie, I see a woman who spent her childhood trailing behind her big sisters because she got short-changed on the love and attention she deserved. I imagine she tried lots of things, desperately trying to please just so someone would love her. For some reason she settled on aprons and flowers, and when she gives those things, she's speaking her love language. So don't go around telling folks not to hear her."

The gentle twinkle in his eye only irritated Carlene more. How dare he imply that Nolie wasn't loved enough!

"Y-you"—she stammered, searching for a way to hurt him the way he'd hurt her—"no wonder nobody wants you to pastor their church."

She braced for his anger, but he shook his head, then looked at her with a smile hidden in his eyes. "Maybe I deserve that, maybe not. All I know is that sometimes it takes an outsider to point out the obvious thing we've been too blind to see. Like the deacon who finally gathered enough courage to tell me that my all-consuming devotion to ministry was making my wife miserable. I tried to set things right, but by then it was too late."

Carlene hadn't expected such raw honesty. She swallowed hard, feeling her cheeks burn as though she'd wandered in front of a searing flame.

"I've a feeling," Erik went on, "that Miss Nolie will stop sewing aprons when she finds something she'd rather do with her time. Then she'll be as preoccupied and frazzled as the rest of us, and the folks who got those precious aprons will miss them."

Carlene snorted. "No one is going to miss those aprons. And I can't see Nolie ever being preoccupied and frazzled—"

"Wait till those puppies are born. They're bound to keep her busy."

"*If* those puppies are born," Carlene corrected. "I hope you're right, but in case you're wrong, please don't accept any aprons from Nolie. Or tool belts. Or whatever she might bring out."

He set his jaw. "Does Miss Darlene agree with this?"

"Darlene"—Carlene glanced toward the house—"knows Nolie has a problem. So humor me, please. Don't accept anything from Nolie."

Chapter Sixteen

*N*olie pulled out her calendar and placed a check mark next to the date. Today, three and a half weeks after the mating at the presumed time of ovulation, she was taking Lucy to the vet to see if he could tell whether the dog was expecting.

Erik had agreed to drive them, so she called the dog out of the house and snapped the leash onto her collar. Erik waited beside his truck and opened the passenger door as they approached. "Should I lift Lucille into the cab?"

"She can jump." Nolie tugged Lucy's leash toward the seat. "Up, Luce. We're going for a drive."

The dog leaped into the cab and Nolie followed, helping her big girl settle on the bench seat. Erik walked around and got in, then pulled out of the driveway.

Wrapping both arms around the dog, Nolie noticed that Erik drove like a man who realized he was carrying precious cargo. The longer she knew him, the more convinced she became that he was a hard worker and a good man who'd married a foolish woman.

"Thank you for offering to take us." She ran her free hand over the back of Lucy's ruff. "I was going to ask Carlene, but thought she might be too nervous to drive with a dog drooling on her shoulder."

Erik chuckled. "I don't know; I think your sister's getting pretty brave behind the wheel. She logged some serious mileage on all those trips to Tallahassee."

They rode in silence until Erik cast her a questioning glance. "So—do you think it took?"

"The physical therapy?"

"I'm talking dogs, not sisters."

She laughed. "I sure hope so. I've seen all the signs—morning sickness, a little vomiting, and general restlessness—but for all I know, I could be imagining things. I mean, sometimes dogs throw up and it means absolutely nothing."

He laughed. "Dogs get morning sickness?"

"Just like people, apparently. And Lucy's been off her feed for the past few days . . . and that's normal, too. According to everything I've read, if Lucy is expectin' Doc Hensley should be able to feel and count the babies today. They're supposed to be the size of walnuts."

Erik grinned. "Why not pecans?"

"Beats me. Funny to think of a dog this big ever being the size of a nut, but I guess we all have to start small."

She looked out the window as an unexpected lump rose to her throat. She'd known that Lucy's pregnancy might be an emotional minefield, but she braced herself to deal with unpredictable feelings. She'd been through stressful situations before. After once spending two hours crying in the bathroom at a friend's shower, she learned to send baby gifts instead of subjecting herself to emotional torture. When everything in a woman yearned for a little one to love, anything to do with childbirth strummed a raw nerve.

The joy of expecting puppies might be a long way from the joy of expecting a baby, but Grandma always said that Nolie should do the best she could with what the Lord sent her. He hadn't sent Nolie a family, but he had sent her two gorgeous animals.

When they pulled up to Doc Hensley's house, Nolie opened the door so Lucy could be first out of the truck. After the dog jumped safely to the ground, Nolie followed, then led the way to the smaller building the vet used as his office. A horse whinnied from an adjacent pasture and in a nearby pen, a sunglasses-wearing sow twitched her ears and snorted.

Erik lifted his brows at the sight of the pig. "Why?"

"Sensitive eyes." Nolie opened the office door. "You should see the goggles Doc's dog wears when they go for a ride."

Erik held the door as Nolie led Lucy into the small waiting room. "Doc?"

Doc Hensley had no receptionist, but he was usually within earshot. A moment later he thrust his head out of the curtain that separated the exam room from the waiting area. "Nolie? And Lucy! Come on, bring her in. How'd the test strips work for you?"

As Erik took a seat in the waiting room, Nolie clicked her tongue between her teeth, urging Lucy forward. "They worked great, I think. I've been keeping careful track of everthing, and I'm pretty sure she's preggers. But I'd feel better if you could tell me for sure."

"Well, let's get her weighed, then we'll take a look." The vet coaxed Lucy onto the scale, then squinted at the digital readout. "One hundred twenty pounds. On her last visit she was one hundred fifteen, so she hasn't gained a lot of weight . . . yet."

Because Lucy was too big to fit on the stainless-steel exam table, Doc knelt on the floor and patted his knees. "Lucy, can you sit for me? And lie down?"

Nolie prodded Lucy and the big dog lay down, then lazily rolled onto her back, exposing her belly.

The vet pressed his stethoscope to Lucy's chest. "Heart and lungs sound good." He grinned at Nolie. "Can we change places? I need to do some work down at the south end."

Nolie laughed and traded places with the doctor. As he pressed his big hand on Lucy's abdomen, Nolie crouched to stroke the dog's nose and rub her ears, murmuring reassurances while the doctor palpated and prodded.

"We have a uterus either filled with puppies or filled with tumors," he finally announced. "And since there were no tumors when

I examined her a couple of months ago, I suspect your girl is more than a little pregnant."

Nolie thought she might burst from a sudden surge of happiness. She clapped, then grimaced when Lucy startled. "Sorry, girlie, didn't mean to scare you. But you're gonna be a momma. Isn't that great?"

"I should ask *you* when the puppies are due," Doc Hensley said, still palpating the abdomen. "At this point, you know more about this dog's cycle than I do."

Nolie smiled, glad she'd done her homework. "Since everybody says whelping can take place anytime from the fifty-ninth day to the sixty-fifth, I suppose we should start looking for signs of labor around October twenty-sixth."

Doc pursed his mouth. "The larger breeds tend to take their time, so I'd put her on the far end of that scale. But it looks like you're definitely going to have puppies by the time of the Fall Festival."

"Wow—that's such a busy time of year. I usually make harvest aprons for Darly's friends and little pumpkin aprons to give the trick-or-treaters—"

"Better start sewing now." The vet slid back and leaned against the wall, then folded his hands atop his bent knees. "I know you've never raised a litter—"

"I'm so looking forward to it!"

"—and you may not realize how much work is involved. If you'll notice, Nolie, there are only eight nipples on this dog's belly. I counted a lot more than eight pups."

She froze, paralyzed by his implication. "Did—did you get a final count?"

"I think—I could be wrong because they're slippery little things—but I think I counted at least fifteen. The other day I read about a Leonberger who had eighteen pups, so apparently large litters are not uncommon in this breed."

Nolie slid back and dropped to the hard floor. Fifteen to eighteen puppies? She had trouble imagining that many dogs in one place. "So—so what do I need to do?"

"For now, take good care of this momma. Next month, I suggest you have someone build a nice, roomy whelping box with protective rails along the sides. The rails are important with large breeds, because you don't want the momma lying on pups and suffocating them."

She nodded, her mind racing, then flinched when Erik stepped through the curtain and moved into her peripheral vision. She'd almost forgotten about him.

"Couldn't help overhearing." He crouched and looked Doc Hensley in the eye. "I could make a whelping box. Do you have some kind of blueprint I could follow?"

"I could get you one." The doctor pushed himself off the wall and stood, then moved to his computer. "Give me a sec to find something appropriate and I'll print it out for you."

Nolie smiled at Erik, grateful beyond words. "Thank you. I didn't know how in the world I was going to find something like that."

"Congratulations." He extended his hand to help her up. "It'll be an interesting challenge. Might even be fun."

The old printer on the counter began to grind. "It'll take a minute or two," the vet said, lifting the lid on the cookie jar next to his computer. "How about it, Lucy—you want a treat?"

The dog flipped herself upright, then rose to a sit, as pretty as could be.

Darlene got in the car and tucked her cane into the narrow space between the seat and the door. Buckling her seat belt, she sighed, grateful she'd finally completed her physical therapy. No more twice-a-week rides to Tallahassee with Carlene; no more listening to her sister's suggestions on how to improve everyone from Nolie to the governor.

Darlene had done well at PT; her therapist even said so. Her foot had mended nicely, she was walking with only a cane for support, and she hadn't developed a limp. "You might be tempted to favor that leg," the therapist warned, "and while I wouldn't be foolish, don't let yourself pamper it too much. It's mended, the bones have knit back together, so it needs to bear weight again. Unless it begins to ache, you have to trust it."

She was ready to do exactly that, eager to get back to the business of cooking, tending to her home, and leading her civic committees. Carlene had been a great help over the past few months, but after today Darlene would no longer need her. She could board the first plane back to New York whenever she wanted to.

But of course she wouldn't, at least not yet. She had to finish the semester with her voice students, and Edna Higgins had asked her to crown this year's Miss Buttercup Squash Pageant queen, since she'd won the crown herself more than thirty years ago. But after the festival, Carly had no reason to remain in Peculiar. No reason at all, unless she wanted to stay for Thanksgiving and Christmas.

Darlene's mouth twisted in a wry smile. Maybe she could announce that they wouldn't be celebrating the holidays this year . . .

She waited until Carlene settled behind the wheel and backed out of her parking space before she began a long-overdue conversation. "I want to thank you," she said, shooting a breezy smile across the space between them. "I don't know what I would have done without you these past few months—and I really mean that."

Carlene lifted a brow as if doubting Darlene's sincerity, then she smiled and pulled onto the highway that led back to Peculiar. "I enjoyed it." She pushed up her sleeves for the drive home. "And it's no more than one sister should do for another. If I'd broken my foot, you would have done the same for me."

"Not if it meant going to New York." The words slipped out before Darlene could stop them, but Carlene didn't seem to take offense.

"No," she said, laughing. "I can't see you living in Manhattan. But if I'd broken my foot here, I know you would have taken care of me. You're a natural caregiver, Darlene. I've always admired that about you."

Darlene sat back, stunned by the unexpected compliment. Carlene didn't dish out flattery, and this was high praise indeed.

She cleared her throat, not sure how to respond. "I'm glad to be done with all that PT. Even though the therapist was kinda cute."

"He was, wasn't he?" Carlene grinned and turned on the radio. "Made me wish I were thirty years younger."

Darlene laughed, too, and relaxed to the music, propping her elbow on the door and crossing her steel-reinforced foot over her knee. Time to press on with the matter at hand—reminding Carlene about her plans to return home.

"Don't you miss the big city?" She glanced at her twin. "I can't believe you've managed to stay away this long."

Carlene smiled as a distracted look filled her eyes. "I miss some things," she admitted. "Being able to go out at two a.m. for a cup of hot chocolate. Mingling with all kinds of people speaking different languages, the cosmopolitan feel of things. And the food! Southern cooking is good, but in New York you can get whatever you want, whenever you want it. Chinese food, Indian, Thai, Greek, Italian. And those kosher delis are amazing."

"I can see why you'd miss that," Darlene said. "But it's not like you said good-bye forever. A brief sabbatical would do anybody good. Time away recharges us and gets us ready to go back to work with new energy. I am so looking forward to being able to stand at my own kitchen sink—"

"That reminds me"—Carlene glanced at the left mirror—"I wanted to discuss something with you, something that may not come as a surprise."

Darlene smiled. Here it came, the announcement that Carlene had decided to go home. She mentally rehearsed an appropriate response: *Oh, too bad! Nolie and I might not see you for another five or ten years, but we will carry on somehow . . .*

"I got a call from my broker yesterday," Carlene went on, "and though sales are still sluggish in New York, she's managed to find a tenant for my apartment. So I've arranged to have all my belongings shipped down here. I also spoke to Dr. Carlisle, and he extended my contract with FSU for another semester." A small smile nudged itself onto her mouth. "I guess I don't have to spell it out—it's finally official. I've decided to live permanently in Peculiar. I've come home, Darly, for real and for good. And I'm happy about it, happier than I ever thought I'd be."

Overwhelmed by a rising sense of disbelief, Darlene sat motionless, her face frozen until Carlene looked directly at her. "Well? Aren't you going to say anything?"

"I'm thinking . . . and I'm surprised." Darlene's voice sounded flat in her own ears. "I never dreamed someone like you might want to live in dinky old Peculiar."

Carlene's laughter filled the car like crystalline tinkling. "How you talk! This is my home. Peculiar may be small and quaint, but I'd never call it *dinky*. The people here are larger than life—even you, Darly. Especially you."

Somehow Darlene managed to shape her mouth into what she hoped was a smile, though it felt more like a grimace.

"Since I'm going to be living permanently at Sycamores," Carlene continued, "I've been thinking about how my furniture will fit in the house. I don't have many pieces, but the furniture I'm bringing is nice. I have a Henredon sofa that would look perfect in the living room, so we could get rid of those ancient plaid couches. I'd love to keep Grandmother's bed, but I'd like to paint my bedroom; that Pepto-Bismol pink is completely outdated. I was thinking maybe a pale yellow or a soft shade of green, something to match the trees outside the window . . ."

Darlene closed her eyes, a scream clawing at the back of her throat. This was a nightmare, pure and simple. Carlene wanted to stay and ruin not only Darlene's life, but also the house. How could she? How dare she?

But Darlene wouldn't raise a fuss now; she would wait and talk to Nolie about how they should brace for Hurricane Carlene.

"Paint," she said, speaking with the odd sense of detachment that always accompanied an awareness of impending disaster.

A storm was brewing; she could feel it in her bones.

* * *

With a stiff gait, Darlene walked through the front door, leaned heavily on her cane as she moved to the living room, and finally sank into the sagging plaid couch that had survived two children, a husband, a boyfriend, and unnumbered club meetings. Griffith Junior once threw up on this cushion. Katie spilled a pitcher of Kool-Aid on a pillow. An escaped gerbil gnawed a hole in the thin fabric that used to line the underside, and most of the springs lost their bounce years ago. Even so, Darlene loved the hulking plaid sectional and so did Cary Grant, who usually took his afternoon nap on the backrest.

Until today, nothing had defeated the couch. But in a few words, a mere throwaway sentence, Carlene had condemned the sectional and forced Darlene to see it as it was—an ugly, slightly smelly, uncomfortable eyesore.

She let her head fall to the crocheted afghan draped across the back. How many times had she curled up in this corner and sewed while Griff watched a football game? This was where she waited for Katie to come home from her dates; it was where she fretted when Griffith Junior went camping with his Boy Scout troop. Henry found the courage to kiss her for the first time on this couch, Grandma used to knit in the opposite corner, and when his heart failed him, Griff stretched out here . . . and died.

She had lived a sizable portion of her life on this piece of furniture, but Carlene wanted to toss it out as if it had no significance whatsoever. Darlene wanted to howl in protest, but how could she express her outrage? After all, Sycamores belonged to all three sisters in equal measure, and Carly might well insist that since she'd had no say at all in the past thirty years, she deserved the opportunity to make a few changes now . . .

But why couldn't Carly see that she was ripping apart the fabric of Darlene's life?

Nolie swept into the room, accompanied by her dogs, and halted in midstep. "What's wrong?" she asked, her observant eyes focusing on Darlene's face. "You look like you're coming down with something."

Darlene blinked slowly, then drew a deep breath. "Carlene has decided to stay in Peculiar permanently. She's having all her stuff shipped from New York."

"Wonderful!" Nolie clapped, her face brightening. "That's so exciting!"

Darlene shook her head. "She's already talking about making changes. She wants to get rid of this couch and replace it with some hoity-toity sofa I've never heard of."

Nolie sank onto the padded armrest of Griff's favorite recliner. "Well . . . couches aren't meant to live forever, you know. And truthfully, Darly, that thing has seen better days. The important thing is that Carly's coming home."

"But this couch belongs to *me*." She grimaced at the childlike whine in her voice. "I know this sounds silly, but don't you think it's disrespectful to barge in and start changing things with no regard for others' feelings?"

Nolie leaned forward, bracing her elbows on her knees. "She's not barging in; she's been here over three months. And she's our sister. This is her home, too."

"Yeah, but . . ." Darlene let her voice trail away, knowing that any argument she might offer could be overruled by common sense and the principle of fair play. Yes, Carlene had every right to change a few things, but if she were considerate, she'd ask first.

"The problem," Darlene began again, "is that if Carlene were thoughtful and kind, if she wanted to keep peace in the family, she wouldn't change anything without first asking our opinion. But she dropped this news like a bomb, and the next thing I knew she was talking about painting the pink bedroom and getting rid of my sectional—"

"You can put your couch in the rec room," Nolie said, standing. "And you can go downstairs and sit on it all you like. Don't be so sensitive, Darly. This is a good thing."

Darlene looked up, disbelieving. "You're kidding, right?"

"Not at all." Nolie's smile flashed, dazzling against her tanned skin. "Imagine—the three of us living together for as long as we're allowed to own Sycamores. It'll be just like it used to be when we were kids. You and Carly will be close again, and I'll be the tagalong afterthought struggling to keep up."

She stepped closer and ran the back of her hand over Darlene's cheek. "It'll be okay, Darly. I promise."

But Darlene closed her eyes, unable to find any comfort in her younger sister's words.

Chapter Seventeen

*T*hose who say Florida is one long summertime haven't learned to recognize the signs of each distinct season. Spring may not bring tulips and daffodils, but it awakens the sleeping azaleas and decorates the live oaks with bright green frills. The indisputably muggy months of a Florida summer are cooled by ocean breezes that frequently drive in showers. While winter can be blissfully warm, periodic cold snaps evoke sweetness from heavy-hanging oranges and remind wintering snowbirds why they came south. And while blazing maples and golden beech trees may be rare in a Florida autumn, every sunset glows purple and pink and yellow over the west coast's gentle shores.

Nolie stepped out of the Coif It Up salon and blinked at the overcast autumnal sky. She could feel a cooler tinge in the breeze, but what had accounted for the chilly atmosphere she felt in the salon?

She had gone to the beauty shop for her quarterly hair trim, but after getting out of LuAnn's chair she greeted the other women who worked there and offered each of them one of her new harvest aprons. Irene, the nail tech, was the first to refuse her gift, blowing on her nails and saying she couldn't possibly accept because she would ruin her manicure if she handled fabrics at that particular moment. Nolie offered to leave the apron on a chair, but Irene shook her head, finally saying that she had more stuff in her kitchen drawers than she could ever use. "Thanks, but no thanks," she finished, refusing to meet Nolie's eye as she searched through her nail polishes.

Irene's lack of interest stung, but then Tiffany, the beauty-school intern, also refused even though Nolie had designed a special pink apron just for her, with compartments for scissors, combs, and wrapping papers, plus a roomy pocket for the skinny rods Tiffany used for permanent waves.

Nolie walked away, confused, but her confusion shifted to consternation when LuAnn turned down an apron as well.

"What is this, a conspiracy?" Nolie managed a weak laugh as she looked around the room. She spied Edna Higgins reading a magazine under a hair dryer. "Edna, wouldn't you like a new autumn apron? I found these vintage tablecloths in harvest patterns . . ."

Edna raised her magazine another five inches, obviously pretending the noise of the dryer prevented her from hearing the question. But Nolie knew better—if she'd been sharing a bit of gossip, every woman in the shop would have caught it even if all five dryers were roaring.

Nolie hoisted her bag to her shoulder and fingered the newly trimmed ends of her hair. She hadn't really needed a haircut; she had come to the salon primarily to make apron deliveries.

What was wrong with those women?

She strolled down to the Piggly Wiggly, walked past the line of grocery carts and the giant display of dog food, and waited next to one of the checkout stations. Monisha Brand stood in line with a loaded cart and after smiling hello at Nolie, she cleared her throat and gave Wanda, the cashier, a pointed look. When Wanda turned to see who was standing behind her, Nolie grabbed an apron and came directly to the point. "Wanda, I made a harvest apron for you." She thrust it toward the girl and smiled at Monisha. "I have one for you, too."

"I'm sorry, sugar." Wanda grabbed a sack for Monisha's groceries. "That's mighty sweet of you, but why don't you give it to someone who doesn't already have several aprons?"

Nolie thrust the apron at Monisha. "From the looks of your grocery cart, you're getting ready to do some baking. This apron might help you feel a little more festive."

Monisha sighed, then her mouth curled in an expression not quite a smile. "Bless your heart, Nolie, and thank you, but I just bought a new apron the other day. Sorry, but the Walmart over in Quincy had 'em on sale."

Nolie pressed her lips together and walked around the checkout stand, then headed to the back of the store. The men in the meat department could certainly use aprons—their white uniforms were always a mess by lunchtime. They might feel a little silly wearing turkeys and pumpkins, but the festive harvest season was fast approaching . . .

"Floyd?" She waved to catch the meat manager's eye. "I've got something for you out here."

Floyd Wilkerson, a nice man who regularly attended the First and Only, came out from behind the counter wiping his hands. "Can I help you, Miss Nolie?"

"I made aprons." She pulled a colorful assortment from her bag. "Looks like you and the 'guys could use something to liven up the meat department. The harvest pattern might put shoppers in the mood for holiday baking."

"Well, Nolie, that's right nice of you." Floyd smiled and plucked one of the aprons from her outstretched hands. The design he selected was gathered at the waistband, a decidedly feminine touch, but he was nice enough to humor her—

Until Melvin Brown stepped out from the cutting room and stopped to murmur something in a low voice. The men exchanged whispered comments, then Floyd handed the apron back to Nolie. "Sorry," he said, looking truly apologetic. "But Mel says we're not supposed to wear anything but the official Wiggly white. Regulations, you know. I'm sorry, Nolie. It's awful nice of you to think of us."

Nolie stuffed the aprons back into her bag, then trudged out of the grocery store, her thoughts churning. She'd been joking when she suggested the existence of a conspiracy, but how could anyone deny it? For some unthinkable reason someone had condemned her aprons. But why would anyone do that? How could anyone be so gossipy and cruel?

She stood on the sidewalk and watched a flock of geese cross the sky in a southbound V. Though she loved her home and her town, on days like this she would give anything to sprout wings and fly away with them, but she couldn't leave. Her life was deeply rooted in Peculiar, and now she had to think of Lucy and her soon-coming puppies.

But she would not let her aprons go to waste. She picked up her bicycle and pedaled across the parking lot to the Goodwill donation box. The Goodwill store was in Chattahoochee, so as she dropped off her harvest collection she smiled at the thought of her aprons traveling all the way to the next town and maybe even beyond.

Whoever started that vicious conspiracy had actually broadened her horizons.

After answering the door, Carlene welcomed Bryce Grant, one of her favorite students, and led the way to the baby grand in the living room. She liked each of her students, but Bryce won her heart the first day they met. The striking girl was attractive, but not a stereotypical beauty. Instead of being blonde, blue-eyed, and self-possessed, Bryce had a gangly, coltish charm that revealed itself through sparkling green eyes and spiky black hair. With a model's stick figure and mile-long legs, she would attract attention anywhere, but she hailed from the little town of Sneads and seemed to prefer dogs and horses to recitals and shopping.

"How are you coming on that new aria?" Carlene slid onto the piano bench. "Do you want to consider it for your sophomore recital?"

"Maybe." A dimple winked in the girl's cheek. "But first I'd like to try it somewhere else."

"Such as?"

Bryce's face flamed. "The squash thing. If I can polish that song, I think it'd work well for the talent competition."

Carlene wrestled with a rush of conflicting emotions. "Are you talking about the pageant? Don't take this the wrong way, but you don't seem like a typical contestant."

Bryce lifted her chin. "Maybe it's time to shake the contest up a little."

"There's nothing I'd like better, but the judges don't usually care for political demonstrations. If you're an honest entrant, fine. But if you want to be in the pageant only to make a statement about women's rights, whale fishing, or some other such thing—"

"That's not it at all." Bryce tensed her jaw, betraying a deep frustration. "I want to enter the pageant for real reasons. There's no way I can continue in school without some kind of a scholarship. Unless my parents get financial help, this is going to be my last year."

Carlene pulled off her reading glasses and studied the young woman by the piano. Bryce held her head high, her dark brows startling against her porcelain complexion and smooth skin. Emotion had whipped color into her cheeks, and her full mouth contrasted nicely with her impish chin.

No, she wasn't the typical pageant type. But she had a certain chutzpah, a vibrant spunk, the judges should appreciate.

"Then I wish you well." Carlene gave her a pleased smile. "I'll do all I can to help you. I love the Fall Festival, and the pageant will always hold special memories for me. I won it, you know, about a million years ago."

Bryce's eyes shone. "How'd you do in the Miss Florida gig?"

"Never made it that far." Carlene shrugged. "At the Fall Festival, I impressed a professor who got me an audition for Juilliard, and my audition netted me a scholarship. I left home right after Christmas, so the first runner-up competed for Miss Florida in my place."

"That's too bad."

Carlene laughed. "I never thought so. Winning Miss Florida—a long shot, at best—probably wouldn't have brought me a place on the stage, which was what I wanted more than anything else. So I'm a big believer in the squash thing, but I'm an even bigger believer in following your dream. Just tell me what you want to do, sweetheart, and I'll do my best to help you."

Grinning, Bryce pulled a chair over to the piano, then reached for her notebook filled with rough sketches of pageant-gown possibilities. Carlene pushed her music aside and studied the pictures, determined to help her young protégée succeed.

Happily imagining all the places her aprons might go, Nolie pedaled slowly up Main Street, then turned onto George Washington Carver Avenue and stopped outside Pauline's Diner. More cars than usual filled the parking lot. She paused, wondering if she had forgotten about some special event. Maybe someone was having a birthday lunch, or perhaps a caravan of tourists had wandered into town. If they stopped at Pauline's, they had to be awfully hungry and terribly lost.

Desperate for a cool drink, she parked her bike in a shady spot, then stepped into the diner, tugging the neckline of her blouse away from her damp skin. A group of noisy people had gathered around a booth near the window and after a single glance, she realized the gathering was mostly male.

Must be hunters on their way to prepare a favorite hunting ground. 'Twas nearly the season, after all.

She picked up a menu from the hostess stand and tried to decide what kind of drink she wanted. Sweet tea? Or Coke? A sarsaparilla float might hit the spot . . .

Shirley, the waitress, tore herself from the noisy table and strode over, a blush darkening her cheeks. "Nolie, honey, good to see you. Want a booth over in the shade?"

The moment Shirley said Nolie's name, an odd silence fell over the group near the window. The change registered in Nolie's consciousness, but only when she peered at the men did she realize why they'd stopped talking. These weren't hunters from out of town; most of them were local men who'd gathered around a stranger. The unfamiliar man at the center of the table bore a striking resemblance to Buddy Hopkins's father, with the same narrow face, thinning brown hair, and long hands. But Mr. Hopkins passed last year, which meant that the scarecrow having lunch in Pauline's must be . . . Buddy Hopkins himself.

Darlene pulled a load of dirty linens from the laundry chute and hesitated when she heard a diesel grumble outside the house. Why would a semi pull up at Sycamores? She dropped the sheets and hurried to the front door. The cab's door hung open and the driver had disappeared. A national moving company's logo covered the side of the trailer, opening the door on a memory Darlene had tried to lock away.

Of course. Carlene had rented her apartment and arranged to have her belongings shipped to Sycamores. Judging from the size of this truck, her belongings included more than a few boxes of books and some clothes.

Darlene blinked as tears sprang to her eyes. Nothing about this was fair. Carlene had chosen to make her home in New York, leaving Sycamores to Darlene and Nolie. This house belonged to them now; it was crammed full of their furniture and packed with their memories. Like Nolie and Griff playing checkers on this porch every night after supper; Katie and Griffy Junior struggling down these stone steps when they were toddlers; Griffy running his little cars and trucks over the smooth floor in the foyer; Katie choosing the color of the deep-pink walls Carlene wanted to paint over—

"Hello?"

She was halfway down the front steps when the distinctive rattle of a rising retractable door broke the afternoon's silence. She strode to the back of the truck and peered at two men standing before a load of stacked shelves, boxes, and furniture. One of them had already pulled out a dolly, but he halted, eyes wide, when he spotted her.

"Ms. Caldwell?"

"I'm Mrs. Young, the lady of the house."

The second man consulted a clipboard. "We have a load for Carlene Caldwell, 19485 Lakeview Drive."

Darlene lifted her chin. "Carlene Caldwell is only a guest here. And we have nowhere to put all this"—she gestured to the contents of the truck—"all this stuff."

The man lowered the clipboard. "Not all of it is for you, ma'am, only about half of what you're lookin' at. We drop off one load here, then drive on down to Tampa to deliver the rest."

"I don't care what that piece of paper says. I'm the owner of this property and Ms. Caldwell is simply a guest. She didn't ask before she called you, so you can just close the door and take that load someplace else."

The two men stared at each other, doubt on one man's face, irritation on the other's.

Darlene looked away and set her jaw. Carlene hadn't done a thing to make room for this stuff. She'd given Darlene no warning about when the truck would arrive. She hadn't even had the decency to consider Darlene's or Nolie's feelings about having their home rearranged to suit her needs.

"Just a minute." The man with the clipboard pulled a cell phone from his pocket. "I'm gonna need to make a call."

"Go right ahead. Call your boss, call whoever you want, but I'm not accepting that load." Darlene crossed her arms and walked to the edge of the driveway, where Nolie's sunflowers bobbed in the breeze.

Wasn't this just like Carly? She was always making plans and not giving anyone the details. Putting other people out so she could do whatever she wanted. Like the time she sang in church without telling Momma, or the day in high school when she promised to take Darlene shopping, then forgot to show up because she and Griff went to the A&W instead . . .

Now Carly was inside the house, listening to that skinny girl sing some foreign song, leaving Darlene to deal with her mess because her precious lessons couldn't be interrupted. If Darlene hadn't refused this delivery, she'd be sweating like a mule and trying to squeeze Carly's boxes and furniture into the garage, the rec room, anywhere she could find space. She'd probably have to pull her car out of the garage to free up that area, which meant her pampered Buick would age twice as fast out in the sun . . .

She turned when the front door opened.

"Thank heaven," Carly called, skipping down the steps. "I didn't hear the truck, so I'm glad you phoned. Now, what's the problem with the unloading?"

The foreman, or whatever he was, pointed to Darlene.

Carly stopped, her face going blank with surprise.

"We don't have room to store your stuff here." Darlene kept her voice calm and even. "If you want it, you'll have to find someone else to keep it."

"What do you mean, 'if I want it'?" Carlene's tone veered from disbelief to irritation. "I wouldn't have paid to have everything trucked down here if I didn't want it."

"We have no room."

"You have a dad-burned mansion, for heaven's sake, filled with worn-out furniture. Anyone else would be grateful for some new pieces. This place could use a touch of class."

"This place"—Darlene swallowed, trying not to make a scene in front of the moving men—"is *not* a mansion, but it *is* our home. You don't have the right to use it as a storage facility."

"You seem to be forgetting something, sister." Carlene's lips thinned. "This is my home, too, and I have every right to live here. I have every right to store things here. For six more years, this house is as much mine as it is yours."

"Ladies." The driver with the clipboard stepped forward, his hand upraised. "If you could just find some space—"

"The garage." Carly gave the man an emphatic nod. "Let me get the keys to back out the car."

"Touch my car over my dead body." Darlene took a step toward the Buick. "I'm not leaving my car exposed to the sun and rain. It'd be rusted in a month."

With burning, reproachful eyes Carlene glared at Darlene. Darlene stared back, fury almost choking her, but at that moment Carly's student ran onto the porch, her cheeks flaming and her eyes wide. "May I offer a suggestion?" She cast a hopeful look first at Carlene, then at Darlene. "Maybe you can find a way to compromise. Maybe Ms. Caldwell can store her things in a rental unit until she has a chance to sort through what you all can use and what really isn't needed."

Darlene crossed her arms. "Peculiar doesn't have any such thing."

"Chattahoochee might." The girl turned to the foreman, a beseeching look in her eyes. "Have you ever seen a storage place around here?"

The man tipped his hat back, then lifted his smart phone. After tapping the screen a few times, he looked at Darlene. "There's a public storage facility in Quincy."

"Thirty miles," Carlene said, pressing her hand to her chest. "If I want to look for a scarf or a pair of shoes, I have to drive thirty miles?"

"You love to drive," Darlene shot back. "So what's the big deal?"

Maybe the point scored, or maybe Carlene simply didn't want to fight in front of three outsiders. Whatever her reasons, she nodded, stepped into the house, and returned a moment later with her pocketbook on her arm. "All right," she said to the man with the clipboard. "Let's go to Quincy and get this truck unloaded."

"I'll drive you," the student called, heading toward her car.

As they walked away, Darlene couldn't stop herself from calling out, "How are you going to get home?"

Carlene halted, one foot inside her student's car as she prepared to take the passenger seat. "Why should you care? You obviously don't want me here."

Darlene stiffened, but she bit her tongue as the truck rumbled to life and pulled out of the driveway, the student's economy car chugging along in its wake. Darlene waited until both had disappeared, then she climbed the front steps and wearily closed the door behind her.

Funny . . . though she'd won this battle, Carly's parting comment left a deep wound. How could her sister make her laugh with delight one minute and make her want to strangle her the next?

Swallowing the sob that rose in her throat, Darlene pushed that troubling thought aside and went back to her laundry room.

"Buddy Hopkins."

His name tasted awful in Nolie's mouth, like milk gone sour. The men around the table froze at the sound of her voice, then scattered like chickens who'd glimpsed a hawk.

Now that her heart had gotten through the shock of seeing him again, she slid onto the empty bench across the table and studied the man she once adored. She longed to ask why he ran away, why he married someone else. Why he broke her heart. Didn't he mean all the things he'd told her? He swore he loved her; had he lied? He kissed her and buried his face in her breasts—how could he do those things if he never intended to meet her at the church?

Buddy said hello without meeting her gaze; he mumbled "good to see you" and seemed to talk to her right shoulder. He rambled on about living in Nashville and how much he enjoyed the seasons up north, especially hunting season.

"And how's your wife?" she asked, stifling the urge to ask why he married Joni Leigh Grayson instead of keeping his promise to her.

He shrugged. "Had to leave her a few years ago. I guess we weren't suited. She complained about me drinkin' too much and stayin' out too late, but she was no angel, either—the woman slept all day and complained all night. Spent every penny I made and then some, so I took what I could and left that baggage behind. Now I consider it a lesson well learned—I never should of married her."

He looked at Nolie then, and in his tentative smile Nolie saw an inkling of the boy he used to be, the young man who had charmed her and made her laugh. The secret boyfriend who would appear at her special place by the lake and spend hours listening to her secrets. The boy who talked her into stripping down to her underwear and swimming with him, then lay by her side on a sun-dappled blanket and talked about his goals for the future. She had listened, captivated by his dreams and enthralled by the idea of being his special someone, chosen from all the other girls, more adored than the rest. Momma had once called her an "oops baby," but she knew she would never be an afterthought with Buddy.

She wanted to ask if he remembered the day they went swimming in late August, if he recalled picking her up and carrying her out of the water, then gently lowering her to their blanket. Did he ever think about the time he stretched out beside her, looked up at the tree canopy, and said their spot was holy like a church? Could he have forgotten turning to her and saying, "Why don't ya marry me, Nolie Caldwell?"

Surely he remembered the way her eyes filled with tears and her hands trembled as she stroked his face, how she said yes because she couldn't imagine giving her heart to anyone else. She gave it to Buddy that day, unreservedly and completely, and he accepted it, promising that soon they'd live in a small cottage with a puppy and three kids, a pretty little place where she could grow flowers and keep a passel of dogs if she wanted to.

They set a wedding date together. He told her to make all the arrangements and as they stared into the treetops, they talked about who they wanted to perform the ceremony and who should be invited to the wedding. It would be a small affair, nothing fancy. She'd sew her own dress and pick the flowers for her bouquet. She'd do everything, she promised, and she'd love him forever . . . all he had to do was show up with the license and a ring.

Now, watching Buddy Hopkins from across the table, she could see that he'd led a hard life. But at least he was living . . . while she'd been spending her life on hold. She tried to forgive and forget, and neither had come easily.

She studied him, noting the lines on his forehead, the deep parentheses around his mouth, the splashes of gray at his temples and in his beard. He stared at her, too, through a thick silence that seemed crowded with questions. Was that remorse she saw in his eyes?

"You're looking awful good, Nolie."

Emboldened by his tone, she finally found her courage. "What brings you back to Peculiar?"

The corner of his mouth dipped in a half smile as he toyed with a spoon. "I dunno—curiosity, I guess. I had to drive through here on my way home from a fishing trip, so I thought I'd stop in. Pauline's was always the best place to catch up on everthing in town."

"I reckon it is." She smiled, then lowered her hand until it covered his. "I want to tell you somethin'."

His eyes shone with hope. "Yeah?"

She nodded. "I have spent years dreamin' of the day I'd see you again. Way back when I cried myself to sleep ever night, wondering why you didn't love me anymore, I thought if I could only see you again, I'd fall to my knees and beg you to forgive me for whatever it was that I'd done." She smiled. "In those dreams, you always lifted me up and swore I was forgiven, and that you'd love me forever. But after a while I stopped dreamin' things like that."

"Nolie—"

"Then I told myself that not showing up for our weddin' couldn't be your fault, that you must have been drugged or somethin' like that. I thought maybe Joni Leigh's brothers kidnapped you and made you take her to get a marriage license. I thought maybe you owed them money or somethin'. I reckoned they must of gotten you drunk or high or just stoned enough so you didn't remember that you'd promised to meet me at the church. That you'd promised lots of other things, too."

"Noles—"

"Hush up, Buddy Hopkins, it's my turn to talk."

He clamped his mouth shut and the look in his eyes shifted to wariness.

"For a long time I prayed that if God would bring you back, I'd be the perfect wife. You could have your marriage to Joni Leigh annulled or somethin' and you and I could start fresh with a big church weddin'. I thought maybe if I were a little nicer to people, a little sweeter to my sisters, or a little smarter, none of this would of happened. But it *did* happen, didn't it?"

She tilted her head to study him from a different perspective. "After a while I dreamed about takin' my grandpa's shotgun to wherever you decided to show up. I was goin' to say, 'Buddy Hopkins, did you forget somethin?' and then I was goin' to blow your fool head off." She smiled and patted his hand. "Later I realized that murderin' you wouldn't be exactly Christian. After all, we're supposed to forgive our enemies and pray for those who spitefully use us."

One corner of his mouth twisted upward, though his eyes remained wide and wary.

"So I've been prayin' for you for well over twenty years now. I've prayed that the Lord would keep you safe, that he'd make you happy, and that he'd always give you whatever you needed. All the time." She focused on his face and softened her tone with seriousness. "Are you happy, Buddy?"

He peered at her from behind a thin fringe of bangs as his mouth pulled into a sour grin. "I reckon so."

"Good. Because you're gonna get not only what you need, but also what you truly deserve. I've been prayin' that, too." She patted his hand again, then slid toward the end of the bench. "Sure was good to see you, Buddy."

"Wait." A frantic look entered his eyes as his hand gripped hers. "Are you happy, Nolie?"

"I think I might be." She bit her lower lip, then smiled. "Yes. Yes, despite everthing you did to make me miserable, I am happier than I deserve to be."

She slid out of the booth and walked away, aware that half a dozen curious people were watching her retreat.

Buddy wasn't one of them; she'd bet her last dollar on that.

Carlene waved good-bye to Bryce, then hesitated in the driveway when she saw Nolie pedaling up the road. Nolie came toward her, dust billowing behind her wheels, then she hopped off her bike and grinned at Carlene. "Been out shoppin'?"

"Been over to Quincy. Had to rent a storage unit for my furniture."

"Oh? I guess that's a good idea."

"I had two options: either rent a unit or mud wrestle Darlene for rights to the garage. And between you and me, I don't think I could take her."

Nolie chuckled as she leaned her bike against a tree, then walked with Carlene toward the front porch.

"You look pretty," Carlene offered as they climbed the steps. "But I thought you were going to get a haircut."

Nolie's smile flattened. "Thanks. I did get a trim."

Carlene frowned, unable to miss the shift in Nolie's mood. "Everything okay? You look like you've just heard bad news."

Nolie didn't answer for a minute; then she squeezed Carlene's arm. "I'm fine. I ran into Buddy Hopkins at Pauline's. And as I left, I couldn't help feeling that I dodged a bullet all those years ago." She turned to Carlene, her gaze unusually direct. "Ever think that maybe God allowed you to be hurt in order to protect you from something worse?"

"I don't know. Maybe."

"Momma always said everthing happens for a reason. Too bad it took me so long to realize she was right." She turned, blocking Carlene's path to the front door. "You know, if you talk to Darly about the best way to use your furniture in the house, you may not need to rent that storage unit."

Carlene stiffened. "Did she tell you about the moving van?"

"What moving van?"

"Never mind. I thought Darly might have put words in your mouth."

"Darly didn't tell me anything." Nolie frowned. "I take it the moving van arrived?"

"While you were out, and Darly wasn't happy about it. Then again, Darly isn't exactly happy about my moving back here."

Nolie's eyes brimmed with concern. "She doesn't begrudge you the right to live here . . . but maybe you should tread carefully before changing anything outside your bedroom. Remember, this is the place where Darlene loved her husband and raised her children. It's been her home for years. It's her kingdom, and it's going to be hard for her to step back and let you charge in, even if it's your right to share the throne."

Carlene snapped her mouth shut, stunned by Nolie's insight. Maybe Darly did love her husband here, but she would never have had that husband if Carlene hadn't surrendered him. But Nolie wouldn't know that. She was only a child at the time.

"Sycamores is not a kingdom," Carlene said, her throat tightening. "It's an old house. And it's going to belong to the county in a few years, so none of us should be terribly attached to it. But try telling that to the Queen of Everything in there . . ."

Nolie chuckled. "I never wanted to be queen. I've always let Darly take charge because homemaking is what she loves. It's what she was born to do."

Sighing, Carlene leaned against a column and let her gaze drift toward the gardens. Nolie didn't know even half the story, but maybe she had a point. After all, if their roles had been reversed and Darlene came to New York with the intention of carving out a television career as a Southern Martha Stewart, Carlene might have a little trouble sharing her home.

Amazing how much wisdom resided beneath Nolie's calm exterior.

"Don't worry, I get it." She gave Nolie's hand a gentle squeeze. "All my stuff is over in Quincy now. Maybe I can talk to Darlene and gradually bring things over or sell some items in the classifieds. After all, I'm not in any kind of hurry."

A thoughtful smile curved Nolie's mouth. "I always knew you were a wise woman."

A few days after running into Buddy at Pauline's, Nolie took her dogs outside for one last potty break before bed. A light rain had come out of nowhere, a steady shower, and though the dogs didn't mind, Nolie stepped under the back porch to keep dry. Shivering in the unexpected coolness, she pulled her warm-up jacket around her and startled when Erik said her name.

"Sorry," he added, lowering his sneakered feet from the edge of an iron table. "But I didn't want you to turn around and be scared to death when you saw me here in the dark."

"Nice rain," she said, grateful that the evening shadows hid the blush warming her face. "What are you doing out here in it?"

She saw the glimmer of his smile in the dim light of a porch lamp. "I like coming out at night—it's a great time to think and pray. I like to watch the stars, but tonight the rain caught me by surprise."

"Rain wasn't in the forecast." She dropped into one of the other iron chairs. "And the sky was pretty much cloudless all day." She turned her head away and grimaced—good grief, why did she get so stupid around him? And why was she talking about the weather?

"By the way," Erik said, "I've been meaning to ask you a favor. If you're too busy, though, I wouldn't want to impose."

She turned toward him, relieved that he'd found something to talk about. "What do you need?"

"I could use a tool belt. I saw some at the hardware store, but the pockets were all the same size. I liked the apron you made for working with Lucy . . . with pockets of different sizes, so everything has its place."

"Oh." She smiled, certain that her cheeks were glowing despite the chill. The women at the salon might not want her aprons, but somebody did. "I'd be happy to make one for you."

"No rush." He shifted in his chair. "You can take your time."

"It's not like I have a whole lot to do."

"Just don't call it an apron, okay?" He chuckled. "Wouldn't want to lose any man points."

She laughed, too. "I don't think you're in any danger of that. And thanks."

"For what?"

"For askin'."

He gave her a puzzled look, then cleared his throat. "I heard something downtown today," he said, "but if this is too personal, we don't have to talk about it."

Her pulse quickened. "You heard something about me?"

He stretched his long legs out again, propping them on the edge of an empty chair. "I heard you ran into what's-his-name down at the diner. Everyone's saying you gave him a fair piece of your mind."

"Oh." She smiled. "That's a problem with small towns—there's not much to do, but plenty of people to talk about you when you do it."

"So it's true?"

She watched the rain falling like ink from a dissolving night sky. "I guess so."

Lucy bounded onto the terrace, ran over to Nolie, and smiled, waiting for a pat on the head.

"Ew, Lucy, you're wet." Nolie ran her fingertips through the damp fur on the top of Lucy's skull. "There. Now go play or something."

The dog bounded off again, but not before shaking all the water from her heavy coat. Nolie lifted her arms and ducked, but she still got caught in the sudden shower.

A few feet away in the darkness, Erik laughed softly. "I don't know why she did that. She's out there getting wet again."

"I think it's instinct." Nolie used her sleeve to wipe water droplets from her face. "She instinctively knows when I don't want to get wet."

They sat for a while without speaking, surrounded by the rhythm of rain on the deck over their heads. Then Erik stood and walked toward her.

Her heart sank at the realization that he was leaving. She moved her legs out of the way so he could pass, but he didn't go anywhere. He sat in the empty chair closest to her, the seat lit by lamplight from inside the house.

"Tell me," he said, leaning forward with his elbows braced on his knees, "tell me how you were able to find peace about your situation. How did you forgive the man who hurt you?"

She studied him. Apparently he'd been thinking long and hard about something that disturbed him. The corners of his mouth were tight, and his eyes slightly shiny. Had he been putting himself through this sort of stressful heart searching every night?

"I struggled, yes." She closed her hands to resist the impulse to stroke his cheek. "But when I saw Buddy sitting there, I realized he had already paid a price. And I'm not his judge—I never will be. He has to answer to God, not only for what he did to me, but for how he treated everyone. Knowing that I'm only a tiny piece of the picture—knowing that, I could smile and let it go. I don't really think about him anymore, and I don't hate him. Truthfully, I mostly feel sorry for him."

Erik hung his head. "It sounds so easy when you say it. So . . . sensible."

"I'm not saying what worked for me will work for everyone—I mean, I'm not much of an expert."

"Aren't you?" His mouth twisted in wry amusement. "Let me see—instead of being angry at that church for running me off, I need to realize they've paid a price?"

"They lost you as a minister. And who knows? Maybe what they did soured other people in town. It's not like divorce is all that disgraceful or rare these days."

"And I'm not their judge—they have to answer to God. Because I'm only a tiny piece of the picture." He smiled at her. "Did I get it right?"

"Sounds right to me." She kept her voice light, not wanting to sound like a preacher herself. "But forgiving is something you do, not something that comes to you when you recite the proper words. It's not a magic formula."

"If only it were that easy." Erik straightened, placed his hands on his thighs, and broke into a friendly smile. "And with that, Miss Nolie, I'd better be heading to bed. Your sister wants me to edge the driveway tomorrow, so I need to get an early start."

"Good night, then. Don't get wet." She swung her legs out of the way, but before he left he pressed his hand to her cheek. Afraid to look up, she shivered beneath his touch, then felt a chill of disappointment when his footsteps crossed the terrace and were swallowed up by the wet grass.

She stood to call her dogs as her mind spun with a dozen unasked questions. Why had he touched her? Was touch his way of saying thank you to a friend? Or did his touch—*could* his touch—mean something more?

Chapter Eighteen

*F*our weeks passed, a warm autumn gradually cooling to the more temperate days of October. With a secretive smile, Nolie watched Carlene and Darlene work out a truce about how much furniture could come from Quincy—not much and only with Darlene's approval. But every few days Carlene would borrow the Buick and drive over to fetch a couple of cartons of clothes, books, or photo albums. On those evenings, while Darlene went out to her committee meetings, Carlene and Nolie would sit in the living room and sift through the boxes, looking at albums or sorting through winter clothing Carly would never need in Florida.

Throughout the early weeks of October, Nolie watched Lucy for any signs of change. The dog's belly had begun to balloon, and during the third week of the month she became unusually restless. At Nolie's urging, Erik built the large whelping box, finishing in only a few hours. When he asked Nolie where he should put it, she decided the main floor laundry room would be the best place. The site was warm and sheltered, indoors, and close to the kitchen and running water.

Lucy had been behaving out of sorts for the last several days.

Once Nolie realized the dog was scouting for a place to have her puppies, she led Lucy to the whelping box, now padded with the dog's favorite blanket and several old towels Darlene donated to the cause. Lucy seemed to understand the purpose of the box, and once she discovered this ideal spot, her appetite waned to almost nothing. Nolie's concern intensified.

Saturday morning Lucy's temperature plummeted to 98 degrees, 3 degrees lower than usual—a sure sign, Doc Hensley said, that labor would begin within the next twelve hours.

Saturday afternoon, while most of Peculiar attended the Pumpkin Squash Festival, Nolie sat next to the washing machine with Lucy's head in her lap. She stroked the dog's silky ears and studied the occasional rippling movements in that swollen belly. Nolie had hoped one of her sisters would be around to help with the puppies' birth, but the festival had kept Darlene and Carlene busy for the past week. Carlene was over the moon about being invited to take part in the pageant, and she'd spent days trying to figure out what to wear when she crowned the new Miss Buttercup Squash. Darlene was preoccupied because in addition to her regular organizational duties, she'd also promised to judge the jam contest and the quilting exhibition.

The Miss Buttercup Squash Pageant was scheduled to begin in a few hours, so neither of her sisters was likely to join Nolie in the labor room. Erik wasn't likely to appear, either. The twins had kept him busy hauling quilts and tables and building booths throughout the day. Nolie had hoped he'd come home for dinner, but after working so hard he had every right to stay and eat homemade baked goods, toss a pumpkin or two, and watch the pretty girls sashay across the stage in their pageant gowns.

As the sun sank toward the western horizon, Nolie found herself completely alone with her pets. She never imagined she'd be alone when Lucy needed her most. A wave of melancholy threatened to depress her, but she tamped it down. She had no time for self-pity, not when Lucy needed her.

Outside the laundry room, Ricky whined and scratched at the door. "Sorry, buddy," Nolie called. "But I don't think Lucy's in the mood to see you right now. Why don't you be a good boy and go to your bed?"

She heard silence, then the slow click of his nails on the floor as he moved away. Poor guy. Just like some human fathers, he was being left out of all the excitement.

As Lucy dozed, Nolie studied the dog's belly and looked for signs of labor. She had never witnessed a canine birth, and she wished she'd looked for a few video examples on YouTube. If something went wrong she could always call Doc Hensley, but he and his wife were probably at the festival. She didn't want to interrupt their evening unless she ran headlong into an emergency.

She propped her feet on the huge wooden whelping box that filled most of the available space. A stack of clean towels waited on the washing machine, and the kitchen lay only a few yards away in case she needed to boil water or grab a handful of paper towels . . .

Lucy flinched, then lifted her head and looked toward her tail. Alarm jetted through Nolie as she peered southward and saw a watery stain seeping onto the quilt . . . brownish liquid, like spilled coffee.

Lucy's water had broken.

Nolie pressed her lips together and drew a deep breath. Okay, like it or not, this situation was definitely progressing. Whining, Lucy got to her feet and began to pace, moving from the window to the door and back again. Nolie held her breath. This was good. She'd read that mother dogs often paced to hurry labor along, so perhaps this was exactly what Lucy needed to do. Or was it?

She closed her eyes and wished that Erik would come.

The dog stopped pacing, then lowered herself to the quilt and rolled onto her side, panting steadily. Nolie's tension level rose— human mothers sometimes panted, too, so this was probably normal behavior. While she watched, a lump appeared at the birth canal, then began to emerge. No, not a lump, but a head covered with a thin membrane, undoubtedly the birth sac. Lucy seemed completely unaware of what was happening until the slippery sac dropped like a shining tear onto the quilt. Then Lucy looked to see what she'd produced.

Nolie held her breath. The pup wouldn't be able to breathe unless someone broke through the membrane within seconds. She was willing to do it, but she'd rather Lucy take care of it herself. Her heart thumped almost painfully against her ribs as she pulled on latex gloves and grabbed a towel. If the puppy didn't start breathing soon, she was supposed to rub its chest . . .

Lucy began to lick at the puppy, tugging at the sac with her teeth. Nolie leaned back against the washing machine, stunned by joy and wonder. Incredible the way Lucy knew what to do. She was tearing at the membrane now, fastidiously removing it with her front teeth, delicately chewing the umbilical cord to sever the connection. And the puppy was mewling! Its high-pitched cries echoed in the laundry room and brought tears to Nolie's eyes.

"You did so good, Luce," she whispered, not wanting to interrupt the new mother's ministrations. "What a beautiful baby you have!"

And then, because she promised herself that she'd keep careful records, she wrote the time of the puppy's birth in her journal and reached for the red nail polish. Two Red Toes would be the eldest, born at 4:47 p.m. She prayed he'd be the first of at least a dozen others.

With a fried Twinkie in one hand and a diet soda in the other, Darlene walked along the fair's midway, smiling and nodding at neighbors she hadn't seen in weeks. The ladies of Peculiar had outdone themselves this year, filling more than a dozen booths with autumn wreaths, canned vegetables and jams, scarecrows dressed in harvest fabrics, and lap quilts in every conceivable color combination. Dorothy Rehnquist was selling lovely Christmas decorations, Deborah Dennis had driven all the way from Tallahassee to exhibit her watercolor paintings, and ventriloquist Jake Jones and his dummy were entertaining the children. Nancy Moser's booth had been a surprise hit—she was featuring Dipsy DoodleCanes, hand-painted canes that were both useful and artistic. Darlene bought one, happy to toss her institutional model into the nearest trash bin.

She smiled at several familiar faces—out-of-towners she didn't know by name but recognized from previous festivals. In the parking lot, she spotted several cars with Georgia and Alabama license plates, proving that the reputation of their little celebration had spread into neighboring states. Next to the parking area, in portable booths at the south end of the fairground, Tommy McNally's carnival barkers sold winding lengths of red tickets to children and teenagers who wanted to take a spin on the Tilt-A-Whirl or the merry-go-round.

"Hey, Darlene!" an unfamiliar woman shouted. "Good to see you out and about. Love your cane!"

Darlene hesitated—was the woman being sarcastic? But since her cane *was* adorable, she gave the woman a smile. "Thank you!"

She finished her Twinkie—an indulgence she would never serve but loved to eat—tossed the wrapper into a trash can, and headed toward the corn-dog stand where Henry was supposed to be working. As she passed the stage where the Miss Buttercup Squash Pageant would begin in a couple of hours, she stopped in midstride. Henry stood in front of the stage, his head bent in conversation with Carlene. What was he doing here? This was the dinner hour; he should be frantically serving corn dogs and French fries and fried Oreos to starving festivalgoers. Yet here he stood, his face crinkling with laughter, one hand resting protectively on Carlene's shoulder.

A wave of painful memories swept over Darlene, nearly choking her. She spun around and started to retrace her steps to the parking lot, where she wouldn't have to guard her expression as she fought against the onslaught of bitterness Henry and Carlene had unleashed.

"Miss Darlene?" She stopped in her tracks as a male voice called her name, then turned. Erik stood near a booth a few feet away, and he was motioning her over. Why couldn't the world leave her alone for a few minutes?

Slowly her unwilling feet carried her toward him. She recognized the woman inside the booth—for years Myra Masters had been renting retail space at the festival to sell her homemade clothing. "Myra." She nodded a greeting, then looked at Erik. "Are you lost or something?"

He grinned, apparently missing her sarcasm. "Look at that." He pointed to a sundress hanging on the wall of Myra's display. "Isn't that material the exact color of Nolie's eyes?"

Darlene stepped back and laughed to cover her annoyance with Erik and men in general. "I wouldn't say her eyes are fire-engine red."

"Not that one; the one behind it. The light blue one."

She gave the dress a brief distracted glance and forced a smile. "Yeah, okay, maybe. What of it?"

"I was thinkin' about getting it for her. She's been workin' really hard lately, and I thought . . . well, I thought she deserved some kind of reward."

Darlene stared at him—hadn't they all been working hard?— then she barked a laugh. "You could buy it for her, but she won't wear it. You know she only wears white."

"Maybe it's time to change that."

"Yeah, okay, and maybe it's time for me to run for president."

She forced a laugh, but apparently it didn't fool her handyman. He examined her face with considerable absorption, then took hold of her elbow and pulled her toward the shade of an oak tree.

"Let's get you out of the sun, Miss Darlene. You're looking a mite flushed."

"I'm fine, Erik. Honestly."

"Really?" He released her, then slid both hands into his pockets. "I know it's not my place to ask, but it seems to me that something's got you upset. I don't need to know details, but could I help?"

She widened her eyes in feigned surprise. "Has something upset *me*? Of course not, everthing's fine, just fine."

"Miss Darlene." He underlined her name with rebuke. "You may think you're talking to a handyman, but I'm a pastor first and foremost, and I know when people are trying to cover something up. You came walking by here at about ninety miles an hour. Something tells me you weren't trying to get in some exercise."

She studied him, wondering if she should take another stab at evading the question. But the set of his chin suggested a stubborn streak, and she didn't think she'd be successful.

So she blew out a breath and let him have it. "It's Henry. I know he's falling for Carlene, and there's nothing I can do to stop him. He's always buzzing around her, and even though she says she's not trying to entice him, how can she help it? I know she secretly hates me because I married Griffith. And Henry! Just when I get to the place where I think I might be ready to get married again, he starts spending time with Carlene. And he's always using that daughter of his as an excuse. His interest in me is nearly gone—if he ever had any real interest, that is. Why should he marry me when he could have the *famous* Caldwell girl?"

She paused, breathless, when the minister put his hand on her arm. "I think I get the picture."

"Then you understand why I'm constantly frustrated."

He lifted one eyebrow. "I understand a lot of things."

"But what can I *do*? I've talked to Henry and I've tried to talk to Carlene, but there's a wall between us and I can't get through it. She pretends to be all sweet and nice, but I know she resents me for marrying her old boyfriend. If she didn't, she'd have kept us in her life. She put a lot more between us than mere miles. I'd love to be close to her again, but how can I? I wish she'd go back to New York, but she keeps coming up with excuses to make my life miserable, first one thing and then the other, and it didn't help when I broke my blasted foot—"

Erik turned slightly, then folded one arm across his chest and pressed his index finger to his lips. "Someone"—he waggled his finger at her—"recently told me that holding a grudge is completely wrong for a Christian. You're a Christian, aren't you, Miss Darlene?"

She blinked. How could he see the hidden problem—that Carlene was holding a grudge—and miss the obvious? Didn't he know her at all? "Of course I am."

"Good, good, I thought so. So as a believer, you want to clear the air between you and your sister, right?"

Darlene frowned. What did the man have up his sleeve? "Of course. It'd be nice to make things right."

"Good. You said she resents you. You said she put things between you. So why not talk to her about those things and uncover the root of the problem?"

Momentarily speechless, Darlene stared right through the man. Talk to Carly about the past? Talk about how and why Darlene snatched Griff up the moment Carly's back was turned? A conversation like that would stir up too much pain and heartache. "That"— she cleared her throat—"would be difficult."

"Why?" The minister's brown eyes probed hers. "You two used to be close. You're twins. Nolie says you did everything together when you were younger."

She sighed. "We did."

"Then what came between you? Was it just the boyfriend?"

Darlene looked down and rubbed her nose. "We drifted apart long before Griff."

"When did this drifting apart begin? Can you remember?"

Of course she remembered. She had begun to feel like an outsider the day Carly sang that solo in church. People buzzed about Carly afterward, the phone rang all that afternoon, and Momma began to look at Carly with an excited glow in her eyes. Within days Carly had been exalted, while Darly slipped to run-of-the-mill.

"I remember," she said, a hair of irritation in her voice. "Everything changed when we learned Carly could sing. Within a few months, she became a diva."

"I see." The preacher's eyes warmed slightly, and the hint of a smile implied that she'd just solved her problem. "Is it possible, Miss Darlene, that you resented your sister for getting so much attention?"

"It's not all my fault. Carly could be a real snot—you don't know how bad she could be."

"Maybe so, but we're not responsible for what others do. Jesus tells us to forgive, so we're responsible for our own actions. We have to forgive the ones who hurt us . . . even if they never admit that they hurt us."

Darlene bit her lip until it throbbed with her pulse. Could the preacher be right? His advice sounded so logical, but she'd never considered her role in the estrangement. She never realized that by forgiving Carly she could free herself from all the problems of her past.

She could forgive Carly for being a diva. For being talented. And for loving Griff first.

She swallowed hard and looked up at the minister. "Is that what they teach you in seminary?"

He smiled. "Actually, I learned it from Nolie."

As Darlene stared into space, the preacher patted her on the shoulder and turned back toward the midway. "You know what they say about still waters running deep. See you back at the house, Miss Darlene."

By six o'clock, seven puppies had arrived in the whelping box. They were appearing every ten minutes now, almost as regular as clockwork. Lucy attended to her duty so vigorously, licking and chewing and biting, that Nolie worried about the new momma's strength giving out before all the puppies arrived.

The new arrivals' mewling must have alarmed Ricky, who was still waiting outside the room. Nolie could hear him pacing, and occasionally he put his face to the crack beneath the door and chuffed so loudly that Nolie laughed. Anyone who said dogs couldn't communicate had never lived with one.

Whenever Lucy rolled onto her side, the pups clamped onto her teats with remarkable tenacity, but as soon as she turned or stood to attend to a new arrival, the other pups began to cry and wriggle over the quilt, blindly searching for the life-giving milk.

"I think," Nolie murmured, "I may need some help here, Luce. I'm going to have to get some formula . . ."

She startled at the sound of a slamming door. Fortunately, it was soon followed by a familiar male voice. "Nolie?"

Thank heaven, Erik had come back.

"I'm in the laundry room," she cried, trusting that Ricky would show him the way. "Lucy's in labor!"

A few moments later, the laundry-room door opened. Erik stared at the scene for a moment, then eased himself through the opening, keeping Ricky outside. "Wow." He looked exhausted, his jeans were dirty, and he was burdened with a rectangular box and a white bag, but his tired face brightened at the sight of so many squirming puppies. "How's she doing? How are *you* doing?"

"I'm fine, but I'm worried." Nolie used the back of her hand to rub her nose, then pointed at Lucy's still-swollen belly. "She's getting tired, and I'm afraid she can't keep this up for much longer. I've got puppies coming every ten minutes."

Erik set his box on the dryer, then placed the white bag on the floor at Nolie's side. "I brought you a couple of corn dogs, in case you were craving festival food."

"Thanks. I am hungry, so I'll eat when I can grab a minute."

Erik crouched to get a better look at the new arrivals. "They're bigger than I thought they'd be."

"Most of them are about a pound." Nolie gestured to the diet scale she was using to weigh the newborns. "Leos are big dogs, after all."

He glanced at Nolie's list and the bottles of nail polish, then grinned. "What are you going to do when you run out of colors?"

"Double up," she said. "Red/pink, Black/green, whatever I have to do. I think I can get several color combinations out of these few bottles."

"I'm sure you can." Erik stood and braced his hands on his hips. "So what can I do to help?"

She looked at him, disbelieving. "You're tired. You have to be exhausted. And this wasn't on Darlene's list of handyman chores."

"Maybe I don't want to be Darlene's handyman tonight." His voice softened as his gaze met hers. "Maybe I just want to be Nolie's . . . right-hand man."

She blinked, wanting to take the time to analyze his words, to ponder their meaning and motivation, but time was a luxury she didn't have. She'd think about his comment later, when she'd be better able to decide if he was being genuine or glib.

"Bless your heart." She smiled in dazed relief. "I have some canine-milk replacer and a couple of bottles on the kitchen table—could you mix up a batch of formula? Doc Hensley said all the pups need to nurse at least a little while to get the momma's antibodies, but we can feed the older ones from a bottle."

"I think I can manage that." Erik squeezed her shoulder, then headed toward the door. "Be back soon to give you a hand."

Nolie exhaled a grateful sigh as she watched him go. He didn't have to come into the house. He could have gone to the guesthouse, relaxed, had a nice night.

But he had thought of her. He had brought her something to eat, and he had come to check on her. Surely that meant something. She tilted her head, wondering, then found herself distracted as yet another puppy poked his nose into the world.

Chapter Nineteen

$\mathscr{S}$tanding in the wings of the makeshift stage, an electric tingle raced up Carlene's spine as Bryce stepped into the spotlight. The girl smiled at the judges sitting in center seats in the front row, the same place they'd occupied when Carlene sang in the Miss Buttercup Squash Pageant. She'd sung a soulful version of "Somewhere over the Rainbow" and practically knocked them off their benches, but Bryce would impress them far more singing "All I Ask of You" from *Phantom*. She had practiced until every inflection and pitch was perfect; no one else's talent would come close in showmanship, crowd appeal, or technical quality.

Carlene held her breath as the prerecorded accompaniment began. With a confidence that belied her years, Bryce took the microphone, positioned it in exactly the right spot, and began to sing. The lovely aria floated over the crowd, and Carlene tilted her head to study the judges' reactions. The female judge, another voice teacher from the university, folded her hands, closed her eyes, and nodded along; both men settled back in their seats and smiled. And why wouldn't they?

On that rough stage, Bryce looked like an angel hovering above a pumpkin patch. The single spotlight caught the sequins on her ivory dress and bounced back in a thousand bright flashes; the fabric of her gown moved like a second skin as she gestured with her toned arms and perfectly manicured hands. Unlike the other girls' long hair that seemed to grow down their backs without rhyme or reason, Bryce's short cut framed her face, highlighting her long neck and slender shoulders. The girl appeared confident, every inch a natural performer, in every aspect a queen.

If she didn't win the title tonight, every person present would suspect that the judges had been paid off.

As Bryce's voice soared above the audience of mothers, fathers, and sugar-hyped children, Carlene closed her eyes and drifted on a tide of memory. She could almost feel the cool metal of the microphone against her palm and the plank boards of the old stage creaking beneath the soles of her new high heels. Thirty-two years ago her heart had pounded so fiercely that the locket on her necklace thumped against her sternum, but she'd spent months rehearsing, so she wasn't afraid.

She took the stage in an emerald one-shouldered dress, her hair carefully curled and sprayed into place. Like Bryce, she made certain to smile at the judges before beginning her song. The accompaniment track began to play, she inhaled to expand her diaphragm, then filled her lungs as she looked for the faces of her family in the audience.

Somewhere over the rainbow . . .

She found Momma and eight-year-old Nolie sitting with Grandma in the third row, their faces tense with secondhand anxiety. Mr. Williams, her voice teacher, sat behind them with his wife, but though Carlene kept searching, she couldn't find Darlene. She couldn't find Griff, either, but she really didn't expect to see him as long as the rides remained open. He had always been more interested in fun and games than in her music.

Hard to believe, though, that she couldn't find Darly in the audience. Momma made a special point of making sure everyone got to the festival on time, stressing that the pageant would begin sharply at seven.

So what had Darlene been doing when she should have been cheering for her twin sister?

The resulting burst of applause at Bryce's soaring final note snapped Carlene back to the present. She clapped until her hands reddened, and felt tears sting her eyes when Bryce looked directly at her and blew a kiss.

This—the knowledge that she'd made a significant difference in someone else's life—was worth a thousand Broadway performances.

Nolie suspected that at least one puppy remained in Lucy's womb, but after nearly an hour it hadn't appeared. She could see Lucy straining and panting, but no matter how hard she tried, the puppy wouldn't be born. The poor mother was exhausted, and the other puppies' crying unnerved both Lucy and Nolie.

Frantic with worry, Nolie scooped up four puppies and deposited them in a wicker laundry basket. Erik had already carried a basketful of puppies to his truck, so they might have to make several more trips. But how were they going to transport all these dogs to the veterinary hospital?

"Stop and think, girl." She paused in the doorway and leaned her head against the frame, her thoughts spinning. If Lucy were a Pekinese or a beagle, it'd be easy to pick her up, put her and the puppies in Erik's truck, and head to the vet's office. But Lucy weighed nearly two hundred pounds now, and fifteen hungry puppies were crying for food and warmth and the comfort of their mother . . .

How was she supposed to safely pack them up? She couldn't. No one could.

She lowered her basket and put the puppies back into the whelping box. Erik came around the corner as she straightened. "We're not going to the vet's office," she told him, her voice trembling. "You should bring those other puppies back. I'm going to track down Doc Hensley and ask him to come here."

Erik's Adam's apple bobbed as he swallowed hard. "What if Lucy needs surgery?"

"Maybe Doc will have an idea about that, because I don't have a clue." She strode to the phone in the kitchen and dialed the vet's number. A recorded voice announced that her call was being forwarded, then she heard Doc's scratchy greeting. "Hello?"

She blurted out her story in a rush. "I'm sure there's still another pup," she said, "and Lucy can't deliver it. I'm really worried."

A long exhalation rolled over the telephone line. "Okay—keep Momma calm and try to get her to rest between contractions. I have to go to the office, but I'll be out that way as soon as I can get there. Do you have formula and bottles for the other pups?"

"I do."

"You can start feedin' 'em, then. Just a couple of ounces, but we need to help because we don't want to wear Lucy out. Hold on, Nolie, I'm on my way."

God bless that man. Nolie hung up and leaned against the counter, bracing her hands on the edge. Of all the mistakes she had ever made, surely this was the biggest of them. She would never forgive herself if she lost Lucy. If Lucy died, most of the pups would die, too—Nolie would never be able to successfully care for fifteen puppies around the clock. Like human babies, they ate every couple of hours; they needed their momma to teach them things, and Nolie didn't know what a human should be doing in this situation, let alone a momma dog . . .

Erik returned with the first basket of puppies and set it on the counter. When Nolie didn't look up, he reached out and lifted her chin. "Can't the doctor come?" he asked, his voice soft with dread.

She swiped at the wetness on her cheeks. "He's coming. He has to go to the office first, though, to pick up supplies." She straightened and pushed a few frazzled strands of hair away from her face. "He said I should start feeding the puppies. I'm going to have to keep a chart to know who's been fed and who hasn't—"

"I'll help." Erik headed toward the laundry room with the basket of squalling pups. "Just tell me what to do."

Nolie sniffed and followed him, feeling some of the burden roll off her shoulders. This was proving to be one of the most difficult situations she'd ever faced, but with Erik's help, she just might find the strength to endure it.

Still floating on a cloud of bliss after crowning Bryce this year's Miss Buttercup Squash queen, Carlene flinched when her cell phone rang. Who would call her this late on a Friday night?

She glanced at Darlene, who was creeping along the highway because the sun had set. "Are you expecting to hear from anyone?"

Darlene snorted. "Why would anyone call me on your phone?"

Carlene shrugged, knowing her sister had a point. But no one should be calling *her* now, either. Bryce was busy celebrating with her family, the Fall Festival organizers were heading home to flannel nightgowns and cups of cocoa, and her New York acquaintances were either eating dinner or stretching their legs during a show's intermission.

She glanced at the caller ID. At first the name didn't register, then recognition hit like a bolt from the blue.

She pressed the *talk* button. "Hello?"

"Miss Caldwell? Morty Risen here, from Turner, Risen, and Field. I've news about your lawsuit, and wanted to let you know as soon as possible."

She caught her breath, not sure she could handle any more bulletins from New York. Bad enough that she'd never work on Broadway again, but if she'd also lost her malpractice case she might be looking at steep legal fees she couldn't afford to pay. Considering that she earned an average of twenty dollars per voice lesson, she'd need years to pay off a sizable bill.

Keenly aware that Darlene was listening, she braced for the worst. "I'm ready."

The lawyer didn't laugh. "Your doctor's insurance company wants to settle, as I knew they would. They offered two point two million in damages, so I told them I had to take the offer to you. We can counter, and my instinct is to do that, but I'm required to present you with every offer before I give them a response."

Her breath caught in her lungs. "Two point—how'd they come up with that figure?"

"They have actuaries who compute these things—they take your earning potential, your current salary, plus a list of incidental considerations and possibilities. I believe we could get more if we push back. I'm thinking that four million is a more appropriate number."

"I just—let me think a moment, please." She pressed her fingertips to her temple as her mind raced. Her agreement with the lawyer's agency stipulated that one-third of any settlement would go to the firm, so would the remainder leave her enough to live on? She didn't need a fortune.

"I trust you, Mr. Risen. If you think that's a fair settlement, I'll take it. If you think it's unfair, then feel free to push back, but I don't think I need much more."

"I still think we could press for four—"

"I was never a star, which the other attorney is bound to point out if you ask for too much. I have no illusions about my talent, and I'm not greedy. Three is more than enough. I'd be grateful to walk away with two."

"Very well, I'll ask for an even three. Dealing in round numbers is always best, don't you think?"

Three million dollars . . . with one million going to her attorney, one to her bank account, and one for a dream project that had begun to take shape in the back of her mind. Yes, round numbers suited her very well.

"Thank you," Carlene said. "I'll wait to hear from you, then. Have a good night." She clicked off the phone and dropped it back into her purse, then folded her arms and sighed. From across the car, she could almost smell Darlene's smoldering curiosity.

"Well?" Darlene tossed her a quick glance. "Is Mr. Risen somebody from FSU? Is he trying to get you to take more voice students?"

Carlene laughed, amazed at the way her sister's mind worked. "Hardly. He's from New York."

"A friend, then?"

"I've never actually met the man."

"But you said you trusted him—"

"He's an attorney, all right? He's handling some legal affairs for me, and I have to trust him to take care of things because I'm not in New York at the moment."

"Well." Darlene lifted her chin and stared out at the dark road, chilliness surrounding her like a blanket. "Excuse me for being concerned about my twin. It's not like I meant to pry."

Carlene lifted her gaze to the ceiling and shook her head, then looked out the passenger window and smiled.

As tense as a bow string, Nolie watched Doc Hensley roll Lucy onto her side and slowly run his gloved hand over her distended abdomen. "I hope I don't have to do a C-section." He kept his voice low and soothing. "I understand why you couldn't bring her into the office, but these aren't the most sanitary conditions."

"Please, Doc," Nolie begged, "just save her. I don't know what I'll do if she doesn't survive this."

"She's tired, but she's not a quitter. She's okay, this girl." When Doc slipped a gloved finger into the birth canal, Nolie moved closer, desperate to help if she could.

"I have to operate." The vet's voice went grim. "There's a big puppy inside. We can't take a chance on it dying and Lucy risking infection." He looked over at Nolie. "Can you get someone in here to help?"

"Erik?"

She lifted her voice, but Erik hadn't gone far. He appeared in the doorway almost instantly, his expression serious. "What can I do?"

Doc Hensley glanced at him, then pulled a length of plastic tubing from his surgical kit. "You can pretend you're an IV pole. Hang on." Moving with a swiftness Nolie rarely saw in the older man, the vet slid a needle into Lucy's front leg, then attached the needle to the tubing and the tubing to a bag of liquid. "Just hold the bag," the vet told Erik. "You don't faint at the sight of blood, do you?"

Erik managed a lopsided smile. "I haven't yet."

"Good man. Let's keep it that way." Doc Hensley pulled a snout-shaped gas mask from his bag and fitted it to Lucy's nose. Then he looked at Nolie. "Okay, missy. Your job is to sit at this end and make sure this mask stays fitted over her muzzle. Gas will flow from the canister, so you don't have to worry about that. Just make sure Lucy doesn't wake up in the middle of things."

Nolie nodded and scooted toward Lucy's head. "Got it. I'm ready."

With the gas flowing and the mask securely fitted to Lucy's face, the dog went to sleep. When Doc was sure Lucy was unconscious, he lifted the last of the roaming puppies and put it with the others in laundry baskets, covered the baskets with blankets, and then rolled Lucy onto her back. With padded ties he anchored her front legs to the frame supporting the laundry sink and her back legs to a kitchen chair, then he put on his surgical mask and sprayed antiseptic over the length of Lucy's belly. He unfolded a sterile drape with a long opening and placed it over the big belly. Then, with a quickness that caught Nolie by surprise, he sliced Lucy open.

Nolie looked away, unable to watch, as Doc worked on her beloved dog. Behind her, she could hear Erik murmuring something, and only after listening intently did she realize that he was praying. For her. And for her dogs.

"It's a good thing we're doin' this," Doc said, his voice muffled by his mask. "I see more than one puppy inside."

Nolie's heart went cold and still. Had she made a mistake by waiting too long to call the doctor? Had all the unborn puppies died? Erik must think her a fool for even attempting this.

"Erik, hang that bag on the doorknob, will you?" Doc said a minute later. "And rub this puppy down for me. I'll cut the cord in a sec."

When the puppy began to cry, Nolie closed her eyes, relieved that Number Sixteen had made it safely into the world.

Number Seventeen soon followed. The doctor also handed this

puppy off to Erik, who rubbed it briskly and laughed when the little creature began to protest.

"And here's our troublemaker."

Unable to resist, Nolie turned to watch. She gasped as Doc cradled another pup in his gloved hands. She had never seen such a huge puppy. She bit her lip and looked at the vet, almost afraid to ask. "Is it . . . deformed?"

Doc wore a somber expression as he broke the sac and wrapped the pup in a towel. He rubbed the puppy's chest with almost frantic motions, encouraging it to breathe, but the poor thing didn't move.

"Was it in the birth canal too long?" Nolie asked. "Did it suffocate? Is that why it's all swollen?"

Doc Hensley shook his head. "This puppy never got into the birth canal. He's simply too big because he's swollen."

"Water retention?" Erik guessed.

Doc Hensley nodded. "We call them water puppies. We don't know exactly what causes the condition, but pups rarely survive when they're this severely bloated. This little guy never had a chance."

He lowered the motionless puppy to a clean towel, covered it, and proceeded to stitch Lucy's incisions with amazing speed and dexterity. Nolie had always thought herself skilled with a needle and thread, but Doc was expert in an entirely different way.

Her eyes brimmed with tears. She felt terrible for the puppy they lost, but she would have lost Lucy and all three unborn puppies if Doc Hensley hadn't come. She looked at the squirming babies. Lucy had become a mother seventeen times in the space of a few hours, but she would need help. The poor momma dog couldn't do this alone.

And what would she have done without Erik? She glanced over at him—he was still holding Number Seventeen, his eyes sparkling with wonder and delight.

Carlene could not have been more surprised when she and Darlene returned to the house. The kitchen they'd left only a few hours earlier had been transformed into a canine emergency room, complete with a masked surgeon, a lanky surgical assistant, and an anxious nurse who hovered over three wicker baskets on the kitchen island, each filled with squirming brown and black puppies.

Nolie apologized to Darlene for the mess and promised to clean up when she could find a minute, but Darlene immediately pulled on rubber gloves and grabbed a bottle of bleach from the butler's pantry. "By the way," she said, splashing bleach onto a sponge, "Bernita, Edna, and Mary Thomas want to know if you'll be making Christmas aprons this year. Seems they all want one."

Nolie lifted a brow, then shook her head. "I'll get to those," she said absently, "when I can find a little time to breathe."

Carlene shook her head—so much for trying to force Nolie out of her rut. Leaving Darly to her cleaning, she strolled out of the kitchen and went in search of a quiet space.

Still basking in the satisfaction of a job well done and the good report from her lawyer, she walked through the living room and pressed her hands to the dark windows overlooking the gardens and back lawn. She and her sisters ought to host a bonfire or a picnic to celebrate Bryce's victory. The girl had entertained the audience; she had wowed the judges, and several people pulled Carlene aside and predicted that Bryce would win Miss Florida.

Who could say? Carlene might be mentoring a future Miss America. She smiled at the idea, then remembered the item Bryce had given her as the lights went out and the last of the pageant organizers went home.

"No matter what happened tonight," she whispered as she pressed a small package into Carlene's hand, "I wanted you to have this."

Momentarily speechless with surprise, Carlene had ripped off the bright wrapping paper and discovered a small plaque engraved with a simple tribute: *To Carlene Caldwell, who taught me how to shine. If I find any success in life, I owe it to you.—Bryce Grant*

As she read those words and saw the sparkle in Bryce's green eyes, Carlene felt like she'd just been crowned Buttercup Squash queen all over again.

So why not share her accomplishment with the family?

She pulled the plaque from her purse and looked for a suitable location to display it. The living room hadn't changed much over the years; those faded photos had probably been hanging over the fireplace for ages. One photo of Darlene, Griff, and their children was so old, Katie and Griffy Jr. appeared to be in elementary school. Surely Darlene wouldn't mind if Carlene replaced the picture with this small memento.

She took the photo from the wall, blew dust off the frame, and set it on an end table. Then she hung her plaque in that spot, approving of the way it blended with the other family artifacts. The display wasn't the most artistic arrangement she'd ever seen, but at least it added variety to the line of posed pictures. More than that, the plaque assured Carlene that she'd found a purpose in this community . . . and was making a home for herself in Peculiar.

Humming, she picked up the deposed photo and propped it against a stack of books on the shelf. The family picture suited that spot quite nicely.

She climbed the stairs to get ready for bed, hoping to dream of future pageants and tiaras and girls with sparkling voices.

Chapter Twenty

$\mathcal{S}$unday morning, Carlene woke and stretched in her bed, luxuriating in the rare sense of solitude. Soon Nolie would be off to her church du jour, and Darlene would head to the First and Only, which meant Carlene could enjoy having the kitchen to herself. After a cup of coffee and a pastry from Darlene's never-empty dessert stand, she might shower and walk over to the Methodist assembly, where services started at eleven and ended promptly at noon. With any luck, she might beat her sisters back to the house.

She slipped on her robe and padded downstairs, craving a dose of caffeine. She hadn't realized how much the pageant would take out of her. Now that the event was over, she felt as though a load had been lifted from her shoulders.

As soon as she landed on the first floor, she realized she'd been mistaken about being alone. She heard the hum of adult voices and above that, the high-pitched squeal of hungry living things.

She groaned. Of course. Lucy had given birth last night, so Nolie would be reluctant to leave the new mother. But who was with her?

Carlene cinched the belt of her robe tighter and followed the sound, tiptoeing through the kitchen. Cary Grant crouched on the counter in the butler's pantry, his golden gaze fixed on the goings-on in the next room. And no wonder—Lucy, Ricky, Nolie, and Erik were sprawled on the laundry-room floor, surrounded by more squirming puppies than Carlene had ever seen in one place.

"Oh, my." Her jaw dropped. "Did Lucy explode?"

"She's the proud mother of seventeen." Nolie flashed a brief but triumphant smile, then returned her attention to the puppy she was bottle-feeding. "I don't know what we would have done if Doc Hensley hadn't come over to help deliver the last three."

"We could have had eighteen pups," Erik added, his face looking even thinner than usual, "but one of 'em was stillborn."

"A water puppy." Nolie shook her head. "Poor thing."

Despite the tragic news of a lost pup, Carlene couldn't help smiling at the scene. Something new had developed between Nolie and Erik—she heard it in Erik's "we." She also saw it in the way Erik's eyes followed Nolie, and in the way Nolie's voice softened whenever she looked at the minister. Carlene and Darlene had been half-joking when they suggested that Erik might make a good partner for Nolie, but who knew what might develop?

The dogs looked as weary as the humans. Lucy lay asleep on her side, but Ricky sat upright, squirming uncomfortably as confused pups kept trying to nurse at his belly.

Nolie followed Carlene's gaze and laughed. "They'll figure it out eventually, but Ricky's a good dad. I have to watch him, though, to make sure he doesn't lie down on one of the puppies. He could smother one without realizing it."

Carlene watched the scene for a few more minutes, then lifted her hands and backed out of the room. "I'll leave you two to take care of this new family. I came in search of coffee."

"There's a pot on the counter," Erik called. "Help yourself."

Carlene lifted a brow and retreated to the kitchen. Erik had certainly made himself at home . . . and he and Nolie seemed like a solid team. She poured herself a cup of coffee, then snagged one of Darlene's pastries. Because the puppies' squealing carried into the kitchen, she placed her breakfast on a saucer and carried it into the living room, then closed the swinging door. For at least a few moments she wanted to sit and reflect on the events of last night. The experience had been such a high point—and who could have imagined that a small-town festival would bring one of the greatest joys of her career?

She sank into a wingback chair and set her plate on the adjacent table. She let her head drop to the back of the cushion as she sipped her coffee, relishing the silence, then smiled in a moment of déjà vu.

She'd sat and sipped coffee in this chair before. The day before she left for Juilliard, she got up and came downstairs, wanting to enjoy the quiet house before everyone got caught up in packing her off. A bedraggled Christmas tree stood in the corner, shedding pine needles every time someone brushed it. All that remained beneath the tree was Momma's hand-stitched tree skirt. It looked as if it were ready to be picked up and packed away . . . just as Carlene was ready to pick up her bags and head to New York.

She closed her eyes and let the memory sweep over her, prickling her skin like the ghost of Christmas past.

Her mind took her back to January 1981 and the snowy morning she began classes at Juilliard. She left the dorm and sloshed to class over wet sidewalks and snow-crusted lawns. The trench coat she'd bought in Tallahassee wasn't nearly thick enough, and the pink nylon sweater she wore with flowered pants did little to keep her warm. She hadn't thought to buy a pair of boots, so by the time she reached class, her shoes and socks were soaked and her toes felt like icicles.

She draped her coat over the back of her chair and slid into her seat, aware that curious glances kept darting in her direction. The other students all wore black—black jeans, black sweaters, black scarves, and black boots—with the occasional touch of red or ivory.

The girl in front of her turned and flashed a quick smile. "Hi. New arrival?"

Carlene nodded, almost afraid to speak. The girls in her dorm had already laughed at her accent, so how could she answer without provoking hilarity in the classroom? "I'm Carlene," she managed to say. "And obviously, I just fell off the turnip truck."

The students around her laughed—not *at* her, but *with* her, and that proved to be the brightest moment in months of painful adjustment. The first few weeks at Juilliard proved that her accent was unsuitable for professional singing, her clothes inappropriate for the fashion capital of the nation, and her point of view too provincial to be worthy of a hearing.

At least, she told herself, she had a talent. She met her voice teacher, who seemed nice enough, and sang a simple art song for his evaluation. She expected him to respond with high praise, but when she finished the man folded his hands and made a face, shuddering as he proclaimed they had a *lot* of work to do.

The girls in her dorm might have provided a bit of comfort, but they treated her with downright scorn. As Carlene left her room to go practice one evening, the other girls surrounded her like a pack of wolves surrounding an injured deer. One by one, under the pretense of "helpfulness," her detractors offered comments on why her clothing was unsuitable, unattractive, and unstylish. Carlene tried to remain strong under the rain of criticism, but finally ran back to her room in tears.

Accustomed to praise and affirmation from her friends and family, Carlene struggled through those first weeks away from home. She tried to keep her head up as her teachers derided her accent, her roommate ignored her, and few people acknowledged her talent. Every night she sat alone at a corner table in the dining hall and ate, struggling to fill the empty space that ached for Sycamores, family, and friends.

After dinner, when she should have been studying music theory or humanities, she wrote tear-streaked letters to Griff and Darly, confessing that she was a hayseed who didn't belong at Juilliard and would *never* belong in New York. They wrote back—Darly more than Griff—sending short, newsy letters that encouraged her to think positively, work hard, and sing her heart out.

"And when you come home for spring break," Darlene teased in one note, "be prepared for a big surprise."

Griff's early letters had been filled with declarations of how much he missed her and how he wanted to hold her. Near the end of January, he wrote that he couldn't imagine life without her. "If you really want to sing on Broadway," he declared, "I'll find a way to come to you. Because Peculiar isn't the same without you, Carly, and I'm going crazy with missing you."

He had asked Carly to marry him before the Miss Buttercup Squash Pageant, but she told him she had to finish school before walking down the aisle. After six weeks at Juilliard, however, she wanted nothing more than to go home and marry the love of her life. Making it in New York might be a career goal for some people, but not for her.

The hope of a future with Griff was all that kept Carlene going— that, and the promise of a vacation. Spring break fell in mid-March, and Momma agreed to buy Carlene a round-trip plane ticket. She almost asked her mother to make the ticket one-way, but knew she couldn't broach the subject of quitting school over the phone. Momma would want her to at least finish the semester, so Carly would have to tough it out until May. Her heart soared with the knowledge that Griff waited for her in Peculiar.

And he did . . . just not as she'd expected.

The old feelings of betrayal surfaced in her consciousness like a powerful riptide that threatened to pull her under. She took a quick breath and sent her gaze roving over the mantel, searching for safe, neutral objects: dusty figurines, Momma's lace doilies, old photos of Grandpa and Grandma . . .

Her eyes froze on the spot where last night she hung her plaque. The small treasure had been replaced by the photo she'd propped against the bookshelf. She looked automatically to the bookshelf, expecting to see that the two items had changed places, but her plaque was nowhere in sight.

What in blazes? She rose and searched the mantel, the bookshelves, the tables and their drawers. Finally, she found the plaque in a slot of the antique magazine holder Darlene kept by the sofa. The memento had been tucked away so no one could see it, where no one could appreciate it.

Carlene picked up the plaque, her blood sparking as she curled her fingers around its sweet inscription.

Darlene's brain buzzed with thoughts as she pulled up next to Erik's pickup and put the Buick in park. She had a dozen items on her Sunday afternoon to-do list, and the most crucial item was the roast currently bubbling in the slow cooker. She'd put it in early so the meat would be ready when she got home from church. If Nolie and Erik could tear themselves away from those squalling puppies, they should all be ready to sit down for dinner by one o'clock.

She let herself into the house, dropped her pocketbook and Bible on the chair by the door, and hummed "Bringing in the Sheaves" as she moved to the counter, where the aroma of roasting beef wafted from the slow cooker. When she realized she could hear the pitiful cries of Nolie's puppies even from the sink, she shut the door that led to the butler's pantry and the laundry room, but the noise continued. She sighed, realizing those high-pitched squeals would penetrate the house no matter how many doors she closed.

She lifted the slow cooker's lid and poked the roast with a fork. Ah, perfectly tender. The potatoes were soft, the carrots beautiful. Whoever invented the Crock-Pot deserved the undying gratitude of all Sunday cooks.

Drawn, no doubt, by the scent of roasting meat, Cary Grant rubbed against her ankles, circling in a figure eight as he purred against her legs. "Yes, I see you," she told the cat. "And I'll get you a snack *after* the family gets their Sunday dinner."

She took four plates from the cabinet and turned, about to set the table, but hesitated when she spotted Carlene standing in the doorway that led to the living room. Her sister's mouth was tight, her arms folded. Fury flickered in her eyes like heat lightning.

"Oh!" Darlene dropped the plates on the table, then pressed her hand to her heart. "You scared me, standing there like that."

"Before you do anything else, Darly, would you come into the living room? I want to ask you something."

A shiver of premonition raced up Darlene's spine. What had she done now? Whatever it was, she didn't want to talk about it.

She grabbed an apron from the pantry. "Can it wait?" She turned to the flatware drawer and started counting out knives. "I want to get dinner on the table before the roast dries out—"

"This won't take long. But I intend to have my say."

Darlene dropped the silverware as guilt thundered at the back of her mind. She couldn't imagine many situations with the power to inject that sort of ire into Carlene's expression. Her sister could be upset about Darlene's unwillingness to paint the living room or the discovery that Cary Grant had coughed up a hair ball on her bedspread, but neither of those situations seemed likely to fire up Carlene to this degree. So what had?

Carlene spun through the swinging door and disappeared into the living room, leaving Darlene in the kitchen. What to do? She couldn't refuse to talk; Carly would only press the matter until the entire house knew about whatever had upset her. And if her issue led to something personal, Nolie and Erik didn't need to know about it. Some matters didn't need to be made public.

But Momma always said chickens came home to roost.

Swallowing hard, Darlene followed her sister into the living room. She propped her arms on the back of the wing chair and tried on a smile that felt two sizes too small. "What did you want to ask me about?"

Wordlessly, Carlene pointed to the pictures over the fireplace. "Last night I hung a small plaque on that wall. By the time I came downstairs this morning, it had disappeared." She shifted her gaze to Darlene's face. "Did you move it?"

A rush of heat toasted Darlene's chest even as her knees weakened with relief. What a time to have a hot flash! And how could Carly be so upset over something as silly as a plaque? She glanced around, searching for something she could use as a fan, but came up empty-handed.

"You took down our family photo." She reluctantly met Carlene's ice-pick gaze. "I put it back where it belonged."

Carlene's nostrils flared. "Ten of your family photos are already scattered around this room; I counted. The one picture I moved was ancient history, and I'm sure you never look at it."

"How do you know what I look at? I look at everything because this is my *home*; I raised my family here. You can't saunter in and start moving things around whenever you get the urge."

"Isn't this my home, too?"

"And didn't I give you a room upstairs? I don't care what you do in your room, but you moved a picture that belonged to *my family*." She felt a rush of vengeful pleasure at the words, knowing that in this area, at least, she was more blessed than her sister.

But Carlene hadn't finished. "Your family doesn't live here anymore." Her eyes flashed. "Now the 'family' at Sycamores is you and me and Nolie. Why can't I have a little space on the wall? Why must you begrudge me one tiny rectangle over the fireplace?"

"I don't begrudge you anything."

"Yes, you do. I think you hate the idea of my living in Peculiar. You keep hinting that I should go back to New York, so I know you don't want me around. But this is my home, too. Sycamores belongs to all of us."

"Don't you think I know that?"

"You don't behave as if you do. You're so . . . so *stingy* with this house and with your friendship. We used to be close, Darly, but I haven't felt close to you since I came home. You smile and act as though everything's fine between us, but even after all I did to help you during your convalescence, you still behave as though you resent the air I breathe."

Darlene clenched her hands. "What you did for me? What you *did*? Do you think I don't know you only stayed to help because you wanted everyone to see you as some kind of Florence Nightingale? You *liked* it when they said how noble you are, how sweet you were to help poor Darlene hobble from her bed to the toilet. And in the meantime you flirted with my boyfriend; you laughed and teased and tried to snatch him right from under my nose—"

"I did not!" Carlene's nostrils flared again. "I don't want your boyfriend! Henry's a nice man, but he's not my type at all."

"I heard you two carrying on in the kitchen while you were baking. You're always hanging on his arm, looking up at him like he's the cream in your coffee. The poor man is so addled he doesn't even realize what you're doing—"

"I'm not doing anything!" Carlene's mouth opened and closed as though she couldn't believe a word she was hearing. "Henry and I worked together in the kitchen that night because I couldn't follow your cupcake recipe. He bailed me out because unlike you, I can't cook. We were trying only to uphold your reputation as the world's best cupcaker."

"You weren't making cupcakes last night." Darlene tossed the words like stones. "I stood by the stage and saw you talking to Henry before the pageant. You were touching his arm, looking up at him and smiling—"

"Would you rather I frowned at him?" Carlene lifted her gaze to the ceiling. "Good grief, Darly, he's practically part of the family. I have no romantic interest in him, none at all."

"If you don't," Darlene countered, "then why don't you go back to New York? I was hoping—good grief, I was *praying*—that once you saw the pageant you'd miss performing so much you'd want to go back to your fancy big city. Life was so much easier for me when you lived in another state."

"Really? Because life in New York wasn't easy for me at all."

Darlene stared, puzzled by her sister's admission.

"Weren't you happier in New York?" She stepped closer. "You had a job you loved; you had your own place; you were a Broadway star, for heaven's sake—"

"I wasn't a star." Carlene sniffed. "I keep trying to tell you that."

"You're a star to us Peculiar folks." Darlene softened her voice. "And things would be easier for everyone if you just went back to

Manhattan. That's your real home, isn't it? That's where your friends are, your work, your life—"

"I can't work anymore and my friends, if you can call them that, have scattered to other shows." A rueful smile crept onto Carly's face. "For thirty years, I've been making temporary friendships that end when the final curtain comes down. Once a show is finished, the other actors aren't your friends anymore; they're your competition." She sank to the edge of the wing chair and stared mindlessly at the carpet, her faint smile holding a touch of wistfulness. "I didn't want to tell anyone because I don't want pity, but you might as well know. I can't go back to New York because I can't sing anymore. I don't think I'll ever sing again."

Carlene focused on her twin through a haze of tears. Could Darlene ever understand the trauma she experienced in losing her voice? Darlene had no comparable skills; she would never wake up one morning unable to bake, decorate, or organize. Even if she were in a wheelchair, she'd be able to tell people what to do. She'd probably sit up in her coffin to direct her funeral.

Darlene crinkled her brow and sank into the opposite wing chair. "I don't understand. Did you get kicked out of your union or something?"

"I lost my talent." Carlene's voice broke. "I had surgery on my vocal cords. Something went wrong, and now I can't sing."

Darlene shrugged. "Your voice will come back. It always came back after you caught a cold."

"It won't come back this time. I haven't sung a decent high note in over a year." She drew a deep shuddering breath and released the secret she'd harbored far too long. "I can't go back to Manhattan because I don't have a life in New York anymore. My apartment has been leased, my friends have scattered, and my agent is busy with other clients. The only thing I have in New York is a pretty good lawyer who doesn't even know what I look like."

Two deep lines appeared between Darlene's brows. "I don't believe you can't sing. You teach voice lessons. I've heard you teaching Bryce and those other kids."

"You don't have to be a great singer to teach; you only have to be able to demonstrate techniques and I can do that in my lower register. But no one would hire me to sing onstage, not anymore. So you see"—she gave Darlene a rueful smile—"I'm at a crossroad. I honestly didn't intend to stay when I first came down here, but the longer I lived at Sycamores, the more I thought that this is where I might want to spend the rest of my life. I could do something useful here; I could teach. But I can no longer be useful in New York."

Her revelation apparently extinguished the fire in Darlene's heart. She sat back in her chair, her face tight with consternation. "I had no idea."

"I didn't want you to know. Pride, I guess." Carlene tilted her head. "And I didn't mean to cause you grief, Darly. I should have realized you'd be attached to the way things are in the house. And I like Henry as a friend, nothing more. I've tried marriage and I have no interest in repeating the experience, at least not anytime soon. I can see where you might want to marry again, though. Obviously, you and Griff had a great marriage and raised a wonderful family."

She looked up, expecting to see that she'd mollified Darly's indignation, but instead Darlene turned her head and brought her hand to her mouth.

"Darly?" Carlene leaned forward. "Are you okay?"

"No." The word came out strangled. "No, I'm not okay. And you can stop pretending that you don't know why I'm not."

Carlene frowned and studied her sister. When Darlene's shoulders began to shake in silent sobs, she stood and bridged the gap between them, kneeling on the floor in front of Darlene's chair. "What's wrong?" she whispered, looking into her twin's tear-streaked face. "Honestly, I have no idea why you're upset."

"Don't you?" Darlene's chin quivered. "Don't you remember what happened the night you were crowned Miss Buttercup Squash?"

Carlene searched her memory. "I remember the pageant, the judges, being crowned, and being happy. I remember Momma and

Grandma waiting for me, and I remember letting Nolie wear my tiara on the way home . . ."

"Do you remember me?" Darlene peered at her through teary eyes. "Do you remember anything about me that night?"

Carlene shook her head. "No, and I'm sorry about that. But I'm sure you were there, supporting me with the rest of the family."

Darlene erupted into fresh noisy tears that sent Carlene spiraling back to the long-ago week she'd come home for spring break and learned she would be serving as maid of honor in Darlene's wedding. Darly cried then, too, but whether from shame, joy, or embarrassment, Carlene couldn't tell.

"I know we should have said something," Darly had sputtered while Griff sat on the sofa, unwilling to meet Carlene's gaze. "But we didn't know how to tell you, so Momma suggested that we let it be a surprise. Neither of us could imagine getting married without you, Carly, so we decided to schedule the wedding during your spring break."

When Carlene didn't—couldn't—answer, Darly rose and walked forward to take her sister's hand. "Please be happy for me," she whispered, her eyes dark and pleading. "I've been so thrilled for you because you're off fulfilling your dream. Don't you think you can be a little bit thrilled for me? All I've ever wanted to be is a wife and mother."

Somehow Carly managed a trembling smile. Darly gave her hand another squeeze, then turned and tucked her finger into the collar of Griff's shirt, pulling him off the couch and into the kitchen.

Momma watched them go, then shook her head. "I'm so sorry." Her gaze moved into Carlene's, then she looked away, seeking safer territory. "They're both so young. We don't want this spread around, of course, but Darly's pregnant. If we didn't need to act so quickly, I'd have tried to talk her out of gettin' married."

The news edged Carly's teeth. "Griff?"

"I'm afraid so, honey. No question about it."

Carlene didn't think she could be any more shocked. But this confirmation sent a flash of grief ripping through her before it melded with the sorrow that had occupied her heart ever since getting off the airplane and seeing Darly holding Griff's hand.

Feeling sick, she left the living room.

Griff tried to talk to her later that night. Though Darly watched him like a hawk through dinner and kitchen cleanup, he slipped away when Carlene stepped onto the terrace for a breath of fresh air. "Carly," he stammered, his voice in tatters, "I'm so sorry."

She almost pressed her finger to his lips, but withdrew her hand at the last instant. He was no longer hers to touch.

"You don't need to explain." She tried to smile, but her mouth wavered as if it had a mind of its own. "It hurts, but I understand. I wasn't here. Darly stepped into my place, and you welcomed her. I . . . I wish you both the best."

He let out a deep sigh and tunneled his fingers through his hair. "I never meant for this to happen. My feelings for you haven't—"

"Stop. I can't—I won't—hear any more. I won't have anyone saying you were disloyal to my sister only days before her wedding."

"Not even if I say I will always love you?"

A sob caught in her throat, but she managed to shove it down. "Please don't say that." She turned from the sight of his tortured face, ready to lie, to confuse, to do anything but tell him the raw truth. "I can't—I can't afford to be distracted from my goals. I need to focus on my music."

"But Carly—"

"That's enough, Griff. If you say another word, you'll tear out my heart and hurt Darlene. If you care for us at all, you won't do that." And because she cared for him, she would never tell him so.

To his credit, he didn't speak again. With deep shadows beneath his eyes, he touched her shoulder and walked back into the house to tell Darly good night.

Four days later, Carly stood in the paneled vestibule of the First and Only.

"Over here, Juanita and Nolie. Cindy?" Aunt Verna stood outside the ladies' room, a wedding program in her hand. "Honey, your makeup looks fine, so get in line. Carlene? Come on, girl, you have to walk in right before the bride. Keep an eye on those children, will you? I'm not sure Glennette will remember to toss the petals. Lately all little Stevie wants to do is pick his nose."

Carlene stared at her bouquet of red roses and pink carnations. A nearby table held a stack of leftover programs, the guest book, and a big box of pink rosebuds, cunningly folded to conceal small handfuls of rice. Carlene felt her mouth quirk with relief—at least she hadn't had to attend the rosebud-making party.

Aunt Verna herded the bridal attendants toward the door to the sanctuary. As a junior bridesmaid, eight-year-old Nolie would walk down the aisle first. Juanita and Cindy took their places in front of Carlene. Aunt Verna grabbed the hands of the ring bearer and flower girl, two squirmy preschoolers, and positioned them behind Carlene.

Cindy Beeker turned toward Carlene. "You haven't said much about New York. Are you lovin' it up there?"

Carlene forced a smile. "It's interesting."

Cindy's eyelashes fluttered. "I was floored, absolutely floored, when Darly called and asked me to be in her weddin.' 'Course I've always known she was partial to Griffith, but for the longest time I thought he was your boyfriend. My momma said he must have been datin' Darly all the time he was hangin' out at Sycamores."

Carlene made a sound like several consonants strung together, but Cindy didn't seem to notice.

"Did you see Darly's ring? Such a pretty little stone, but it looks so much bigger with all that mirror around it. Momma says Griff will probably replace it once he gets a job. By the way, has he said anything about where he'll be workin'? 'Course he won't start until after graduation, but I'm so impressed. Griff and Darly are the first from our class to get married. Don't tell anyone"—she lowered her voice— "but I might be the second. I've been seein' Tommy Nance for the last few weeks, and things are gettin' mighty serious."

The organ began to play the wedding march. The door to the sanctuary swung open and Aunt Verna pointed to Nolie, who began her slow walk down the aisle.

Carlene closed her eyes. If she didn't love Darly, she would toss this bouquet and run out the door. She was here for her sister, but who was here for *her*? Her heart had been shattered and her future plans ruined. All because she'd taken time to follow the dream that she'd been expected to follow.

But what if she didn't want that dream?

Momma would say this was how things were meant to be. Carlene was meant for stardom and the stage. Griff was a small-town guy, so he needed a wife like Darly. She would give him a home and family and make him feel like a king. She would raise his children—Carlene struggled to subdue the spasm that threatened to send fresh tears streaming over her cheeks—and be the wife he'd always wanted.

Aunt Verna nudged Juanita, sending her down the aisle.

As inexplicable as it seemed, Griff and Darly had been drawn to each other, they had fallen in love, and they had conceived a child. So it was only natural and right that they be married, and that they should live at Sycamores. If Carlene could find a way to bear the pain, she could be happy for the bride and groom.

Carlene opened her eyes and gulped deep breaths as Cindy started down the aisle.

Darly mustn't see tears on her sister's cheeks. She must never know how deeply Carlene loved Griff. She must be led to believe that Carly thought of Griff as a high school fling with a simple country boy. She must never know that Carly had been ready to give up her scholarship and her dreams of Broadway to be with Griff.

Carlene squared her shoulders. Today she would practice everything she'd learned in her acting class. She'd smile. She'd summon up happiness from someplace deep within. And if the agony became unbearable, she would retire to the ladies' room, lock herself in a stall, and cry.

Aunt Verna smiled. "Carly, honey, get ready. 'Cause it's time for 'Here Comes the Bride.'"

Without turning, Carlene knew the door to the ladies' room had swung open. The air filled with the rustle of fabric and the heavy scent of flowers because Darlene had stepped out to claim her husband.

Relying on the talent that had brought her to that moment, Carlene lifted her chin, slapped on a smile, and began her long walk down the aisle.

Once she stopped crying, Darlene pressed her hands to her face and breathed deeply, the sound of her labored breaths filling her ears. Should she tell Carly the truth? She obviously hadn't discovered it, but if they were going to establish a new honesty with each other, sooner or later the truth would come out. She would realize Darlene had plotted against her and purposely stolen Griff away.

Darlene waited until her emotions steadied, then drew a long quivering breath. "When you were dating Griff," she said, keeping her gaze on the table, on the window, anywhere but on Carlene's face, "I was jealous because I had a secret crush on him. I'd loved him ever since our freshman year when he'd meet us at the bus stop. But he never gave me the time of day; he only seemed to notice you."

Carlene shook her head. "You didn't have to be jealous. Clearly, he liked you, too."

"But he adored you," Darlene insisted. "Everyone knew it. And when y'all started dating in our junior year, I thought I'd die every time he came to the front door for you and not me. But over the summer you got busy preparing for the pageant. Momma gave you all her attention; she worried about your dress, your shoes, your hair, your music. Grandma spent all her time watching her TV programs and Nolie was just a kid, so I had lots of free time. Griff would come over to see you, but then you'd run off to a dress fitting or a music lesson, so he and I spent a lot of time playing pool in the rec room."

Carlene nodded. "I remember him being over here a lot that summer."

"He was completely in love with you, though. Half the time he was with me he was talking about you, asking what kind of flowers you liked, who your favorite singer was, what color you liked best.

I knew he thought of me as a kid sister and I was okay with that, as long as I was able to be with him."

Carlene looked up, her eyes soft and large. "And then you became good friends. And after I left, your friendship grew into something deeper."

"Not exactly." Darlene cleared her throat as Carlene's brow lifted. "The night of the festival, before the pageant, Griff and I went for a ride on the Ferris wheel. When we reached the top, I kissed him. He was stunned at first, but then—honestly, Carly, I think he was only desperate for you and sick about the possibility of your leaving. He was eighteen, brimming over with hormones, and so in love. On the Ferris wheel that night I think—I know—he closed his eyes and pretended I was you."

Doubt flitted into Carlene's eyes. "But we're nothing alike."

"Don't you think I know that? But I wore your perfume, and I'm pretty sure I was wearing one of your sweaters. Anyway, we didn't go to the pageant. We went to the parking lot instead."

"You left the festival?"

"Actually . . . we didn't go anywhere."

A faint line appeared between Carlene's brows. "Let me understand what you're saying—you deliberately made a pass at my boyfriend?"

Darlene lowered her gaze. "I felt bad about it later, but at the time all I could think about was how jealous I was. You had everything—the best boyfriend, the best clothes, the best teachers. Grandma even made sure you got the best pieces of fried chicken at dinner. You were the star, and I was always standing in your shadow."

"None of that was my doing, Darly."

Darlene narrowed her eyes and studied her sister. Carlene's countenance was open and guileless—she probably believed every word she was saying. She might never realize how she'd lapped up the attention, or how Darlene felt growing up as the less-gifted twin.

But all that was over. Darlene had struggled, and she had forgiven the past. And anything forgiven might as well be forgotten.

"I wasn't thinking about you that night," she went on. "I wanted Griff, so I took him."

Carlene didn't speak, but from the corner of her eye Darlene saw her sister's hand rise to cover her mouth.

"The next morning I felt guilty about what we did, and so did Griff. He called and apologized all over the place, saying he'd been wrong to take advantage of me and it would never happen again. The thing was, though, I took advantage of him. I think he realized it, though he was too much of a gentleman to point it out. Anyway, he stopped coming over. You barely noticed, though, because by then you were focused on your Juilliard audition."

She turned in time to see Carlene close her eyes. "I went to New York right after that," Carly said, "clearing the way for you. How long did you wait before you pounced?"

Darlene shook her head. "That's not . . . quite what happened." She hesitated, unable to lift her gaze as the ugly truth came spilling out. "I don't know if you ever counted up the months, but I didn't get pregnant after you went to school. Katie was conceived on pageant night, so in January, after you were gone, I called Griff and asked him to come over. I met him outside and walked him down to the lake so no one would overhear what I had to say."

Carlene's squint tightened. "Is that where you told him that you'd set a trap?"

Darlene winced, but she'd known the truth would hurt. She deserved it. "That's where I told him I was going to have his baby in a few more months. And that's where he cried and said God was punishing him for what he'd done. That's when I knew he'd marry me if I wanted him to, but he'd never love me, not really. He'd always be in love with you, and I would always be the sister he settled for. I'd always be second best."

The empty air between them vibrated, the silence filled with strain. When Carlene didn't immediately respond, Darlene shifted her watery gaze and stared at the portrait of Chase Caldwell on the mantel. "Momma said we should get married, of course, so Griff did the honorable thing and proposed. But I knew he'd been writing you, and I knew you'd wonder how he could go from lovin' you one month to marryin' me a few weeks later. But"—she shrugged—"if you wondered, you never said anything about it. I was always grateful for that. If I couldn't have a husband who loved me, at least I had a sister who did."

She took a deep breath and exhaled it with a shudder. She'd finally shared her secret, exposing it to the one she betrayed. In a minute, Carly would scream, or throw something, or say that marrying a man who didn't love her was what Darlene deserved for stealing the only man who'd ever really held her heart.

She lifted her gaze, braced to see horror or disdain or fury on her sister's face. She never had a chance to look, however, because Carlene rose and left the room.

Coming home had been a tragic miscalculation. Carlene hurried through the kitchen and pushed the screen door that led to the back porch. She needed air, and lots of it, or she would faint.

She moved onto the deck, then braced her hands against the railing and leaned forward, straining to fill her lungs with oxygen.

For years she had chalked Griff's defection up to time and opportunity. He wanted to get married and he didn't want to wait. Carly was gone while Darly remained at home, so Griff seized the opportunity to marry another Caldwell girl, the one who suited him better.

So Carlene quietly congratulated herself on her generosity of spirit—she'd been willing to give up the man she loved because another woman would be better for him. But Darlene had just blown away the delusions and half truths. Griff didn't just happen to fall in love with the sister who would be better for him; he'd been caught in a trap. So he meant what he said when he told Carlene he'd love her forever.

The realization sent a ribbon of pure white pain ripping through her head.

If only she'd known! She'd . . . what? What would she have done differently? She wouldn't have come home and married Griff because Katie, dear Katie, needed her father. Griff wouldn't have stuck around for a few years and then divorced Darly because he was a faithful man, a good man, who wouldn't hurt a loving woman like that.

Knowing of Darlene's treachery wouldn't change a thing for Carly and Griff. On Buttercup Squash Pageant night their paths forked, never to entwine again.

No, Darlene's manipulation wouldn't change a thing in Carlene's past, but it could still change her future. Why should she stay in Peculiar with such a devious woman? Darly might have found peace in confession, but that confession hadn't done anything to ease the struggles in Carlene's heart.

Maybe she no longer had a place at Sycamores or even in Peculiar. Everyone had been happy to see her at first, but after that? Nothing. She hadn't been appreciated at the Peculiar Community Theater, and not a single committee asked her to join. Darly didn't even have room for Carlene on the mantel.

So she should leave. She could go to Tallahassee, rent an apartment, and try to forget Peculiar even existed. She might drive through town to meet Nolie from time to time, but she could die happy without ever seeing Darlene again . . .

Or could she?

She wrapped her arms around herself and stared out at the shimmering lake. At the thought of leaving this place, loneliness crept into her mood like a fog. Darlene and Nolie weren't disposable. She couldn't toss them away like so many of the colleagues she'd known in New York. They were her sisters and, like it or not, they held her past, her present, and, undoubtedly, her future.

She was born in Peculiar and of Peculiar. She would always be, as the townsfolk liked to say, *a Peculiar person*.

And this was where she needed to stay.

She had loved Griffith Young with the unspoiled ardor and devotion of youth. Young love might be innocent, but theirs had risen from years of friendship, deep conversations, and long walks along the lake. She knew Griff loved her because his eyes glowed when she sang, and because he beamed when she beat him in games of rec-room pool.

Griff had been proud of her . . . like Daddy had been proud of her. And she wanted to please Griff just as she'd always wanted to please her father. Wasn't that love?

But Griff came to love Darly, too. Seeing the evidence of his affection—the children, the sound of his voice when he called Darly's name, the way he looked at his wife from the head of the table—had been enough to send Carlene running to Aunt Verna's house. She hadn't been able to visit Sycamores *because* Griff loved Darly, and knowing the truth hurt.

Rage faded from her heart as she considered the undeniable facts. Griff had loved them both, but in different ways. And he wouldn't want her to be furious with Darly. So she had a choice—vent her anger or let it go; rail against the past . . . or forgive it.

She never found another love to equal that one, but Darlene couldn't be faulted for that. Darlene had fallen in love and gone after her goal with the same determination and grit Carlene often employed to win a Broadway part.

They really weren't so different, after all.

She needed to go back in the living room and talk to her sister. Part of her yearned to protest the injustice of Darlene's actions, but another part wanted to comfort Darlene and assure her that Griff's love had been real.

She climbed the back-porch staircases and stepped into her bedroom, then opened the door to the small storage space under the attic eaves. Several of her moving cartons stood in the semidarkness, still taped shut, but at least she'd had the foresight to clearly label them. She found the one marked *LR desk* and tore it open, then pulled out a small cedar box and spilled its contents. She shuffled through several letters and notes, looking for a particular postmark, and finally found the one she wanted.

By some miracle, Darlene was still sitting in the wing chair, her eyes red and puffy. Carlene moved to the couch, the unopened letter in her pocket. She tried to close her throat over a rising sob, but quickly

surrendered and began to cry in a helpless and completely unattractive sound. She couldn't remember the last time she felt such raw
emotions—not even losing her voice shook her like the tumult roil-
ing in her heart.

"Carly"—Darlene's voice, hoarse and ragged, reached her ear—"I
wouldn't blame you for being furious. But before you hate me, know
that Griff never really loved me. I don't think he ever got over you,
and that's the gospel truth. He was like a man doing penance. He only
married me to pay for his sin and to give Katie a father—"

"Darly, would you shut up?" Carlene lifted her head and swiped
tears from her cheeks. She looked at her sister, who now wore a mask
of shock.

"I'm sorry for snapping at you." Carlene cleared her throat. "But
I needed time to think. You sprang that story on me so suddenly."

Darlene nodded slightly, then pulled a tissue from her pocket
and blew her nose. "Everbody in town is always quick to say that
Griff was a great husband and father to our kids, but they didn't
know him like I did."

Carlene looked away, recognizing the quicksand behind those
words. She could not let herself get caught up in Darlene's fears.

"I know I complained about you not coming home very often,
but secretly I was glad you stayed away," Darly went on, oblivious
to Carlene's silence. "As long as you weren't around, everone could
believe Griff loved me because he played the part so well. But if you
walked through the door, I knew his expression would give him away
and everone would see the truth."

Carlene looked at the worn carpeting that had serviced three
generations of Caldwells. How many secrets had been revealed on
this rug, and how many concealed? Darlene seemed to believe that
confession brought relief, but maybe every truth didn't need to be
exposed. In some cases, maybe love won the day when the truth
remained cloaked.

She lifted her head and looked at her sister's tear-streaked face.
"Darly," she managed to whisper, "Griff loved you. Didn't he tell you
so all the time?"

Darlene shrugged and looked away. "He played the part of a lovin' husband, but that's what people expected. And he was a good man. Once we married, he never looked at another woman—though he certainly would have if you'd been around."

"Honey, he loved you. I'm sure he did."

Darlene snorted. "I was married to the man. I knew him better than anyone."

"Did you?" Carlene pulled the envelope from her pocket. "I want to read you something."

Darlene stared at the letter, thought working in her eyes. "What's that?"

"A letter from Griff."

Darlene blinked. "How—how often did Griff write you?"

"I don't know. He dropped a note every now and then."

"But why?"

"Maybe because I was his sister-in-law. Maybe because I was his friend. He sent this note in June 2007."

Darlene's brows furrowed. "That was right before he died."

"That's why I kept it." Along with all the others. Along with a few secrets of her own.

She unfolded the typewritten page and began to read:

Dear Carlene:

Great news from Sycamores! On June second, Katie and her husband had their first baby, a seven-pound, two-ounce boy named Matthew James Jennings. Darly and I are over the moon about being grandparents, and I'm sure she'll send you a picture as soon as she has reprints made. She has covered our dresser in pictures of the little guy. He's nearly as handsome as his granddad, though he'll definitely look better once his head stops looking like a football.

I'm tickled by the idea of being a grandpa, but Darly is torn between feeling delighted and feeling too young to be called "Grandma."

The old homestead is still standing, if you're curious. We will always have a guest room with your name on it, if you want to visit.

Katie and Carl are still living in Minnesota, of course, and Carl is still working for that dairyman. I don't know how they milk cows in all that snow, but apparently they've got things figured out.

Griffith Jr. and Kitty have settled in California. No word of grandkids from them yet, but we'll give them time. I just hope the idea of earthquakes doesn't make them as nervous as it does me.

Nolie's doing well; you should see her summer garden. People come from all over the county just to ride up our driveway and gawk at her sunflowers.

I'm good; still working for the paper mill over in Tallahassee.

And Darlene is—well, I wish you could see her. She takes such good care of me, the house, the kids, and most of the folks in Peculiar. I don't know what any of us would do without her. She's more precious than gold, a mite more temperamental, and a whole lot more useful. God has been awfully good to me, but the nicest thing he ever did was send Darlene my way.

Come on down to visit, if you're able to get a break. If you're not, Darly and Nolie send their love.

Your bro-in-law,
Griff

Carlene lowered the letter.

"Some birth announcement." Darlene sniffed. "He didn't even mention how long the baby was."

"I didn't dig this out to prove how much he loved Matthew," Carlene answered, folding the page. "I read it to show you how much he loved *you*. I don't know how he felt in the beginning, but clearly he grew to love you and the life you created together. I became a sister-in-law. He loved you, and his world revolved around your family. After you married, you were *never* second-best."

Darlene sniffed again, then her mouth trembled into a smile. She lifted her hand to her eyes and slowly, carefully, wiped tears from her lower lashes, then she looked at Carlene. "You know, my pot roast is going to dry out if I don't take care of it."

Carlene felt her mouth twist. Dear Darlene, always finding refuge in domesticity. "Okay. Take care of it. But Darly, if you don't want me around, just—"

"We want you here with us." A trace of unguarded tenderness shone in Darly's eyes as she looked at Carlene. "People always have to adjust, but don't put us through that again by going away. We'd miss you too much."

"Okay." Carlene leaned back and waved her sister away.

Darlene got up and walked toward the kitchen, but stopped just before the swinging door. "Thank you," she said, her gaze fixed on the door frame. "Thank you for sharing that letter with me."

Carlene let her go, then unfolded the letter again. She hadn't handed it to Darlene because love wouldn't allow her to share all the thoughts on Griff's heart.

She scanned the paragraphs she hadn't read aloud:

> Not a day goes by that I don't think of you, Carly. Not a day passes that I don't stand on the driveway, face the northern horizon, and wonder what you're doing up there in the big city. I have a life in Peculiar, a life that fits like a comfortable old coat, but ever once in a while I dream of the life you and I might have shared. Last night I dreamed we were together in a taxi, and you were holding some kind of fancy award, a huge statue that nearly took up all the room in the back seat.
>
> Then I woke to find Darlene beside me. I love my

family, God knows I do, and maybe I'm living the life he
intended for me. But I miss you, Carly, and hope you'll set
aside a few dozen years for me in eternity.

We have a lot of catchin' up to do.

Pressing the crisp pages to her heart, Carlene's mouth curved in
a trembling smile.

Chapter Twenty-one

Nolie spent Sunday in a haze of exhaustion, coming out of the laundry-turned-puppy nursery only when Darlene or Carlene ordered her to take a nap. Memories of Saturday night and Sunday blurred into an endless cycle of caring for Lucy, placating Ricky, and bottle-feeding a continuous parade of puppies.

But Sunday night she slept . . . because Erik appeared in the laundry room after dinner and told her to go upstairs and get some rest. When she protested, pointing out that he wasn't responsible for her dogs, he replied that he was the official hired hand; since she and her sisters hired him to work, she might as well let him carry his share of the load.

His logic made about as much sense as taking a cat to obedience classes, but she didn't have the strength to argue.

By Monday morning, she had begun to feel a little more like herself. She stood in the laundry room again, a cup of coffee in one hand and a toaster pastry in the other. She set her coffee cup on the dryer, then nibbled on her breakfast and watched the puppies gather around their mother.

Lucy seemed to be doing well. Doc Hensley had promised to stop by later to check on her, but the incision looked clean and the new mother made no attempt to lick at her stitches. The puppies, however, were another matter. They crowded around Lucy's belly, piling on top of one another in their search for breakfast.

A few puppies lay in another pile in a corner of the whelping box. Nolie would bottle-feed those slugabeds, and perhaps she could convince Darly or Carly to do a little foster mothering once she got up.

She swallowed the last bite of her pastry, then turned to drink her coffee. As she picked up her mug, she noticed a rectangular box on the dryer . . . why did it look familiar? Darlene never kept boxes in the laundry room, and Carlene never entered the laundry room unless she was desperate for clean clothes. But as a memory focused, Nolie realized she hadn't seen the box with one of her sisters, but with Erik. He'd been carrying it when he came back from the festival Saturday night.

Nolie fingered the box, tempted to peek inside. The box was unmarked and accessible, not taped or tied shut. Anyone might be expected to look inside, but Nolie didn't want to pry. The box belonged to Erik, and in all the confusion and excitement he'd forgotten to pick it up. The man had done so much for her family; she didn't need to pay him back by snooping through his things.

Still . . . she *could* look inside and then drop it by the guesthouse along with a note: "Sorry, but this must be yours . . ." or some such thing. Erik wouldn't hold that against her, not even if the box was filled with underwear or something else that might prove embarrassing. More likely, though, he'd picked up a new dress shirt for an interview or done a little Christmas shopping at the festival. After all, the man likely had siblings and friends she knew nothing about.

Unable to resist a moment longer, she set her mug on the washer and slowly lifted the box lid. Inside she found smooth white tissue paper, artfully folded, so she parted the crinkly papers to see . . . a lace-trimmed something in a heavenly shade of blue. She blinked in astonished silence, then lifted the fabric from the box, shook out the folds, and held the garment against her. The exquisitely tailored sundress would fit her perfectly, but it couldn't be intended for her or anyone else in this family. Too colorful for her, too small for Darlene, and too young for Carlene, the dress was clearly intended for someone outside the Caldwell clan.

She swallowed a sudden surge of disappointment, then gave herself a stern rebuke. Was she wallowing in self-pity again? She had to stop this nonsense, nip it in the bud. For all she knew, Erik bought this for a woman in Chattahoochee, or perhaps this dress was intended for one of his sisters, a niece, or some girl who needed something nice to wear to church . . .

She slammed the door on her wild imaginings and folded the dress, then put it back in the box. She noticed a tag at the neckline: *Hand stitched by Myra, with love.*

Well, that explained it. Obviously, Erik had seen this Myra in a booth at the carnival, admired her work, and felt compelled to buy something to encourage the poor lady. Maybe this was the only item she sold all day. Maybe Erik was only acting as a minister when he bought this dress, so he might not even care who ended up with it.

It probably meant nothing, but she still had to return it to him. She'd drop it by the guesthouse once she finished the first puppy feeding, and she would behave as if she had no idea what the box contained. If he wanted her to know, he'd tell her. If he had a girlfriend, he'd tell her. He'd always been honest with her, hadn't he?

Consoling herself with her plan, she sat on the floor and opened her journal, ready to record the day's feedings.

By five o'clock, a deep and peaceful weariness had settled on Nolie like a quilt. She'd fed the puppies every two hours, making sure to rotate them between the bottle and mother's milk. Now all the puppies slept in a huddle as Ricky watched over them from outside the whelping box. Lucy had taken advantage of the puppies' nap time to stand and eat her dinner, wolfing it down as if she was ravenous.

Nolie looked at the stretch of empty floor by her side. She was tempted to grab a clean towel for a pillow and take a nap, but Darlene might have a heart attack if she came into the laundry room and found Nolie unconscious on the floor. Better to resist the encroaching tide of exhaustion and leave the room. Better to go search for caffeine.

She walked through the butler's pantry and entered the kitchen, finding Darlene at the sink. Darly hummed as she washed a few dishes, clearly happy to be back at her old routine. "Supper will be ready in about twenty minutes," she said, lifting a brow as Nolie walked by. "You wanna get washed up before we eat?"

Nolie stopped and looked at her clothes. Her white knit shirt was stained with puppy formula; her white jeans unmistakably soiled. "Wow. I didn't realize I was so filthy."

"Hate to say it, hon, but you smell, too." Darlene shook her head. "You can use the big tub in my room if you want the whirlpool jets."

"I'm afraid they'd put me to sleep." Nolie managed a smile, then snapped her fingers. "That reminds me—I need to do something before I forget. And don't worry. I'll be as fresh as a daisy for dinner."

She turned and retraced her steps, then grabbed Erik's box from the dryer. She would set it by the guesthouse door so he'd find it the next time he ventured out. After being up all night with the pups, though, he might not show himself until tomorrow morning . . .

She hurried past Darlene, eager to avoid offending her sister's olfactory sense, and went out the screen door, letting it slam behind her. Though the air contained the hint of a coming cold snap, the sun was a blinding blur in the west. She squinted and walked toward it, anxious to deposit the box and hurry upstairs to a warm bath.

No sooner had she bent to place the box by the stoop than the door opened. Erik stood in front of her, unexpected and attractive, his hair still wet from a shower. She inhaled the clean scent of soap and took a quick step back. "You—you left this," she stammered, taking another step away from Mr. Clean. "I'm a mess, but I wanted to bring it back before it got lost in all the puppy stuff."

He picked up the box, surprise blossoming on his face. The tip of his nose went pink as he held the box toward her. "I'm sorry. I should have taped a note on it. This is for you, Magnolia."

Startled by the use of her full Christian name, Nolie stared, heat creeping into her face—what should she do? Should she confess that she'd looked inside and knew such a beautiful dress couldn't be for her? Or should she play dumb?

But he hadn't said, *I bought this for you.* Someone at the festival could have asked him to deliver it. Maybe it was a gift, or maybe someone wanted alterations done.

She frowned and accepted the box. "Were there any instructions included? I mean, what am I supposed to do with this?"

Erik leaned against the door frame and crossed his arms, laughing softly. "You're supposed to wear it."

Her brain stuttered. "But—but it's not—"

"I know it's not your usual thing"—a faintly eager look flashed across his face—"but the minute I saw it I knew it had been made for you. That dress is the exact color of your eyes."

She stiffened, momentarily abashed. "I shouldn't accept a gift like this. It's . . . too personal."

"Nolie." He spoke in a low voice that was both powerful and gentle. "We have birthed puppies together. We've laughed together, shared secrets together, and prayed together. I thought we were . . . good friends."

She wavered, torn between what her heart wanted and what people might say; then her heart won.

Smiling, she hugged the box to her chest . . . while managing to remain a safe distance away. She'd thank him more appropriately once she'd had a chance to clean up.

Their little family—Carlene, Darlene, Erik, and a freshly bathed Nolie—had just gathered around the dinner table when Darlene heard the sound of a car in the driveway. "Hang on," she told the others as she moved toward the back door, "let me stick my head out the door and see who that is. We might need to set another place at the table."

Carlene groaned. "Whoever it is, I hope they come in quickly. I'm starving and those chicken enchiladas look delicious."

"As good as something you'd find in Manhattan?" Nolie asked, a teasing light in her eye.

"Better than." Carlene grinned. "It's hard to find an enchilada cart on Sixth Avenue."

A few moments later Darlene happily led Henry into the kitchen.

"I guess you need that other place setting." Carlene moved to the cupboard while Erik slid his plate and silverware to the far end, making room for Henry beside Darlene.

Nolie got up to get a glass. "I'll pour him some tea. You want a lot of ice, Henry?"

"If you don't mind." Henry grabbed the back of the chair Erik vacated, then pulled off his ball cap and stood under the kitchen light, his scalp shining through the thin layer on the top of his head.

Darlene sank into her seat and studied him. Henry didn't seem like himself. He'd stuttered when he asked if she minded him coming to dinner, and he was standing like a soldier behind that chair . . .

"Henry?" She softened her voice. "Somethin' on your mind?"

He cleared his throat as a dark flush mantled his cheeks. "The thing is, Darlene, I came here to tell you something."

"I'm listening." She looked at Henry and lifted a brow, then motioned for the bowl of sweet corn. "Could you pass that, Erik? Thanks."

"The thing is," Henry began again, watching the corn move from Erik to Nolie to Darlene, "I've talked to Gretel and put my foot down. I told her that I want to be happy, that she's got her whole life ahead of her, and that if it's any consolation, I love her a lot, but I love you, too."

Darlene lowered the bowl with a solid thunk. "Would you mind repeatin' that?"

Henry's shoulders rose as he drew in a deep breath. "I don't think I can, so here's the bottom line: I love you. I want to marry you. I was thinkin' we could get married during the holidays 'cause Gretel will be home from college. But if she's not on board with this weddin', she can just stay home while we get hitched. Because I love you, Darlene

Caldwell Young, and I want you to be Peculiar's Mrs. Mayor. Will you do me the honor of marrying me on Christmas Day?"

Darlene looked at Carlene, her jaw dropping as a warm glow flowed through her. Henry loved her. Even though Carlene had been around for months, Henry chose *her*. Even though his daughter pitched a fit every time he mentioned Darlene, Henry stuck up for her.

Henry wanted to marry her, and not because he had to. Not because of anything he thought she had—

Her thoughts hit a wall. Some folks would say Henry fancied living in a fine old lakeside house surrounded by valuable acres.

"I suppose"—she looked away, lest he see the fear in her eyes—"I suppose you'll want to live here after we're married? At least until our time runs out?"

Henry cleared his throat again. "I know this place has special meanin' for you, Darly, but I hope you'll understand when I say that it has no such meanin' for me. In fact, sometimes I feel right inadequate when I'm here, livin' in Chase Caldwell's shadow and all. No, I want you to come into my home, or if you'd druther, let's find a little place together. Wherever we are, that'll be home for us. That's what I'm thinkin'. And here—" He reached into his pocket and pulled out a small velvet box. "I got this here ring for you, if you'll accept it."

Red faced, awkward, and absurdly sincere, he dipped his head and held the box toward her. Her heart turned over the way it always did when he looked at her like that. She stood and opened her arms, a relieved cry breaking from her lips. "Yes, Henry Hooper, I will marry you!"

Carlene, Nolie, and Erik applauded as his arms went around her and their lips met.

After offering the happy couple congratulations and good wishes, Nolie settled down to eat. Henry's proposal had caught everyone by surprise, but Darlene was practically glowing as she heaped food onto her new fiancé's plate. Try though she might, however, Nolie couldn't imagine Sycamores without Darlene at the helm. How were she and Carly supposed to adjust to life without her?

She roused herself from the weariness that threatened to weigh her down and forced herself to pass the enchiladas. Her eyes burned from sleeplessness and exhaustion, but the noise from the laundry room had subsided to the occasional squeak and chuff. The puppies and their parents were sleeping peacefully, so maybe she could use this quiet time to think . . .

Then for no apparent reason, Erik stood. "I'll be right back; it occurred to me that nobody brought in today's mail." He looked around the room as if expecting someone to contradict him. When no one did, he gestured to the door. "Don't wait for me, please. Go ahead and eat."

After Erik left, Darlene's smile faded as she looked at Nolie. "You have bags under both eyes. I think your bags have bags."

Nolie managed a scowl. "Thanks, sis."

"I mean, I don't think I've ever seen you looking so tired." Darlene tsked as she scooped out an enchilada. "Hand me your plate, Nolie, and let me give you a nice helping of this dish. You could use a little more meat on your bones."

"Speaking of bones," Carlene said, her voice light as she picked up her fork, "this smells wonderful, Darly. Just the thing for a celebration."

Nolie looked from one sister to the other, again noticing a subterranean shift in their relationship. Carly was not usually this pleasant around Darly, and Darly never basked in Carly's praise . . . but she was beaming now.

"I just hope the chicken's not undercooked." Darlene spooned up another helping and smiled at Carlene. "Want more? Move your plate over here so I don't dribble cheese all over the tablecloth."

Nolie leaned forward and peered more intently at her sisters. "Okay," she said, her voice flat. "Where are the twins and what have you done to them?"

Darly and Carly both looked at her, their faces matching reflections of surprise.

"What are you talking about?" A dimple winked in Darly's cheek. "Would you like some corn with your enchilada?"

Nolie shook her head.

"Try the bread." Carly took a roll for herself. "It smells wonderful."

Nolie chewed her lower lip, then unfolded her napkin. If they didn't want to talk, fine, she wouldn't question whatever had happened between them. Maybe this was the long overdue change she'd been praying for.

"By the way"—Darlene dropped another enchilada onto Henry's plate—"those puppies are adorable. I couldn't believe Erik stayed up all night to help with them."

"Definitely above and beyond the call of duty," Carlene agreed. She looked directly at Darlene. "But I don't think he'd stay awake all night if *I* needed help with something."

Nolie expected Darlene to respond with a sharp comment, but she laughed. "I think you're right. But let's not forget, the man is a gentleman."

"And a minister," Henry added. "I'm not surprised he'd go the extra mile."

Nolie studied the food on her plate. After the confusing events of the afternoon, she seemed to be treading water in a conversation far over her head. Let them joke or insinuate or whatever they were doing; she wanted only to eat and take a nap—anyplace *but* the laundry-room floor.

Erik came back into the house, pausing to wipe his feet on the doormat. He dropped a stack of mail on the counter, then thrust a single white envelope into his back pocket. The letter had already been torn open, Nolie noticed, and Erik's dark brow was furrowed with thought.

"Thank you for getting the mail." Darlene folded her hands. "Now eat before your food gets cold."

"Grace," Nolie interrupted. "We haven't said grace yet."

"That's right." Carlene dropped her fork and looked at Erik. "Would you mind leading us?"

He sat, propped his elbows on the table, and bowed his head.

"Thank you, Father, for your daily provision, and thank you for the warm hospitality of this home. Bless us and lead us according to your will. In Jesus' name we pray, amen."

They began to eat, but Nolie was so tired she barely tasted her food. She ate because she knew she needed nourishment, but while her sisters and Henry talked about the upcoming wedding, Nolie's thoughts revolved around sweet sleep.

Except when she looked at Erik. The man usually joined in the conversation, but tonight he focused on his food, shoveling in corn, enchilada, salad, and bread without pausing. Nolie attributed his silence to exhaustion; like her, he was probably ready to drop in his tracks. Unless he had something else on his mind . . . like a blue sundress?

For no reason she could name, the thought of that dress gave birth to a cold panic that started between her shoulder blades and trickled down her backbone. She couldn't bring herself to wear it, at least not anytime soon. The dress was too new, her feelings about it too uncertain to subject the garment to her sisters' scrutiny. She needed time to think, to analyze Erik's motivation, and to examine it in a mirror to see if it could possibly reflect her true self . . .

Which meant she'd have to figure out who she was . . . if she could.

When everyone had cleared their plates, Darlene stood and brought over her special carrot cake. Erik cleared his throat. "I guess this is as good a time as any for an announcement," he said, looking first at Darlene, then at Carlene. "You know that for the past several months I've been sending my resume to various churches. I haven't had much success in that area, so a few weeks ago I applied for a position as a chaplain at the Florida State Penitentiary. I figured they wouldn't care that I'm divorced since I wouldn't be ministering primarily to families. I was right—they've offered me a job."

Stunned, Nolie looked at her sisters. Darlene's eyes appeared to be in danger of falling out of her head, and Carlene's face had gone idiotic with surprise. Nolie closed her eyes, too amazed and shaken to interpret what Erik just said. He was leaving them? He never promised to stay forever, but she couldn't imagine the guesthouse without him in it.

"I haven't given the warden a final answer," he went on, "but he'd like me to report to Starke during the last week of December so I can get settled before beginning work on January first. That's when the present chaplain officially retires."

Henry found his voice first. "What kind of work would you be doin' there?"

Erik smiled. "The usual sort of thing, I expect. A lot of counseling, leading Bible studies, talking to families. And takin' care of people on death row—the chaplain has to attend every execution. That's a sobering thought, but if a man ever needed an opportunity to get right with God, surely that time is when he's only a few minutes from meeting his eternal destiny."

"Isn't that dangerous work?" Confusion and concern warred in Carlene's eyes. "Sometimes they have those horrible riots and take people hostage—"

"Driving down a Florida highway can be dangerous," Erik said. "Either we trust the Lord to protect us or we don't."

The kitchen swelled with silence as Nolie tried to make sense of what he was saying. She felt the pressure of curious looks—from Darlene, Carlene, Henry, even Erik. They all expected her to say something, to visibly react, but what could she say? Erik was a free man and he never made any promises to the family or to her—

"Magnolia"—Erik's hushed voice cut the silence—"would you step outside and talk to me?"

Nolie didn't know how it was possible, but Darly looked even more shocked than before. "You want her to leave in the middle of dinner?"

Nolie glanced at Henry and Carlene, both of whom were watching her as if she were about to lay an egg; then she nodded. "Yes, I will."

"Thank you."

She moved her napkin from her lap to the table, pushed back her chair, and stood. After one last glance at her bewildered sisters, she moved silently toward the back door. Nolie walked to the edge of the porch and stared through the screen. The lawn looked as it always had; the lake shone with the same majestic quiet it had displayed for years. A pair of ducks splashed at the water's edge, just as generations of ducks had before these two . . .

"Nolie." Erik's voice was heavy with some emotion she couldn't—didn't want to—identify.

"Darlene's never going to forgive you for interrupting her supper," she said, not daring to look at him. "She's real particular about the dinner hour."

He moved to her side. "Nolie, I need to take this job."

She kept her gaze focused on the lake, but she could see him, feel him, with every nerve in her body. "So take it. I'm glad you found what you were lookin' for."

"I've been called to minister and this is the door God opened," he said, "but I never thought I'd find myself reluctant to move ahead when the time came. I want to go, Nolie, and I'm excited by the challenge, but there's a part of me that would hate to leave you. You've made me wonder if maybe I should forget about God's call and just settle here. But I can't do that, and I don't think you—well, never mind. You have to do what you feel led to do."

She felt a wry smile curve her lips. "Is that why you bought me the dress? As sort of a farewell present?"

"Not at all—I didn't know I'd be leaving until a few minutes ago. But I'm hoping, Nolie, and I've been praying that when I leave, you'll go with me."

She blinked, her eyes stinging at this unexpected announcement. Then her lips puckered with annoyance. "If this is your idea of a joke, Erik Payne, you can just leave now."

"You think I'm joking?"

"Aren't you?"

"I've never been more serious."

"Ha."

"Nolie—please, look at me. I can't talk to the side of your head and say everything I want to say."

She drew in a deep breath, then slowly, unwillingly, turned to face him—and his eyes. The eyes she'd first seen as wounded, but she now saw as lovely and loving . . .

"I've come to care for you in a most profound way." A trace of unguarded tenderness shone in his eyes. "I've never met anyone like you, and the thought of leaving you is killing me. So marry me, please. Marry me soon, so we can make plans for our new life."

She lifted her hand, placed it flat against his chest, and forced a smile. "You don't want to marry some stupid girl from the sticks."

"You're right—but I haven't met any stupid girls lately. I have met a wonderful, wise, and loving woman from a town rich with tradition."

She studied his face, wanting to memorize every detail before he left. "You should marry that woman, whoever she is."

"She's *you*, Magnolia Caldwell. I don't know why you think of yourself as stupid, but I've learned so much from you. Your words, your actions, the way you forgive . . . I don't think I'd be ready to go back into ministry if not for what I've learned here. So marry me, Nolie. Come with me to Starke."

"Leave Sycamores?" Surprise siphoned the blood from her head, making the world spin. She clutched at the porch railing. "How can I leave my home? I'm tied to this place; I have my gardens and the dogs and all those puppies. Plus people know me here, and they need me."

"You can plant new gardens and you can bring the dogs. You were always going to find homes for those puppies, weren't you? If not, you can bring the pups, too. Wherever you go, people will know you and need you. I know you, Nolie, and I know you are the most loving, generous woman I've ever met. You'd be a wonderful minister's wife, but more than that, you're the woman I want to protect and serve for the rest of my days. You deserve to be loved . . . and I want to love you more than almost anything else in the world."

Somehow his hands found her waist and held her steady against the spinning blur of house and landscape. Her head slipped to his shoulder and he supported her as his breath fanned her ear. "I know you're tied to this place, but I know you can break free. It's time for you to cut the apron strings and step into the wide world. Heaven knows it needs more people like you."

A hot tear escaped her lashes. "But my parents and grandparents lived and died here."

"Nolie." He grabbed her shoulders, held her in an almost fierce grip, and bent to peer into her eyes. "You can't make a place for yourself under the sun if you keep nesting in the shade of the family tree. Come out, Nolie, and come away with me. Please."

His steady gaze bore into her in silent expectation, forcing her to close her eyes in order to think. Leave Sycamores? She never thought she'd be able to do it until she *had* to, but Darly was as tied to this place as she was and Darly had decided to take a leap of faith . . . a leap of love.

As for herself . . . she'd pinned all her hopes upon a mirage, and wasted years mourning something that never existed. But a good man now stood before her, a man who adored and understood her . . . a man she couldn't imagine not seeing every morning.

Here was love.

She made her own decision to leap in that instant. Opening her eyes, she looked at him, delighted by the heartrending tenderness of his gaze. "Yes. The Ricardos and I will marry you."

A shiver rippled through her as he sealed their covenant with his lips.

Chapter Twenty-two

Darlene gripped Carlene's hand as the bridal march began to play. Along with the other invited guests, she stood and turned to watch Ricky trot down the aisle, curled ribbons dangling from his collar and mingling in his thick brown fur. In his mouth, he carried a basket filled with rose petals and a box holding two wedding bands.

Erik had worked with the dog for days, training him to carry the basket without spilling any of the contents. Nolie wanted both dogs in her bridal party, but Doc Hensley convinced her that even though the puppies were five weeks old, Lucy wasn't ready to be away from them. Darlene had sighed in relief when she learned that Lucy and her offspring would remain in the house—no bride should have to share her day with a passel of scene-stealing puppies.

"Here she comes," she whispered, elbowing Carlene. "And doesn't she look pretty?"

Nolie came down the back-porch steps and crossed the terrace, her arm tucked through Henry's bent elbow.

"She's never looked more beautiful," Carlene said, her smile as wide as a church door. "That shade of blue was made for her."

Darlene wasn't completely convinced that wearing the blue sundress was a good idea—she thought people might assume Nolie was a less-than-chaste bride—but Nolie said she'd been wearing white for too long; she wanted to add color to her life. So she wore the sundress and carried a bouquet of bright yellow sunflowers, every blossom cut from her garden.

Nolie hadn't listened to Darlene's advice about the wedding dress or the venue, but she did heed her suggestion about the minister. Reverend Tommy Lee Joseph stood in front of a vine-draped arbor on the lakeshore, only a few feet from where the Sycamores's dock used to stand. Orlain Jones, organist for the First and Only, played a portable keyboard and Bernita Creveling, who had always accepted Nolie's aprons with gratitude and delight, stood near the pastor as matron of honor. Henry would serve as Erik's best man.

Nolie had asked her sisters to stand up with her, but Carlene begged off by saying she was too old to be in a wedding party. Darlene declined, too, saying she didn't want to have to buy another fancy dress, seeing as how she had a wedding gown of her own to purchase. Nolie understood, but Darlene couldn't help feeling a little wistful as her younger sister walked past, bright yellow petals falling from her bouquet as she moved by.

A few of Erik's relatives had driven up from all across the country. They stood in a gathering, all of them tall and lanky, all of them studying the bride they'd barely had a chance to meet.

A tangled knot of emotions formed a solid lump in Darlene's throat: Joy, because Nolie and Erik deserved every happiness. A tinge of regret, because Momma would have loved to witness this wedding. Guilt, because for too long Darlene had assumed Nolie would never marry. Even a thread of jealousy because Nolie was getting married first. Darlene had to wait until Christmas . . .

A chilly breeze blew off the lake, ruffling the wavelets that lapped at the shore and fluttering the short veil Nolie wore over her hair.

"Henry looks handsome," Darlene murmured, not really caring

if Carlene heard. Thoughts of the man who would become her husband in twenty-four days kept spinning in her head, along with a checklist of things she still had to do to prepare for Christmas and the big event.

"Dearly beloved . . ." Darlene leaned closer to Carlene as the minister began the familiar ceremony. Reverend Tommy Lee asked who gave the bride away and Henry said, "Her sisters and I," then formally took Nolie's arm and placed it on Erik's. Then Henry stepped to the side and locked his hands, giving Erik a wink and a "me, too" grin.

Darlene tried to control herself, but as the ceremony progressed her chin quivered and her eyes filled in spite of her efforts. The past few weeks had brought so many fresh realizations: her life with Griff hadn't been a complete sham; Carlene wasn't the invincible superstar everyone supposed; and Henry honestly loved her. His love, coupled with Carlene's forgiveness and Nolie's wisdom, had given Darlene the courage to step out and claim the life she wanted instead of the one she inherited.

She watched through a veil of tears as Nolie and Erik repeated their vows. When their heads drew together for the traditional kiss, she squeezed Carly's hand.

"I'm going to miss her," she whispered. "I'll even miss those big hairy dogs."

"You can always visit," Carlene pointed out. "Starke is only three hours away."

"Things won't be the same. But that's okay—change is good, right?"

Carlene nodded. "It must be. It's what brought us together again."

If the English language were more reasonable, Carlene told herself as she waited for the happy newlyweds on the front porch, the word *love* would be as big as the hearts of those who learned how to offer it.

"They're coming!" Nolie cried.

"Here!" Darcie Hooper, Henry's sister, pressed a small bag of birdseed into Carlene's palm. "Get ready to shower them!"

Carlene untied the ribbon, then hastily tossed a handful of sunflower seeds over Darlene's and Henry's heads. The happy couple dashed through the rain of good wishes, then hurried down the steps and into Henry's car, now decorated with shaving cream and crepe-paper streamers. As dozens of well-wishers, including Darly's children, stood on the steps and called their farewells, Carlene leaned against a pillar and realized that she missed Darly already.

She and Darlene had been busy with wedding preparations over the past few days, but they keenly felt Nolie's absence. "Feels like a hole in your sock," Darly said. "Your toe keeps working at it because you know something's not right."

But it *was* right that Nolie be married and happy. Just as it was right and wonderful that Darly found love again.

Just as Carlene had. But she'd found it with her sisters.

She stood on tiptoe and searched for Nolie and Erik. She spotted them standing a few feet away—their hands mingling, their heads pressed together in a celebratory kiss of their own.

Henry tucked Darlene into the passenger seat, then ran around the car. He managed a quick wave before getting in and starting the engine; then the car pulled away, off to the airport and a week-long honeymoon in Paris. Darlene had finally run out of excuses to avoid using the airline tickets her children had given her.

"Have a wonderful time, sister," Carlene whispered. "I will miss you something fierce."

She pulled herself off the pillar as the cluster of guests began to break up. Half a dozen women offered to stay behind and help clear away the remnants of the reception, but she turned them down. "Darly would have my head if I made her wedding guests clean up," she said, softening her words with a smile. "So y'all run on home and enjoy the rest of your Christmas. I'll be fine here, just fine."

Before leaving, Nolie rushed forward and gave Carlene an affectionate hug. "I'm so happy," she said, squeezing Carlene's shoulder. "I never dreamed love could be like this."

"How are the Ricardos?"

Nolie's eyes sparkled as she stepped back and reached for Erik's hand. "All but two of the pups have gone to wonderful homes around Starke. And the other two—I think we're going to keep them. Our house is big enough for lots of dogs, with a fenced yard and lots of room to romp . . ."

"Lots of room for kids, too." Carlene smiled when Nolie blushed. "Be sure to call if it looks like I'm going to be an auntie. Thank you for coming, both of you. It's so good to see you."

She gave Nolie another hug, then hugged Erik, too. Before leaving, Nolie pulled a small envelope from her purse and slid it into the pocket of Carlene's hostess apron. "I'm so glad you're wearing it," she whispered, smiling as she stepped away.

Carlene stood on the porch and waved as the new Reverend and Mrs. Payne held hands and walked down the sidewalk, making their way to the pickup.

Gretel Hooper was among the last to leave. "Thank you," she said, turning to face Carlene on the porch. "The wedding was awfully nice."

"Darlene will be glad to hear you enjoyed it," Carlene answered. "She planned everything."

Gretel nodded stiffly, then walked down the stairs, her back ramrod straight. Carlene shook her head as she watched her go. The girl could choose to be happy or sad about her father's remarriage, but life would be a lot more pleasant if she chose happiness.

When the last guest had gone, Carlene stood on the porch and thought about her home. The porch lay in deep shade at this hour, but beyond it simmered a sun-drenched garden where roses nodded their heavy heads and sunflowers still followed the blazing torch in the sky. Next to the sunflowers, Nolie's gladiolas nodded drowsily and her roses stood unadorned, stripped of every last blossom and bud for Darly's wedding.

Carlene smiled. Several people at the wedding had asked what she intended to do with Sycamores now that the big old house would serve as home to just one of the Caldwell sisters. She shrugged and said she was still considering what to do next, but her plan had been taking shape for months.

With five years remaining on the Caldwell clock, she would open a music academy. With its wealth of large bedrooms and the sprawling space downstairs, the place could house at least ten students and two other faculty members. Young musicians who wished to sing or play could come during the summer or for a fall term, where they would learn what a professional performer's life entailed. Carlene could hire Darly to cater a couple of meals a day, and the entire lower floor could be carved into practice rooms.

Lately she had come to realize how much Peculiar had given her—family, faith, and now, a future—so why shouldn't she give something back?

Having a prestigious music academy in the area would be a feather in Jackson County's cap, so when Sycamores became county property, Carlene would promptly offer to buy it with the proceeds from her lawsuit. The school would continue under her direction, and Jackson County would benefit from a much-appreciated financial windfall. County officials could do a lot more with money than with an aging homestead.

She shivered in a frisson of anticipation. Such potential, just waiting to be explored. Just like the second half of her life.

She turned, about to go into the house, then remembered the card in her pocket. How like Nolie to hand deliver a thank-you card instead of sticking it in the mailbox.

Carlene opened the envelope, then lifted the cover of the plain white card. In her distinctive script, Nolie had written a simple quote:

Eden is that old-fashioned house we dwell in every day
without suspecting our abode until we drive away.
                                          —Emily Dickinson

"How right you are, little sister." Carlene pressed the card to her chest and smiled. "How very right you are."

Author's Note

While Peculiar, Florida, does not really exist, Peculiar, Missouri, does. I trust that the people who live near Chattahoochee and Tallahassee will forgive me for populating their area with a fictional town.

Writers—novelists particularly—tend to mine their personal experiences for story material, and I am no exception. But since I have never broken any bone (with the possible exception of a finger I recently caught in a rattrap), I must thank my friend Robin Lee Hatcher for allowing me to interview her about her bones, casts, and physical therapy. Robin, I'm so glad you're back on your feet!

This novel would not exist if my agent, Danielle Egan-Miller, had not given my stalled brain several nudges in the right direction. Thanks are also due to her associate, Joanna MacKenzie, for her suggestions on the manuscript in progress.

Special thanks and hugs to the kind and caring staff at Animal Hospital of Seminole, Florida, who not only answered my question about nursing canines and C-sections, but also came to my dogs' aid on many occasions.

I hope you enjoy your stay in Peculiar as much as I have.

Darlene's Very Vanilla Cupcakes*

Cupcakes:

1½ cups self-rising flour

1¼ cups all-purpose flour

1 cup (2 sticks) unsalted butter, softened and at room temperature

2 cups sugar

4 large eggs at room temperature

1 cup whole milk

1 teaspoon vanilla extract

Preheat oven to 350 degrees.

Line muffin tins with cupcake papers (makes at least twenty-four standard cupcakes).

In a small bowl, combine the two flours. Set aside.

In a large bowl, at medium speed with an electric mixer, cream the butter until smooth. Slowly add the sugar and beat until fluffy, about three minutes. Add the eggs, one at a time, beating well after each addition. Add the dry ingredients in three parts, alternating with

*Adapted from a recipe in Allysa Torey's *More From Magnolia: Recipes from the World-Famous Bakery and Allysa Torey's Home Kitchen* (New York: Simon & Schuster, 2004), 127.

the milk and vanilla. With each addition, beat until the ingredients are incorporated and stop. Do not overbeat.

Using a rubber spatula, scrape the batter from the sides of the bowl to make sure the ingredients are well blended. Then, using an ice-cream scoop, carefully spoon the batter into the cupcake liners, filling them about three-quarters full. Bake for twenty to twenty-five minutes, or until a piece of uncooked spaghetti inserted into the center of one cupcake comes out clean. (Spaghetti is wonderful to use when testing the doneness of Bundt cakes—just don't eat the spaghetti.)

Cool the cupcakes in tins for fifteen minutes. Remove from the tins and cool completely on a wire rack before icing.

Vanilla Buttercream Frosting:

1 cup (2 sticks) unsalted butter, softened and at room temperature
6 to 8 cups confectioners' sugar
½ cup milk
2 teaspoons vanilla extract

Place the butter in a large mixing bowl. Add four cups of the sugar and then the milk and vanilla. On the medium speed of an electric mixer, beat until smooth and creamy, about three to five minutes. Gradually add the remaining sugar, one cup at a time, beating well after each addition (about two minutes), until the icing is thick enough to be of good spreading consistency. You may not need to add all of the sugar.

If desired, add a few drops of food coloring and mix thoroughly. (Use and store the icing at room temperature because icing will set if chilled.) Icing can be stored in an airtight container for up to three days.

Yield: enough for two dozen cupcakes

Mayor Henry Hooper's Favorite Toffee-Mocha Cream Torte[*]

For cake:

2 sticks unsalted butter, softened and at room temperature

2 cups white sugar

2 eggs at room temperature

1½ teaspoons vanilla extract

2⅔ cups all-purpose flour (unbleached is best)

¾ cup baking cocoa

2 teaspoons baking soda

¼ teaspoon salt

1 cup buttermilk

2 teaspoons instant-coffee granules (Darlene suggests Starbucks or Nescafé)

1 cup boiling water

---

*Adapted from a recipe in *Taste of Home Baking Classics,* edited by Janet Briggs (Greendale, WI: Reiman Media Group, 2008), 189.

For topping:

½ teaspoon instant-coffee granules

1 teaspoon hot water

2 cups heavy whipping cream

3 tablespoons light-brown sugar

6 Heath candy bars (1.4 ounces each), crushed

Preheat oven to 350 degrees. Grease and flour three nine-inch round baking pans.

In a large bowl, cream butter and sugar until light and fluffy. Beat in eggs, one at a time, beating well after each addition. Beat in vanilla. Combine the flour, cocoa, baking soda, and salt; add to creamed mixture alternately with buttermilk, beating well after each addition. Dissolve coffee in boiling water; add to batter. Beat for two minutes.

Pour batter into three round baking pans. Bake for sixteen to twenty minutes or until a tester comes out clean. Cool for ten minutes before removing from pans to wire racks to cool completely.

While cake is cooling, in a large bowl dissolve coffee granules in hot water; cool. Add cream and brown sugar. Beat until stiff peaks form.

Place the bottom cake layer on a serving plate; top with 1⅓ cups topping and then sprinkle with ½ cup of the crushed candy bars. Repeat layers twice—cake will be topped with topping and candy bars. Store in the refrigerator.

Makes twelve to fourteen servings.

1. Have you ever lived in a small town like Peculiar? What are some of the advantages of small-town life? Disadvantages?

2. The title, *Five Miles South of Peculiar,* is literal, intending to imply that Sycamores is five miles south of the town. But could the title also refer to any of the characters?

3. The story is told through the third-person viewpoints of the three sisters—Carlene, Darlene, and Nolie. Could you identify with one character more than the others? Why or why not? Did it help you to be "inside the heads" of all three characters?

4. In most novels, characters begin in one place and end up in quite another, usually the result of changes in their situations and/or their characters. Where did each of these characters begin? How were they changed by the end of the story?

5. Why do you think Nolie asked Henry to invite Carlene to Darlene's citywide surprise birthday party? Why did she show him that picture of the twins as infants?

6. Would your church (if you have one) hire a minister who had been divorced? Why or why not? How did you feel about Erik Payne's predicament?

7. Why do you think Nolie wanted to wear only white? How does

color influence your mood? How does it affect the people around you?

8. Both Carlene and Darlene think of the tall sycamore trees as "sentinels," but Darlene thinks of them as malicious guards while Carlene sees them as benevolent guardians. Why the difference in perspectives?

9. When Carlene convinced people not to accept any more of Nolie's aprons, Nolie is upset, but takes comfort in the thought that "whoever started that nasty conspiracy" might have "broadened her horizons." What motivated Carlene to speak to people about Nolie's aprons? And what was the actual effect of her action? Were Nolie's horizons broadened? In what way?

10. Nolie gleans some wisdom about forgiveness and passes it to Carlene . . . and, inadvertently, the other principal characters. What sorts of things are difficult to forgive? Is it always beneficial to forgive those who have wronged us?

11. What have you taken away from this book?

A Conversation with Angela Hunt

1. Returning to Peculiar after a successful Broadway career was difficult for Carlene. Have you ever had a similar experience when returning home as an accomplished author?

   Not really. Carlene and I have one thing in common—neither of us is world famous, so we're not likely to be mobbed in the supermarket. I have some friends who are true celebrities—folks who can't step out in public without being photographed or asked for autographs—and I'm actually grateful that I've never had to deal with that sort of thing. Neither has Carlene.

2. Do you have any siblings? How is your personal experience with—or observations of—sibling rivalry similar to or different from the rivalry between Darlene, Carlene, and Nolie?

   I have two younger sisters, and we are quite different and spaced years apart, so we never fought over boyfriends or anything like that. Thank goodness! Because Darlene and Carlene were treated as "two of a kind" in their early years, it's no wonder they fell in love with the same man.

3. The scene where Nolie's dog gives birth to puppies is so vivid! Do you have any experience breeding dogs? Can you tell your readers more about your pet mastiffs?

I love dogs, but have had no actual experience breeding them— for one reason or another, none of my mastiff pups has been what I'd consider suitable for breeding (the breed is prone to hip and joint problems and I've encountered both in my pups). But I frequently watch Animal Planet TV and learn from other "dog people." Dogs are such an amazing God-given gift. I might consider breeding someday, but my homeowners association would frown on me raising bear-sized dogs in my tiny backyard. . . .

4. In *Five Miles South of Peculiar,* many of the characters have lost their way and are looking for a home. How do you define home? What makes a home—physically or metaphorically?

The saying may be a cliché, but it's true: home is where the heart is. Where your loved ones are. And, I think, where your history lies. Because the people who knew you growing up have memories of you stored away. For good or bad, they can tell part of your story. If you had amnesia, they could help you find yourself, and surely that's part of what makes a person feel rooted and at home. (Goodness, I think there's another novel somewhere in those ruminations. . . .)

5. Did you do any kind of research before writing *Five Miles South of Peculiar?* Did you learn anything surprising or unexpected while writing this book?

Writing any book requires at least some research, even if it's only learning what sort of flora and fauna grows in a certain geographical region. But I sewed several aprons before writing this book (getting into the mood) and bought more cupcake cookbooks than I'll ever use. I've been a singer, so I already knew a lot about vocal cords and performance, but I did do a bit of reading about the throat surgery that cost Julie Andrews her singing voice. And Leonbergers—they are a real breed, beautiful dogs, and I might just have to get one someday. When I'm back under my HOA's two-pet limit, that is.

6. On your website, www.AngelaHuntBooks.com, you have a special section for readers where you have reading group guides and information about scheduling a conference call to "Ask Angie." Are you in a book club yourself?

I started a book club in our little neighborhood about eight years ago, and it's been a marvelously rewarding experience. These women have taught me more about what makes a book appeal to a reader than any writer's class I've ever taken. And no, we don't read my books. We read everything from *New York Times* bestsellers to young adult novels, and we learn something from every selection. And from each woman who attends (we'd welcome men, too, if we could ever find any willing to come), I learn how to make a story appeal not to literary purists or other writers or academicians, but to *readers*. I love that.

7. How important are parables in your writing? Do you have a favorite?

I love parables—in fact, I'd say that's probably my mission as a writer. Some of my stories are more metaphorical than others, but nearly all of them have hidden meanings that relate to spiritual realities. When Jesus wanted to teach the crowds following him, he didn't speak in overtly religious terms, but usually told secular stories that related to common people's lives: stories of housewives and farmers and brides and grooms and poor widows and wealthy men. Those who were led by the Spirit caught his spiritual meanings; the others simply enjoyed the story. I learned long ago that the Spirit can speak through my stories in ways I never intended, so I'm thrilled to let him work as he will. As to favorite parables, I love the story of the lost sheep and the tale of the four soils. That one—no pun intended—is deep, and it took me a while to fully understand it.

8. The men in *Five Miles South of Peculiar,* with the exception of one, are strong, patient, kind Christian men. Were any of them inspired by individuals from your own life?

They are the kind of men my father was—not given to a lot of talk, but honest, loyal, hardworking, salt-of-the-earth types. They are more comfortable showing their feelings through action, not words.

9. You completed your master of biblical studies in theology degree in 2006 and completed your doctorate in 2008. What was the experience of returning to school like? How has your higher education influenced your writing?

I went back to school because I was writing about deeper theological topics and I felt a huge responsibility to "get it right." The things I learned not only deepened my writing but gave me several new book ideas. I'm still learning, and should complete my ThD this year . . . if I get my dissertation finished.

10. Which is more difficult for your characters in *Five Miles South of Peculiar*: forgiving each other, or forgiving themselves? What about for yourself?

Carlene and Darlene do carry burdens of guilt, but they also carry little scorecards marked with wrongs committed by the other. And while forgiving oneself can be difficult, I think human nature struggles to forgive others—we are so prone to carry grudges, nurse our wounds, and chafe under perceived injustices. In my own life, I've found that it's easy to say, "I forgive that offense," and then dredge it up again a few months later—what, did my forgiveness expire? I have to keep reminding myself that Jesus said he'll forgive as I do (Matthew 6:14), and I don't want him remembering my failings as readily as I remember others'.

Forgiveness would be so much easier if we could entirely forget.

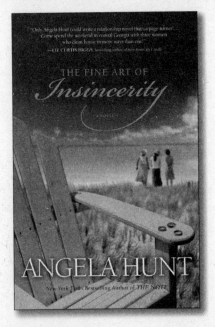